Harry Bentley's

Second Chance

Harry Bentley's

Second Chance

A Yada Yada Brothers Novel

Dave Jackson

CASTLE
ROCK
CREATIVE
Evanston, Illinois 60202

Published in Evanston, Illinois. Castle Rock Creative, Inc.

Publisher's Note: This novel is a work of fiction. Names, characters, places, and incidents are either products of the author's imagination or used fictitiously. All characters are fictional, and any similarity to people living or dead is purely coincidental.

ISBN: 978-0-9820544-0-6

Printed in the United States of America

For a complete listing of
books by Dave and Neta Jackson
please visit www.daveneta.com

What Is a Parallel Novel?

Dave and Neta Jackson are doing something new in Christian fiction—"parallel novels," two stories taking place in the same time frame, the same neighborhood, involving some of the same characters living through their own dramas and crises but interacting with and affecting one another ... just the way it happens in real life.

Growing out of Neta Jackson's best-selling Yada Yada Prayer Group novels come two brand-new stories sprinkled with familiar faces and places from the Yada Yada world: Dave's *Harry Bentley's Second Chance* is a Yada Yada Brothers novel, and Neta's *Where Do I Go?* begins her Yada Yada House of Hope series.

It's something only a husband-and-wife writing team could pull off.

Read either story first. Each stands on its own.

In *Where Do I Go?* Gabrielle Fairbanks has nearly lost touch with the carefree, spirited young woman she was when she married Philip sixteen years ago. But when she moves to Chicago to accommodate Philip's ambition, Gabby longs for the chance to find real purpose in her own life.

A chance encounter with a homeless woman suddenly opens a door she never expected. The women of Manna House Women's Shelter need a program director—and she has the right credentials. Gabby's in her element, feeling God's call on her life at last, even though Philip doesn't like the changes he sees in her. But she never anticipated his ultimatum: quit her job at the shelter, or risk divorce and losing custody of their sons.

As for *Harry Bentley's Second Chance* ... well, dive in and find out!

To the brothers in my own men's group:
Carl, Carlton, Dave M., Fred, Gary, Ken, Larry,
Nelson, Nevin, Peter, Rick, Rommel, Steve, and Tony.

They are *not* characters in this book,
but they've supported me all the way.

Prologue

Cindy Kaplan pulled the unmarked cruiser into the lot behind Chicago Police Headquarters and found a parking space. She left the engine running, the whine of the air conditioner cycling on and off to beat the summer's heat. Still, sweat glistened on the bald head of the older black man sitting beside her. In the six years they'd been the salt-and-pepper duo in the elite anti-gang unit, she'd seen the frown lines between his eyebrows deepen into permanent grooves. They'd watched each other's back, covered for one another, and saved each other's life more than once, but now she was afraid she was losing him.

"Harry," she sighed, brushing back the shock of straight, ash brown hair that fell perpetually over her right eye, "you know you don't have to do this. What's to be gained? Really … think about it. Even if you make your case against Fagan, your career's over the moment anyone finds out you blew the whistle."

She saw him glance at her, then he sighed. "Cindy … in all the time we've ridden together, when was the last time I backed down over somethin' like this?"

She shrugged. "Well, when was the last time we ever faced something like this? I know you're a straight-up guy, but this is different. Different than anything we ever faced before. Fagan's popped guys for less."

"Oh, come on." He tugged at the protective vest under his shirt that always seemed too tight in hot weather. "Don't inflate on me now, partner. We don't *know* that for sure 'bout Fagan."

"Maybe not, but we've heard it more than once. Why take the chance? I mean, given what we've actually seen Fagan do, why wouldn't he smoke you if you tanked his little racket?"

She watched the big man lean forward again, cradling his head in his large hands, his elbows on his knees, his face inches from the air-conditioning duct in the cruiser's dash. She could imagine him sitting like that in his apartment for hours struggling over what to do, and she knew if she talked him out of it now, she might save his life but crush the self-respect he had rebuilt.

When he leaned back, he stared straight ahead. "Look, Cindy. I'm goin' on up in there to make my report like I said. I'm a lot of things, but I'm no quitter. What Fagan and his crew been doin' ain't right, and someone's gotta shut him down. You young. You got your whole career 'heada you, and I wouldn't be s'pectin' you to put that on the line. But me? It don't matter what happen to me no more. This is just somethin' I gotta do. Know what I'm sayin'?"

He turned and looked at her, dark eyes glistening. She could tell his emotions were churning when his speech got a little "homey," as he called it. She broke eye contact, not wanting to embarrass him.

"Don't worry 'bout it," he added, his voice growing husky. "No way am I gonna drag you into this. I'll make sure of that."

"Harry, that's not what I'm saying. It's you I'm concerned about."

"I know, and I 'preciate it. But I gotta do it. No way 'round it."

She heard the door click open. He turned once more and gave her a mock salute, grinning like a schoolboy. "See you. I shouldn't be too long." Then he stepped out of the cruiser and headed for the Office of Professional Standards.

Detective Bentley, please sit down."

It was a warmly decorated conference room, not a police interrogation cell like so many in which Harry had spent hours questioning suspects. But as he took his seat on the other side of the polished mahogany table from the three "suits," he felt like he was as much on the grill as any perp.

"I understand from this report that you feel there have been a few problems in your Special Operations Section."

"That's what it says. But ..." Harry looked back and forth at the three of them. "Perhaps you gentlemen would be so kind as to let me know just who I'm speaking with before we dig in too deep."

"Of course. I'm Captain Roger Gilson, chief investigator for the IPRA. And"—he motioned to the man to his right—"this is my assistant, Carl Handley." He turned to his left. "Bill Frazer sits in on these hearings as counsel for the city. And that little tape recorder between us is here in place of hiring another court recorder. Tight budget, you know."

Harry Bentley slid his chair in a little closer. "You did say this was the IPRA, the *Independent*"—he emphasized the word as he raised one eyebrow—"Police Review Authority, right? Even though two of you are from the department and Frazier, here, represents the city?"

"*Entirely* independent." Gilson waved both hands over the table like an umpire signaling Safe. "We have no contact with any of the line officers, completely insulated. And we take orders from no one, not even the mayor's office."

Harry rolled his eyes … *Not in Chicago*. He took a deep breath and plunged on. "As you can see from my report, I've been in the SOS for six years. At first we were doing a lot of good putting away dope pushers and gangbangers. And there are still good men and women in the unit, don't get me wrong. But it's been taken over by rogues, particularly …" Harry took a deep breath. "Particularly Matty Fagan."

"What do you mean, 'taken over'? This Fagan, he's your boss, isn't he?"

"Yeah, Lieutenant Matthew Fagan. Irish, you know. Likes to be called Matty. But … well, if you read my report, it details three raids where we had no warrants but broke into citizens' homes anyway. On two of those occasions we found large quantities of drugs, cash, and weapons. We confiscated them all but did not make any arrests—probably couldn't have made them stick without warrants. But a short time later, all that contraband disappeared, back onto the streets. Then—"

"Mr. Bentley," interrupted Frazier, the lawyer, "you lost me there for a minute. How do you *know* this money and dope and guns ended up back on the street?"

Harry rubbed his hand across his smooth head. "I don't have any proof about the drugs, but they did disappear. And I'm sure the money went into the pockets of a few members of the unit, because they talked about it—"

"Wait, they *talked about it*? And you think they'll admit to that?" Frazier snorted.

"Course not. But the guns … there I have evidence. I recorded the serial numbers from those guns, and three weeks later I pulled one off a perp. The number matched! It's even in my arrest report."

The three investigators looked at one another. "Harry," said Captain Gilson, his voice confidential, "would you consider any of the men in your unit your enemies? Any, uh, racial problems going on?"

Harry's gut clinched. He wasn't about to dignify that one with a direct answer. "Captain, look at my report again. We had no warrant for the third incident either. Didn't find any drugs *or* weapons. But we did find more than six thousand dollars in a Ziploc bag in the back of an old woman's freezer. Fagan walked out of the house with that woman's money in his pocket. No criminals apprehended. No arrest. Just a raid!"

"Why didn't you say something at the time?"

"I did. But Fagan shrugged it off. 'It's drug money, Bentley. Those gangbangers do it all the time—stash their cash with grandma, auntie, or their girlfriend, wherever they think we won't look. Well, we looked … and finders, keepers!' That's what Fagan said."

Gilson leaned toward his assistant and mumbled out of the side of his mouth, "Fagan's probably right."

Harry heard him."You think so?" Intensity furrowed his brow even deeper as he hunched forward over the table. "You think I don't know that happens all the time? I'm no rookie. But that's not what happened *this* time. I'm tellin' you, this old woman wasn't holdin'. Even if she was—whether that was drug money or not—Lieutenant Fagan had no right barging in and taking it for himself. This kind of thing happens all the time with him. The guys talk, but on these three occasions—the ones in my report—I was there. I saw it go down. And I'm willing to testify."

Captain Gilson busied himself flipping through Harry's report. "Okay, okay, Bentley. Let's say everything in your report is accurate—"

"It is!"

"All right." Gilson held up his hand. "I just want to ask why are you entering a complaint *now*?" He turned both palms up in a helpless gesture. "A lot of people might consider your unit a service to the community, even if it does cut a few corners, know what I mean? They're happy for an all-out war on the scumbags. But here you are, turning on your own. Why?"

Harry leaned back in the chair. Good question. He had a lot to lose. But he shook his head. "I … I got a kid, or at least I had a kid … I lost him to the streets. I joined the SOS to make a difference … but what do I find? The SOS is at the rotten core of the whole problem. That's why!"

CINDY WATCHED HARRY BENTLEY push open the glass door of the office building and stride across the parking lot, his tread heavy, head forward. Uh-oh. Didn't look like it went too well. What would Harry do, now that he had made his play?

"Hey, partner. How'd it go?"

"Uh, okay, I guess. Let's roll."

"Nah, nah, nah. You don't get by me with that." She put the cruiser in gear and turned to back out of the parking spot. "Come on. Spill it. What'd they say? They gonna open an investigation?"

"Yeah, but …"

"Yeah, but what? Didn't they believe you? What happened?"

"They probably believed me, but I'm not so sure how eager they are to bust it open. They're more worried about the bad press it'll give the department."

"But they're gonna do it? Right?"

"They gotta do it since I made a formal report. But …"

"But what? Come on, man, don't make me pull thread by thread. What happened?"

Cindy watched Harry out of the corner of her eye as she turned into traffic along 35th Street. He leaned back against the headrest. "They want me off the force."

"What?"

"Ah, it kinda makes sense. They say if the time comes I have to testify, I'll be seen as a more independent witness … nothing to gain or lose."

"So how's that gonna happen?"

"Take early retirement. I got twenty years in, so they can put out the word that I was 'encouraged' to retire because of … of …" He turned and stared out the side window.

"Because of what?"

"Because of the problems I was havin'."

"You mean the drinking? But you're on top of that now! You've been in AA for over a year. Everybody knows that."

"Yeah, I know. They're just saying it'd be a good cover. No one would suspect me of being the whistle-blower until the hearing. But believe me, Cindy …" He shook his head. "I don't wanna go out with a cloud hanging over my head either way—for still having a problem or for being a whistle-blower."

"But Harry, it's not a bad plan. It might keep you alive, you know. And besides, you'd have your pension. You're not *that* old. You could start over, a new career, whole new life. It'd be like a second chance. Man, you oughta go for it! And you know I'll come around and check on you from time to time." She grinned.

"Yeah, maybe."

Cindy looked over at him. It *was* a good plan, but she knew the downside. Even if Fagan and his gang got sent upriver, Harry had broken the blue code of silence. Once it got out that he was the whistle-blower, there wouldn't be a precinct in the whole city where he could go in and get a cup of coffee.

Chapter 1

EIGHT MONTHS, AND HARRY STILL HAD TO REMIND HIMSELF not to strap on his Glock when he got out of bed each morning. But he was beginning to adjust to his new job as doorman for Richmond Towers, an upscale high-rise on Chicago's lakefront. Occasionally he could read on the job, and now that he had landed the day shift, he could relax and get other stuff done in the evenings. "Copacetic" is what his grandmama would have called it—with just enough interesting characters around to stave off boredom.

Like now. He watched through the rain-streaked floor-to-ceiling windows as a hunched figure dragged something toward the door. A second figure emerged out of the mist, limping along behind. Harry stepped quickly around his chest-high desk to confront them both just as they came inside the revolving door.

"Hey! Get that rickety cart outta here," he barked at the homeless derelict hauling all her worldly possessions. "Lady, you can't come in here. Residents only."

But the person behind the frizzle-haired woman looked slightly familiar—late-thirties, attractive, in spite of the dripping ringlets hanging down around her face. She grimaced and waggled her fingers toward him in a tentative wave. "Uh, she's with me, Mr. Bentley … Mrs. Fairbanks."

Fairbanks? Harry looked more closely. "Fairbanks? Penthouse?" He nodded toward the old woman, frowning as deeply as ever. "Whatchu doin' with this old bag lady?" Then he noticed a bloody rag around the younger woman's bare foot. "Are you all right, ma'am? What happened to your foot?"

"It's all right, Mr. Bentley. I, uh, we just need to get up to the, uh, apartment and get into some dry clothes." She smiled and flipped up her ID card with a *ta-da* flourish, then swiped it through the scanner that opened the glass security door leading to the elevators.

Harry walked back around his crescent-shaped desk and settled onto his high-backed stool. Some of these rich people were a piece of work. He could keep the riffraff out of any place, but making nice to the residents at the same time could get complicated. Like the kid on twenty-two who kept bringing in his punk friends, smelling of dope and banging their skateboards against the walls. Harry raked his knuckles over the wiry gray horseshoe beard that ran along his jawline and wished the management would create clearer guidelines.

The house phone rang, and he picked up the black receiver. "Richmond Towers. Can I help you?"

"Is this Harold Josiah Bentley?"

He hesitated. "Who's askin'?"

"My name is Leslie Stuart, and I'm calling from the Department of Children and Family Services. I need you to verify whether I'm speaking to Harold Josiah Bentley."

"I'm Bentley. But did you say DCFS? I don't have any kids." He pulled the receiver away from his ear and frowned at it, the grooves in his forehead growing deeper. "How'd you get this number, anyway?"

The woman was quiet for a moment. "Do you have a son named Rodney?"

Rodney! Harry stiffened. It had been ten years. What had Rodney done now? Hearing someone coming through the revolving door, Harry swung around on his stool and lowered his voice. "Look, can't talk now. Got people here. Besides, this phone's supposed to be for internal use only. No personal calls." He slammed down the receiver and stood up with a placid smile on his face.

"Oh, Mr. Bentley, I'm so glad you're here," said a white-haired woman. She was probably the same age as Harry, but he thought of her as much older. "I forgot my cash. Could you run out and pay the cabby for me? I'll take care of you later."

Knowing he hadn't been "taken care of" since the last time, Harry still smiled broadly and said, "Happy to, Mrs. Worthington. How much does he need?"

"Oh, I think it was fifteen-something. But be sure to give him a dollar tip. You know, Mr. Bentley, I want to thank you so much. That kid who works here on the weekends when you're gone would never be so nice."

Harry went out and tossed a twenty through the window of the cab and came back in before his shiny dome could catch too many raindrops. The phone was already ringing again. He reached over his counter and picked it up more slowly this time. "*Richmond Towers* ..." He emphasized the name. "Can I help you?"

"Mr. Bentley, I do need to speak to you today." He recognized the voice as the lady with DCFS. "If this phone's not good, do you have another number where I could reach you?"

"Yes, but I'm on duty right now. Can't this wait? Couldn't you call me some other time ... like on Saturday? I'm off Saturday."

"I'd rather not work on Saturday if I don't have to, Mr. Bentley. Look, we need to talk ASAP, so can't we just do it now?"

Harry blew through pursed lips and gave her his cell number. Within a minute his *Law and Order* ring tone sounded.

"Now, Mr. Bentley, if you would just confirm your birth date for me, we can—"

"Wait a minute. Before I confirm *anything*, what's this about?"

There was a deep sigh on the other end of the line. "It's about your son, Rodney. With him not making bail, he's likely to be in Cook County for—"

"What'd he do?"

"Well ... for now he's pled innocent, so his case will take at least six months. In fact, it could be a couple years before he's sentenced. And who knows what after that. So we've gotta place your grandson in foster—"

"*Grandson*? What grandson?"

"Rodney's nine-year-old son, DaShawn ... You do know about DaShawn, don't you?"

Harry's shoulders slumped. Rodney had a kid? "Uh, I kinda lost touch with Rodney some time ago."

"Listen, Mr. Bentley, I need you to confirm your date of birth before we continue. Confidentiality, you understand. Wouldn't want to be discussing these matters with the wrong person. So when were you born?"

Harry Bentley swiveled around on his stool so that his back was to the revolving door. He sighed again. Dealing with Rodney always meant drama. "February 23, 1948. When did he have a baby?"

"February 23, 1948? Okaaay"—she dragged out the word as though she were checking the date—"and you *are* Harold Josiah Bentley, right?"

"Yes, yes, and I was born on the south side and served as one of Chicago's finest for twenty years. You wanna do a background check on me?" He cringed as soon as he'd said it. He didn't need anyone plowing through his past, turning up the supposed reason he'd been encouraged to retire from the force.

"A background check won't be necessary at this time, Mr. Bentley, but if you could come down to DCFS tomorrow, we'd like to talk about the possibility of you taking the boy."

"Wait a minute. Wait a minute. What about the mama? Why don't she take the kid?—Hold on. I got a call on the other line." He laid down the cell and spun around to pick up the house phone, even though his cell continued to emit the tinny scratch of Ms. Stuart's voice as it lay on the desk.

"Richmond Towers."

"Mr. Bentley?"

"Yes." At least *this* call was an internal one.

"Yes, it's, uh, Mrs. Fairbanks. Top floor. Do you know the whereabouts of a homeless shelter for women in the area?"

Harry chuckled to himself. So the "pet" she'd brought home wasn't working out so well. "Yeah, I think there's one just a couple blocks from the Sheridan El stop."

"Is that nearby?"

Harry began to give directions when Mrs. Fairbanks cut in again. "All right. Thanks—no wait. Could you call a cab for my, uh, friend?"

"Sure," Harry said.

"Thanks. We'll be down in a few."

Harry hung up and glanced at his cell. He was tempted to close it, but he picked it up. "You still there?"

"Sure am—"

"Hang on. There's somethin' else I gotta do."

He laid it back down and called the cab.

Finally, he picked up the cell. "Okay, Ms. Stuart, now … Oh, yeah. Why isn't that boy with his mother?"

"She's in rehab. Crack. So can you come down?"

Harry rested his elbows on the counter, head in hands. "Ms. Stuart, I'm not off until Saturday—"

"Then Saturday'll have to do. *I'll* come in on *my* day off. You be here—100 West Randolph—at 10 a.m. and give the security my name, Leslie Stuart."

She hung up before Harry could object. He slapped the desk. He'd left himself wide open for that one, mentioning he'd be off Saturday. Maybe he shouldn't show up … but he knew he would.

In a few minutes, Mrs. Fairbanks came down with the bag lady in tow and handed him a ten to put the old woman in the waiting cab.

THAT SATURDAY, THE BRISK and businesslike Leslie Stuart—pale eyes, long, straight dishwater blonde hair—asked a lot of questions: Yes, he had a pension from the police department, and he also worked full time. No, he wasn't married. His ex—her name was Willa Mae—left him ten years ago because of the pressures of being a detective. No, he didn't know where she was or whether she had gone back to using her maiden name of Taylor. And Harry didn't offer the information that back then he'd also had a little trouble with the bottle, because all that was behind him now … at least as long as he attended an occasional meeting. His apartment was small, but, yes, there was a second bedroom. No it wasn't empty; it was his *den* and gonna stay that way!

"Listen, Ms. Stuart, I haven't agreed to take this kid, so I don't know why you're asking all these questions."

"I'm asking all these questions so I can know whether we even *want* to consider you for custody of your grandson. Our first goal in a situation like this is always relative foster care. But I need to know whether you qualify."

Qualify? Why wouldn't he qualify? But then he felt a stab in his gut: he hadn't been there for Rodney, and now his son was in jail.

Ms. Stuart wanted to schedule a home visit.

"A home visit?"

Somehow, Harry managed to get out of her office without making any commitments.

Where are *you* off to, Mrs. Fairbanks, all twinkletoes today?" Harry called out to the curlyhead from the penthouse as she bounced through the lobby the next Thursday morning.

She spun around with a laugh. "I'm interviewing for a job, Mr. Bentley. Wish me luck!"

Yeah, well, she'd need it. "What are you up to now, might I ask?"

"That shelter you told me about needs a program director—and I'm it!" She giggled. "Seriously, Mr. Bentley, I'm a qualified CTRS and this job seems just right for me."

He put down the newspaper he'd been reading and pursed his lips. "Oh, it does, does it? What do you know about homeless people, Mrs. Fairbanks?—no disrespect intended."

She grimaced and glanced around as though looking for someone to answer for her. "Well, good point. Not much. But I'd like to learn. And one thing I do know, Mr. Bentley—*everyone*, rich or poor, male or female, young or old, needs to feel useful, needs purposeful activities or work to occupy their time." She chewed on her lip. "Including me."

Harry smiled. "Good luck then, Mrs. Fairbanks. I'll be lifting up a prayer for you today." It seemed like the thing to say—something his mom would say—though Harry knew he'd never do it. Didn't know how. "Want me to call you a cab?" Now that he *could* do.

"No thanks. I'm taking the El. I did it once, think I can do it again." She waved and pushed through the revolving door onto Sheridan Road.

Harry shook his head. Oh to be young and idealistic again … and with that much energy. Though he knew sometimes such energetic do-gooders could end up doing harm.

But when she returned that afternoon, he tried to respond with enthusiasm. "Ah. There she is. Are you now gainfully employed, Mrs. Fairbanks?"

She screwed up her face. "I'll find out Monday. But in the meantime, I'm going to work on my business wardrobe—shred a few of my jeans, forget to wash my clothes … what?"

Oh boy, just as he'd feared. "Homelessness is not a joke, Mrs. Fairbanks. If you don't know that by now, forget the job. They don't need do-gooders down at that shelter." He held his breath. Was that too harsh?

Her face reddened, but she seemed to recover. "I was just kidding around, Mr. Bentley." And she stomped off toward the elevator.

A few moments later she was back, standing before his half-moon desk. "Mr. Bentley? You were right. My comment was inappropriate. I apologize."

He hardly knew what to say. "That's big of you, Mrs. Fairbanks. Maybe you'll do all right in that job after all." He grinned and stroked his short, grizzled beard in wizened evaluation. "You've got guts, gotta say that."

Chapter 2

THE PERSISTENT MS. STUART wouldn't let Harry alone. She had been calling every other day that week and finally said she would come by to see him on Saturday, April 22.

"It'll be a waste of your time. I won't be home!"

"Listen, Harry, DaShawn's got promise. He's a good student. Don't lose him in the system."

"Yeah, and whose system is that?"

"See you next Saturday, Harry."

"Don't think so."

But on the off-chance she'd show up anyway, he decided not to be there. When Saturday came, he did his grocery shopping at Dominick's down the street from Richmond Towers and went around back where his nephew worked stock, wasting as much of his time as he dared. Then he drove up to Evanston to check on his elderly mother—boy, he already had a "social work" job with her. He'd have to find more support for her soon, maybe even move her to a retirement home.

Still killing time, he decided to drive down to the south side. At the very least he ought to visit Rodney at Cook County. Online he'd discovered Rodney was in Division 9, but the charges against him were not listed, just that he had been denied bail. *Denied bail?* The social worker had suggested that he hadn't been able to *make* bail, but if he had been *denied* bail, his offense—or charge, Harry reminded himself, since he hadn't been convicted yet—must've been pretty serious. Where had he failed in raising that kid?

Harry hated this kind of drama. He stood stiffly in line at the jail along with all the wives and mothers and girlfriends and children who'd come to visit inmates. Not many visitors looked like fathers. No wonder most of the children in the room were completely out of control. What was the chance Rodney's boy "had promise" coming from a home with a crack addict for a mom and a con for a father? Maybe Ms. Stuart had just been selling him on taking the boy to make her own job easier with a quick placement.

The overweight deputy behind the window clicked through the computer screen when Harry told him who he wanted to see. "He doesn't have anyone on his visitor list," the man said without looking up.

"Yeah, yeah ... *visitor list.* I know the routine. But I'm his father."

"Sorry. If he didn't list you, he doesn't want to see you."

"He didn't know I was coming. Look." Harry pulled out his membership card for the Retired Chicago Police Association and pushed it through the opening to join his driver's license he'd already submitted. "I'm CPD, retired. Can't you just call him down here?"

The deputy shoved the cards back without even looking at them. "I'll put in the call, but he don't have to come down. Step into the room to your right. Put all your personal items, including your belt, in a locker and wait until your name is called."

Harry waited for three hours while groups of about a dozen people at a time were buzzed through the heavy steel door into the next room for visitation. When his name was not among the last batch, he headed home.

Before he knew it, he was pulling in behind his apartment building with no memory of the drive. It was as if he'd been totally drunk, blacked out. But his mind had been busy reviewing his own life as a father—him working too many hours, coming home wound tighter than a guitar string … when he managed to come home at all, so determined *his* kid wouldn't end up on the street that he often came down too hard on Rodney. Not a good scene! He swallowed hard as he got out of his black-and-silver RAV4 and wiped his eyes, looking around to be sure no one noticed.

Well, what's done is done. You can't change the past, he told himself.

Nevertheless, on Monday he wired one hundred dollars by Western Union to the commissary account of Bentley, Rodney, jail ID #2006-0008021 at CCDOC, Illinois. Then he wished he hadn't. It was probably just throwing good money after bad.

All that week Harry successfully dodged more calls from Ms. Stuart. He wasn't going to be bullied into a responsibility he hadn't asked for. But he was thinking more and more about his own son. On the last Saturday of the month he went back down to Cook County Jail and found that Rodney had finally added his name to his list. He was called with the second batch of visitors. After going through a metal detector and being searched, a guard directed him down a beige corridor with a dozen cubicles on the left. In each cubicle was a round metal stool anchored to the floor. In the third one from the end, Harry faced a window of thick glass with a single three-inch grill at mouth level. The fine-meshed screen in the grill was so packed with dirt and lint that Harry could not see any pinpricks of light through it.

"Keep your hands and mouths and all other body parts off the glass," the guard said loudly. "We don't have time to be cleaning up your smears. If you get up off the stool, your time's up and you're outta here. If you have children with you and they leave the cubicle, your time's up and you're outta here. Do not speak to or interact with the people in the adjoining booth. You are under audio and video surveillance the entire time. Anything you or an inmate says in this facility is admissible in court."

In about five minutes, a line of men dressed in CCDOC tan smocks and pants paraded in under the supervision of two guards on the other side of the glass. Rodney shuffled in third and sat down opposite Harry on a similar stool.

"Hey," Harry said.

"Hey." Rodney looked off to the side. It was almost impossible to hear him through the clogged grill.

"So, how'd you get in here?"

"I sure didn't ..." His voice trailed off.

"Speak up! Can't hear you."

"I *said*, I sure didn't pay no hundred bucks like you did."

"Come on, Rodney. I just wanted to see you."

"So ... now you've seen me."

Harry studied his son, who still hadn't made eye contact with him. In spite of a scar above his right eye that Harry didn't remember, he said, "You're lookin' pretty good."

"Yeah, well you know we get three squares a day. Like for lunch today we got what they call 'mush'—potatoes and rice with some green Jell-O on the side."

"Ha. So much for coddling prisoners with gourmet dining."

Rodney finally made eye contact with Harry. They stared at each other for a few moments.

"What's your case?"

"You oughta know. You're a cop. Throw in a little of this, a little of that, drop some evidence on you, and make a case. It's all trumped up."

"The computer says you were denied bail. That's more than a simple drug bust. What'd you do, Rodney?"

"You think I'm gonna tell you? You once said you'd drop a dime on me before you'd buy me new Nikes."

Harry winced. "Okay then, what'd they *charge* you with?"

Rodney shook his head. "You look it up." He got up suddenly and left.

Harry sat there. If he were to hire a good attorney, he probably could get a second bond hearing and bail his son out, but should he? Not if his son wouldn't even tell him what the charge was. He could be a murderer or child molester or something. It was the same old standoff. He never could get through to that kid.

By the second Friday in May it seemed like the DCFS woman had finally given up. Marvelous inventions—voice mail and caller ID—you could avoid just about anyone you didn't want to talk to.

Harry took the day off, redeeming a little comp time for some of the evenings he had worked late. He had a dentist appointment at 10:30 and could use the afternoon to catch up on things at the apartment.

He arrived home two hours later with a flappy lip and headed for the bathroom to see if his lip looked as fat as it felt. He was making faces at himself in the mirror when his apartment doorbell sounded.

The intercom from downstairs wasn't working, and he wasn't expecting anyone, so he let it ring. But they wouldn't quit … probably some salesperson. Finally, after the fourth ring, he buzzed the person up and went to stand in his open doorway to see who it was, not wanting to admit some unknown person to the building.

He heard them climbing the stairs, and then from around the corner appeared Ms. Stuart, grinning like he should be proud of her for doing two flights of stairs without puffing.

"Hello, Mr. Bentley. Called you at work, but they said you had the day off. We were beginning to think you'd moved to Florida, but here you are."

"Huh," he mumbled, wanting to say, *"Wherever I go, there you are!"* but he bit it off. Harry looked down. The "we" Leslie Stuart mentioned was a brown-skinned boy following her who sported a huge Afro, the size of which Harry hadn't seen since the seventies.

Ms. Stuart came on until she stood right before Harry. "Well, can we come in?"

"Mm. Guess so." He swung the door wider and stepped out of the way. "And this is …?" He watched the hair float by him like a bouncing halo. It had to be at least six inches long.

"This is DaShawn! Shake hands with your grandfather, DaShawn."

The hair stopped, pivoted, and from underneath a boy looked up at him, and then extended his hand. A nice, firm grip.

"Uh … how you doin', young man?"

"Aiight."

Leslie Stuart cleared her throat. "DaShawn!"

"Oh, yeah. I'm fine, sir."

"Hm." Harry gestured across the room. "You all, go ahead and take a seat on the couch, there." He picked up the papers from his TV chair. "Wasn't expecting company." He massaged his lip with his tongue. Could they tell it was still numb?

"So, DaShawn. This is my crib. Not much, but …" Should he offer a tour? "Living room, eating area, kitchen." He gestured toward the obvious in the open-floor plan of the compact apartment.

"Down the hall there, bathroom is on the right, then my bedroom and the den. Just enough for one person." He glowered at Leslie Stuart, pausing. "You all want some water or something?"

The boy shrugged, causing his halo to bounce. Harry retrieved three bottles of water from the refrigerator, studying the boy as he passed them out. Other than the big hair, DaShawn was a replica of Rodney at the same age. Same caramel-smooth skin. Same distinct eyebrows and strong forehead. Same little smirk. But the social worker had said *this* boy was a "good student." Rodney had never been a good student.

"You like school?"

"Yeah, pretty much."

That was something to which most nine-year-olds wouldn't admit these days. Maybe DaShawn did have promise.

Harry made small talk, asking about where he was staying, what sports he liked, but all Harry could see was Rodney in the boy's every gesture and expression. Somehow the memory of a certain spring evening haunted Harry. Rodney had asked if he would come to his basketball game the next night. The park district team was in the round-robin playoffs. "You got it, sport!" But the next day he had a big blowout with his captain and was so mad by the time he got off duty, he headed straight for Dugan's, the only Irish pub in Greektown. By the time he left, he was plastered and got stopped on the way home. He would have received a DUI if he hadn't flashed his badge.

"You didn't show up. You never *show up!"* was all Rodney had said. Harry's stomach rolled over with the memory. Perhaps even Rodney had promise. He couldn't remember. If he could just relive those years ...

"You know, I'm not under so much stress anymore." He glanced at the DCFS woman, having almost mentioned AA. "Let's just say, things are different now, Rodney. Maybe—"

"I'm not *Rodney*! That's my old man."

"Right! Right. DaShawn." Harry stabbed the air with his finger. "It's just that you look ... ah, forget it. I'll get it right: *DaShawn*."

Rodney's childhood was gone, and maybe there was nothing Harry could do for him. But after seeing DaShawn—his own flesh and blood—he really didn't want the boy lost in the system.

The rest of the conversation was a blur until Leslie Stuart stood and said, "We should probably get going. I'll call you later, Mr. Bentley." In a matter of moments, she and DaShawn were out the door.

He closed it behind them and drifted back across the living room as though lost in a stupor. Did that just happen? Maybe it had been a reaction to the Novocain. His lip was back to normal now.

Given the woman's persistence, Harry expected a call on Monday, but it came late that same afternoon, apparently as soon as Leslie Stuart got back to the office. Didn't this woman know when to quit? It was Friday, after all!

"So are you going to take him?"

"*Take him?* How can I answer that after a thirty-minute visit?" But Harry had wrestled with that very question ever since the boy left.

"Good," Stuart said. "At least that's not an outright *no*."

"Ms. Stuart, you are the pushiest woman I've ever met. How can I take him? I work full time—don't get home till seven. What am I supposed to do?"

She didn't answer ... making him deal with his own questions.

He shook his head. "Look, I don't want the boy to get lost in the system any more than you do. Maybe you could find a good family, and I could have him visit me sometimes on weekends."

"That won't do it, Mr. Bentley. And I think you know it."

"All right. All right."

Leslie Stuart waited two beats. "*All right* as in visits won't do it, or *all right* as in you'll take the boy?"

"*All right* as in I'll consider it."

"Fair enough, Mr. Bentley. Call you Monday."

Harry sighed as his phone went dead. A two-day break. But his mind gave him no vacation. He immediately started arguing with himself.

He wanted to do right by his grandson, but what if the boy developed an attitude like Rodney? As a cop, his radar was well tuned. The kid wouldn't get away with much, but Harry knew the boy needed more than a cop. He needed a relationship with a man who loved him, and Harry wasn't sure he knew how to do that.

His heart pounded. How could a kid do that to him? He should calm down. He needed a … no, he wasn't going down that alley. But he needed something to get his mind off the whole question. In the months since he had retired from the police force, Harry had been surprised to discover that his circle of friends included only cops. He hardly knew anyone else anymore. But under the circumstances, he couldn't continue hanging out with them. So where was he to go?

Wait … what day was this? Friday? That Fairbanks woman had invited him to what she called "Fun Night" at the homeless shelter where she worked. He smiled to himself as he recalled how that spunky curlyhead from the penthouse had found a place for the old bag lady—whether she wanted it or not—and then ended up working there herself.

Mrs. Fairbanks, now she was all right. Maybe he *would* go by there this evening. At least, it'd be something to do.

Chapter 3

IT WAS NEARLY 8 P.M. BEFORE HARRY BENTLEY ARRIVED at the shelter. And just as Mrs. Fairbanks had said, the place looked like a small church crunched between three-story brick buildings, but the construction was obviously new. On the steps were a couple of "brothers." One, a wiry fellow in a red T-shirt and jeans, was sitting halfway up the steps smoking a cigarette, cupping the butt in his hand as though he didn't want anyone to see it. He was talking to a taller, professionally dressed man who stood down on the sidewalk with one foot on the first step, hands in his pockets.

"Hey, how you doin'?" He nodded to both men and jerked his thumb toward the building. "Is this that women's shelter?"

The standing man turned. "This is Manna House, if that's what you mean. What can we do for you?"

"Well, I …" Harry stopped, realizing for the first time how out of place he might appear. "You see, this woman—name's Fairbanks—who lives in the building where I work, told me they were having a party here tonight, and …" He shrugged, palms up. "Oh, man, this sounds a little whacked out, but she invited me to drop by." Harry laughed like it was just a joke.

The two men looked at one another and joined in with half laughs. The one standing said, "Well, if Gabby Fairbanks invited you ..." He stuck out his hand. "I'm Peter Douglass. And this is Carl Hickman."

Carl extended his fist and bumped knuckles with Harry. "Yo, man."

"Bentley, Harry Bentley."

Carl grinned up at him as he ran his hand over his own balding head. "You *Harry*, huh?"

"Hey, you'll be there soon enough, bro." They all laughed, and Harry began to relax. "You guys goin' to this party thing?"

"We just come out for some air." Carl took a drag on his cigarette.

"I'm on the board of Manna House," Peter explained. "Several of us drop by to help out whenever we can."

Just then a van pulled up, the engine missing on at least one cylinder as it puffed blue smoke from the tailpipe. A middle-aged white couple was inside. The driver leaned out the window. "Josh and Edesa here yet?"

"Yep," said Carl. "They been here from the start." As the van began to pull away, Carl called again, "Hey Denny, ain't you guys comin'?"

"Soon as I can find a place to park this thing." Carl got up and flipped his cigarette butt to the curb. "Well, Harry Bentley, you ready to chance it?"

"Chance what?"

Carl grinned. "God only knows." And turned toward the shelter.

Harry shrugged. "Sure." What was so "chancy" about a party with the staff and residents of a homeless shelter? He followed the other two men up the steps as Peter punched the door buzzer.

Harry followed them through the foyer and into a large room decorated with crepe paper streamers and pulsing with a Latin beat from a boom box turned too loud for its small speakers. There must have been thirty people in lines dancing in unison, but Harry stuck close to the curlyheaded white woman who had let them in.

Mrs. Fairbanks grinned at him, her face as bright as a sunflower. "Still can't believe you made it, Mr. Bentley! You actually made it! But go ahead." She nodded toward the dancers. "Pick up the step."

"Ha!" He ignored her suggestion and looked around like he was in a museum, even though the walls, floor, and lights were rather utilitarian. "This is quite a place you got here."

Mrs. Fairbanks leaned closer to be heard above the music and laughter. "Yeah, and it's busier than you might expect." Just then the song ended, and everyone stopped, some waving their hands at their faces to cool off.

"Listen up, everyone," his hostess called. "I want you to meet a good friend of mine. This is Mr. Bentley from my building."

Everyone clapped as Harry did a modest wave. "Harry'll do. Just call me Harry."

"Well, Mr. Harry," said a young woman with tiny braids that hung to her shoulders. She emerged from the group and came toward Harry with an outstretched hand. "Come on and join in. All we're doin' is the Macarena. In fact, all you mens, get on out here now and show us your stuff."

Harry had never danced the Macarena and looked to Carl and Peter for an escape, but both of the men he had come in with gave a helpless shrug as they were pulled into the lines. What else could Harry do?

He'd been a good dancer in his day, but the sequence of steps, turns, arm motions, and dips seemed more like the stepping he'd seen kids do on the street. At first he felt lost until he decided to concentrate on duplicating the movements of just one person—a woman next to him who was more his age and size. Her movements were so graceful and understated, it took all the intimidation out of them, and soon Harry was in the groove.

She smiled at him, then turned away, causing her long gold earrings to swing against the warm brown of her cheeks. Harry couldn't help thinking that she looked as regal as the royal blue caftan she wore.

When the dance ended and everyone clapped, Mrs. Fairbanks said loudly enough to be heard, "Not too shabby, Mr. Bentley. See, it didn't take you long."

"Ha! If you'd been doing the Mashed Potato, well *then* you'd have really seen somethin'."

"Mashed Potato? What's the Mashed Potato?" said the girl with tiny braids.

"Oh, come on, now. You don't know what the Mashed Potato is? But I guess you wouldn't. Probably before your time." Harry gave a sly glance at the sister in blue. "Who else knows that oldie but goodie?"

With a dropped jaw, the woman gave a wide-eyed look of mock horror. "Hey, I was only ten when that one came out!" But she broke into a couple of moves.

Everyone cheered, and the tall white kid on the boom box punched the button. In a hot minute Harry and the blue queen were twisting heel and toe in perfect rhythm as the rest of the revelers gathered around, clapping to the beat.

"All right! All right now! Come on, the rest of you join in. This ain't no exhibition, and it's a lot easier than that … that Macaroni, or whatever you were doing before."

Whooping and hollering, half the group stepped up. When the music finally cut out, Harry mopped his face with his handkerchief. "I guess I even broke a sweat on that one," he joked, following his dance partner toward the refreshment table. "Guess you heard, my name's Harry Bentley. And you are … ?"

"Estelle. Estelle Williams."

"Thank you for the dance, Miss Williams."

She laughed. "Please, just Estelle."

"It's a deal if I can be just Harry."

"All right, *Just Harry*." She laughed again.

As they both filled paper cups with punch, Harry stole a few glances at Estelle. Such a warm smile, and he liked the way her full hair fell, streaked with silver, almost to her shoulders. Very classy. He almost asked whether she worked at the shelter, but what if she lived there? No, couldn't be. She couldn't be a homeless person. But if he couldn't ask what she did, what kind of small talk could he initiate to get to know her?

She came to his rescue as they found a couple of chairs and sat down. "So, sounds like you know our Gabby."

"Gabby? Oh, you mean Mrs. Fairbanks." Odd. The two names didn't go together. "Yeah ... I met her when she moved into Richmond Towers." Did he want to admit to being a step-and-fetch-it doorman? "Actually, I'm retired. Chicago PD. But I took a job as doorman in that building. Just somethin' to do, you know. Like they say, *use it or lose it*, so I try to keep busy."

"Chicago PD? Hm."

This was a good time to change the subject. "And you?" he asked, pretty sure she couldn't be a homeless person. "What brings you here?"

"Who me?" She laughed again and waved a hand. "Oh, God brought me here. Actually, I volunteer to make lunch for Manna House. So I'm here most every day."

"Oh, that's great." Whew, she wasn't a resident. "Always good to give back to the community."

"Amen, brother. And I owe a lot to Manna House. Had to make myself useful, you know. It was the least I could do."

"Oh yeah. Know what you mean." But he didn't. Why'd she *owe* them? "So, what do you do with the rest of your time?"

She arched an eyebrow as if he were asking too many questions. But still she answered. "I'm a certified nurse assistant. I do elder care. That's the God part. See, when I first came to Manna House, I didn't really have any marketable skills, but after the shelter burned down and we all had to find other places to live, the woman I ended up sharing an apartment with helped me get certified. She's a social worker, so she knew all about the CNA programs offered by various colleges."

Harry's mind was spinning. He'd noticed she wore no ring, but these days, what did that prove? But if she shared an apartment with another woman, she wasn't married. She did elder care. Hm, interesting. But what was that about having to find alternative housing after the shelter burned down?

"So there was a fire? Wow." He looked around. "Did a killer job restorin' this place. Looks like new."

"That's 'cause it is. Had to be completely rebuilt. Let's see, that was after New Year's, 2004. I'd only been here a short time, but boy, when your home burns down, it's a real crisis."

"You lived here?"

"Yep." Her lips tightened.

Harry knew he'd put his foot in it. Better change the subject quick. "So … Estelle, you said you do elder care. That's like taking care of old people or something? You work in a nursing home?"

She shook her head. "No. I do private care."

"Well, I could sure use some of that!"

"Harry Bentley!" She rolled her eyes and shook her head. "I know you ain't that old, so don't go flirtin' with me, now."

"No, no! I didn't mean it that way." He held up his hand and laughed. "I meant for my mama. She's gettin' on in years, and I'm gonna have to find somethin' for her before long. But she don't want to go to no home."

"I understand. Maybe I can give you some ideas. There are a lot of senior services available most people don't know about."

"That'd be good."

The party had been going on without them, and Harry had noticed that Mrs. Fairbanks—everybody at Manna House called her Gabby—was doing a great job. More games, more dancing, lots of laughing, but the time had come to wrap things up.

"Guess we better help out." He got up and joined the other men, folding up the chairs and clearing the snack table.

As the volunteers and guests began saying good-bye to the residents and drifting toward the door, Harry made sure he walked beside Estelle.

"I'd be glad to see you home, if you'd like." Stupid! He hadn't driven his car, but he could call a cab.

"Oh, no. That's okay, Harry. Thanks for the offer, but I already called my housemate. She wanted to be here tonight, but she ran into some unexpected job thing, takin' a kid to his mama's or somethin'. She'll be along any minute now to pick me up. Probably needs a taxi license, she does so much runnin' around!"

"Yeah, try getting one of those in Chicago."

Estelle's laughing response drew Harry in until he realized he was grinning as broadly as a clown while he descended the steps of Manna House. Though the blustery forty-degree wind didn't invite hanging out, he decided to wait with Estelle until her ride came.

"Hey, Harry." Peter Douglas, one of the guys who'd greeted him when he first arrived, stuck out his hand. "Looks like you had a good evening. Glad you came."

"Yeah. Me too."

"Say, some of us get together at my place on Tuesday nights for Bible study. All the guys you saw here tonight and a few others. We'd sure be glad for you to join us."

"Ah, I don't know. Haven't been to church in a while."

Peter laughed. "Well, this ain't church, though church is good. We just read a little of the Word and talk about what it means, then pray for each other."

"Well, uh"—Harry looked down and shook his head—"I haven't done much prayin' either, I guess."

"Oh, that's okay. Never too young to start."

They both laughed.

"You know, one of the best things about getting together with the guys is we're often going through similar stuff—how to raise our kids, challenges on the job, where'd all the money go?—what everyone faces, but a lot of guys feel like they're in it alone. You oughta come, give it a try. Here's my card. It's got my home address. Tuesdays at seven."

"Thanks. I'll see 'bout it."

A snappy Hyundai Accent pulled up to the curb, its finish gleaming candy-apple red below the copper-toned streetlights. "Estelle, let's go!"

"Oh, here's my ride. It was good to meet you, Mr. ... *Just Harry*."

"Same here," he grinned as he walked her to the car.

But when he opened the car door and the dome light came on, Harry did a double take. Could *this* be Estelle's housemate? She'd said she was a social worker, but ... *Leslie Stuart*?!

Chapter 4

THE VOICE FROM WITHIN THE CAR SQUALLED, "Harry Bentley? What are *you* doing here?"

Harry's eyes had not played tricks on him! It *was* Leslie Stuart!

"I … I, uh, just came to the party." Like she didn't think he had a right. "I was *invited*."

"Harry," Estelle's calming voice prodded from behind, "it's kind of cold out here. Mind if I get in?"

He moved out of the way and offered her his hand.

"You two know each other?" Estelle arched that eyebrow.

Harry shook his head, then admitted, "Well … yeah, kinda—"

"I've been working with his grandson … professionally."

"Really? Well, she's a pistol, Harry. Whatever it is, she'll have that grandson of yours set up in no time."

"Yeah. No doubt." Harry bent down as Estelle settled into the passenger seat of the Hyundai and pulled the safety belt across her. "It was good meetin' you, Miss Williams."

"It's Estelle, Harry!… Goodnight, now." She shut the door, and the car pulled away.

Harry stared after the retreating taillights as he rubbed his hand over his smooth head. It felt like someone was choreographing his life, and he wasn't sure he liked it.

HARRY SPENT SUNDAY AT HIS MOTHER'S, it being Mother's Day and all. He brought a rotisserie chicken from Dominick's, whipped up some instant mashed potatoes, and even cooked a bag of frozen green beans—the most cooking he'd done in a month. But the kiss his mother planted on his cheek was worth it. She seemed thinner than ever, and he had noticed that her left hand shook at times.

What was he going to do?

When she fell asleep in her recliner after dinner while watching some preacher on TV, Harry gathered up her dirty clothes to take to the Laundromat. Looking around, he realized the apartment was filthy. Oh great! The woman he'd hired to come in and clean had left a message on his cell two weeks before that she was quitting. But with all the stuff going on about Rodney's kid, he'd forgotten it. He sat down on the sofa and watched his mother breathing heavily, mouth half open. He'd gone through all his acquaintances. So now who could he get?

Estelle Williams. He was sure she didn't do cleaning, but she did elder care, and she'd said she could help him line up various services. Whew. With his mother needing him on one end, and Leslie Stuart trying to get him to take his grandson on the other, he felt like a sandwich some kid had sat on. His mom already needed more help than he'd been giving. He couldn't take on another responsibility.

That's what he would tell Leslie Stuart when she called.

On Monday, Harry turned his cell phone off. Not wanting to deal with the whole mess, he was determined to hang up if she called Richmond Towers. But by evening, there had been no call.

Just before it was time for his replacement to go on duty—the kid was perpetually late—Gabby Fairbanks came in, getting a suitcase large enough for a two-week trip to the Bahamas caught in the revolving doors. Harry was just about to go help her when she freed it and called out, "Hello, Mr. Bentley! Thanks for coming to our Fun Night at the shelter." She beamed. "You were definitely the life of the party."

Harry nodded toward her. "Thank you for inviting me, Mrs. Fairbanks. I looked for you this morning but didn't see you. Did you"—he tipped his head toward the giant suitcase—"go somewhere this weekend?"

She grinned again. "Yes. I flew back to Virginia to see my boys for Mother's Day. They'll be coming next week. Afraid your job may never be the same. They're lively."

"Mm. Wonder who they get that from?... Oh, by the way." Harry looked up toward the ceiling, though there was nothing there but the light fixtures. "The woman named Estelle ... I think she's a volunteer at the shelter. Seemed like a mighty fine woman. I was, uh, wondering if you happen to have her phone number. She said something about doing elder care, and I thought maybe sometime I could talk to her about my, um, mother, in case she, you know, needed some in-home care. Just in case."

Harry looked back at Mrs. Fairbanks in time to see a little smirk curl the corners of her mouth. All right, now what had he done?

"Mr. Bentley! Elder care, my foot. I do believe you have a crush on Miss Estelle Williams!"

"What? Ah, no, no, no. You see, I was just over to my mother's yesterday, and she's not managing very well by herself, so I thought Miss Williams might be able to give me some suggestions. Know what I mean?" He stood watching the curlyhead, realizing he hadn't erased her little smirk. "No, no. You see, you don't understand. Now don't you go sayin' nothin'—"

She held up her free hand, a ring of keys hanging from her thumb. "I'll phone her number to you tomorrow. Okay?"

THAT EVENING, BACK IN HIS OWN PLACE, Harry turned on his cell, but there were no messages from Ms. Stuart. What could that mean? Had she given up on him? Had she done a background check and decided he didn't qualify for being DaShawn's foster parent? Or was she just playing a game with him, waiting until he was so curious, he'd phone her?

Well, he wouldn't play that game. Let her wait. He pulled the two pieces of leftover Giordano's pizza out of the refrigerator and tossed them into the toaster oven. But what would he say when Stuart did call ... presuming she still wanted him to take DaShawn?

Maybe Estelle—or Miss Williams; after all, this *was* just business, right?—could help him line up the help he needed for his mother: weekly cleaning, maybe some personal care, or even a visiting nurse once a month or so, just to make sure she was doing okay physically. And how about that food thing for the elderly, what did they call it? Hot Wheels? No, those were the little cars Rodney used to play with. But it was some kind of "wheels." Ah, well. Estelle would know.

He thought about Estelle moving in that line dance at the party when she first caught his eye with her grace and her regal ... yeah, it was a kind of regal beauty. Grace and beauty. She had grace and beauty, and he could sense it was more than skin-deep. She had a calmness he coveted.

Well, enough of that. As soon as he got her phone number, he'd give her a call.

And if he got things lined up for his mother, perhaps he could clear out the den, get rid of a few things, and move the rest into his bedroom or the living room. Bethune Elementary School was a pretty good school. He could probably get DaShawn in there.

He'd been at Richmond Towers long enough now to be in charge of scheduling. He wouldn't mess with Tony Gomez, the night doorman; he had a family, and his hours suited him. But if that evening kid wanted to keep his job, he'd have to shape up. And if Harry needed to take a day off when DaShawn was out of school, the kid could pick up the slack. Heaven knows he had covered for that lazy kid often enough. What was his name again? Harry could never remember it. Oh, yeah, Balor Draven. What kind of a name was that?

He sniffed. Something was burning. *Oh no. The pizza.* Snatching it out of the toaster oven, Harry waved his hand and licked his burned fingers. One thing that would sure have to change if DaShawn came: he'd need to take cooking more seriously. No more of this fast food, leftovers, and carryout. The boy'd need decent meals. Heck, he needed decent meals himself.

But those were just practical things. They weren't the main issue. The real issue was himself. Could he be a father to the boy? Could he give himself in that way? What was it Peter Douglass had said at the party about the men's group … they sometimes discussed how to raise kids? Huh. He could probably use a whole lot of that if he took in DaShawn. Fact was, he wished he had someone to talk to about the whole idea. Was he crazy to even consider the plan? But that was personal business. How could he discuss personal business with complete strangers? Most of his friends had been on the force, and he hadn't even seen Cindy for a couple of months. And besides, she was a woman. What would she know about being a dad … or being a granddad to a young boy whose real dad—his own son—was in jail?

Carl Hickman—the brother he'd met at the party—he looked like he'd been around the block a few times. Harry had no idea whether he was a father or what kind of a father he might be, but he could probably understand. And, come to think of it, it might be easier to talk to a stranger about things like that. At least they wouldn't be judging him by his past.

On Tuesday, Harry left his cell phone on, and this time Leslie Stuart did call, about two in the afternoon. "Hello, Mr. Bentley. Sorry I didn't get back to you yesterday. I got a little behind, and something new has come up."

Something new? Harry steeled himself to hear that DaShawn's temporary foster parent had died or faced some other emergency that meant he had to take DaShawn immediately. Big-time pressure! Instead, she said, "DaShawn's mother is out of rehab. I don't know how she got out early, but I checked, and she's out legal. She wants the boy. So looks like you're off the hook for the time being, Mr. Bentley."

Harry sat in silence on his stool in the Richmond Towers' lobby.

"Harry ... did you hear what I said?"

"Yeah, yeah. I heard you. But ... but what's that mean? He gonna live with her?" Harry sensed the tension rising in himself. "Where she be? I mean, does she have a place? Is this good for DaShawn? You said she was a crackhead. There's no way she can care for him proper."

"I'd tend to agree, Mr. Bentley. But she *is* his mother, and there's a lot of red tape in declaring a mother unfit unless we can demonstrate actual neglect or criminal behavior."

"*Criminal behavior*? Last I checked, drugs were still illegal! Where's DaShawn now?"

"Oh, he's with her. Been there since Friday night, actually. That's why I couldn't make it to the party. I got the word at the office right after I talked to you on the phone. Spent most of yesterday mopping up the paperwork, trying to make sure it wouldn't all fall apart before I called you."

"Before you called me? You shoulda called me first thing!" He took the phone away from his ear and cleared his throat and thought for a moment. "Where'd you say she lives?"

"Near west side."

"No, I mean the actual address. I ... I'm gonna want to drop in and see DaShawn sometime, see how he's doin'." He shook his head. It'd be the least he could do. "Now that I know I'm his grandpa, and all."

"Let me see here. I should know the number. Oh, here it is." She gave him the address on West Flournoy. "Unit 317. She doesn't have a phone, or at least wouldn't give me the number. It's just south of Garfield Park, on the other side of the Eisenhower."

"Yeah, I know that area." Harry scribbled the address on a scrap of paper. "Pretty hard core. No way a kid can grow up 'round there and make anything of himself. He'll be dead or in jail before he's eighteen."

"You're probably right about that, Mr. Bentley. Sorry, but there's not much we can do now. I'll try to keep a watch on the case for you, though."

"Thanks. And what's her name—the mother, I mean?"

"Donita Stevens."

"Stevens, huh? So she wouldn't even take Rodney's name?"

"They weren't married, Mr. Bentley."

"Figures. Well, thanks."

"Hey, what did you think of Manna House?"

"Oh, that was pretty good. Seems like a real nice place. I don't know if Miss Williams told you, but I dropped by the party because a woman from my building works there."

"You mean your apartment building?"

"No, no. Richmond Towers, here, where I work. She lives up in the penthouse. Real ... guess you'd say they're fairly well off. I think she wanted to do some charitable work or somethin'. But she threw a nice party."

"Yeah, that's what Estelle said. Said she had a *real* good time." She emphasized *real*. "Well, Mr. Bentley. Let's keep in touch."

"All right. See ya."

He closed his phone and spun around on the stool. So Estelle "had a *real* good time," did she? She'd spent almost the entire evening talking to him. Hm. Harry smiled.

His thoughts circled back to DaShawn, and the image of the boy's hair floating along like a cloud around his head. Well, his head wouldn't remain in the clouds for long if he stayed with his mother. Boy, how'd she get out of rehab? Harry knew crack addicts. Unless they really worked the program, went all the way through, the pipe would get 'em again the first time they faced any kind of a challenge. It was just too tough.

And DaShawn would be right in the middle of it!

The question was not only how his mother got out of the program early, but why? Maybe she never intended to get straight in the first place. If that was the case, she'd already be dirty. Harry thought about that for a few minutes, imagining DaShawn having to fend for himself—making his own meals, doing his laundry, getting himself off to school—with his mama passed out or ... or doing whatever she did to get her next fix. And what would that be? Turning tricks? Hustling? Dealing?

Maybe Fagan's raiding parties weren't such a bad idea, after all.

Wait a minute. That was it! If she got busted again, she'd be put away for sure, no question. And DaShawn would be out of the mess! It'd have to be a clean bust, though, not one of those stupid raids Fagan went on, stealing the dope and roughing people up without making an arrest that could stick.

But Harry was not on the force anymore. Could Cindy see that it was a clean bust? What if he went to visit DaShawn, kept his eyes open, maybe snooped around a little until he came up with enough information for Cindy to obtain a valid warrant? Then if Ms. what's-her-name—Donita Stevens—got raided, that could result in a good bust, one that would stick.

But what if Fagan found out? Or what if Gilson and the IPRA investigators found out he was messing with police business again? Would that blow open their whole investigation? Which was more important: getting his grandson out of a bad situation, or bringing down a dirty cop and his gang of thugs?

Harry's heart was pounding. No more copacetic for him! And what would happen to DaShawn? That would pretty much settle the question of whether or not he would have to take the boy, now wouldn't it?

Chapter 5

It was Leslie Stuart's voice: "Hi, this is Estelle and Stu. We're not available to take your call right now, so please leave a message and your number and we'll call back as soon as possible."

Stu? Was that what she called herself? Harry slapped his cell closed. That Fairbanks woman had given him Estelle's number, all right, her *home* number. What was she trying to do? First, she had teased him about Estelle being too young for him, when he wasn't even sixty yet. And now this!

Harry remembered her giggling, *"But she did give me permission to pass on this number."* Yeah, a number Leslie Stuart could listen in on! No way was he going to leave a message for Estelle that the social worker might hear. But how else was he going to get in touch with Estelle?

The shelter! It was the middle of the day. He could call her there. Or better yet, he could go by and see her. It'd be nice to see her again. No, that might not work. They might not want men hanging around a women's shelter. He'd better call.

He dug out the fat Chicago phone book from the bottom drawer of his desk and flipped through it until he found the number for Manna House. When he called, the person who answered told him

Miss Williams was busy serving lunch and asked if she could call him back.

Harry waited, greeting the Richmond Tower residents and helping with various courtesies. And he waited some more, threatening at one point to call the cops on a salesman who wouldn't take "No Solicitors" for an answer. And still he waited. Perhaps Miss Williams hadn't had as good a time at the Fun Night as he imagined.

And then in the middle of the afternoon, the *Law and Order* tweedle of his cell sounded. The caller ID said Manna House.

"Bentley here."

"Harry?"

He smiled to himself. "So how ya doin' Miss Williams?"

"Hm. This is *Estelle*, Harry, just returnin' your call. What can I do for you?"

"It's about my mother. You remember I told you she was elderly, and I'm needin' more support for her. So I was wonderin' if you'd be willing to give me some pointers. I'm not expecting you to take her on or nothin', but I don't even know where to turn for the things she needs, and I'm not able to do it all myself, anymore."

"I'd be glad to do what I can, Harry, but—"

"Great. What if we talked about it over dinner?" He hadn't even planned that one. It just came out and made him feel like a nervous schoolboy when it did. Certainly she'd turn him down, keep it all business.

"Well, I could probably be more help if I met your mother first and could see where she lives, maybe do an informal assessment."

Harry's heart dimmed. She was right. He should have known better. And she probably wasn't interested in dinner either.

"But after that," continued Estelle's rolling contralto voice, "I'd be happy to go somewhere so we could talk."

Whew. Lights off! Lights on! "Then dinner it is. Could I pick you up Friday evening about six? We could go over to my mom's for a while, then out for a bite."

"I'd be honored, Harry."

She gave him her address in the Rogers Park neighborhood and said good-bye, leaving him wondering why he had put it off until Friday. Why hadn't he said tomorrow … or even tonight?

Harry dropped by his mother's place after work to straighten things up. No reason to show Estelle the downside of everything.

He worked until midnight cleaning the apartment, scrubbing the toilet, and throwing away spoiled food from the refrigerator. It was a wonder his mother hadn't died of food poisoning. Then he went through her mail, putting bills in one pile, past-due bills in another, and chucking all the junk mail. Boy, they sure did prey on the elderly, trying to get them to sign up for bogus insurance plans, "As-seen-on-TV" crap, and appeals from religious organizations to "receive a hundredfold, just by contributing to …"

If there was a God—and Harry didn't doubt there was. It had been the only way he had made AA work. He just wasn't on direct speaking terms with God at the moment. But if there was a God, Harry wouldn't mind if someone called down a little fire on the junk mailers, especially those who took advantage of old people.

Lightning ricocheted through the orange clouds above Chicago as Harry drove home. Maybe it was one of the bright flashes that caused him to notice a familiar unmarked cruiser in front of The Office, a small bar on Touhy Avenue, named to give customers an excuse for why they weren't yet home from work. Harry checked the license plate as he rolled past. Cindy's cruiser! He'd left a message on her cell saying he was working at Richmond Towers, but she hadn't stopped by, even though she'd promised to check in on him from time to time. Why was that? They'd been tight for too long for her not to care.

But now there she was, probably sitting in there with her new partner. He pulled into a parking spot halfway down the block. The thunderstorm had opened up, dumping buckets. He'd be soaked by the time he got to the door of the bar. And how could he get a private word with her without her new partner listening in? Nevertheless, he jumped out of his RAV4 and made a run for it.

Slamming through the door, he shook the water off and wiped it from his brow with the back of his hand. Three people sat at the bar, but ... ah, there she was at a table near the back. She was facing him; her new partner sat with his back to the door—not too smart. Harry waved.

"Harry!" Cindy stood up and came to greet him. Her partner followed, looking more like an Iowa farm boy with a buzz haircut and rosy cheeks than a Chicago cop. But he walked with the stiffness acquired from too many doughnuts and too many hours logged sitting in a cruiser.

"Harry, how you doin'? It's been, what? Nine months? I thought you'd dropped off the face of the earth."

"No, just learnin' how to retire. I'm actually over at Richmond Towers, big high-rise right on the lakefront."

"Wow! Some digs!" She was doing something with her eyes, darting them toward her partner as her brow twitched tiny frowns.

"Nah. I don't live there. I'm still in the old crib. But I picked up a gig at Richmond Towers as a doorman."

"Oh, yeah, I got your message about that. You, a doorman? So what's that about? You spying on the rich and famous?"

Harry shrugged. "What can I say? But hey, you gonna introduce me?"

"Oh, yeah. Sorry. This is Art McAlister, my new partner. Harry Bentley, the dinosaur of Special Ops."

They shook hands. McAlister's grip was firm, but he didn't try to prove anything.

"Nice to meet you. Cindy's always sayin', *Harry this!* or *Harry that!* Now I know where all that comes from." He grinned. "Oops!" He reached for his vibrating cell phone. "Sorry. Probably my wife." He walked back toward the table where he and Cindy had been sitting.

"She's always calling him."

"So how's it goin'?"

Cindy glanced over her shoulder. "I think Fagan got him assigned to keep an eye on me. That's why I haven't dropped in to see you. But so far, nothing else has changed."

Harry studied McAlister, who seemed to be deep in an urgent conversation on his cell. "Cindy," he said, still watching McAlister, "I need you to do me a favor, and I don't have time to explain all the details. But if I gave you an address and told you where on the premises you could find some dope, could you get a warrant and arrange a legitimate bust? I mean, it's got to be a good collar, because the whole point is to put this person away."

"I suppose it could be arranged, but Harry, that's rather unorthodox for 'Mr. Clean,' don't you think? I mean, using the law for some personal agenda."

"Oh, she's dirty, no question! This wouldn't be a plant or anything. In fact, all this would come down to would be a parole violation, but I need her off the street. And technically, I'm a private citizen now, just reporting information about some illegal, controlled substances."

"I don't know, Harry. What's this about? At the very least, you owe me—"

"So McAlister," Harry looked over Cindy's shoulder and nodded toward the approaching cop, "you got everything straightened out?"

"Oh, yeah! Just the kids." He waved his hand as though shooing a fly as he rejoined Harry and Cindy. "I don't know why my wife can't handle that stuff." He stretched, pulling his shoulders back and yawning. "So, Bentley, want a beer? On me. 'Course, we're on the job, so it's more coffee for us."

"No, thanks. You on the job, and me on the wagon." He grinned broadly.

"Oh, yeah. Heard 'bout that. Good for you."

"Thanks. Hey, sounds like the storm's let up, so I better get goin'. See you all later. Cindy, give me a call, okay? You got my cell."

Outside, the storm had already blown itself out over the lake, leaving behind nothing but full gutters and a light drizzle. Harry walked slowly to his car and climbed in, oblivious of getting damp.

Was he doing the right thing? Even Cindy had raised the question. But she didn't understand what was at stake. He had to get DaShawn out of that situation, and if DCFS couldn't help, he'd do it himself!

He sat there as the windows fogged up. "Oh, God, what am I supposed to do?" Was that a prayer? He sure wished he could consult with God … or at least someone who could provide a little perspective. Maybe he ought to drop in on that Bible study and see if those guys really did know something about talking to God.

Chapter 6

HARRY SHAVED THE WHITE FUZZ that still cropped out like a wreath around the back of his head. He grinned at himself in the mirror. If Estelle Williams said anything about his bald head, he'd point out that he wasn't follically challenged; his hair had simply migrated to his chin. Harry liked his new look since retiring from the police force, where beards were not welcome unless you were undercover or had a religious excuse. He trimmed his silver chin curtain, turning from side to side to make sure it was even and neat. Then he slipped into a pair of black slacks and put on a long-sleeved purple dress shirt. The May evening would still be chilly, so he'd wear his dress leather jacket. But should he wear that gold chain around his neck? He didn't want to fling the bling, but a gold chain might look nice inside his open collar. Yeah, and Estelle would appreciate it, too … he hoped.

When Harry arrived at Estelle's apartment, he hesitated to ring the bell, remembering she lived with Leslie Stuart, but what else could he do? The intercom crackled, and then Estelle's voice broke through. "Be right down."

Whew. He peered through the glass door from the entryway into the building and in a moment saw a lady in green come down the stairs with some kind of a brown fuzzy scarf thrown around her shoulders for an evening wrap. Harry grinned. The gold loops hanging from her ears made him glad he had on his gold chain. Tonight Estelle's hair was twisted and piled on top of her head in ways Harry couldn't even imagine, and to him, she looked like a queen.

"How ya doin', Miss Estelle?" he said when she opened the door.

"Oh, I'm still kickin', Just Harry." She gave him a smirk. "Still kickin', just not quite so high."

He held the outer door and walked her to his RAV4.

When they arrived at his mother's cramped apartment, Harry introduced Estelle to his mother, Wanda Bentley, a frail senior with dark leathery skin whose black-and-gray wig was on straight today. She sat staring at the TV through rheumy eyes as though she hadn't heard them come in, until Estelle touched her shoulder and introduced herself. Then she looked up. "Oh, it's so good of you to come see me, Miss Williams. You know, I don't get company much anymore." She looked around the room. "Oh my, please excuse this mess."

"That's all right, Mother Bentley. And you can just call me Estelle."

Harry realized his own expression involuntarily mirrored the bright smile that spread across his mother's face. He moved a kitchen chair close for Estelle to sit within arm's length of his mother. Once she was settled, Estelle opened a small notebook and took notes as she asked questions about how often his mother got out, whether she had been sick lately, what she liked to eat, what she liked or didn't like about the most recent cleaning woman. His mother answered all the questions even though her attention seemed to drift repeatedly to the game show on the TV.

As the interview continued, Harry thought about his grandson. If he could get things set up better for his mother, maybe taking in DaShawn wouldn't seem so overwhelming. He tried to think of things they could do together. He'd have to help the kid with homework, he knew that. But what else did kids do these days? Computer games? Sports? He couldn't let him run the streets.

Wait a minute ... He watched Estelle working with his mother. She was somethin' else. He'd better not let this one get away, but ... but if he had a boy to take care of, how could he possibly go out on a date like tonight?

From time to time, Estelle pulled him from his reverie to provide information about his mother—like the date of her next doctor's appointment and what medications she was taking.

"This has been good. This has been good, Mother Bentley," said Estelle, closing her notebook. "Now listen, honey, I'm going to help Harry plan some better ways to support you, so it's important to know you as well as I can." She stood up. "Would you mind if I looked around for a few minutes? I won't move anything, 'cause I know it's important for you to know where everything is."

"You better not move anything!" Harry's mother shook her finger in the air. "That's what's wrong with those cleaning people. They hide things on me all the time. And they steal my toilet paper. I don't know why they can't buy their own."

"Harry, why don't you read your mother her mail or something, while I check out a few things."

Harry picked up the mail that had accumulated on the table, wondering why the TV wasn't sufficient to occupy his mother. Nevertheless, he flipped through the mail. Bills, a booklet of coupons—Harry laughed. "How 'bout this, Mama. Twenty percent off resurfacing your driveway if you respond before the end of May. You only got twelve days!"

His mother wrung her hands and pulled her gaze from the TV screen. "Do you think it needs it?"

"No, Mama. I was just kiddin'. Your building has a parking lot, and you don't have to do anything about it." He ripped open a hand-addressed envelope. "But here's somethin'. A birthday card from"—he opened the card—"from Ethel. You remember your friend Ethel?"

"Of course. She was by just the other day."

"I don't think so, but it's a nice card, nonetheless. Says, 'Birthday? Get over 'em! I have. That's why this is late.' Then she wrote, 'Congratulations on your eighty-eighth.'" He handed the card to his mother as Estelle came back into the room.

"Well, Mother Bentley, I think that's all. It's been a pleasure to get to know you." She bent down and gave the old woman a hug.

Harry's mother turned up to her, seemingly free of the TV for a change. "When you comin' back?"

"Hm. Not sure, Mother Bentley. We'll have to see, but you take care, now. Okay?"

"Harry, bring me some more toilet paper next time you come. This time I'm gonna hide it where they can't find it."

Back in the car, Harry cleared his throat. "Well, that went well. I really want to thank you. But before you tell me what you think might help her, you ever been to the Dixie Kitchen up in Evanston?"

"Can't say as I have, but if *Dixie* means Southern, I'm game."

"Actually, it's more Cajun, if that's okay. The real name is the Dixie Kitchen and Bait Shop, but I 'spect we can ask 'em to hold the crawlers." He glanced over at her as he turned north on Clark.

Her eyebrow went up. "It's not the crawlers I'm worried 'bout. Just make sure them crawdads ain't still kickin' in my étouffée."

They both laughed.

As they drove, Estelle opened her notebook and began ticking off things Harry could do to improve life for his mother. Sign her up for Meals on Wheels. (*So it wasn't "Hot Wheels," after all.*) Be sure the things she needed weren't stored too high for her to reach. Remove all the throw rugs and extension cords so there would be nothing for her to trip over. "Falls are one of the most dangerous things for the elderly, you know. If a fall don't kill 'em outright, hitting their head or somethin', a broken hip can send them to a nursing home for the rest of their days. And we wouldn't want that, right? And you need somebody for personal care, to help her with her hair and nails. That means so much to an older person."

As helpful as Estelle's suggestions sounded, Harry felt overwhelmed. He'd need a full-time scheduler to manage them all.

"Does she have any friends who live in assisted living?"

"I don't know."

"Try to find out, and take her for visits. A good facility can be a blessing 'cause it provides and coordinates all the services older people need. Too many elderly fear they're just the first step to a nursing home, but assisted living actually extends basic independence for as long as possible."

Harry appreciated Estelle's suggestions, but as he parked his RAV4 on Church Street in Evanston, he was happy to see her close her notebook and slide it back into her ample purse.

The Dixie Kitchen and Bait Shop fulfilled the "bait shop" half of its name through its funky décor—there were no crawlers on the menu or in an icebox in the corner. But an old wooden fishing boat did hang from the ceiling, "Rent-a-Rod" fishing poles for twenty-five cents leaned in the screened porch, jars of home-canned peaches and tomatoes sat in open cupboards, and bright tin signs for everything from Genuine NeHi Orange Crush to Burma Shave patched the weathered clapboard walls. Mismatched wooden chairs, checkered tablecloths, and Zydeco music made Harry feel like he was in an authentic Southern diner as they sampled complimentary johnnycakes and selected peach-glazed chicken wings and fried green tomatoes for appetizers. Estelle ordered her étouffée and a side of greens while Harry got crawfish fritters with jalapeño jelly and a side of slaw.

"So were you pining for Mississippi or something when you suggested comin' here?" Estelle asked.

"Not me, sister." Harry wiped some of the "heat" off his lips with a checkered napkin. "Halsted and 115th is as far south as I ever lived, but this is just like Mama's cooking, especially the johnnycakes. We used to have 'em every Sunday morning before church. But she can't really cook now, so I have to come to a place like this to get 'home cookin'."

"Hm. No doubt." Estelle traced figure-eights in her étouffée with her spoon, then looked up at him. "Do johnnycakes every Sunday morning before church mean you were raised in church? I noticed your mama's Bible is well used."

"Oh, yeah. Mama loves church. She'd still be there all day every Sunday if she could."

"Uh-huh. Maybe that's one of the things you could arrange for her. I'm sure it'd mean a lot. What about you, Harry?"

"Who, me?" He shrugged and watched a young waitress weave her shapely behind between the tables. "Guess I kind of let church slide when I was on the force. A cop's schedule is crazy, you know. Never nothin' you can ever depend on." He laughed nervously. "When I was home on a Sunday morning, it was mostly for sleepin'."

"Mm-hm." She nodded her head knowingly. "So, what's your excuse now?"

Whew! This lady didn't stop. "Uh, well, like I said, just got out of the habit, I s'pose."

This time she shook her head like he'd just played a deal-breaker.

"Harry, neither of us is a spring chicken, so I'm gonna be straight up with you right from the get-go. I love your company, and this"—she waved a hand to indicate the funky restaurant—"makes a great evening. But I need to tell ya ... Jesus comes first. Know what I'm sayin'?"

Harry shrugged. "Sure. I don't mind." He paused as an accordion's wail washed a Zydeco waltz over him. "I mean, if you want to pray over your food or go to church or give money to TV preachers"—he tried to think of all the things his mother did—"I'm good with that.... Fact, I'd even go to church with you."

"Hm. That'd be nice, Harry, but ..." Estelle tipped her head back and softly tapped her lips with the tips of her fingers, then fixed him with her dark eyes. "I'm not just talkin' church. Bible says, 'Can two walk together, except they agree?' Sooner or later there'd be a partin' of the ways. And I don't need that."

What was she getting at? "But don't the Bible say somewhere, 'Love covers a multitude of sins'?" Harry was sure he'd heard that somewhere, maybe in Sunday school as a kid.

Estelle erupted in a full-throated laugh, causing patrons at the adjoining table to glance over and smile. "Oh, Harry, you're too much." Her laugh subsided. "I'm not talkin' 'bout no sin here. You an' me ... we just need to be on the same page if anything's to come of this." She waggled a finger back and forth between them.

Same page? He'd be glad to be on her page. But ... He leaned forward and spoke softly, not wanting to entertain their neighbors any further. "Uh, maybe we're getting ahead of ourselves, know what I'm sayin'? How 'bout …" He tried to think. "What if we just went to a movie Sunday night? I hear *The Da Vinci Code*'s out. I read it was about Jesus or something."

Estelle grinned and shook her head. "Don't think we should start with that one, Harry. 'Sides, I need to be at the Sunday Evening Praise at Manna House this week. But, hey"—her eyes got wide—"could you come to that?"

"Is that like the Fun Night, a little Macaroni and Mashed Potato?" Harry swiveled his shoulders and grinned.

"No Mashed Potato, but you better believe we get down sometimes. Actually, it's church for the shelter women, and this Sunday my real church is leadin' it, so I gotta be there. Why don'tcha come?"

"Ah, I don't know." He rubbed his hand over his head. "You know, me and church … well, that was a long time ago. But, hey, I'll think about it."

The waitress came with the check, and Harry dug the plastic out of his wallet. "So, what's your church?"

"SouledOut Community Church. Meets in that mall just west of the Howard El station."

"Church? Never seen no church in there."

"S'pose it's easy to miss. But the name's on the door … ever since the two churches merged."

"*Merged?* That's a new one. You usually hear of churches splittin'."

"Yeah, and this was white and black too—Uptown Community and New Morning Christian."

"That must've been some trick."

"Or God."

"Well now, there you go!" He raised both hands, and froze. He'd almost said, *If God can put a white and a black church together, we oughta be a snap.* Whoa! That was going too far. He broke into a hearty laugh, thinking about what most people considered "too far" on a first date.

"Okay, Harry Bentley, you gonna let me in on your little joke, or what?"

"Nah, nah. Nothin'."

"Now, Harry, don't you go makin' me call your mama. 'Cause you know I got her number."

Chapter 7

HEY, MAMA. IT'S ME."

"Harry, when you gonna come see me?"

"Mama, I was there just last night. Brought that Miss Estelle Williams over to meet you. Talk about what you be needin'. Don't you remember?"

"Oh, yeah. I sure do 'member her. Very nice, Harry. But when you gonna bring me that toilet paper I need?"

"Mama, you still got plenty. You don't need no more. What I'm calling about is to ask if you want to go to church tomorrow."

"But Harry, they tore down Mt. Zion with the urban renewal."

"Mama, that was back in the seventies. You haven't gone there for a long time. How 'bout that other church you were attendin', up here on the north side? I could take you by there tomorrow if you want."

"Oh, I don't know, Harry. That preacher didn't even come to see me when I was in the hospital with my gall bladder. Why don't I jus' go wit' you to your church tomorrow? I'd like that."

"Uh … uh, Mama, I'm not gonna be able to make it tomorrow. I was just offerin' you a ride. But maybe another day, okay?"

"All right, Harry. Now, you tell that Miss Estelle hi for me, you hear?"

"Sure will, Mama. Bye."

HARRY WAITED UNTIL SATURDAY EVENING to drive down into the city and out the Eisenhower to Donita Stevens's place on the near west side. He figured by that time on a Saturday, she'd be out doin' "her thang," and he'd have his best chance to visit DaShawn and case her apartment. He found the address and parked half a block away. The building didn't look as bad as he had imagined, but the scars around the neighborhood and the guys hanging out on the corners still showed this was no place to bring a boy up right.

A skinny old man stood in the vestibule swaying back and forth like his meds were off. He was sucking on the butt of an unlit cigarette through lips that had caved in where teeth should have been. Harry paid him no mind as he checked the buttons for 317.

"I got me a key." The old man had moved to Harry's side. "Let you in for a buck."

Harry looked at him as he pushed the button. "We'll see."

The apartment buzzer seemed to work, and in a moment a youthful voice came through the intercom. "Yeah."

"DaShawn, this is your Grandpa Bentley. Buzz me up."

There was a long silence. "Donita, she say I cain't have nobody up in here when she be out."

"'Course not, and that's a good rule. But I'm your grandpa. She just meant that for kids and strangers. Come on, now. Buzz me up."

Another long silence. Finally, the door buzzed. Harry gave the old man a *sorry* shrug and went in to climb the dark stairs and find unit 317. He knocked, and the door opened three inches, the length of the security chain. Floating in the gloom within, Harry could see

DaShawn's soft hair, but it was too dark to see the features of his face.

"Hi…." He stalled as though he didn't know what to call Harry.

"Hi, yourself. You gonna let me in?"

"Oh, yeah." The door closed while the chain rattled, then swung wide.

Harry stepped in and looked around. The only light came from the TV and a light from what looked like the bathroom down the hall. He flipped the wall switch, and a bare bulb in an overhead fixture illuminated the joint living and dining rooms. There wasn't much furniture—an old plastic sofa and a coffee table in the living room, with the TV balanced on a rickety stand against the opposite wall. A table, two chairs, and a single, unmade bed sat in the dining room. A scarred-up skateboard lay on the foot of the bed, and boxes were stacked in the corner. Harry was actually surprised that the place wasn't worse. It was nearly empty.

"So this where you sleep?" He pointed toward the bed with the skateboard.

"Yeah. Donita says she might put a wall across the living room and give me the end with the windows."

Harry paused. The boy hadn't even called his mother, Mom. What was with that? "Well, don't hold your breath. This is a rental, and she could get put out for that. She gone for long?"

DaShawn shrugged.

Harry took a few steps around the living room, looking at the miscellaneous stuff in the corners. "You got any toys or anything?"

"Some … under the bed. Hector says he might get me a Nintendo if I'm good."

"Hector! Who's Hector?"

"Donita's … friend."

"Friend, huh? Yeah, I 'spect he is." More likely her pimp.

DaShawn didn't respond.

"So, you had anything to eat?"

"Not yet."

Harry went into the kitchen, the boy following. He switched on a bluish florescent light and opened the refrigerator. Some beer, half-empty bottles of ketchup and mustard, a half loaf of white bread. Harry squeezed it—hard, probably moldy. He checked the freezer, all the while keeping his eyes out for drugs. Nothing.

"What do you usually eat?"

DaShawn shrugged. "Sometimes she send me over to the store. They got wings."

"This late?"

"Whatchu mean? Sun ain't even down yet."

"Yeah, but stuff happens."

"Ah man, I be out lots later than this all the time."

Harry grimaced. Probably so, but not on his okay. On the other hand, if he wanted to search the apartment, what could be better? "How far's the store?"

"Around the corner." DaShawn pointed north, toward the expressway.

Harry sighed, dug in his pocket, and pulled out a five. "Go get us some wings and a couple Cokes. And hurry right back. I don't want to have to come after you."

The boy left his hand outstretched, the crumpled five still in it. "It's gonna take more'n that. The wings are five-sixty-nine. Cokes a dollar-twenty-nine. Plus, how 'bout fries?"

At least the kid could add. Harry retrieved the five and slapped a twenty in its place, thinking he'd have to adjust his budget if he took in this kid.

As soon as the boy grabbed his skateboard and went out the door, Harry headed into Donita's bedroom and immediately tripped on something in the dark. He recovered and found a light. What he'd tripped over was a duffle of dirty laundry sitting in the middle of the floor. It actually smelled. He looked around. Bingo! Right there on the top of a small three-drawer dresser was a pipe, a soot-blackened spoon, and a candle, all the hardware necessary to get Donita's bail revoked ... if the judge had any sense. But Harry wanted more. She had to have a stash somewhere, something that even the most lenient judge couldn't overlook, something Donita couldn't claim was left over from the "old days."

He pulled open the drawers—mostly empty. No drugs. He punched the pillow and threw back the blanket. He tossed the closet and lifted the mattress. The whole apartment was so empty there weren't the hundreds of hiding places one usually encountered in a suspect's home. He went into the bathroom, opened the medicine cabinet, and lifted the lid on the toilet tank. Nothing!

He was standing there thinking when he heard the front door handle clatter and the door swing open. That kid was fast—

"DaShawn! Whatchu doin', boy? You in my room?"

Harry eased the bathroom door shut as the woman came down the hall.

"Hey, boy, you better get your butt out here right now. Don't you go hidin' up in there on me, now. DaShawn! I know you been in my room, 'cause I didn't leave no light on. So quit playin' wit' me, you hear!"

Fists pounded the door while Harry stood there wondering what to do.

"DaShawn, I swear, if'n you don't open this door right now, I'm gonna bust it down, and then I'm gonna bust your butt till you can't sit for a week! You hear me, now? Open up!"

What else could Harry do? He flushed the toilet and opened the door.

The light-skinned woman in red-hot shorts, platform heels, and no more than half a tank top screamed and leaped back. "Who you? Whatchu doin' in my apartment? Get out! Get out right now!" Her long blonde weave swung back and forth as she shook her head and yelled.

Harry held up both hands and took a step toward her.

She backed up. "I'm warnin' you, man. Hector gonna be all over you. Where's my boy? DaShawn!" she yelled. "Where you at, boy?"

"Listen, listen to me, now." Harry took another step into the hall. "I'm DaShawn's grandpa. Harry Bentley ... Rodney's father. I just came by to visit DaShawn—"

"Where he at? DaShawn! You better tell me where he at right now or you gonna be in a world of hurt, mister!"

Harry laughed. "Take it easy, lady." He took a step back, down the hall toward her bedroom, hoping to reduce the threat, but she advanced, just keeping out of his reach. Harry tried lowering his voice. "Now nobody's gonna be in a world of hurt, and you ain't gonna do nothin' 'bout nothin'. So just calm down."

"That what you think. Where my boy?" Her decibels increased as she stepped toward him, her finger in his face. "He said DCFS gonna give him to somebody. That you? No way! Did that white bee come up in here and take him away?"

Harry sighed deeply and retreated another step. This woman was ought of control. "Look, ma'am. He's all right. I just sent him over to the store to get us some wings. He'll be right back. If you want, I'll go after him."

"*If I want?* What I want is you outta my house, right this minute." She was wagging her head from side to side like a sassy teen. "How do I know you ain't some gangbanger up in here tryin' to rob me of all my valuables?"

Yeah, like what? "Do I look like a gangbanger?"

Just then the door opened again, and DaShawn came in with a bag in his arm.

Donita wheeled around. "Where you been? How come you be out wit'out tellin' me? And who tol' you to let strangers up in here? You outta you mind, boy? I gonna thrash you good. Get in that bathroom and drop your pants. Move!"

Harry reached out. "Now hold on—"

She turned on him. "Don't you interfere. This ain't none of you business." She swung back around, grabbed DaShawn by the collar—causing the bag of wings, Cokes, and fries to fly—and pulled him into the bathroom. Then she turned and yelled at Harry, "I don't give a flyin' fig who you are. You better be out that door before I come out this bathroom!"

Slam!

Harry stood there while the yelling continued from inside. But he didn't hear any hitting and no cries from DaShawn. The boy shouldn't have to endure such a berating, but it had probably happened all too often before, and it might be difficult to get a charge of abuse to stick if the yelling was not accompanied by anything physical. What should he do? Bash the door open? Pull the kid out and take him home tonight? Yeah, and how long could he keep him under those circumstances?

No, the only hope was to get Donita recommitted for possession, and just the paraphernalia—while illegal—might not be enough. He was sure she was dirty, but where was her stash? He turned and looked through her bedroom door one more time, scanning the room as the yelling in the bathroom continued. On the floor in front of him was the duffle of dirty clothes. He fell to his knees and pawed through the laundry. Nothing!

But there was a zipper on the end of the bag. He felt it—a pouch. Inside, he found the mother lode: three bags of freebase cocaine. He zipped the pouch closed and walked down the hall. But as he passed the bathroom door where the lecture had subsided to a angry grumble, he couldn't help yelling, "You hurt that boy, and I'll have you up on charges!"

"You think so? You get outta here or I'll call 911, and we'll see who's up on charges!"

Oh, yeah. Harry laughed to himself as he left and slammed the front door.

Downstairs the toothless old man was still in the vestibule, swaying back and forth and grinning. "Guess she told you. You ain't gonna get that boy after all, are you?"

Harry gritted his teeth. "I'll get him. You just wait and see." He hit the outer door with the palm of his hand and walked through it.

"Hey, how 'bout my buck?"

Harry turned and scowled back at him. "What buck? I got in on my own."

Chapter 8

HARRY PUNCHED IN CINDY'S CELL NUMBER and arranged to meet her at Bakers Square on the corner of Touhy and Western. "And be sure you come alone," he added.

He made it back through the Loop and was up to the restaurant by 10:20, staking out a booth where he nursed his endless cup of coffee while he waited for Cindy. Most of the patrons had cleared out, and it was nearly 11 p.m. before she showed. Greetings, small talk, and after the pie and more coffee arrived, she fixed him with a frank stare. "So, what's up Harry? Is this about that collar you wanted me to make?"

"Yeah, and you're gonna have to move on it quick, 'cause there's a good chance the evidence'll walk."

Her cool stare continued with no more than a *convince-me* lift of one eyebrow.

"Okay, okay. Here's the situation." He explained the whole story—from the DCFS calls and the discovery that he had a grandson to Donita's tirade at finding him in her apartment.

When he was done, Cindy leaned back and folded her arms. "So you're tellin' me you're willing to take on raising a kid you don't know, don't have a relationship with, and him headin' into his teen years. You're crazier than I thought, Harry."

"What am I supposed to do? He's blood, Cindy, and you know what'll happen to him if I leave him out there on the west side with someone like that … like his mother."

"Yeah. Well, you may be right, but why don't you go through DCFS or file a child endangerment complaint like any other citizen?"

Harry rolled his eyes. "You know all that would get me would be a fight with the mother that could drag on for weeks. Without hard evidence, I'd probably lose. But even if I didn't, in the meantime she'd poison him against me so bad I'd have no chance of workin' with the boy. No, the quickest way to rescue him is to charge the mother with a parole violation."

Cindy continued to stare at him.

"It's legitimate! She's in violation, Cindy. And that's no place for a boy."

"All right. All right. So you said the drugs are in the end pouch of some sports bag kickin' around her bedroom floor?"

"And she's likely to stash it someplace more secure. That's why you've gotta move ASAP. Who knows, she might be fixin' to sell it, but one way or another, it won't stay in that bag for long."

"Okay, Harry. Just this once, but don't be tryin' something like this to solve all your little domestic disputes."

"*All my domestic disputes*? You know I lost them ten years ago."

She gulped the last of her coffee and stood up. "Come on. Let's drop by the 24th District Station. You can fill out an affidavit for a search warrant. But I'm gonna have to tell Fagan what I'm doin' cause even after a judge signs it, I can't serve it alone. It'll at least be McAlister and probably backup as well." She frowned and brushed away the shock of hair that had fallen over her right eye.

"But you're probably in luck. Fagan's not likely to even glance at the warrant, so I should be able to keep your name out of it. I'll do everything I can to make sure it's a good bust."

"That's all I'm askin'. You'll let me know when it's goin' down, right?"

"Since when have I ever left you out?"

HARRY SAT AROUND HIS APARTMENT all day Sunday, bored as a rock, then went to work at Richmond Towers Monday and Tuesday feeling nervous as an electric charge. Why didn't Cindy call? She had to get over there pretty soon, or his information wouldn't be any good! Still no call. On Tuesday afternoon his cell rang and he flipped it open as fast as a gunslinger. But it turned out to be Peter Douglass, the African-American brother Harry met at the Manna House Fun Night.

"Hey Harry, hope you don't mind me calling. Estelle Williams gave me your number." *What was she doing passing on his number?* "Reminded me to ask you about our men's meeting this evening. Whaddaya say?"

"Uh …" If Estelle suggested Peter call him, she was obviously thinking about him. That was good. But wasn't that men's meeting a Bible study? Sounded like she was trying to pull him into her religious stuff. On the other hand, he was the one who volunteered to go to church with her. But this wouldn't be *with her*. Still, he'd left behind all his old CPD friends, and evenings got pretty long. Those guys seemed pretty cool to hang with.

"Harry, you still there?"

"Yeah, sorry. I was just thinkin' 'bout whether I was free tonight."

"Well, are you?"

"Yeah, guess so. What time was that again?"

"Seven. My place. You still got my card?"

"Uh, no. Think I lost it."

Peter gave him the address. "Great. We'll see you then."

HARRY KNEW THE NEIGHBORHOOD. His old boss, Fagan, lived just a few streets over and had thrown a backyard barbecue for the team one Labor Day before all the corruption had started. Things had been looking up back then. Street parking was still as hard to find. When Harry had squeezed his RAV4 into a spot so tight he wasn't sure he'd ever get out, he climbed the stairs to Peter Douglass's third-floor apartment and received a back-slapping welcome from the five men who were already there.

Harry glanced around, recognizing a woman's touch that was missing in his apartment: elegant art prints on the walls, shiny wood floors—Harry slipped off his shoes to add to the pile near the door—bright area rugs, modern beige-and-black furniture, bookcases filled with hardcover books, and drapes over the windows. Harry started to take a seat on a loveseat nestled into the bay window at the front of the room, but Peter caught his arm. "Nah, nah. Come on over a little closer. We got plenty of soft seats."

Harry selected a vacant overstuffed armchair. It was under a large quilt hanging on the wall. He turned to look up at it. Each square seemed to be in a different style, depicting various scenes or designs.

"That's our wedding quilt," Peter offered. "Made by a bunch of my wife's friends. She'll have to tell you about it someday."

That put Harry a little more at ease, presuming he would come back again.

Of the five men, Harry had already met two: Peter Douglass and Carl Hickman—the brothers at the shelter party. The other three guys were white, and Harry realized he'd seen two of them as well at the party. As they introduced themselves again, Harry picked up on a few more details. Denny Baxter was middle-aged, an athletic director at a local high school. The younger guy was his son, Josh. There was also an older Jewish man named Ben Garfield, a little dumpy and brusque, with a "rubber face" that could go from a sunshine smile to a haunted frown. Harry put him in his midsixties. Surprisingly, the oldest guy and the youngest guy in the group were both new fathers. Ben said he and his wife had two-year-old twins. "*Oy vey.* They run circles around us," he groused. "Believe me, parenthood is for the young." He jerked a thumb at Josh.

Turned out that Josh and his wife were in the middle of adopting an eight-month-old baby of an addict mom who OD-ed. As the lanky, twenty-something dad described her, Harry remembered some of the women at the party passing around a dark-haired little beauty.

He listened as the other men offered these new fathers bits of encouragement, but they both still sounded overwhelmed. Harry knew how that felt.

"Harry, you got family?" Peter asked.

"Uh ... yeah." Why was Peter checking his business in front of these guys? Harry glanced around, but no one seemed particularly on alert. He hesitated, trying to think what he could contribute that wouldn't get too deep. "Well, one thing I learned—guess you could say the hard way—is you gotta be there. Know what I'm sayin'? I was in the home, but I wasn't really there, you know?"

"You right about that," Carl Hickman put in. "I ain't no perfect dad, and that used to get me so down, I ended up sleepin' all the time. But that only made it worse. Wouldn't have no job now if it weren't for Peter. And I still can't kick these cancer sticks." He slapped the pack in his shirt pocket. "But here I am, can't let my failures wipe me out. You know what the Word says, 'Though a righteous man falls seven times, he …'" Carl left it hanging, and several of the other guys finished the verse with: "'… he rises again.'"

Harry leaned back in his chair. His own comment had been received as valid. He thought about the group: A kid with a crack baby and a guy older than himself with two toddlers. Maybe he wasn't so crazy after all to think of taking in DaShawn … if he had some guys like this to encourage him.

He jumped when his cell phone rang and fumbled in his pocket to find it.

The other guys laughed. "Hey, man. That's some ring tone—*Ta-Dum.*"

"Sorry." Harry wanted to shut it off and forget it, but he didn't dare. What if it were Cindy? He flipped it open and saw it was his mother. Boy, this was his life … pulled in all directions at the same time. He glanced around at the other men.

"No problem, Harry. Just step in there if you want." Peter gestured with his eyes toward the dining room.

"'Scuse me, gentlemen."

He got up and slipped into the next room, sparsely furnished—his was cluttered with more stuff than he had places to put it—but here the dark table was set off by a single vase of flowers in the center. He'd have to remember that.

He put the phone to his ear. "Yeah, Mama."

"Harry, that you? Why you take so long to answer me?"

"I'm busy, Mama. Can't talk right now. I'm … I'm in a Bible study." That ought to impress her.

"That don't sound like you, Harry. Is that really you?"

"Yes, Mama."

"Well, then, I just gotta tell ya, they took all my toilet paper again. Can you bring me some more?"

"Who's *they*?"

"That cleaning lady. She always be takin' my toilet paper."

"Mama, there hasn't been any cleaning lady there this week. Look in the cabinet under the bathroom sink. You got plenty there."

"You sure, baby?" Her voice got thin. "Harry, can you just bring me some extra? I'll hide it under the bed. They never look there. Dust bunnies and a whole lot more. It'a be safe."

"Okay, Mama. But I gotta go now. I'm in a Bible study."

He punched the End button, set the phone to vibrate, and closed it.

When he returned to the living room, the chit-chat had drifted to the brawl that had broken out the previous Saturday at the Crosstown Classic between the Chicago White Sox and Chicago Cubs. "Started when the two catchers got into it." Ben snorted. "That what's-his-face, the Sox catcher, he went after Barrett."

"Nah, nah, nah." Josh waved his hands in front of his face. "It was Michael Barrett clocked Pierzynski."

"*Ah, meshugaas*. You never saw what Pierzynski did before that."

"Ben, Ben. You just sayin' that 'cause you're a Cubs fan."

"Darn right, I'm a Cubs fan. And one of these years ..."

They batted it back and forth a few more times until Denny Baxter suggested it was time to get into "the Word," as he called it. Harry didn't have a Bible, but Peter Douglass offered him one and helped him find the book of James, chapter one.

It had been a long time since Harry had read anything from the Bible, and he was mildly surprised at how practical it sounded. The explanation that troubles and trials strengthen a person by building perseverance until a person becomes mature made sense. The verse that followed was hopeful: "If any of you lacks wisdom, he should ask God, who gives generously to all without finding fault, and it will be given to him." But then came the qualifier that gave

Harry that familiar, left-out feeling: "But when he asks, he must believe and not doubt, because he who doubts is like a wave of the sea, blown and tossed by the wind. That man should not think he will receive anything from the Lord; he is a double-minded man, unstable in all he does."

Yeah, well, Harry knew he pretty much mimicked that wave in the sea. Just look at how many times he had gone back and forth about DaShawn.

After they'd talked about the first chapter, the guys went around asking the others to pray for them about different things. The young Baxter kid and the old Jewish guy both said they needed a big dose of that wisdom for parenting. Peter Douglass said he needed wisdom for his business. His biggest client was on the verge of going belly-up, but they owed him big bucks. If he squeezed them, that might be the last straw. But if he didn't act soon, they might declare bankruptcy anyway, and then he'd get little or nothing.

When everyone else had spoken, Carl Hickman turned to Harry. "So, what's up with you, bro? Anything you want us to pray for?"

Harry scratched the beard that ran along his chin. "Guess I could use some of that wisdom too." As briefly as possible, he told them his grandson might be coming to live with him.

"What's his name?" Denny asked. "I'd like to pray for him by name."

"DaShawn. He's my son's boy. My son … you might say he's out of circulation for a while."

Carl nodded his head. "I hear ya. And DaShawn, when might he be comin'?"

"Could be anytime. Just don't know."

"Then we'll keep prayin' on that," promised Carl.

Chapter 9

At 12:18 on Wednesday afternoon, the lobby of Richmond Towers turned into an evacuation center, or at least that's what it seemed like when Mrs. Fairbanks came stumbling out of the elevator with her enormous suitcase in tow, getting its wheels caught in the gap between the inner and outer doors. Harry hurried over to help her, finding the size of the luggage was matched by its weight.

"Are we fleeing the penthouse with everything we own, Mrs. Fairbanks?"

Her face reddened to match her hair. "No, we're gonna go get our boys from Virginia. But I'm afraid we're running a little late. Could you get us a cab, Mr. Bentley? I have to go back up for a moment."

No sooner had Harry freed the luggage than the elevator doors closed on her.

Boys from Virginia? Oh, yeah. She'd gone to see them a couple of weeks ago. Strange family, boys living a thousand miles away. Harry thought about the conversation among the men the night before about the importance of a father being present. Well, at least he hadn't been a thousand miles away while Rodney grew up. But he might as well have been.

Harry made the call and asked for rush service. The cab was waiting when Mr. and Mrs. Fairbanks came down, him looking cool and calm, with one small piece of luggage and her frazzled as she juggled a large purse and another small bag while she tried to put on a sweater.

Harry grabbed the handle of the large suitcase. "I'll get this for you, ma'am." Why was that arrogant lug walking straight to the cab as though his wife and her things were no concern of his?

"Thank you, Mr. Bentley," Mrs. Fairbanks said as she handed him a five.

As Harry watched the cab pulled away, he removed his cap and wiped his hand over his head. There went a carload of trouble.

CINDY'S CALL FINALLY CAME LATER THAT AFTERNOON while Harry was still at work.

"Tomorrow morning at six."

"Six? That's before coffee and doughnuts, your time."

"Harry, you want her to be in, don't you? You know that's the best time to avoid a big row. The least chance of her fleein' or flushin' it. I'll let you know how it goes down."

But Harry was not going to wait to find out. He immediately called Tony Gomez, the night doorman at Richmond Towers, and told him to cover for him until he got there the next morning.

"But Señor Bentley, I gotta get home in time to get the kids off to school."

"Can't your wife cover for you just this once?"

"I don't know, man. She's usually trying to get out the door herself about that time, know what I mean?" Harry let the question hang, and finally Gomez said, "Okay, I'll see what I can do. But you gotta get there soon as you can, man. And you owe me one."

Sleep was like the pennant in July for the Cubs. It kept slipping further and further away until at 3 a.m., Harry gave up. He showered, shaved his head, dressed, had some toast and coffee, but it wasn't yet four. Back in the bathroom he trimmed his beard and was going to brush his teeth, but decided he still felt hungry, so he went out and scrambled a few eggs, had more coffee, and tried to watch the news on CNN. Finally at five, with the day just beginning to turn the sky out over the lake a pale yellow, Harry got in his RAV4 and headed for the west side.

He found a parking spot on St. Louis where he could still see the front of Donita's building on Flournoy. A couple windows in the stairway were open, as was a window in what had to be Donita's living room. He scrunched down in his seat so he could just barely see through his steering wheel and lowered his driver's-side window so he could hear. In all the years he'd done stakeouts he couldn't remember ever feeling this nervous, not even when he was a rookie.

It was still ten to six, and the whole neighborhood was as quiet as a small prairie town. One homeless guy pushed a shopping cart down the middle of the street, stopping right in front of the apartment building Harry was watching. He fiddled with a boom box he had perched on top of his pile of worldly belongings. It popped and scratched, but it refused to bring in a station until the man gave up and continued on down the street, cursing, "All you all ..." He yelled at those who lived in the apartments on one side of the street and then to those on the other side. Equal treatment for everyone who was getting his day off to a bad start.

The quiet returned except for the occasional bark of some nearby dog. Maybe it wasn't as bad a neighborhood as Harry had thought. Very little graffiti on the buildings, grass along the parkways—at least in spots—with a decent number of trees. And most of the parked cars looked like they might even run. No signs of personal pride in their homes, though. No flower gardens by the doors. No window boxes outside the apartments.

A woman came out of a building and hurried down St. Louis right past him—probably hoping to catch the El that ran down the center of the Eisenhower Expressway. She was much too heavy to look good walking that fast. Now Estelle, she'd never do that. He smiled. If things ever worked out with her, he and Estelle and DaShawn could make a pretty solid family. Certainly better than the tension he'd had with Willa Mae. Of course, he needed to keep things in perspective. It was part of the program, and as Step 1 said, it was his powerlessness over alcohol that had made his life unmanageable. He couldn't blame the mess on anyone else. But things were different now. He was different now, and with the help of someone as solid as Estelle, the potential was even greater.

He glanced at his watch: 6:23. Still no raid. Still no Cindy.

Harry pulled out his cell and opened it. Dark screen. He punched the Talk button and the screen flashed for a moment, then went dark again. He sighed and shook his head. The battery! In all his anticipation of what this day might bring, he had forgotten to plug in his phone last night. How stupid! How could he have done that at a time like this? He needed to find out where Cindy was. Maybe she had been trying to call him. Was this thing going down or not?

And then he saw them—two cars rolling slowly west on Flournoy, one a dull black and the other a light sandy green. Cops. They stopped silently in front of Donita's apartment building, and Harry hunkered down even lower in his seat. The front doors on both cars opened simultaneously without even a click that Harry could hear, and four cops got out.

One was Fagan, and Harry recognized two of the other guys. He didn't know the fourth man. Probably a new guy on the task force.

But there was no Cindy!

Perhaps she was in the backseat of one of the cars. The kaleidoscope of reflections on the cruiser windows obscured any view of what was inside, but Harry didn't hold his breath. He glanced back down the street, hoping for a third car. No luck. Fagan was already giving instructions to two of the men to head down the gangway between the buildings to cover the back. And he and his partner were headed for the front door, a small bar in his hand that he would use to force the lock on the entry door so they wouldn't have to announce their arrival by intercom.

Harry grabbed his door handle and lunged forward, thinking to intercept the squad, then stopped himself. This wasn't how he had planned it. But what could he do? He'd blow the whole play if he showed himself. No, he had to let it unwind. Cindy surely had obtained a warrant, and probably Fagan had it with him. He might still pull off a good collar, and that's all Harry wanted. It wasn't as though Fagan never followed proper police procedure. Having a good arrest record had been important to the SOS from the very beginning. It was only because of the rogue raids that Harry had blown a whistle.

He froze, mouth open, listening for the eruption he knew was to come. His whole body hummed with tension, though when he stretched out his hands, they appeared steady. What was taking them so long? Surely they were up to the third floor by now.

And then he heard it. Not the familiar bellowing of, "Police! Open up!" But yelling like a cat lifted by its tail; he knew it was Donita. At first he could decipher a few of her words: "Who do you think you are?" "Get out!" "I don't care. Get out!" Then it turned to screaming punctuated by Fagan and the other cops yelling demands. "Where is it? We ain't playin', girl! You better cough it up if you want to live."

Harry's gut flip-flopped when he heard her screams choked off by thuds he knew were body blows. She was getting beaten. He jumped from his car and ran toward the building. He didn't like Donita, but she sure didn't deserve a beating. He had to stop it.

Halfway across the intersection, and almost to the door of the apartment, Harry heard the team thudding down the stairs. "Come on. Come on, hurry it up. Let's get outta here!" And then they burst through the front door and hurried toward their getaway vehicles without even glancing to the side where Harry had ducked momentarily behind the corner of a parked van.

Donita was not with them.

They had not made an arrest but only one of their infamous raids.

Harry stayed where he was while the cars roared past. Windows from surrounding apartments flew up.

"Hey, hold it down out there?"

"What's happenin'?"

"Call 911."

"Them was the cops, fool. What you 'spect 911 to do?"

Harry slipped into the building and hit the intercom for Donita's apartment as the neighbors argued it out.

"Come on. Come on, DaShawn. Somebody buzz me in."

There was no response. Harry grabbed the door handle and yanked. It flung open. Obviously, Fagan had broken the lock. Harry climbed the stairs two at a time, wishing he could still leap three.

The door to 317 stood open, soft crying coming from inside. Harry stepped in to see Donita sprawled unconscious on the floor, bleeding from the mouth. DaShawn was huddled in the corner, crying.

Chapter 10

HARRY KNELT BESIDE DONITA and held two fingers to her neck. Her pulse was still strong, and the bleeding from her mouth appeared to be from a badly cut lip rather than something internal. Still, she was unconscious and had obviously taken some pretty hard hits.

"Call 911, DaShawn.

Sniff, sniff. "I can't, Grandpa."

Harry looked over at him sharply. That was the first time anyone had ever called him *grandpa*. "Why not? She needs help."

"He took"—sniff, sniff—"he took the phone."

"Who took the phone?" Harry was checking for obvious broken bones, being careful not to move Donita's torso or neck.

"That man"—*sniff*—"the one who was hittin' her. He thought I was callin' the cops. But I wasn't. I really wasn't. I was just—"

Donita's left forearm looked suspiciously misaligned. Harry looked up. "Don't you have some other phone? We need an ambulance here, boy."

"We don't got no other phone, and that was Donita's new Razr. She gonna be real mad."

Harry jumped up and ran to the open window. He spotted a woman still looking out of her window across the street. "Hey, call 911. We need some help up in here."

"Already did."

"Well, call back and specify that we need an ambulance, and right away."

He returned to check Donita's breathing. It seemed steady, but a huge blackish bruise was building on the side of her face. Suddenly, Donita began to retch, and then she vomited.

In spite of the risk of a neck or back injury, Harry had to keep her airway clear. He lifted her up by the middle so that her head was low and hit her on the back between the shoulder blades to dislodge anything she might have aspirated.

DaShawn began to cry again. "Don't hit her no more, Grandpa. Don't hit her."

"It's okay, son. I ain't hurtin' her. I just don't want her to choke."

When it was clear that she was breathing freely, he lowered her to the floor again. The cryptic dispatch messages of a police radio sounded from the street below. Harry went again to the window and called to the two men getting out of a blue-and-white cruiser. "Up here, 317. And call an ambulance."

"It's on the way."

He returned to Donita. She was just beginning to regain consciousness, moaning, and bringing her hand to her bruised face. She started to try to rise.

"No, stay down. Help'll be here in a minute."

"You! Whatchu doin' here?"

"I was ... I was just comin' over to see DaShawn when I heard a bunch of screamin' up in here. So I came on up and found you like this. Now lie still."

The sound of talking and heavy footsteps came up the stairwell. Donita raised up on one arm and looked around the room, a look of bewilderment and then fear crossing her face. "You with that guy who beat me?"

"No way. I just got here."

"Yeah, right." Her expression turned sullen.

The chatter of police radio communications accompanied the two uniforms who came through the door. They turned down the volume.

"So what happened here?"

Harry started to answer and then hesitated. How could he report what he really knew about what had gone down?

Donita suddenly pointed a finger at Harry. "He busted in here and beat me up! You gotta arrest him." Her boiler was already up to full steam.

"What? I heard you screamin' in here and came up to see what was happening."

"That's a lie. He wants my boy. He was over here the other day tryin' to get him. But I wouldn't give him up, so he came back and tried to beat me into submission."

"That's insane! I'm a—"

"Sir, please keep your hands in plain sight and stand over there. And lady, you just stay right there on the floor until the paramedics get here. No, no. You stay down there."

Harry tried again. "Look, officers, I'm CPD, retired. I was just gonna show you my ID. Can I retrieve my wallet?"

"Turn around so we can see what you are getting."

Harry complied, moving slowly. He withdrew his wallet, opened it, and turned back around.

Donita was still running at the mouth. "I don't care what he is. He was in here ta take my boy, and he beat me up. I wanna press charges. Ain't you people heard of bad cops before, beatin' up folks? It's all the time on the news."

"Mr. Bentley, is it true that you wanted to take the boy?"

"Look, I'm the boy's grandpa, and I—"

"Yeah. See? He was here the other day and woulda taken him then if I hadn't gotten home in time to stop him. DCFS won't give him no custody, so he be fixin' to kidnap the boy."

Harry was reaching his limits. "Donita, you're talkin' crazy. Somebody beat you up, all right, but it wasn't me, and they knocked you silly, so will you just shut your mouth?" He turned to the cop. "Ask the boy what happened. He was here."

"Who beat up your mama, son?"

"This man came in and—"

"This man?"

"No, no—"

Donita yelled at DaShawn. "Shut up, stupid." Then to the cop. "He don't know nothin'. Look at him whimperin' over there. He's afraid he'll get beat up too. That's why he'll say anything. Don't pay him no mind. I don't care what he says …" She tried again to rise up. "Ow, ow. I think he busted my arm."

"Lady, please remain right there where you are."

"You got no right makin' me stay down here in my own puke." She continued getting to her feet. "I'm telling ya. This is the jerk who beat me up, and I wanna press charges."

"Okay, okay. Everybody calm down, now. The paramedics are here and, ma'am, you need to go to the hospital. So that's the first thing that's gonna happen."

Two female cops followed the paramedics into the room.

The lead officer turned to Harry. "Sir, if you'll come with me, we'll get out of their way. And Jennings, you bring the boy down." He addressed the female officers who had just come to the door, and Harry heard him tell them to accompany Donita to the hospital and file her complaint if she insisted on it. The cop shielded his mouth with his hand, but Harry still heard him say, "Don't encourage her. This is just a domestic thing."

IT WAS NOON BEFORE HARRY FINALLY CLIMBED back into his RAV4 and drove away from the area. By then Donita had been carted off to Stroger Hospital, someone from DCFS had collected DaShawn—it wasn't Leslie Stuart, though Harry made sure the woman knew that Ms. Stuart was his case manager—and Harry, backed up by DaShawn, had convinced the officers he hadn't beaten up the boy's mother ... though he was careful not to mention Fagan or the fact that Donita had been beaten by on-duty police. Instead, he encouraged the theory that her pimp may have been the perp, and she was just trying to protect him by accusing Harry.

Though the officers accepted that line as probable, they reminded Harry that if Donita persisted in filing charges, he would have to appear in court. He knew that, but it didn't worry him too much. Surely when the dust settled, Donita would drop her ridiculous accusations.

TONY GOMEZ, THE NIGHT DOORMAN, was livid when Harry finally got back to Richmond Towers. Harry raised both hands. "Sorry. I had an emergency. Wasn't anything else I could do."

"Ah, man, you have no idea what my wife's like when I don't come home on time. It messes up everything with the kids, and she ends up accusing me of being out with some *chica*."

"Hey, I'm sorry, man. You want me to call her?"

"No, no. Just don't ever do that to me again. Okay, man?" And Gomez was out the door.

Harry didn't like people being mad at him. But today he had worse things to worry about. He sat on his stool with his elbows on the desk and his head in his hands. Driving all the way up from the west side he'd been going over what had happened.

Whether or not Fagan and his men had declared themselves as police, Donita was plenty street-smart. She'd have known if the thugs who beat her up were cops ... so why accuse him? Why didn't she start singing "police brutality" from the outset?

Fagan. He'd probably threatened her so bad she was afraid to finger him. Maybe she'd been through this before and knew the cops managed to keep their shields shiny. Still, why accuse him? Why not blame it on her pimp?

Okay, he knew why. She was afraid he might gain custody of DaShawn, so she decided to kill two birds with one stone: come up with a plausible "perp" for her beating that didn't accuse Fagan, and put Harry out of the running for DaShawn at the same time.

Harry raised his head. A resident was coming through the revolving door. He smiled broadly. "Good afternoon, Mrs. Worthington. How you doin' today?"

The white-haired woman didn't even glance his way as she walked across the lobby, through the security door, and pushed the elevator button. "Harry, did UPS drop off a package for me today?"

"Can't say as they did, Mrs. Worthington. But then I—"

She raised her hand as the elevator door closed behind her, never having made eye contact with Harry.

Harry snorted and shook his head. *Serves her right if UPS came before I got here today. If she don't want a polite answer, she can remain ignorant!* He took a deep breath, trying to get rid of some of the tension. He felt wound as tight as when he used to come home from work and had no more patience for his family.

Maybe he ought to go to an AA meeting tonight. It had been some time, and he knew these feelings. Ha, he was in no shape to take on the care of a kid. And yet, what would happen to his grandson? DaShawn had called him *grandpa* back there in the apartment. Made him feel good, and it showed the kid had some respect for him. Harry shook his head. The kid's life was so chaotic, he might be the only stability in the boy's whole universe.

An ounce of respect for an island of stability, that was worth something. Something to build on. He ought to call that social worker—Ms. Stuart—and check on what was happening. He pulled out his cell and flipped it open. Still dead … obviously. After a moment's hesitation, he glanced around the lobby as though someone might be spying on him, then picked up the house phone and dialed.

"Ms. Stuart? Harry Bentley. I presume someone told you what happened this morning with my grandson, DaShawn. I was just calling to see if you knew if he's okay and … and where you plan to place him."

"Yes. They brought him in just a little while ago with some story that you beat up his mother. Tell me that didn't happen, Harry."

"It didn't! But did he say that? He knows better—"

"No, no. Not the boy, Mr. Bentley. It's on the police report. DaShawn insists it wasn't you. So what really happened, Harry?"

Harry sighed. "That's a long story." He stopped. This wasn't a conversation to be having over the phone or in a place where someone might walk in and overhear him.

When he didn't volunteer to get into the "long story," Leslie Stuart said, "Why don't you tell me this evening when I bring DaShawn by your place, okay?"

"DaShawn? My place?"

"That's right. He has to have someplace to stay, and you're next on the list. I'm not inclined to send him to another foster home right now. He's been bounced around so many times."

"This evening?"

"Yes, this evening. I'll come by your apartment about seven."

The line clicked dead, and Harry sat there shaking his head. How could things turn around so quickly? He didn't even have any food in the house. Or a bed for DaShawn to sleep on.

He wasn't ready.

Chapter 11

BALOR DRAVEN WAS LATE relieving Harry at the Richmond Towers front desk. Talk about a paleface; this guy must've washed with bleach and dyed his hair black. But he looked you in the eye. At least, it seemed that way until you noticed his mouth was hanging open. Then it was more like the lights were on but no one was home.

"You have some kind of an emergency that kept you, Mr. Draven?"

"No. Why? You got some kind of an emergency that you gotta get out the door right on the hour? Lighten up, man." He flung his leather jacket into the corner.

"Where's your uniform jacket?"

"Too hot."

"That's why they air-condition this lobby for us. We're supposed to wear our uniforms."

"Well, you don't wear your cap sometimes. Look, here's my cap." He pulled open the bottom desk drawer and produced a crumpled duty cap. He breathed on the dull brim, wiped it across his shirt, and put the cap on his head ... a little askew.

Harry struggled with whether to respond or get out the door. The door won. Thoughts rattled around in his head like marbles in a can. He had to shop at Dominick's. And where would DaShawn sleep? It'd have to be the couch for tonight and maybe a few more until he could clear out his den and find a bed. Should he buy a new one or look in the paper for a used one? He wanted to get off on the right foot with DaShawn, but buying furniture could cost big bucks, and he didn't have so many of those. And what kind would DaShawn want? A kid's bed, like a NASCAR bed, or just a regular one?

Uh-oh! Tomorrow was Friday. He couldn't leave the kid alone at home. What would Ms. Social Services say about that? He'd need at least the whole day to get all this stuff done and DaShawn settled. But he'd pretty much just blown his chances of getting Draven to fill in for him.

By this time, Harry was at his car. He climbed in and punched the number for Tony Gomez into his cell phone before starting his engine.

"Hey Tony, any chance you could fill in for me tomorrow? I got kind of a … an emergency." Yeah, he could call it an emergency in spite of Draven's attitude.

"Gee, I don't know, man. That'd be a double shift, and I'm already kind of short on sleep."

"Yeah, but you'd get some overtime, and you could catch up on your sleep later. Whaddaya say, man? Can you help me out here?"

"I guess. If I tell my wife ahead of time, she'd probably be okay with it."

"Hey thanks, man. You just saved my bacon. Sometime I'll break it all down for you as to what this is all about. Okay, *amigo*?"

Harry closed his cell and started his car. Whew! One down, but how many more to go? Harry had no idea.

The light on his phone answering machine was blinking when he got home, demanding to be heard. Harry pressed the button and began putting away groceries.

"Harry, this is Matty, your old team leader, remember? Of course you remember, but not in the way I want you to remember me. Know what I mean? Word has it, you've been spreading some very nasty rumors about me, Harry." Harry froze with a half gallon of milk in his hand. *"That needs to stop. In fact, you got twenty-four hours to retract those lies, or ... Well, let's not go there, 'cause I know you're gonna do the right thing. Okay?"* The answering machine beeped the end of the message.

Harry left the milk on the counter and returned to the machine, fighting with whether to listen to the message again or delete it. Cindy had warned him about Fagan's intimidation, but he didn't want to give in to it, not even a little bit. He pressed the Delete button. How had that guy found out about the investigation? There had to be a leak in the Review Board. He stood there trembling inside from some kind of stew of anger, apprehension, and bewilderment. He'd known it was risky to report on Fagan, but there was always the hope that government would work right ... this one time ... for you at least. People needed some kind of faith that justice would prevail.

His thoughts were cut off when the doorbell rang. He glanced at the clock as he put the milk in the refrigerator—quarter past seven. Had to be DaShawn and that social worker lady. At least some things were going right. He buzzed them up and pushed Fagan's call out of his mind as he stood there with the door open until they came in.

"Ms. Stuart. DaShawn."

The boy had a bulging backpack and three heavy-duty paper grocery bags with loop handles on the top. Harry couldn't help thinking about the bag lady the Fairbanks woman had let into Richmond Towers. And here was his own grandson, just as homeless. He took a deep breath. DaShawn wouldn't be homeless for long!

"Here, son, you can put your stuff right in here. You got anything else out in the car?"

"No, that's it, Grandpa."

Ah, there it was again ... *Grandpa*. Something deep inside Harry stirred when the boy called him Grandpa. Must be that he was blood.

"Well, my man, we'll get you situated here soon as we can. But for a night or two, you're gonna have to sleep on the couch. You good with that?"

DaShawn went over and plopped down on the couch, bouncing a couple of times like he was testing it. "No problem, and I can watch TV right from here." He flopped back, head on the armrest, feet up on the cushions. "You got cable?"

"Yeah, but ..." Harry hadn't thought about whether his package included channels that weren't appropriate for kids. Wasn't there some way to block those? He raised his eyebrows and took a deep breath. "Yeah, well, we'll have to see about the TV."

"DaShawn," said Ms. Stuart, "why don't you get out your Game Boy and play with it while we talk."

She turned to Harry. "We have some paperwork to fill out. Okay to use your table?"

"Sure." He pulled out a chair and then sat around the corner from her.

"Now you understand, this is just temporary, Mr. Bentley, until we can process everything—"

"Whaddaya mean, *temporary*? Where's Donita in all this?"

"I'm not completely sure about her. You know I'm on your side. I'd like to remove her from the picture. But sometimes that isn't so easy to do."

"She's a prostitute, you know."

"We're looking into that, but for right now, DaShawn's with you. Let's see, I gathered most of the preliminary information previously, so all we've got to do this evening is ..." She laid several pages before Harry. "Now, if you'll just sign and date each sheet at the bottom, I'll get outta here and leave you gentlemen to your first evening together."

As Harry signed, he glanced up at her and was met with the broadest smile he'd ever seen on her face. It crossed his mind again that this was probably the easiest solution for her. But then, maybe he shouldn't be so cynical. It was now also what he wanted, and hopefully—he looked over at DaShawn who was busy exercising his thumbs on his beeping, handheld video game—hopefully it was the best thing for his grandson as well.

They spent most of the next morning boxing up stuff from Harry's den and carrying it down to his storage locker. DaShawn was surprisingly helpful, only dropping out to play his Game Boy when Harry took too long deciding what to pack and what not to pack.

They finished and went shopping for a bed, stopping on the way at McDonald's for lunch.

"So DaShawn, you want to tell me what happened in your mom's apartment yesterday before I came up in there?"

DaShawn shrugged and popped three ketchup-dipped fries into his mouth. "Those guys just come in and started beatin' on her. I done tol' the cops about a hundred times."

"Yeah? And where were you when they came in?"

"Sittin' on the couch, watchin' TV."

"At six-thirty in the morning?"

The boy twisted his head to look out the window, his floating halo of hair catching up a split second later. "Jus' the Cartoon Channel."

"Then what happened?"

"They shut off the TV and started goin' through everything, dumpin' it all over the floor. That's when Donita come outta the bathroom and started yellin' at 'em. They might not've hit her if she hadn't been screamin' at 'em." He gave Harry a *who-knows?* grimace. He looked down and sucked hard on his shake.

Harry waited a moment, but DaShawn was silent as though the story was all over "So what happened next?" Harry nudged. "When I came up, you were over in the corner. How'd you get there?"

"That big guy knock' me over there."

"He hit you?" Harry gritted his teeth. Fagan had to be stopped. The gall of him hitting a child and then using intimidation to quash an investigation. Harry was glad he had deleted that phone message. He wouldn't cave to that scumbag no matter what.

"Yeah, he hit me," DaShawn said, "but it didn't really hurt. He was tryin' to knock the phone outta my hand 'cause he thought I was callin' 911. But I wasn't, Grandpa. I weren't callin' no cops."

"Yeah. You said that before. But if you weren't dialin' 911, what were you doin'?"

"Takin' a video of him hittin' Donita."

"You what?"

"I was recordin' him. Her new Razr has video capture."

"*Video capture*? You mean like a movie, action and sound and all?"

"Yeah. It be off the hook, man. All new features. She paid big bucks for that Razr. And she gonna be mad, real mad. She'll be outta her mind when she finds he got it."

"Now just hold on a minute." Harry's mind was spinning. If there was actually a video of Fagan beating a suspect … "But you're sayin' Fa— I mean, that man took her phone?"

"Yeah. After he knocked me over in the corner, the phone fell on the floor, and he grabbed it up and put it in his pocket."

"You actually saw him put in his pocket?"

DaShawn nodded, hair and all.

"But first you think you got some kind of movie of him hitting your mom? How long?"

"How long, what?"

"How long was the movie?"

DaShawn shrugged. "I dunno. He hit her three, four times 'fore he saw me. Then he hit her more later. He started kickin' her." The boy stopped, put down his burger, and took a deep breath as he stared down at the napkins and papers on the table.

"It's okay, son." Harry reached across and rested his hand on the boy's arm. It was the first time he had touched him except for a pat on the back for carrying the boxes down to the locker. "That's okay. I understand."

Harry waited a few moments, then leaned back. "Let me ask you one more thing. Did you tell the cops you took a video of that man?"

"No. They never asked me."

"And did that man hit Donita with both hands?"

DaShawn pursed his lips and squinted his eyes for a moment as though he was thinking. "He had a bunch of stuff in one hand, so he was hittin' her with the other."

"Stuff, whaddya mean *stuff*?"

"White baggies ... Donita's freebase stash."

Harry leaned up and put his elbow on the table, supporting his bowed head with his hand. A nine-year-old shouldn't be so familiar with illegal drugs that he could recognize them by names. But this was getting deep. Somewhere there was a cell phone with a video showing Fagan not only beating a suspect he never arrested but holding bags of drugs he never registered as evidence. If Harry could find that phone, he could nail the sucker!

He looked up to see his grandson dip the last of the fries in the ketchup. "Was Donita dealing?" he asked.

"Yeah. And that's what the guy wanted, the money."

"Did he get it?"

DaShawn shook his head. "She don't keep no money. She say it all be Hector's money."

Harry considered the scenario DaShawn had described in stop-frame. "You think those little baggies would show up on your movie?"

DaShawn shrugged. "He was holdin' 'em right in her face, yellin' at her."

Harry turned and stared out the window for a while. If DaShawn's story was true—and Harry could think of no reason why the kid would lie—then that little movie could be the magic bullet to put Fagan away for good. But … "DaShawn, are you sure that man picked up the phone? Any chance it could have gotten kicked under the couch or something?"

"I tol' ya, Grandpa. I seen him put it in his pocket."

Harry sat there, nodding his head, considering the implications. What if … ? If Fagan thought DaShawn was trying to phone the police, then there wouldn't be any reason for him to search the phone's memory for an incriminating video. Heck, Fagan might not even know cell phones could take videos. Harry hadn't heard of that before. But DaShawn was positive this new gadget had that capability, and these days, kids were always two steps ahead of adults when it came to technology stuff.

"You ever take any other videos with that phone?"

"Oh yeah, lots. Though Donita don't like me playin' wit' it."

"And they come out so you can actually see things, I mean, are they as good as … as the still pictures you can take with a cell?"

"Yeah. Why, Grandpa?"

"I'm just thinkin' … thinkin' about how to get that phone back."

"Tha'd be good, Grandpa. Then Donita won't be so mad at me. 'Cause when she gets mad …"

"We'll have to see." Harry's mind was running like an Internet search engine. If Fagan didn't know about the video, then to him, all he had was a phone he didn't dare use for fear that it could be traced and identify him. So maybe he flipped it into the backseat of his car where it would still be kicking around on the floor. Or maybe he might have emptied his pockets when he got home and left it on his dresser. Or what if he tossed it out the window of his car or into the trash, never to be found again?

"What'd the phone look like? Donita's new phone?"

"It was a new Razr, a flip phone, but pink."

"Pink? Never seen a pink phone."

"Yeah, hot pink. She's got hot pink everything. Like these little plastic short shorts and pink high heels and this pink pushup—" He was gesturing with his hands in front of his chest.

"All right, all right. Got the picture." He hadn't remembered seeing anything pink, but then it fit. What that poor kid had gone through!

One thing was fairly certain: Fagan wouldn't have logged that phone in as evidence back at headquarters. There would be no report of that morning's raid by the CPD's elite anti-gang and drug taskforce. So Donita's cell phone was floating around out there somewhere, and with any luck it still contained the perfect evidence to put Fagan away for a very long time.

Harry stood up.

"Okay, DaShawn, let's go find you a bed. You want a bunk bed so you can have a friend over sometime for a sleepover?"

Chapter 12

SATURDAY WAS LIKE CHRISTMAS for Harry and DaShawn, buying stuff, eating large, and running around as if they didn't get it all now, there'd be no chance later. Harry began to relax and laugh easier as the sense began to grow within him that maybe he could do this … and even like it.

But Monday loomed. How was he going to enroll DaShawn and make arrangements for his care after school? Man, what was the matter with him? He hadn't thought through all this. It wasn't so much that DaShawn couldn't miss a few more days of school. This year had already been pretty messed up for him. According to Leslie Stuart, he had missed a couple of weeks when Rodney was arrested. Then he had to switch schools to the west side when he went to live with Donita, and now he was facing another school and less than a month before summer vacation.

The more immediate problem was, if DaShawn wasn't in school, what would Harry do with him while he was at work? And when would he find the time on a weekday to enroll him in school? He'd already used up a little goodwill with Gomez on Friday, so he couldn't keep expecting him to fill in. Should he call Leslie Stuart and ask if she had any suggestions? Certainly other parents ran into this kind of a problem. Harry hesitated. He didn't want to go running to her with every little detail. Who else knew about schools and might be able to advise him?

Baxter, that white guy from the men's group. He worked at a high school. What was he? An athletic director or something? But how to get in touch with him? The only phone number Harry had was for Peter Douglass.

It was time to be fixing dinner—Harry had no idea what to cook—and DaShawn was watching TV, but if Harry wanted to contact Peter, he'd better try calling now. Who knew how hard it would be to catch him?

Peter Douglass answered on the third ring. "Hey, Harry. How you doin'?"

"Couldn't be better. Couldnt' be better." Though at the moment, he sure could. "But, hey, you got the number for Baxter?"

"Which one? Denny or Josh?"

"The older guy. The one who works at the high school."

"Sure, let me find it for you here." Then in a voice not meant for Harry, he mumbled, "Baxter, Baxter, Denny and Jodi. Ah, here we go." But instead of reading off the number, without missing a beat, asked, "So what's up, anyway?"

"Uh ..." Harry hesitated, thinking the number was coming. "Uh, remember in group how I said my grandson might be comin'? Well, he's here, and I got to get him enrolled in school."

"Hey, that's great. A real answer to prayer. Is he in high school?"

"No, no. He's only nine years old, but I don't know anything about schools anymore, so I thought I'd ask Denny if he could refer me to someone."

"Well, sure, but hold on a moment ..."

Harry waited. It sounded like Peter had his hand over the receiver and was talking to someone. What was that he'd said, *An answer to our prayers*? Answered prayer had never crossed Harry's mind. But … maybe it was so.

"Hey, Harry, you there?"

"Yep."

"Here's Denny's number." Peter rattled it off while Harry wrote it down. "But you know, Harry, you might want to talk to my wife, Avis. She's the principal at Bethune Elementary, which is probably where your grandson would go anyway."

"Really? That'd be great. That's where I was hoping to send him."

In a moment a woman came on the line. "Hello, this is Avis. How can I help you?" Harry tried to match her measured tones with one of the people he had met at the Fun Night. But he just couldn't fit the voice with a face. At first he felt embarrassed explaining his dilemma of not being able to get time off work Monday morning to enroll DaShawn in school, but under the circumstances, it seemed better just to lay it all out there. Perhaps there was some way he could enroll DaShawn in the evening or something, in which case, he'd just have to take the boy to work with him for a day or so. Who knew what the manager of Richmond Towers would say about that. But who said Mr. Martin needed to find out? He and his secretary, Gretchen, were busy keeping the units full and seldom did more than walk through the lobby on the way to their office down the hall.

"Well, Monday's Memorial Day, Mr. Bentley, so there's no school."

Harry slapped his head. Of course, Memorial Day!

"But I'll tell you what." Avis Douglass had his attention. "I have to go in early on Tuesday. If you bring your grandson by about seven-thirty, you could sign a couple of things, then we'll take care of other details later. We can probably get his immunization records and grades forwarded to us from his previous school. Shouldn't be too hard."

When Harry hung up the phone, he felt like he'd sunk the winning three-pointer in a tight game. It was all working out just like, just like … Wait a minute. Could it actually be that the brothers' prayers had something to do with it?

Things seemed to be going so well with DaShawn that Harry decided Sunday was a good day for an outing. He phoned Estelle Williams.

"Estelle, seein' as how it's likely to get into the nineties this afternoon, I was wondering if I could tempt you with a cool, refreshing cruise on Lake Michigan?"

"What? Mr. Bentley, since when does a retired Chicago police officer own a boat?"

"Well now, first off, it's Harry, remember? And second, there *are* cops who own boats, and some pretty nice ones, too, I might add. But truth be known, I was proposing a little outing on the four-masted sailing schooner, known as the *Windy*. It departs from Navy Pier every couple hours for a pleasant turn along Chicago's beautiful lakefront. Whaddya say?"

"Well, I don't know. I got church this morning, and I was just fixin' to head out."

"No problem, mon." He said it like a happy islander. "How 'bout we do it in de afte'noon? Whatchu say, mon?"

"Hey, don't you be pullin' no Jamaican *patois* on me, Harry Bentley. Besides, I'll be busy till at least one o'clock."

"Then I'll pick you up at one-thirty. How's that? We'll grab a bite and then head on down."

"Honestly, Harry! I don't think I have any sailing clothes. It's not the kind of thing I've done much of."

"Of course not. But this is a gentlemanly … I mean ladylike sailing. We're not going to be bobbing around out there with spray flying across the deck. Any pair of slacks and soft-soled shoes will do. But you might want a hat."

"And I don't s'pose you mean a churchgoin' hat. Right?"

Harry laughed. "No, not a church-goin' hat. Just something to keep the sun off your beautiful face." Harry could tell she was going to say yes.

"Humph! Well ... how long this cruise likely to last?"

"Oh, just an hour and a half or so. Promise to have you home before dark. How's that?"

"Okay, Harry."

"Great!" He almost hung up. "Oh wait, one more thing. I'll be bringing a young friend of mine I want you to meet."

"*A friend?* Now, Harry Bentley, I done told you I ain't playin' around. I got more life behind me than to go, so I don't plan to be wastin' what's left competin' with some young thang you decided to pick up along the way. If that's what you're about, you can just get outta my face. Ya hear!"

And the line went dead.

Harry couldn't help laughing out loud, then caught his breath that Estelle had misunderstood him so.

"What's so funny, Grandpa?" DaShawn came shuffling into the kitchen, his hair mashed down on one side and a little nappy.

"Weren't nothin'. Just had a funny phone call."

He hit Redial and waited while the phone rang and rang. *Come on ... pick it up.*

"What do you want?"

"Estelle, just hold on, now. My young friend is my nine-year-old grandson." He held his breath through a silence that felt too long. "I just want you to meet him is all. He's a cool kid." Harry smiled at DaShawn and caught a little grin back.

More silence.

"Estelle? You still there?"

"I'm sorry, Harry." There was a deep sigh on the other end of the line. "I don't know what got into me. Must be hormones or somethin'. I was way out of line. Forgive me?"

Estelle seemed to take a shine to DaShawn as soon as she met him, even putting her arm around him when they were sitting on the deck of the *Windy* while Harry took pictures of two happy people against a backdrop of thin white clouds, streaked like cornrows over Chicago's skyline.

Something as satisfying as his Mama's pudding seemed to slip down inside Harry as he watched DaShawn and Estelle pointing out various buildings along the Chicago skyline. And just for a minute he caught that expression on DaShawn's face that looked so much like Rodney. It was like turning the clock back to let him try it all over again and perhaps get it right this time.

Estelle broke into a full and easy laugh at some joke DaShawn made, and Harry had to tell himself, *Don't go there!* when he began imagining the three of them making a happy family together.

But why not go there?

When the worst thing to happen all afternoon was DaShawn dropping his lemon ice over the railing into the lake, Harry figured the day just … well, as DaShawn put it on the way home, "It rocked, Grandpa."

The alarm hadn't yet gone off Memorial Day morning when Harry was awakened by someone banging on the door of his apartment. What was going on? No one had buzzed his intercom. Had to be a neighbor with an emergency.

"Hold on a minute," he mumbled. Pretty soon they'd be waking up DaShawn, and after staying up late watching *Batman* the night before, Harry had planned to let him sleep as long as possible before getting him up and taking him to work with him for the day. Harry stood up, pulling on a pair of pants, his body protesting in every joint. Whew. He still wasn't over carrying furniture up three flights of stairs and then putting it together two days before. That's what it was like being fifty-eight years old. You just didn't bounce back so fast.

"I'm coming."

He opened the door to see two uniforms standing there. One he recognized—Jerry Guzman—from when he worked the streets before he made detective and got assigned to the anti-gang unit. He blinked. "Guzman? What are you guys doing here?"

The other officer took the lead. "Harold Josiah Bentley? We have a warrant for your arrest—"

Harry threw up his hands as a barrier. "Wait a minute! If this is some kind of a joke, it's sure the wrong time to pull it." He glanced at his watch.

Guzman grimaced. "Sorry, Harry. I didn't realize it was you. Fact is, I didn't even look that closely at the name on the warrant. I mean, never heard you called ..." He unfolded the paper and glanced at it. "*Harold Josiah,* and you know there's gotta be a dozen Harold Bentleys in the city."

"So this is all a big mistake, right? Now get the heck outta here before you wake up the whole building." He shooed at them with his hands and started to close the door.

Gozman stiff-armed the door. "Can't do that Harry. Sorry, but we do have to serve this warrant on you. If it's a mistake, maybe you can work it out down at the station, but for now, we gotta take you in."

"Take me in? You ain't takin' me nowhere!"

The other officer stepped up. "Harold Bentley, you are under arrest for assault and battery and attempted kidnapping. You have the right to remain—"

"Ah shut up. You think I don't know my rights?" Harry turned away from the door, allowing the officers to follow him into the apartment.

Just then, DaShawn came shuffling out of his bedroom. His eyes got big. "Grandpa. What they doin' here? Grandpa?"

"Oh, these fools are making a big mistake. Don't worry 'bout it, son. I'll tell you later. Go on back to bed, now."

He spoke calmly while his insides exploded. The beautiful experience from yesterday was shattering in slow motion into a thousand pieces like some priceless Ming vase, sharp edges cutting everywhere. This couldn't be happening to him.

"But Grandpa—" The boy's face was wrenched in terror.

"I said get back in your room. This don't concern you, boy!"

Harry recognized the change that came into DaShawn's eyes. It was all too like the look Rodney used to give him when he came down too hard—hurt, afraid, angry—Harry couldn't pin it down, but he knew it when he saw it. And he remembered the destruction it foretold.

When DaShawn had slinked back to his room, Harry turned to the cops. He had to put his world back together again, stop the detonation at the spark. "So who's the complainant, and what were those charges again?"

Guzman looked at the warrant. "Let's see, it was a Donita Stevens on West Flournoy, and the charges are assault and battery with attempted kidnapping."

"*Kidnapping!* You gotta be kiddin' me. Well, you know this is all bogus, 'cause that Donita done lost her mind!"

Chapter 13

THE OTHER COP—Harry noticed his nametag said "Heinrich"—took out his cuffs. "Sir, would you turn around, please, and put your hands behind—"

"That's not gonna be necessary," injected Guzman. "Is it, Harry?"

"You try to put those cuffs on me, I'll throw you both down the stairs. Now can't we just work this out?" Somehow he had to rewind this thing.

"Well, I hope you can work it out, Harry, but we can't do it here. We gotta bring you in and book you."

"No you don't." Harry glanced toward DaShawn's room. No boy. That was good, but he was still feeling frantic. He needed another option. "Look, all you gotta do is say you couldn't find me."

"Then what? Somebody else'll pick you up. And they might not be so understanding, know what I mean? What then?"

"That'll be my problem." He needed the time. "Look, you boys go on about your business, writin' parking tickets or whatever you do. I'll come in voluntarily soon … by tomorrow and get this thing worked out. Okay?"

"I don't know …"

"Look guys, I got my grandson here. You saw. And if I don't show, you know where I live, right?"

The two cops looked at each other, and Heinrich shrugged.

"Okay, Harry," said Guzman. "But you better show, 'cause once we walk out that door, you got an outstanding warrant against you. And if you don't surrender voluntarily, make no mistake about it, we *will* be back!"

Once the cops were gone, Harry drifted into the kitchen, almost in a daze, and put coffee on. He stood there, his heart pounding like he'd run a mile. Blasted woman! He didn't have time for this drama. He watched the coffee a few moments. Coffee ... what he needed was a few stiff drinks, something to help him calm down and focus on how to get out of this.

Wait a minute ... stiff drinks in the morning? He hadn't been that bad for years. Maybe he better go to a meeting, but he had no time for that, not now. He'd just have to gut it out and remember that he didn't want to repeat what had happened with Rodney.

He should've known, though. Any involvement with Rodney had always meant drama, and here it was happening all over again. He was trying to help out his son's son, and what did he get for his efforts? He got arrested and charged with a felony!

He poured himself a cup of joe and looked in on DaShawn. His grandson was not in bed. Where'd he gone? Harry turned back to the bathroom. The door stood open, the light off.

"DaShawn? Where you at, son?"

"In here, Grandpa," came a faint voice. "They gone yet?"

Harry went back into the bedroom and opened the closet door. There sat DaShawn huddled in the corner on the floor, tears streaking down his face.

Harry's heart instantly melted … then boiled with anger at the nerve of that woman. "Come on out, son. They're gone, and you don't need to worry. I'm going to get all this worked out." He helped the boy up and wrapped his arms around him.

They clung to each other for a moment. The last time the boy had seen cops come to the house, they had beat up his mother. And who knew how often something like that had happened before, maybe even before breakfast, like this morning. No child should have to be rousted out of his night's sleep to that kind of a nightmare.

Harry released him, and his grandson sat on the bed, his head hanging so Harry couldn't see his eyes. This was going to be harder than Harry had bargained for, but he would fight it. He'd been given a second chance, and it was time to make the most of it. And no cop, no sleazebag Donita, and no one else was going to take it away from him.

Harry checked his watch. "It's gettin' late. You better get cleaned up and dressed. I gotta get to work. We'll grab somethin' to eat on the way. Okay?" He tousled DaShawn's hair, and realized when the boy pulled back and gave him a mock frown through his tears that the move wasn't welcome. "Well, anyway, come on. Let's go or we'll be rushing to get out the door."

It was rush, rush, rush anyway. Harry had forgotten how slowly a nine-year-old could move.

They rode to work in silence, Harry's mind bouncing between how he was going to deal with the charges against himself and plans for Tuesday and what time they would have to leave the next morning to get DaShawn into school. Harry knew a cauldron of anger bubbled just under the surface, and he didn't know how to turn down the heat, so for now, he'd better just leave the lid on.

As for DaShawn, well, who knew what he was thinking?

As they turned into the parking garage for Richmond Towers, Harry pointed through the window of his car. "This is where I work, but see that Dominick's down the street? They have like a coffee shop in there. I'm gonna give you some money, and I want you to go on down there and get yourself some breakfast. There's rolls and milk and stuff, but I want you to get fruit too. Okay? And then you're to come right back up here. No wanderin' around or hangin' out. Understand?"

DaShawn nodded his head, the 'fro bouncing. "Can I get pizza?"

"For breakfast? What's the matter with you, boy? Pizza ain't no breakfast food. They wouldn't even have any this time of morning."

"Sometimes they got leftovers from the night before. Donita gets it half price."

"Oh, man, you gonna make me lose my coffee and doughnuts. No, you get some good food. You hear? Some fruit—a banana and orange juice, maybe a bagel."

Harry had no idea whether he could keep DaShawn entertained for a whole day while he took care of the residents coming in and out. But there were no other options. He glanced outside. The clouds suggested rain, and sending him off alone down to the beach probably wasn't a good idea, anyway. While DaShawn was gone to get some breakfast, he went to the closet and got out the small black-and-white TV he sometimes used for watching ball games. He slid one of the lobby chairs around behind his desk and tucked it into the corner and set up the TV a few feet away on a box. If the management didn't like this arrangement, Mr. Martin could find another doorman. He had taken this low-key job mostly for something to do, but for a career police officer in the elite anti-gang unit, it was often more boring than an all-night stakeout … and not even a partner to talk to.

With a semi-private space set up for DaShawn, Harry straightened his blue uniform, pulled his cap a little lower over his eyes, and went around to the front of his tall, half-circle desk to straighten the brochures in the rack when he heard the elevator ding and its doors opened. All right, workday had started. No more time for stewing about his problems. Put on a face for the residents.

Mrs. Fairbanks emerged from the elevator, smiling like she'd won the lottery. A couple of juveniles followed with faces so sour that *they* must have been the ones to give her their winning ticket.

"Boys," she said, "I'd like you to meet my friend, Mr. Bentley. You'll see a lot of him. He *rules* this roost."

"Mrs. Fairbanks." Harry removed his cap. "You're back from Virginia, I see. And this must be the young man who just graduated from middle school." Harry held out his hand to the older one. "Congratulations, young man. And welcome to Chicago."

The handshake Harry received felt like Jell-O. *O-kay*. He turned to the younger one. "What about you, young man? Do you have a name, or should I give you a street name? Like your mom." If he was going to raise a kid, he'd better learn how to break through. Maybe a little humor would work. He looked from side to side, as if casing the lobby for spies. "Her street name is Firecracker."

"Wha—what?" Mrs. Fairbanks giggled.

Harry glanced at her and noted her cheeks turning red. He leaned down to be on the boy's eye level and patted his own bald head. "You know. The, um, hair." He rolled his eyes toward Mrs. Fairbanks.

The younger boy laughed out loud. "Nah. My dad calls her Mop Top. But only when he's in a really good mood." He held out his hand and gave Harry a decent shake. "I'm Paul. He's P.J."

Ah, maybe he was making some headway. He faced the older one. "Ah. Now what would that stand for? Pearl Jam? Para Jumper?... I know. Peter Jackson! *Lord of the Rings*—"

Uh-oh. The boy's eyes flashed. "No. It stands for Philip Fairbanks, *Junior*." With a look as bored as Draven's death face, he turned to Mrs. Fairbanks. "Come *on*, Mom. I thought we were going to do something."

Whoa, a foul ball. Harry reached into his pocket and pulled out a couple of coupons. "Well, then. Maybe these will come in handy. Good for free doughnuts or ice cream at the Dunkin' Donuts a couple of blocks north of here." He had planned to give them to DaShawn, but the distance in a strange neighborhood was a little far for a boy alone. The younger boy's eyes lit up as he took the coupons, but the older one gave no more than a nod. Still, Harry didn't think it had been a complete strikeout. He looked out the glass front of the building. "And it seems to have stopped raining. Just in time."

Harry smiled, put his cap back on, and turned as the mother and two boys headed for the revolving door just as DaShawn was coming in the other side. "Oh, Mrs. Fairbanks, here comes someone I'd like *you* to meet." But she was already out the door and didn't hear him. Maybe just as well. Some other time when those Fairbanks boys weren't being as arrogant as their father, maybe they—at least the younger one—could become friends with DaShawn.

The morning passed at its usual pace with Harry "makin' nice" to all the residents while DaShawn watched TV and played his Game Boy. No one from building management even walked through the lobby. Everything seemed to be working out. But school would be over in a few weeks, and then what would he do with DaShawn? He couldn't bring him to Richmond Towers every day. The kid would go crazy, and surely someone would complain. Maybe he could find a day-camp program for him, or maybe his mother could keep him some of the time. She was elderly, but they might be good for each other.

Sitting on his stool behind the desk, Harry had almost dozed off while reading the *Tribune* sports page when he heard the swish of the revolving doors. He jerked alert and slid off his stool to greet the person.

It was Leslie Stuart, dressed in a light gray pantsuit and white blouse. But the thing that caught Harry's eye was the red beret cocked jauntily on her head. Harry also noticed the string of silver studs down the outside edge of her left ear. Funny, he hadn't seen those earrings before. Maybe it was the way she'd tucked her straight blonde hair behind her ear.

"Well, well, to what do we owe this visit? Spying on me for Miss Williams to make sure I'm on the job?"

"Funny, Mr. Bentley, but the day I spy for Estelle will be the last day we share the same apartment, and perhaps the last day of my life on God's green earth."

"Ha. I hear ya." Harry frowned. The social worker still hadn't yet looked him in the eye. "Everything okay, Ms. Stuart?"

She sighed deeply and finally fixed him with a dead-pan stare. "We've got problems, Harry."

"So what else is new?"

"No, I'm serious. With you being charged with assault and kidnapping, we can't leave the boy with you."

"What are you talkin' about?" Harry looked down to see that DaShawn had come up to stand beside him and realized there was no way to insulate the boy from what was going on. "How'd you hear about that?" he asked Leslie Stuart. "You got a hotline to the Chicago PD?"

"No, and in fact, who knows when we would've heard about it if it hadn't been for the ..." She rolled her eyes toward DaShawn as though avoiding the mention of Donita's name would somehow protect him from reality. "She gave us a call and insisted he be removed from the premises of a 'felon,' as she called you."

"Ha, she's the only one who's ever been convicted of a felony. I'm still innocent … until proven guilty, and that's not gonna happen. This is totally bogus. Judge'll throw it out like that." He snapped his fingers, wishing he really could make it disappear that fast. "No problem."

"But it is a problem, Mr. Benley, a serious problem. And I wouldn't be so sure about getting it thrown out. Seems like the state's attorney is taking considerable interest in your case. Probably all the media attention on bad cops. Maybe they want to make an example of you or something."

Harry shook his head. "You don't need to worry about all that. It'll all blow away soon enough." But would it? That cauldron was bubbling in his stomach again.

"I hope you're right, Mr. Bentley. But in the meantime, I'm going to have to take DaShawn."

"Take me where?" DaShawn spoke up, resting his chin on the desk counter, his hair shading his face like the crown of a mushroom.

Harry frowned. "Now wait a minute. You ain't givin' him back to that Donita. I'm here to tell ya!"

"No, not if we can help it. When she was in the hospital, they took a blood sample, and we're trying to get an injunction to test it for drugs. But with all the new privacy laws, that's not easy. In the meantime, we've made an administrative decision not to send him back there … for now."

"Then why don't you just make another administrative decision to leave him with me, and we can forget all this crap?"

"You know that's not the way it works, Mr. Bentley, not when the welfare of a child is at stake." She turned to DaShawn. "For now, I'll just be taking you down to the office. We'll see what we can do for tonight."

"*Now*? *Tonight*? What you talkin' about, *now*? You ain't takin' him right now. I got due process."

"Yeah, well, being a former cop, you of all people should know 'due process' doesn't always give your due. Sometimes we intervene and sort it out later."

Harry looked down at his grandson. This wasn't fair. "Well, you can't take him right now. All his stuff is back at the apartment."

She sighed and looked at her watch. "Okay. What time do you get off work?"

"Five, if that knucklehead gets here on time."

She looked at her watch again, as though she hadn't seen it a moment before. "I've got another appointment today. I'll go take care of it and be by your apartment about six. Have him ready." She headed toward the revolving doors. Just before they folded her into their sweep, she turned back. "You know I hate doing this to you … to the both of you. But I can't help it."

Chapter 14

Grandpa, how come—"

"How should I know?" Harry snapped without even hearing out the boy's question. He went back around his desk, perched himself on his stool, and snapped open the *Tribune* again. MAYDAZE! MAYDAZE! MAYDAZE! POPUP BOUNCES OFF RAMÍREZ'S HEAD IN MOST BIZARRE LOSS YET. BRAVES 13, CUBS 12. Yeah, yeah, yeah. Sunday's game probably began the Cubs' annual streak of bad luck. Maybe Harry's too. He closed his eyes and tried to breathe. What was he going to do with all this? In only two days with the boy, his whole world had exploded.

He opened his eyes and glanced over at DaShawn. The boy was in the chair where he'd spent most of the day, but he wasn't watching the murmuring TV with its insipid laugh track. Instead, his feet were pulled up on the seat, his arms around his knees, and his face was buried in his arms. Harry studied the boy for a moment and saw his shoulders lurch. Oh no, what were those? Sobs? Well, that's all he needed, a blubbering kid. He had to get out of this mess. Bring some copacetic back into his life.

But when Harry spoke, his tone was tempered with the memory of the day his own father left for the last time, a day that brought peace to his home, but a peace like the dashed hopes of urban renewal when it tore down all the apartments and stores in the old neighborhood, leaving nothing but vacant lots covered by broken bottles and crushed bricks … for years.

"DaShawn? What is it, son? You okay?" Harry tried to rub out the deep frown lines in his own forehead.

The fluffy head came up to reveal a tear-streaked face. "How come I cain't stay wit' you, Grandpa? I'll tell 'em you didn't do none of those things Donita says."

"I know. It's just that with Donita tellin' them lies, they gotta check it out. Don't you worry, though. We'll get it straightened out, directly. And meantime, I'll keep your room waitin' for you … promise. I won't turn it back into no den. Deal?"

DaShawn nodded, sniffed deeply, and wiped his eyes with the back of his hands.

Harry felt like he ought to go over and give the boy a hug, but he didn't. He felt awkward and wanted to dial everything down a little.

After Leslie Stuart collected DaShawn that evening with most of the boy's belongings—DaShawn said he didn't want to take everything with him because he was coming back real soon, "Right, Grandpa?"—Harry just sat at his table, staring across the room as he reviewed the day's events. But doing so was like cranking a generator that threw sparks somewhere deep inside him. In a few moments he was up and pacing around the apartment.

He probably ought to retain an attorney. He picked up the phone and began to dial a number. In most cases, only fools tried to fight their own legal battles without representation, but after twenty years as a cop, Harry knew his way around. He slammed it back down again. A lawyer would cost five thousand dollars if he cost a buck. And this was such a crazy charge, it wouldn't last a minute. In fact, he looked at the clock on the wall of the kitchen—6:20. Maybe he ought to go down to the station right now and get this over with. He had to do something. It was Monday evening, Memorial Day, and there probably wouldn't be a judge around to set his bail, but he had an idea, a better idea. He wouldn't need a judge. He grabbed his hat and keys.

At the Clark Street police station, he presented himself to the desk sergeant and told him why he was there ... and that he was a retired Chicago police officer and this was a totally fabricated charge.

The sergeant sat there, elbows on his desk, hands folded while he chewed on his tongue like he had heard it all before. He dug through some papers in the stacker on his desk and pulled out a folder and looked through it. "Still gotta book you, 'cause I'm not a judge, and I didn't issue this warrant."

"Yeah, but you can see it's a waste of time, right?"

"Maybe yours, but as for me, this is what your tax dollars pay for. Come on back."

He got up and led Harry back to the processing room, where another officer took over, filling out more paperwork, taking Harry's mug shots, and fingerprinting him. In all his years as a cop, Harry had never seriously considered how it felt to be arrested ... especially if you weren't guilty, which almost every perp claimed. Resentment gurgled in his stomach like he'd eaten some bad food. His face felt hot. Was he embarrassed at being booked for a felony? It was a phony charge, but it was on him ... He scrubbed with the paper towels to get the ink off his fingers. He'd go home with black fingers. What if someone saw that?

"Okay," said the officer, "come on, I'll see if I can't get you into one of our better rooms for the night."

Harry stepped back. "Wait a minute. I'm not stayin' here."

"Oh come on, man. You know the drill. You gotta make bail before we can let you go."

"Not necessarily." This was Harry's gamble. If he was held over, he'd miss work in the morning while they sent him into some municipal court to await a judge's schedule. It could be all day before he was released. But … "Hey, take me to the captain. It's within his purview to issue a police-set bond, an I-bond, and let me go tonight."

"A what-bond?"

"An individual bond, releasing me on my personal recognizance."

"Oh, sure." The officer laughed as he stuffed the papers into a folder. "Yeah, we might do that for a first-offense DUI, but buddy, you're up for assault and battery and attempted kidnapping. That's high octane. No way can we set bond for charges like that."

"Look at the warrant. Does it specify the bond?"

The officer flipped through the paperwork again, then looked up and shrugged.

"See? This is a bogus charge. I'm a retired police officer—here's my card—and I surrendered voluntarily. There's no way I'm any kind of a flight risk. Take me to your captain. He'll understand."

The captain required just as much convincing as the intake officer, even though he'd heard Harry's name before and knew he served on the anti-gang unit. But finally, he told the officer to have Harry fill out the additional paperwork for a personal recognizance bond and let him go.

Harry scribbled in the information for the blanks. He didn't care if anyone could read it. He was outta there!

When he was done and the papers were stamped, the officer handed Harry his copies. "Okay, you're got a preliminary hearing a week from tomorrow, nine-thirty at the Belmont courthouse."

He reached over and pointed to the top sheet in Harry's hand. "There's all the specifics. It'll be Judge Hollingsworth."

Yeah, yeah. Harry scowled at the man, willing the furrows deeper into his forehead. He could read.

"Well ... don't be late. You'll receive a certified copy of all this through the mail in a few days. Good luck."

When Harry finally got home at quarter till midnight, he flopped across his bed without even kicking off his shoes. He lay there for a long time thinking of all the things he could have said or done, wondering if he should have hired an attorney. But then, he got out, didn't he? And he hadn't spent the money. Back and forth. Finally, he dozed off, awaking some hours later to slip out of his clothes and into bed. He turned out the lights, but he couldn't fall back asleep.

He felt lonelier than when Willa Mae had left him. Even she wasn't around to talk to—not that he had ever confided in her much. All he could think about was DaShawn. How had he let that little boy get his hooks so deep in only four days?

At work the next day, Harry tried several times to call Leslie Stuart to find out where she'd placed DaShawn. When his cell rang in the afternoon, he answered without even checking the caller ID.

"Hey Harry, my man," said a male voice on the other end of the line. "What's happenin'? We gonna see you tonight?"

"Who's this?" Harry pulled the phone away from his ear to see the ID. People didn't even take the time to identify themselves these days.

"Carl, Carl Hickman," came the tinny voice until Harry put the phone back to his ear. "You know, from the men's Bible study. We was hopin' you'd join us again tonight. Whaddya say?"

Bible study? Oh, yeah. "Uh … don't know 'bout tonight. I'm kinda havin' to field some chaos around here. Don't think I can make it."

"Yeah. I know what that's like. Life can be a bee sometimes, can't it? But hey, if you're up against it, how can we pray for you? We wanna stand with you, man."

"Ah, it's no big deal. Just need some time to work things out."

"This about that grandbaby you said might come live with you?"

"Well, yeah." Harry hesitated to say more. On the other hand, if there was ever a time when he needed some prayer—if prayer could do any good … "Yeah. He was with me for a few days, but now DCFS put him somewhere else. So … guess you could pray that I'd get him back."

"We'll do that, my man. But hey, if it turns out you can break away, you drop on by now, ya hear? You a part of us, now, that's fo' sure."

"Yeah. I'll try."

Harry closed his phone. Maybe he should go. It'd be better than sitting around his apartment all evening waiting for Leslie Stuart to get back to him. And there wasn't much he could do when she called, no matter what she told him.

He sat at his desk, staring at its marble surface as though he could think his way through it into some other dimension, a dimension where he could figure out life. Those guys in the Bible study seemed to have a fix on life … at least a little. It was sure different than hanging out with his old CPD cohorts, but these guys were all right. He could tell Carl Hickman was street-smart, probably had a monkey on his back at some point, but all of them seemed to think they'd found the secret in the Bible. What was it Carl had said about it? *It's not a bunch of rules or a bag of fortune cookies. It's about God controlling my life.* Harry leaned back from his desk and shook his head. Those guys sometimes talked like they had God's personal cell phone number.

Harry had never been able to envision God in such personal terms. Even AA's Step 3 seemed a little too much like science fiction or hocus-pocus when it talked about turning his life over to a "higher power." He affirmed the step only to work the program—which he knew he needed—but what did it really mean?

What if those guys were right?

What was it he'd said to himself a few days ago, that it felt like someone was choreographing his life? What if that's exactly what was happening? What if all that'd gone down the last few weeks—discovering he had a grandson, thinking he was getting a second chance, even meeting Estelle and getting some help with his mom—what if all that was God arranging things? After all, it was because of Estelle that he'd even tried the Bible study last week. Maybe everything was more connected than he realized. He'd told himself he wasn't so sure he liked someone choreographing his life, but truth be told, nobody was forcing him to do anything. He didn't have to go to that party at Manna House. He didn't have to date Estelle. He didn't have to go to the Bible study. And he didn't have to get involved with his grandson. Those were all his choices. Maybe—

"Mr. Bentley! You okay?"

He looked up to see the Firecracker. "Uh … Mrs. Fairbanks. Sorry, I didn't hear you." He looked beyond her to see her oldest son grab the younger one in a headlock and nearly take him down. He hoped they wouldn't kick over a lamp with their horseplay. "I didn't notice you and the boys come in. What can I do for you?"

"Nothing. Just wanted to say hi." She turned. "P.J., cut that out right now. Sorry, Mr. Bentley. They're out of school already, so I've had 'em down at the shelter all day, and I think they need to get out and let off some steam. We're going up to change and then head down to the beach for a while before I fix supper."

Harry winced. *School!* DaShawn was supposed to be *in* school today. Man. Life was a mess.

Leslie Stuart still hadn't called by the time Harry got home and heated a microwave dinner. He watched the news while he ate but couldn't imagine himself sitting around the rest of the evening waiting for the phone to ring like some teenage girl hoping for a prom date. He'd go to that Bible study and take his cell with him. She knew that number as well as his home phone, and the guys hadn't seemed to mind last time when he'd gotten a call during the meeting. He laughed about that crazy call from his mother about the toilet paper.

Oh no! He still hadn't taken any more over to her. But he knew she wasn't out. He'd get more for her tomorrow.

There was a new guy at the Bible study, at least new to Harry. The other guys seemed to know him, though it was obvious from their exuberance at seeing him that he wasn't too regular in attendance. To Harry, that was good. It took the pressure off him.

Ricardo was short, stocky, and maybe midforties or midfifties. Hard to tell.

"He plays in a band," announced the Jewish guy, when introducing him. "One of those Mexican ones with all sizes of guitars and trumpets, and you know the guy shaking the little rattles. Whaddya call your kinda band, Ricardo?"

"Mariachi."

"Yeah, that's it. *Oy vey*, you oughta hear 'em."

Harry shook hands all around but noticed that most of the other guys hugged each other. It was almost a chest bounce with a slap on the back. But for now, the handshake was good enough for him.

Once they all found seats in Peter Douglass's living room, Carl Hickman leaned forward. "Harry told me he could still use some prayer for his grandbaby." He turned to Harry. "Why don't you tell what's up and how we can pray."

"Well ..." Harry looked around the circle. Last time they had prayed at the end, but ... "DaShawn came to stay with me over the weekend, but DCFS picked him up again last evening, and ... well—" Harry blinked and blinked again. He paused for a moment, then cleared his throat. "Guess I'd like to have him back. I set up a room for him an' everything." Everyone remained silent. What else could he say? "They just came and took him away."

"Ah, that's cold, man," Carl said. "We lost our baby to DCFS for, what was it?" He looked around like everyone there knew the details. "Something like five or six years. DCFS gone and actually lost her. Couldn't even track down where they put her."

"But tell him how you got her back," said Denny Baxter.

"Oh, yeah. With the help of Stu. Yeah, we got her back. Carla's the brightest thing in our house these days."

Wait a minute. Did he say, *With the help of Stu*? That was the housemate's name on Estelle's answering machine: *Hi, this is Estelle and Stu, we're not available to take your call right now, so please leave a message....* Harry frowned. "That wouldn't be Leslie Stuart, the social worker, would it?"

"One and the same. You know her?" Without waiting for Harry to answer, Carl went on. "Don't know if we'd've ever found Carla if it weren't for Stu. Gotta confess, that was back in the day, ya know, when I wasn't much use to the family, truth be told. But

Stu, now she tracked Carla down. So we're grateful, know what I'm sayin'?"

"Yeah, I hear ya." Harry brought up a hand to rub his forehead, breaking eye contact, hoping the conversation would move on.

Peter Douglass picked it up and reported on his business, but Harry didn't pay much attention. This circle was getting tight, maybe too tight. Or was that God again, choreographing his life?

"Harry, you need a Bible again?" Denny Baxter's question brought Harry out of his reverie. "Man, we're gonna have to get you one of your own. Peter, you still got a loaner for him?"

The passage for the evening was from Psalm 119, beginning at verse 129. Peter helped Harry find the place in the Bible where they read:

Your statutes are wonderful;
therefore I obey them.
The unfolding of your words gives light;
it gives understanding to the simple.
I open my mouth and pant,
longing for your commands.
Turn to me and have mercy on me,
as you always do to those who love your name.
Direct my footsteps according to your word;
let no sin rule over me.

There was lots of conversation about the first two verses and how good God's Word was. Harry wondered whether those "words" would give *him* light about what he should do. He didn't like to think of himself as "simple," and yet in this situation with his grandson … well, he had to admit he hadn't done so well the first time around.

Harry was thinking about that until they got down to the last verse and read again, "Direct my footsteps according to your word."

"Hey," said Josh Baxter, "that's just like that Donnie McClurkin song we were singing in choir at SouledOut last Sunday. How's it go?" The young man answered himself in a nice tenor ...

Order my steps in your Word, dear Lord
Lead me, guide me every day ...

Carl tipped his head to the side and began waving his hand like he was leading a choir. "All right, all right, now. Look out, pretty soon we gonna be havin' church up in here. Come on, now, you gettin' it!"

As Josh's tenor faded out, Peter leaned forward, pointing with his index finger. "And then it says, *'I want to walk worthy ... according to your will.'*"

"That's right. That's right!"

Everyone broke out clapping and laughing. Harry joined in. On the one hand, it was good, but he also felt a little uncomfortable for being carried along by the group's enthusiasm. He had to consider those earlier words: *"Order my steps in your Word."* Is that what had been happening to him? Had God somehow been directing his steps, bringing things into his life that invited him to take notice that the world did not turn by chance? Was God really interested in Harry Bentley ... enough to engage him personally? He wished it could be so.

Chapter 15

HARRY GOT HOME SHORTLY BEFORE TEN to find the light on his answering machine blinking. He punched the button.

"Mr. Bentley, this is Leslie Stuart getting back to you about DaShawn. I'm not supposed to tell you where we've placed your grandson—policy, you know; we can talk about that later—but I just wanted to let you know that he's in a good home … temporarily, we hope. Right? I guess that's about it. I'll keep in touch."

A moment of silence followed and Harry felt encouraged that she continued to say she was on his side. He almost hit the Erase button—

"Oh, one more thing: This isn't really my business, and your attorney may already be aware of this from pretrial discovery, but in case you haven't heard, Donita Stevens came up with two witnesses to support her claim that you were trying to kidnap DaShawn … Just thought you ought to know as soon as possible. Hope everything is going okay and you can get this settled quickly."

The answering machine beeped, signaling the end of the message.

Two witnesses? What two witnesses? This was crazy. What was that woman trying to do? She was a prostitute and a junkie, for heaven's sake! Why did she even want the kid?

The charge was obviously bogus, but having been a cop for twenty years, Harry knew such cases could suddenly spin out of control—innocent people ruled guilty, and guilty people set free. For the first time, he began to worry about his actual case. He could end up in some real deep brown stuff, and it wouldn't be chocolate. Maybe he should get a lawyer, after all. No. The first thing he needed to do was find out who those witnesses were and what they'd sworn to ... if they even existed.

He punched in the number for Cindy Kaplan's cell phone. The hour was late, but his former partner owed him an explanation for what went wrong with the raid. Why hadn't she been there?

He waited through five rings before she answered.

"Hey Cindy. It's Harry. How you doin'?"

"I'm on the job."

Silence hung heavy. She was probably on a raid.

"We need to talk, Cindy. Could you come by my work tomorrow morning, say about ten?" By then most of the residents would have left for the day and everything should have quieted down.

"See what I can do."

"By yourself, okay? And Cindy, there's something I want you to check out before—" But the line had gone dead. He was tempted to call her back, but she probably couldn't talk right then, and he didn't want to raise suspicions by pestering her.

The next morning, Harry said, "Good morning." "How you doin'?" "Have a good day," to all the residents like a mom seeing her kids off to school. Things had slowed down when his cell phone finally *Ta-dum*-ed. He checked the caller ID. Oh, ho, Estelle Williams!

"Hello."

"Harry, it's Estelle. You gotta come quick. Something's wrong with your mother, and I don't know what's happened."

"Whaddya mean? Where are you?"

"Outside her apartment. I can hear the TV and something like her callin', maybe for help, but she won't come to the door, and I can't get in. I'm afraid she's fallen. You gotta get over here."

"Okay, uh ... " There was no one to fill in for him, not even anyone in the management office. *Huh.* These rich residents would have to get themselves in and out the door by themselves for once. If his boss, Mr. Martin, couldn't understand, Harry'd go find another job. "I'll be right there, Estelle. You wait, okay?"

Harry wrote, *"Sorry, be back soon"* on a sheet of thick paper, folded it into an A-frame, and put it on his desk—then he ran to his car. Why was it in life that things seemed to come in waves—everything going smoothly for a while and then everything falling apart? It seemed such a truism to Harry, that he drove with extra care—even though he was on his way to a crisis—just to be sure he didn't have a car accident.

When he arrived at his mother's apartment fifteen minutes later, Estelle was standing outside the door, wringing her hands with more anxiety than Harry had ever expected to see from such a together lady.

"I was on my way to my Wednesday client and just dropped by for a minute to see how your mom was doing. But something's wrong Harry. I've got a bad feelin'." Harry fumbled for his keys while she talked. "I heard her cryin' out in there. Remember I told you how falls were one of the most dangerous things for older people? Well—"

Harry pushed open the door. "Mom! Mom! Where you at?"

"In here," came a feeble whimper.

Harry and Estelle burst into the bedroom.

"Oh, my Lord, have mercy," cried Estelle. "Jesus, please let her be all right."

The old woman's shriveled legs were sticking out from under the side of the bed, her fluffy slippers still on her feet. Harry immediately dropped down and grabbed them.

"Don't move her," Estelle said. "She could be injured."

"Mom, you okay?"

"No," came the pitiful cry. "I can't get out."

"But did you fall? Have your hurt yourself?"

"No. Well, I bump my head some."

"How'd you get under there?" asked Estelle.

"I needed toilet paper, but I couldn't reach it. And then … oh, wouldya just get me outta here?" She had recovered some of her spunk.

Harry grabbed her feet again. "I think she's okay."

"No I ain't. I'm stuck! Now get me out."

Harry pulled, and as soon as her head emerged, Estelle rolled her over and helped her sit up, then gave her a gentle hug. "Oh, thank ya Jesus! Thank ya Jesus! I do believe she is okay, after all."

Harry felt the relief as well. At least she wasn't injured.

As soon as Estelle released her, Mother Bentley grabbed her head and turned a ferocious frown on Harry. "Well, I don't think so. You left my hair under there. This lady friend of yours is likely to think I shave my head like you. Why'd you ever do that Harry? You used to have such nice hair."

"Hey, Mama, that's history. Let it go. Here, I'll get your hair." Harry got down on his stomach and squeezed under the bed. How the old woman had managed to do it, he'd never know, but he could see that without something to push against, it would be hard for such a frail person to get back out. He retrieved the wig and came out puffing from the exertion.

He slapped at the wig to brush away a dust bunny. "Here," he said, helping her adjust it. "Why in the world didya crawl under there in the first place, Mama?"

"I tol' ya! Had to get some more toilet paper, 'cause you never brought me any like you said you would."

Harry quit adjusting his mother's hair. She was right. Even when he *had* remembered it, he'd put it off a little longer ... and now this. He shook his head. "Ah, come on now, Mama, you know there ain't no TP under there."

"Oh, yes there is. I put it there."

"Mama ..." Harry kneeled down and looked under the bed again. There was something under there, up near the head of the bed. "Estelle, could you flip the light switch by the door?"

The light went on, and sure enough, there were about six rolls of toilet paper, looking like someone had rolled them under there like bowling balls. He came back up, and while Estelle helped his mom get to her feet and move to her chair in the living room, Harry found the broom and retrieved the toilet paper.

He joined them in the living room and muted the TV. "All right, Mama. I put all that toilet paper in the bathroom. That should last you a good while, and I'll bring some more. But don't you be putting it under the bed no more, ya hear?"

"How'm I gonna keep the cleanin' lady from stealin' them if'n I don't hide 'em?"

"Don't you be worryin' none about that, now. I'll get you some more. I promise."

Estelle brought in a glass of water and gave it to her. "How long were you under there, Mother Bentley?"

"I dunno." Then her face brightened with a smile. "I was under there till you got me out, I reckon."

"I meant, when did you first crawl under there?"

"Oh, let me see … Oprah was startin', an' I wanted to get back to hear 'bout that little girl she was gonna have on."

"Hm." Estelle looked at Harry. "That'd be about ten, just before I got here. So she wasn't under there very long." Estelle got down on the old lady's eye level. "You feelin' okay now, Mother Bentley? You think you can manage?"

"Humph. If Harry would turn the sound back up on my TV, I could manage." She looked up and gave her son a frown.

Harry and Estelle stayed with Mother Bentley awhile longer to make sure she was okay, then left. When they were out in front of the building, Estelle stopped and stood akimbo, hands on her hips. "Harry, you gotta do something." She shook her head. "Your mama shouldn't be livin' alone any longer. She needs daily attention. Why don't you just take her in to live with you?"

"I can't stay home with her all day."

"But at least you could get her set up in the morning and take care of her in the evening. That way you could monitor how she's doing from day to day. I mean, she might not even be eating right. Sometimes that in itself can cause what appears like dementia."

"Yeah, I hear what you're sayin'. But there's no way I can fit her *and* my grandson into my little place."

Estelle sighed. "Oh yeah. Guess that could be a little tight. Maybe you'll just have to get a bigger apartment, Harry." Her puzzled expression brightened. "It'd be cheaper than your mom paying for her own like she is now."

Harry shook his head. "I don't know; I just don't know." He looked off down the street as though there was something interesting about the traffic.

"So, how's it going with your grandson?"

"There's … there's been a complication." He looked back, not knowing what to say next.

"And … ?"

"I don't think I ever told you 'bout how he came to be with me."

"No, I don't think you did."

"Let's see, where to start? A couple weeks ago I got a call at work from this social worker … your housemate, as it so happens, though I didn't know who she was at the time. Fact, I hadn't met you yet." Harry looked at his watch. "You know, Estelle, I really gotta get back to work, but I want to tell you about all this. Do you think we could get together and just talk when we have more time?"

"Hm. That'd probably work. When?"

He would have liked to make it that evening, but he needed to get stuff straightened out about the charges against him, and that might mean some back and forth with Cindy—*Oh no*. He glanced at his watch. She was probably waiting on him right now. "Listen, Estelle, how about if we do dinner again on Friday?"

"Friday? I think Friday would work. Come by about six … and this time, I get to choose where we go."

"Suits me."

"But you're still payin'? Right?"

"Whatever you say, Miss Estelle. See ya then."

Chapter 16

It was 11:15 before Harry got back to Richmond Towers. He grimaced. Cindy might have come and gone already.

Sure enough, when he got to his desk, there was a little frowny face, signed, *Cindy*, on the corner of his sign. He punched her number into his cell.

"Sorry," he said as soon as she answered. Still out of breath, he sucked air. "Where you at now? Could you drop back by?"

"Now? I just left there."

"Great. Then you can't be too far away. This is really important, Cindy. I'm sorry, but I had an emergency with my mother."

"Emergency with your mother, was it, Harry?"

"Yeah, she got herself ... Ah, forget it. Can you just come back for a few minutes? I really need to talk to you."

"Be there in ten. But you owe me, Harry. In fact, your tab is gettin' up toward the limit, know what I mean?"

"See ya."

Harry stood there feeling a little bad. He really did need Cindy's help, but she was right that he'd been asking a lot from her. She'd been the best partner he'd ever had, always selflessly willing to help out the other guy. Harry didn't know why she'd never married. She was attractive enough, but she was also very private about her personal life. All he knew was that she still lived with her parents. He shook his head. Before she knew it, she'd be taking care of them instead of them making a home for her.

WHILE HE WAITED FOR CINDY, Harry stared through the glass to see a cab pull up and Mrs. Worthington climb out and start beckoning to him. Oh no. The amount of groceries that woman wanted him to unload looked like enough to last the rest of the year, and it was only May 31. How could one old lady eat so much?

"So you called me back here to help with those bags?"

Harry turned from the trunk of the cab to see Cindy standing there, the protective vest under her shirt making her look like she had a barrel chest. She brushed back a shock of straight, ash brown hair and crossed her arms.

Harry gestured toward the lobby. "Be with you in a minute. Hey, and thanks for comin'." It felt like he was on probation with everyone these days.

Once he had Mrs. Worthington and all her bags tucked into the elevator, he came back through the glass security door, took off his cap, and sat down in a chair across from where Cindy slouched on a couch.

"Huh, she wanted me to go up there and actually tote those groceries into her kitchen. Probably would have had me putting 'em away, too, if I hadn't said no." He ran his hands over his smooth head, then noticed Cindy was just staring at him. "Sorry. Hey, I hate to lean on you like this, but I really need your help."

His former partner looked at him, her face expressionless, eyes unblinking. Harry knew she was peeved. And she had a right to be since he hadn't been there to meet her earlier, but he had a good excuse. Besides, he wouldn't even be needing her help if ... "So why didn't you do that raid last Thursday?"

"Hey, why are you on *my* case? That was your idea in the first place. You know how things go down sometimes."

"What I know is things got screwed up, really screwed up 'cause Fagan did the raid rather than you."

Her eyes got big. "Did you ask me back here, claimin' *you* needed help just so you could ream me out? What's with you anyway, Harry? I don't have time for this." She stood up, checking to see that her weapon was in place at her side.

"Wait a minute, Cindy. Wait a minute." He reached up and touched her elbow and softened his voice. "Please. Just sit down for a minute." She slowly subsided, and Harry cleared his throat. "Look, I don't know how much you know, but that raid went south. Fagan found the drugs all right, right where I said they'd be, but he didn't make an arrest. Same old, same old. Steal the evidence and beat up the perp. Trouble was, this perp was Donita Stevens, and now she's claimin' I was the one who beat her up, and that I tried to kidnap her son."

"*Kidnap*?"

"Yeah. When I saw Fagan and his crew go in, I knew what was up, so I followed as soon as he left. That's when I found Donita all beat up and called an ambulance. Then she started saying all kinds of foolishness, pinnin' it on me when the uniform cops came. 'Course they didn't believe her. But now she's pressing charges and claims to have two witnesses."

"Who?"

"Got no idea. That's what I need your help for. I need you to see if you can find out from the state's attorney who those witnesses are and whether they're taking this case seriously."

"Why don't you have your own lawyer do it?"

"'Cause I don't have one." How often did he have to explain this? "Why should I spend all that money if this is going to get kicked out as frivolous?"

Cindy frowned. "Not too smart, Harry. You better get representation. You can never tell what will happen when you get in court. Who knows what a judge might do, even if the state's attorney isn't pressing too hard. You know how it is sometimes."

"I know, I know. The judge's hemorrhoids might be bothering him that day or his wife yelled at him. But can you just get me that much information? Then I'll know what I'm up against."

"I'll see what I can do." She stood up. "And Harry, I'm really sorry I couldn't do that raid and come up with a clean collar. Fagan just grabbed it and sent me down to the south side to meet with an informant. What could I say?"

Harry stood with her and put his cap back on. "Yeah, I know. You'd've been there if you could." He walked her to the revolving door.

"So what's with the boy? How are things going with you and your ... grandson, wasn't it?"

Harry laughed and rolled his eyes. "We had a great weekend. Then DCFS heard about these charges and took him away until I can get them dismissed." He held out both hands and shrugged. "That's why I'm in a hurry to get this cleared. Know what I'm sayin'?"

"Really sorry 'bout that, Harry. I'll see what I can do, but all the same, you better get a good lawyer."

"Yeah, I know."

WHEN HARRY GOT HOME FROM WORK Thursday evening, the certified copy of his court date was in the mail and there was a message on his answering machine from Cindy.

"Harry, this is all I could find out. The two witnesses are Joey Jackson and Hector Jiménez. No address for either of them, but Jiménez has a cell phone. Couldn't get much more out of the state's attorney. But they seem to be treatin' this whole thing as routine." There was a pause. *"Good luck, Harry."*

Jiménez, Hector Jiménez. Something about that name rang a bell with Harry. He chewed on it while he went into the kitchen and opened the refrigerator to see what he might eat. Suddenly it hit him. Hector was the name of Donita's pimp. He just hadn't been imagining the guy was Hispanic, and usually pimps kept a low profile when it came to any contact with the law. So why had this guy come forward as a witness?

On the other hand, who knew what Donita had told him? Maybe her story fingered Harry as the one who stole the drugs. In that case, Hector might be more than eager to put the squeeze on Harry.

But who was the other guy, the Joey Jackson dude?

Nothing in the refrigerator interested Harry, but still he stood there staring at its meager contents. Maybe he ought to go back over to the west side and do a little close police work to smoke out this Joey Jackson. Names of the witnesses didn't do him any good without knowing how credible they were.

He slammed the refrigerator door and checked the time—quarter to six. He'd grab a burger on the way.

Harry parked a block away from Donita's building, knowing no good would come of it if she or Hector found him snooping around. On the other hand, as far as he knew, Hector had never seen him and so wouldn't be able to make him even if they passed on the street.

He talked to several people—some coming home from work, kids hanging on the corner, people sitting on their stoop. No one had heard of a Joey Jackson. And the more people he asked, the harder it was to keep his inquiries sufficiently casual to not look like a cop.

In the convenience store—probably the one where DaShawn had gone to buy the wings and Cokes—Harry told the Indian clerk he was trying to find Joey Jackson because they shared a winning lottery ticket.

The clerk's eyes got large. "You were buying this winning ticket here from me?"

"Well, I didn't, but Joey might have. You know him?"

The clerk grabbed up his list to see if his store was up for a bonus for having sold a winning number.

"Look, it's not gonna do you any good if I can't find Joey. Do you know him?"

The clerk continued to study the list. "Yes, I know this person, Joey Jackson. Three times I had him arrested for shoplifting. He tries to steal me blind. How much did he win? It is time now for Gummy to pay back to me."

"Gummy? Did you say Gummy?"

"Yes, yes, Gummy—Joey Jackson. Everybody is calling him Gummy. He steals all the time. He is being worse than the gangs."

"You know where he is?"

"Maybe he is now in jail. How should I know? He is always hanging around stealing from somebody."

"So he lives around here?"

"He is a bum, a homeless bum. You can find him anywhere if you are looking."

The man was so intent on going through the numbers that Harry figured he wouldn't get any more out of him, so he left.

Okay. A homeless bum who goes by the name Gummy.... Wait a minute! Harry went back into the store, causing the bell over the door to jingle.

The clerk's eyes flashed at him. "There is no number here from my store." He slapped the list on the counter. "What are you trying to do? You are trying to steal from me also?"

"No, no." Harry raised both hand for the guy to stop. "Just tell me, is the Gummy you are talking about a toothless old man who has a nervous condition that causes him to sway back and forth when he's standing in one place?"

"Yes, yes. That is the man of whom I am speaking, most definitely. A skinny fellow with no teeth. Mouth all caved in, like this." The clerk made a face by rolling his lips between his teeth and sucking in his cheeks.

"Thanks. That's all I need." It had to be the guy who was loitering in the entryway the first time Harry went to see DaShawn.

Harry walked back to his car. Okay, one of the witnesses against him was a homeless guy whose mental stability could probably be challenged, and the other was a pimp and drug dealer with more than casual connections to Donita. He ought to have it made. No judge would give any weight to that kind of flimsy testimony.

He jumped in his RAV4 and headed home. He was still a pretty good cop, good enough to not need an attorney just to dump a bogus charge.

Chapter 17

HARRY FELT PUMPED ALL DAY FRIDAY. He had a fix on the case Donita was bringing against him—no problem—and he was going out with Estelle that evening. Where would she choose to eat: maybe Jamaican Jerk on Howard, or how about that African Harambee restaurant on Clark? Knowing Estelle, even as little as he did, it would have to be something a little exotic. Maybe she'd want to go to some Indian restaurant on Devon.

He was also feeling eager to tell her about his situation with DaShawn. Estelle was someone who cared, someone who wouldn't put him down for the complications life brought.

Things had slowed down so much in the afternoon that Harry began to doze off at his desk. He had perfected a way to sit there, left elbow on his desk with his chin in his hand so that his head tipped forward just enough so people couldn't see his eyes. Then he would hold his pen in his right hand, poised as though he were filling out some form. The ding from the arriving elevator or the swish from the revolving doors were enough to warn him of an approaching resident in time to greet them with an alert smile.

Harry knew it was a technique familiar to all high school students, and that bugged him. He'd taken a job that required nothing more of him than the ability to shine people on. If he let himself think about it, he could get all stirred up. Too many black people had done that for far too long. Smile nice, be ready to step and fetch it, and talk right. He was more than that. He'd been a professional law enforcement officer, part of an elite unit, but now he'd settled for this. "Retirement" had been a real comedown to the low-key role of a doorman for spoiled rich people. And it was beginning to lose its appeal.

He needed to look for a new job, one that used his skills better—but one flexible enough to allow him to care for DaShawn … and perhaps his mother.

Harry came awake with a start to the whooping and wailing of sirens and horns as though terrorists had attacked his building. He jumped up. It sounded like it was right here in the building somewhere.

The door from the parking garage exploded open and one of his residents came bursting in—Norman Gardner, seventeenth floor. Red faced and pulsing with a blood pressure of at least 260, the man yelled, "Call the police. Call the police right now!"

Then Harry saw he had a couple of kids in tow, one in each hand, gripping them by the collar and dragging them like they were a pair of writhing, terrified rabbits. And bulldog Norman Gardner was the one to put the fear of God in them too. Nearly as wide as he was tall, he had left Vietnam in geography only and still considered himself the toughest supply sergeant alive.

Uh-oh. Harry realized Gardner held the Fairbanks boys in his iron grip.

"Call the police right now!" Gardner stood there puffing, drilling Harry with his beady eyes. "If you don't, I will!"

"Let me go, you jerk! I'll tell my dad," squealed one if the struggling "rabbits."

Harry held up both hands and approached the fray. "Now, no need to call the police. I know the parents. Just let me—"

The little one started to bawl and squirmed, looking past Harry. "Mom! Make him let us go!"

Harry turned to see Mrs. Fairbanks emerging from the revolving doors, her fiery hair wild and her face flushed as if in shock. "Mr. Bentley! What's going on?"

Harry turned back to Gardner for an explanation. The man dropped the boys and began shaking his finger toward Mrs. Fairbanks. "These your kids? You live here? What kind of parent are you, letting them run loose around the building raising Cain?!"

"What—what did they do?… Mr. Bentley?"

But the bulldog wasn't finished. "Snuck into the parking garage and ran around rocking cars, setting off a dozen car alarms." He stabbed his finger at the Fairbanks woman. "You better believe management is going to hear about this!" He spun on his heel, took two paces toward the garage door, and looked back at Harry. "If you can't keep hooligans like these brats from running amuck in our building, mister, I'll have your job!"

Once the door thumped closed, Harry took a deep breath. Kids—did they always have to be getting into trouble?

"I'm sorry, Mr. Bentley. I don't know what got into these two." The woman reached out both arms and drew the kids to her like a mother hen gathering her brood. She looked over their heads at Harry. "But you can be assured that we'll deal with it, and it won't happen again." She then pivoted with one boy on each side and guided them through the security door to the elevators.

Harry returned to his desk, sat down, and put his head in his hands. His heart was pounding as though he'd just made a drug bust, and all it had been was an irate old man and a couple of crazy kids. He chuckled to himself. The "old man" was probably his age, and no wonder that Fairbanks woman's hair stuck out like it did. His would, too, if he had any, and had to manage those kids.

He rubbed his jaw thoughtfully. Maybe he ought to rethink the whole DaShawn thing.

AT FIVE TO SIX THAT EVENING, Harry rang the bell for Estelle's second-floor apartment in the brick two-flat.

The intercom squawked. "Hello, is this Harry?"

Harry grinned. It was Leslie Stuart's voice, but she had never called him Harry before. Must mean Estelle referred to him as Harry often enough to cause the social worker to slip momentarily out of her professional mode.

"Yes. I'm here for Miss Williams."

"Estelle isn't ready quite yet ... You want to come up and wait?"

Harry detected a hint of reservation in her voice. It was a pleasant evening, and he was not inclined to mix his social life with ... with what? His personal life? How could they be separate? And yet he wanted to keep them that way.

He cleared his throat. "That's okay. It's beautiful out here. I'll just wait on the porch." Besides, he needed to keep an eye on his car, which he'd parked in front of a fire hydrant. He leaned on the porch railing, watching some girls across the street jumping rope.

Strawberry shortcake, cherry on top.
How many boyfriends do you got?
One, two, three, four, five ...

Did they include those guys on the corner lagging pennies and walking so bowlegged their knees were wider than their hips—a contortion to keep their pants from falling completely off? Harry hoped not. A few cars came slowly down the narrow street, the drivers seemingly searching for parking spaces. Finally he sat down on the steps—elbows on knees, chin in his palms—and waited.

The door squeaked open, and Harry stood and turned to greet Estelle with a smile. But instead of it being her, or her door, the other door had opened, and it was the guy from the men's Bible study, Denny somebody.

Denny Baxter extended his hand. "Hey, man, how you doin'?"

"Oh, I'm kickin. I'm kickin'. How 'bout you?"

"Can't complain. You here for …?" He gestured with his head toward Estelle's door.

Harry glanced that way as well. "Yeah. Oh, yeah. We been trying to work out some things for my elderly mother, and Miss Williams being someone who works with folks like her, well …"

"Yeah. Hey, that's great."

Harry shrugged. Did Baxter accept his explanation, or had someone been spreading his business around the hood? He stood there feeling awkward for a moment. "So, this where you live?"

"Yeah," said Denny, rubbing the back of his neck. "Yeah, and Stu and Estelle rent the second floor. It's been a good arrangement. But, hey, man," he extended his hand again, "good to see you. I got a game at my school tonight. See ya Tuesday, huh?"

"Yeah, if I can."

Harry watched as Denny went down the steps and got in a van.

"Well *there* you are," came Estelle's velvet voice from behind Harry.

He turned. "Yep. Here I am." He stretched a kink out of his back. "Whoo-ee, you sure do got it goin' on tonight, babe!"

She gave him such a withering frown that Harry knew he better dial it down, but she certainly hadn't been wasting his time by taking a few more minutes to get ready. Wow! Hair done up on top, skin aglow, and some kind of a long lavender gown with black-and-gold trim. Harry wasn't sure he could afford to take her to a restaurant worthy of such magnificence. And who was he to be her escort in his simple slacks and sport shirt?

Harry opened the car door for her. "So, where to?"

"How about Siam Pasta? I feel like some Thai food tonight. You know that little place on Western?"

"Well yeah, but ..." Perhaps she'd read his mind and was taking pity on his wallet. "Hey, have you been to the one up in Evanston?"

"Humph. We went to Evanston last time. You said I could choose, and I want to go to Siam Pasta."

"It's Siam Pasta too. Same food, same people, but they got this fantastic second-floor deck, and tonight would be ideal for outdoor dining. You gotta try it. You sit up there almost in the trees with the breeze blowing. Whaddaya say?"

"All right, since you're payin'. Right?"

"You got it."

To Harry's relief, they were shown to the front corner table on the deck of the restaurant, just as he'd hoped. Trees along the parkway of the two-lane street were tall enough to reach up over the deck, making them feel like they were in a tree house.

They exchanged small talk until their appetizers of lime chicken and crab lagoon arrived. Harry took a few bites, then wiped his mouth and took a deep breath.

"Okay. You asked what was going on with my grandson, so here it is: DCFS took him away because his mother filed charges against me. It's—"

"What?"

"It's not as bad as it sounds. But it is complicated, and some of the things I'm gonna tell you have to be kept in complete confidence." He waited for her nod, then proceeded to explain why he'd retired from the force and—once he realized the kind of life Donita would subject DaShawn to—why he'd decided he had to get his grandson out of her house and out of her neighborhood.

"I wasn't all that interested in taking the boy to begin with, but somehow my heart went out to him once his mother laid claim. Given her background, I realized all that needed to happen to put her out of the picture was for her to be busted for drugs. Being on parole, a violation would be automatic, and then I could have DaShawn." Ugh, it sounded so crass to say it like her misfortune was his gain, but what could he do? He had to rescue the boy.

Their food arrived, ample plates of beef and spicy basil leaves and cashew chicken that they shared family style. But Harry hardly noticed what he was eating as he talked, telling Estelle about his scouting trip when he'd found Donita's drug stash and how he set up his old partner to bust her … and how it all got messed up and now she was accusing him of beating her up and trying to kidnap DaShawn.

Estelle looked astonished. "She can't do that, can she? I mean nobody—at least not a judge—would even listen to her, would they?"

"Huh. That's what I thought, but she came up with two witnesses: her pimp, who wasn't there, and an unstable homeless man who saw me when I first visited DaShawn. She's probably paying him to testify. Wouldn't take much."

"So, when do you go to court?"

"Tuesday, next Tuesday."

"You worried?"

"Nah. It'll all get thrown out." He said it with more bravado than he felt. Somehow his confidence was eroding a little. Maybe he ought to get an attorney like Cindy said.

Harry pushed his plate away and slid his chair back from the table a few inches. "You want some coconut ice cream? Or I think they even got green tea ice cream, whatever that is."

"How 'bout a coffee?"

The coffee was good, hot and soothing going down. Harry eyed Estelle over his cup. "Thanks for listening. So you see how everything is so up in the air right now, the idea of taking in my mom feels out of the question."

"Hm." Estelle nodded her head slowly. "But you gotta do something, Harry. She can't live alone much longer."

"Well, how 'bout you? I mean, could you take her on … as one of your clients? That would help, wouldn't it? If you dropped by every day and made sure everything was going okay, that could be a stopgap until I find a better solution. I'd be glad to pay you your regular rate."

"I don't know, Harry. I'm pretty full up as it is. With volunteering at Manna House and church, I just don't know."

"Well, church. You could take her to church. She would love that. She's always begging me to take her."

"And why don't you?"

"Ah." Harry waved his hand. "Her old church is way down on the south side. And the one she tried to go to up here … it just didn't work out."

Estelle sat there a long moment looking steadily at Harry. "I'll tell you what. I'll go over and help her get ready on Sunday mornings, if you come by and give us both a ride … and come with us."

"Come with you? Where?"

"To my church, of course, SouledOut Community … Don't give me that look, Harry. All those guys you met at the men's Bible study go there. You won't feel alone."

"They do?" He watched her give a single nod. Then he took a deep breath, like he was about to jump into icy Lake Michigan. "Okay, I'll give it a try. But what about during the week?"

Estelle turned her gaze on the pedestrians below along Dempster Street—commuters hurrying home from a late night in a loop office, a young couple walking arm-in-arm and giggling like someone was tickling their toes, a homeless guy trying to sell his last two copies of *Streetwise*.

"I just don't know how I could do it, Harry. They're needin' me more and more at the shelter, and I—"

"Why don't you just tell them you can't do it? You got a new client."

"I can't, Harry. I owe Manna House so much. It wouldn't be right."

Harry recalled the last time she'd said something about "owing" Manna House. It'd been at the Fun Night when they first met—had something to do with her actually living there awhile, but then she'd clammed up.

"So why do you feel so indebted to Manna House?"

She kept her gaze on the traffic on the street below.

"Come on, now Estelle. This is tell-all night. I told you about all the crap in my life—well not all of it, but more than I've told anyone else for a long time. So now it's your turn. What's going on?"

Chapter 18

ESTELLE TOYED WITH HER COFFEE CUP that was obviously getting cold by this time. Her eyebrows were arched as she gazed down into its depths.

"Hey," said Harry, "how 'bout we take a walk down to the lake? You can tell me all about Manna House on the way. Couldn't be a nicer evening." The sun had set, and a long twilight had set in.

"You think it's safe?"

"It's not that late. Besides, I'm a cop, remember?"

"Yeah. You don't have a gun, do you?"

"Well, not on me."

"Whaddaya mean, not on you? You keep one at home?"

Harry shrugged and looked away.

"I thought handguns were illegal in Chicago."

"Hey, don't worry 'bout it. You goin' to the lake with me or not?" When she hesitated, opening her big eyes even wider and turning her head to the side in a little girl pout, he added, "Ah, come on. It'll be okay."

Once they'd crossed under the RTA and El tracks and were beyond the bright lights of Chicago Avenue, Estelle took a deep breath. "Hm. Where to begin? Well, I've got a son too. He's grown, but he was living at home. We had a nice brownstone down on 35th. Bu-u-ut"—she dragged out the word—"he's got some problems, emotional problems. I don't think he'd hurt anyone else, but he began to get belligerent with me. Started pushing me around. Lots of yelling. My friends all said I ought to have him committed, but I couldn't see doing that. I mean, he's my baby, you know." She fell silent, as if lost in thought.

Harry clenched his jaw. She had a *grown* son who was pushing her around? *Huh.* He'd like to get his hands on that jerk. But he kept his mouth shut. He wanted her to keep talking.

"Anyway, one day I tripped, and—Whoops!" She'd no sooner said the word, *tripped,* than she stumbled over a broken corner in the sidewalk. Harry grabbed her arm to steady her.

"Whoa!" Estelle looked back. "Good thing I wasn't wearing heels!"

"Uh, yeah. You'd think the suburbs would keep up their sidewalks better'n that."

He kept hold of her hand … just in case, of course.

She gave him a head-back frown, but didn't withdraw her hand as they crossed the last street, lined on the west with classic mansions, and entered Lake Front Park. The sliver of a new moon dodging between the branches of the elm trees cast eerie shadows across the grass and caused the small waves in Lake Michigan to shimmer like silver silk.

"You want to go sit on the rocks?"

"Sure."

They crossed the park in silence as Harry thought about the nightmare of living with someone who might hurt you. When they got to the rocks, he helped her up onto one of the huge chunks of limestone that protected the park from the lake's crashing storms. Harry had not even clicked on how her long gown might make such a feat impossible, but it was loose and flowing enough that she seemed to manage with ease. Once she was settled, he reached up to get a hand from her. She gave him a good tug as he grunted to make it up onto the waist-high stone he had chosen next to hers. Not a graceful vault, but then he was fifty-eight, and he was still holding her hand as he sat down.

In silence they watched the far, dark horizon where the green and white lights of some small boat crept slowly south. There was no sound of a motor, so perhaps it was a sailboat or maybe just too far out to hear.

"You were saying you tripped one day ..."

"Yeah." She sighed. "I hit my head pretty hard—had to go to the ER and get some stitches. And you know they always ask you whether anyone in your household is bothering you or threatening you or whether you feel afraid? Well, I didn't tell them that Michael had pushed me again, but I knew I had to do something or one of these times I'd get really hurt and he'd get put away. And I didn't want that. So ..." She turned toward him with a *there-you-have-it* expression on her face. "I just left."

"What?! You just left? What'd you do then?"

"That's when I came to Manna House. A friend told me about it, said they wouldn't turn me out just because I owned a house somewhere. They put down I was a victim of domestic violence and took me in. Guess that's why I feel like I owe them."

"Hm." Harry nodded, but it galled him to think of Estelle homeless while her grown son sat up in her house like he owned it. "So, what happened to your house?"

"Still there. Least I have to pay taxes on it every year."

"You're kidding. Does your son still live there?"

"Far as I know."

"You mean you've never gone back to see him?"

"Nope!" Her tone said she didn't want to be challenged. But after a moment she softened. "It's one of those loose ends in life, know what I mean, Harry? We don't like it that way, but for one reason or another, we can't quite figure out how to tuck it in."

Harry turned and studied the bright lights of Chicago to the south. "Yeah, I got a few of those myself."

She pulled her hand free from his and buried her face in her hands for a few moments. Harry had the good sense not to say anything, but simply laid his arm across her shoulder. Finally she raised up and shook her head like she was trying to shake free from something. She stopped and dabbed at the corners of her eyes with the tips of her fingers. "I sometimes worry, you know. I don't think he'd hurt anybody else, but when I hear stuff on the news about someone goin' off on complete strangers, my heart stops until I'm sure it wasn't him. I don't know. I just don't know what I oughta do."

"I hear ya." He couldn't really assure her that would never happen. He'd been on too many calls where someone who couldn't control himself ended up hurting the people he loved and others as well.

She took a deep breath and patted her hair a few times with her hands. "Well, there. We got our laundry out, Mr. Harry Bentley. Ya still speakin' to me?"

"Sure enough am." He gave a gentle tug, and she allowed herself to lean on him a moment.

Harry had a sudden urge to invite her home to his apartment, hold her tight, and just see what might develop ... but he knew that wouldn't work—not with Estelle. In fact, such a move might be the end of a good thing, a very good thing. He should be happy for what a fine evening they'd had so far and build on that.

"S'pose we better be gettin' back. Though I think I could stay out here all night, it's so nice."

"Nice weather, maybe." She let him help her up, wobbling a little on the uneven surface. "But my butt couldn't take it much longer. Those rocks are hard!"

They both laughed, climbed down onto the grass, and meandered back through the trees, Estelle seemingly content to hold his hand all the way back to his car that they'd left near the restaurant.

THERE WAS A NEW MESSAGE on his answering machine when he got home. *"Grandpa! They cut my hair all off.* Sniff, sniff. *Now I'm bald as you ... No, please."* His tone changed. *"I'm just talkin' to my—"* Buzzz.

And that was the end of the message.

Harry played it again. *"Grandpa! They cut my hair all off.* Sniff, sniff. *Now I'm bald as you ... No, please. I'm just talkin' to my —"* Buzzz.

Harry threw his keys across the room and swore. Who'd those people think they were? Where had that Leslie Stuart put his grandson, anyway? Stupid woman! He punched in the phone number. They still had to be up, didn't they? He'd dropped off Estelle only a few minutes ago.

It rang five times. *Oh, God, don't let anything bad have happened to my boy.* The moment someone picked up the phone, Harry barked, "Where'd you send my grandson? You know what they done to him?"

"Uh, Harry, this is Estelle. I think you want Stu, but she's gone to bed ... Huh?" There was some background noise. "Hold on a minute, Harry."

"Hello, Mr. Bentley. What seems to be the problem?" Leslie Stuart came on the line, sounding as groggy as Rip Van Winkle.

"It's DaShawn. Where'd you put him, anyway?"

"I told you I can't give you that address, but—"

"You know what they've done to him? They've mutilated and humiliated him."

"What are you talking about, Mr. Bentley?"

He could tell from her voice that she was wide awake now, so he charged on. "I'm talking about them shaving off all his hair. I just got a phone message where my boy was nearly crying, sayin' that now he's as bald as me."

There was a stifled chuckle on the other end of the line. "Well, if that's true, I'm very sorry, Mr. Bentley. But really, now, you don't think bald is all that bad, do you? Estelle seems to think you're kinda—"

"Don't you be makin' light of this, Ms. Stuart, and I don't give a … You just keep Estelle out of it, okay? This is between you and me. You sent him off to some savages who have no respect for his dignity. There's no excuse for what they done."

"Mr. Bentley, it's almost eleven, and I don't think we can solve this tonight. If what you say is true, I'm truly sorry. I'll check into it first thing tomorrow morning, even though tomorrow is Saturday. Okay? Now I think we all need a little sleep, don't you?"

Harry took several slow, steady breaths. It was true. Nothing could be done about it tonight. But now he knew what it meant when people talked about grinding their teeth.

"Mr. Bentley, you still there?"

"Yeah. So you'll get back to me first thing. Right?"

"I'll do that. You can count on it."

HARRY WAS AWAKE HALF THE NIGHT imagining what had happened to DaShawn. Did they have to hold him down? Was it really shaved? What if they nicked him? If they drew blood, he'd sue 'em, no question! He'd make 'em pay!

Oh God, dear God, please protect that little boy.

Chapter 19

SATURDAY MORNING, HARRY AWOKE EARLY and started coffee. Then he shaved, including his head, showered, dressed, drank some coffee, made the bed—when was Leslie Stuart going to call?—made himself some eggs and toast for a bigger breakfast than usual, washed the dishes and cleaned up the kitchen, poured out the old and put on another pot of coffee. He needed to go grocery shopping, but what if she called while he was gone? He hadn't specified cell or home phone. He hoped she wouldn't try to call Richmond Towers again. Balor Draven probably wouldn't even take a message for him.

He gathered up the week's newspapers and put them out in the recycling bin. It was 8:30 and Leslie Stuart still hadn't called. He drank more coffee and told himself he ought to get a new landline phone that would record caller ID. If he had that feature, he'd be able to call DaShawn back now.

He paced into DaShawn's room—he realized he'd taken to calling it that rather than "the den"—and straightened the bedspread. He peeked under the bed. Maybe the room needed dusting. "Dear God, let that boy be okay," he muttered.

On his way to get the Swiffer, the doorbell rang. He went to the intercom that maintenance had taken two weeks to repair. "Yeah, who is it?"

"Leslie Stuart. Can I come up?"

Well, he wasn't expecting that. He pressed the buzzer. Had she come in person because the situation with DaShawn was worse than he'd even imagined? He held open his door until she had climbed the stairs.

"So what's the deal? Is he okay?" He ushered her in and gestured for her to take a seat on the couch. "Want some coffee?" He was thinking that maybe he had been a little over the top the night before and wanted to show he had it all under control now.

"Coffee would be great." She sat down, positioning a small briefcase by her feet.

"Cream? Sugar?"

"Just a little milk, if you've got it."

Harry hurried with the delivery and sat down across from her with his own mug, freshened and black. He gestured with his free hand to indicate that the ball was in her court.

She took a sip of coffee and looked up at him. "I got a hold of the family where DaShawn is staying this morning. I'm convinced he's all right, but I will make a home visit later today. In the meantime, I asked them what was going on with the hair. They said that the Schaumburg school district where they'd enrolled him—"

"You sent him way out to Schaumburg? What'd you do that for?"

She held up both hands. Harry let out his breath and turned his head to the side, telling himself again to remain calm.

"I sent him out to Schaumburg, Mr. Bentley, because it was the best family I could come up with on such short notice. You know, not every foster family will take this kind of assignment."

"What you're saying is, not every rich white family out in the suburbs is willing to take a little black kid from the city. Right?"

"That's not it. I meant, not everyone is open to such *short-term* assignments. Foster care is challenging enough when you can't be guaranteed long-term relationships with children. And we're still hoping DaShawn will be back with you real soon, now aren't we?"

Harry nodded and leaned forward in his chair.

"Okay then. This was the best family I could find. But as it turned out, the school district has a policy against no distracting hairstyles or clothes. They don't allow kids to dye their hair pink or green or allow big ol' spikey Mohawks, or anything like that. So ..." She shrugged. "When they saw DaShawn's hair, they said it had to go."

Harry stared at her, waiting for more. Then he shook his head. "So you're tellin' me the Department of Children and Family Services condones forcibly shaving a kid's head without any regard for what it might do to his self-image? I mean, how much longer is the school year? One week? Couldn't they even allow an exception for a kid who probably won't be there next year?"

"I doubt that they ever got to the stage of talking about next year, Mr. Bentley. I guess I should also mention that someone from the school was worried about security."

"Security?"

"Yeah." The social worker let slip a dry smile. "Apparently back in the seventies there were a couple instances when kids tried to conceal a knife or a hair pick or something in their hair, supposedly to use as weapons."

Harry threw up his hands. "That's ridiculous! My grandson's only nine years old. So get this: I don't want my grandson stuck in with some honkies out in the 'burbs that don't know 'nough about black pride to stick up for a kid who be ..." Harry paused. He was talking too "homey." "... for a child who was just being black!"

Leslie Stuart reached down and picked up her briefcase, laid it across her knees, then looked up at Harry again. "I'm very sorry about this, Mr. Bentley, but I think DaShawn will survive. He's a good kid and tougher than he might appear. I think the best thing for us to do at this point is to concentrate on getting him back here with you. Agreed?"

"Yeah, an' I'm workin' on that too. I got a hearing Tuesday. Everything should be cleared up then."

"Good." She stood and headed toward the door.

Harry moved to open it for her. "Oh, one more thing," he said. "Can you give me his phone number so I can call him back and talk to him?"

She shook her head. "I'm sorry, we're not supposed to—"

"Come on. He phoned me yesterday, and if I'd been here, I'd have gotten the number then ... or even if I had caller ID, I'd have it now and could call him back anytime I want."

He could see her holding her breath, and then she let it out like a deflating balloon. "All right. I guess it couldn't hurt too much." She opened her briefcase, flipped through a folder, and wrote the number on a slip of paper. "Here. But do me a favor and don't mention where you got this number, okay?"

"You got it ... and thanks. I appreciate this."

As soon as Leslie Stuart left, Harry dialed the number. While the phone rang several times, Harry caught himself saying just under his breath, "Oh, God, please let that boy be okay." Was he actually starting to pray?

A woman answered with a bouncy voice. When Harry asked for DaShawn, she said, "They're over at the park right now, but I'll have him call you as soon as he comes in."

"Is he okay? My grandson, I mean?"

"Well, yeah. As far as I know."

"Then you make sure he calls!"

By noon, eternity seemed half over, and Harry couldn't wait anymore. He dialed and again asked for DaShawn.

"Oh yeah. They just came in. I'll get him for you."

Harry waited, listening to background noise that sounded like the Cleaver family.

"Yeah?"

"Hey, DaShawn. This is your grandpa. How you doin'?"

"Oh, hi Grandpa. You shoulda been here this mornin'. Guess what we did?"

"Not a clue. You tell me." The boy didn't sound so bad, after all.

"We went over to this park where they got these really cool basketball courts, like four of 'em in a row, all run together so it's smooth. Anyway, there were these guys there with model cars. And they're big, man, half the size of a skateboard, and they got like gasoline engines on 'em. I seen electric ones a'fore, and they fast. But these were totally phat, man. Know what I'm sayin'? I mean, they were smokin', for real, Grandpa. Smoke was comin' off their wheels. And the guys set up this race course all around the courts with traffic cones and were drivin' 'em by remote control. You think I can get one someday, Grandpa?"

Harry laughed. "Ah, well. We'll have to see 'bout that." Whatever had happened to the boy's hair yesterday, he sounded okay today. "So how's it goin'? You like where you're stayin'?"

There was a long silence. "It's okay. But you still got my room?"

"Oh yeah. I still got your room here. Even cleaned the floor this mornin'. That way you won't have to do it when you get home. Right?"

"Yeah.... Oops. Gotta go, Grandpa. See you later."

Harry put down the phone and stood there. Perhaps he'd gotten all worked up over nothing. On the other hand, they really shouldn't have cut the boy's hair. What'd it look like, anyway? But it sounded like things were okay, now. He thought back over the sequence of events and pushed the button again on the answering machine: "*Grandpa! They cut my hair all off.* Sniff, sniff. *Now I'm bald as you.... No, please. I'm just talkin' to my—* Buzzz."

Harry had assumed the sniffling was because DaShawn was crying, but maybe he wasn't. Maybe he was just excited. Of course, someone had made him hang up, and Harry didn't like that when the boy was just trying to call his grandfather ... but he knew kids. He'd put down the receiver on Rodney more than once. And Rodney had been pretty angry about it too.

There was one other thing. Harry had prayed about the matter a few times, asking God to protect the boy. Could it have been God who'd turned it all around so that by this morning DaShawn was not only safe but no longer upset? Harry chuckled to himself. Why would God pay any attention to his prayers? He hadn't paid God much attention. But maybe it was time to start. He'd promised to take Estelle and his mother to church Sunday. He'd do that. Maybe he and God could get a little thing going after all. He'd start going to church and keep on with that Bible study, and maybe God would respond in kind, like doing him a few favors.

Wasn't that how religion worked—you do something to appease the gods and they do stuff to help you out? That seemed to be what the TV preachers his mother always watched said: *Send in your seed of one hundred dollars or more and you will receive your hundredfold harvest, pressed down and overflowing!* Argh! They made him so angry, because his mother continued to waste her money on them and had yet to get anything back that he could see.

But here he was, ready to give the same idea a try. Why? He thought for a few moments. Because things had been happening in his life that seemed beyond his reach, and it was time to figure out whether it was coincidence or fate or … or God.

Chapter 20

When Harry arrived at his mother's apartment Sunday morning, Estelle was already there and—as promised—had his mother ready to go. Estelle also looked just as striking as ever. But upon seeing Harry, her eyes got big. "Mm, Harry, don't you look fine in that nice blue suit."

Harry saw her look more closely at the black embroidery on the cuffs and the black piping over the shoulders. He grimaced. "It's actually my work uniform." He hesitated to tell the whole story.

She steaded his mother's arm as they all went out to the car. "You know, Harry, you didn't have to wear your uniform if you don't have a suit. A lot of people dress pretty casual at SouledOut, so you'd have been fine in slacks and one of those nice shirts you always wear."

Harry opened the car door. It was either now or later. No getting out of it. "Actually, Estelle, I probably should've phoned you last night, but I didn't want to make another late call that might wake up Ms. Stuart, so—"

"Oh"—she waved her hand—"you needn't worry 'bout her."

He looked down at the curb a moment, feeling like a kid making a confession for getting home late for dinner. "It's just that I won't be comin' in to church with you and Mama this morning. I can drop you off, but then I gotta go in to work. The weekend guy called in sick last night, so I've got to fill in for him." He looked up at Estelle's blank face. "I'm real sorry."

He closed the door and went around to the driver's side, blowing a silent whistle on the way. He was in for it now. He climbed in and picked up his explanation. "There're only three of us to share the shifts. I've tried to get management to add another doorman as a floater to fill in for times like this, but they just say that's what they pay me a little more for—that and scheduling the other two guys. So there's nothing I can do." He glanced over at Estelle as he pulled out into the street.

"I understand, Harry." She crossed her arms and stared straight ahead. "We'll just do church together next week."

Woo! Harry didn't know whether to be grateful for her understanding or bristle at the edict about next week. Of course, he had every intention of going next week, but ... He glanced over at her again, her sitting there as immovable as a Buddha. He grinned. He liked a strong woman. That hadn't been the problem with his first marriage. Willa Mae had not been a strong personality. In fact, she'd held it all in—except for the pitiful sobbing in the middle of the night that Harry pretended not to hear—until she'd had it. And then she left. Once she was gone, Harry didn't even try to get her back. On the one hand, he knew the real fault lay with himself—the all-consuming job, his drinking, his anger at her and Rodney, and the way he just vegged out in front of the TV when he was home—but he'd also gotten sick and tired of her "poor me" routine.

He couldn't imagine Estelle ever playing that role. In fact, he could tell she never played games at all. He could deal with that, even if there were a few sparks sometimes.

"And Harry, you don't need to worry 'bout gettin' us home. It'll be easy to find a ride with someone else."

Harry got to work just in time to see Mrs. Fairbanks and her two boys loading suitcases into a minivan out in front of Richmond Towers. And there was her husband helping them. He even gave her a peck on the cheek. Oh my, such chivalry. Will wonders never cease? He'd always seemed like such a selfish cad.

"So where are they off to?" Harry asked as Mr. Fairbanks gave the departing van a wave and came inside.

Fairbanks looked Harry up and down as though he couldn't believe the doorman had spoken without being spoken to. "North Dakota. To see her mother." Then he headed through the security door and straight to the elevator.

Well, certainly no small talk there. Harry turned to look over the desk. Balor Draven had dragged one of the overstuffed chairs behind the counter and was sitting in it, slouched down with his head lolling back, mouth half open like he had just downed a keg of beer.

"What took you so long?" Draven said as he pulled himself into more of an upright sitting position. "I told you I was sick."

"And I'm sure it was none of your own doing." Harry grimaced and rolled his eyes. "Go on home. Get some sleep, but you be back for your shift tonight. You hear?"

"Ah, man. Don't know if I can." He got up, put his cap in the desk drawer, and grabbed his jacket. "Not the way I feel right now."

Harry had to admit that Draven's normally pallid face looked unusually green, but maybe this wasn't such a bad thing after all. "All right, Draven. Tell you what, I'll work a double shift for you today and this evening, but you gotta do the same for me Tuesday—my day shift followed by your regular evening shift. And no sittin' around here like you're half dead, either. You be up for it. Understand? 'Cause right now your job's on the line."

Draven raised a finger as he walked toward the door. "You got it, boss."

Once he was gone, Harry got a rag and a spray bottle of Lysol disinfectant and wiped down the desk and any other surfaces Draven might have contaminated, though from the looks of him, the slug probably hadn't covered much territory. Whether it was a bug or overindulgence, Harry didn't want to take a chance on catching whatever ailed Draven.

The next day Harry told Tony Gomez about the plan for Tuesday so Tony would know what to expect.

Tony shook his head. "I just hope he shows."

So did Harry.

ON TUESDAY MORNING, HARRY PULLED into the parking lot beside the Belmont Avenue courthouse fifteen minutes early. He found Judge Samuel Hollingsworth's nearly empty courtroom, checked in with the clerk, and "surrendered" to one of the deputies who ushered him into a side room. Harry noticed the bailiff locked the steel door when he went out. For the first time, Harry felt the chill of incarceration.

Whether the judge was late or other cases were scheduled before Harry's, it was nearly eleven when his case was finally called. The deputy escorted Harry to the defendant's table while the judge conferred with his clerk. Judge Samuel Hollingsworth was a tall, thin man with silver hair, wire-rimmed glasses, and a tan that looked like he spent more time on the golf course than in the courthouse. Harry watched him for a few minutes hoping to get the measure of the man, but he saw no clues.

There were a dozen or so people scattered in the spectator benches—family members of defendants huddled in small groups, a couple of cops, and immediately behind Harry a probable attorney who looked more like an absent-minded professor with electrified hair and the left side of his shirt halfway out of his pants. The man was digging through a bulging, scuffed briefcase, but there was an additional box of files on the bench beside him.

The prosecutor's table next to Harry's was stacked with several piles of folders, but no one sat at it. Where was the state's attorney? Harry heard the door in the back of the courtroom open. He turned to see a middle-aged woman in a gray suit backing in. Beyond her stood a stocky, redheaded man … could it be? Yes, it was Lieutenant Matty Fagan, gesturing with both arms out to his sides as the woman backed farther into the courtroom until she closed the door in his face. Harry chuckled to himself. Yeah, shut that jerk out. His day in court was coming, and Harry would be there to watch. The woman turned and walked briskly forward to the prosecutor's table. Well, how about that? A female assistant state's attorney. Lisa Madigan must have broken the glass ceiling for more women than herself.

Once the deputy reminded everyone that the court was still in session, the clerk announced Harry's case. The procedures that followed were routine, details Harry had observed a hundred times in other people's cases. But now he was there as the defendant.

After the assistant state's attorney outlined the case against him, Harry stood. "Your Honor."

Judge Hollingsworth frowned at Harry and then moved his head to the side to look beyond Harry.

"Uh … Mr. Bernstein." The judged reached out a hand of appeal toward Harry. "Will you be representing this defendant or not? If so, let's get with the program."

"Huh?" came the bewildered response from behind Harry. "Who, him? He's not my client."

The judge leaned back, lifting himself slightly with the arms of the chair to stretch his back. He sighed. "Mr. Bentley, where is your counsel? Don't you have a lawyer?"

"No, Your Honor. The charges against me are so insubstantial that I was certain you would dismiss them as soon as you heard what I have to say. And I am truly sorry this case was ever brought here to waste your time ... and mine."

"This isn't a trial ... yet, Mr. Bentley. That will be the place where evidence is presented and weighed. This is just a preliminary hearing."

"I understand, Your Honor." Harry wiped his hand over his head and realized he had begun to sweat. "However, to determine probable cause, you have to look at two issues: whether a crime was committed and whether I am the likely culprit." Harry paused as he saw the judge raise an eyebrow. He better be careful not to come across as though he was lecturing the judge on his job. Should he back up or proceed with caution? "There's no question that Donita Stevens was severely beaten. I arrived shortly after it happened and summoned help—asked a neighbor to call 911. But there is no evidence whatsoever that I committed this crime or that my grandson, DaShawn *Bentley*"—he emphasized the boy's last name as his own—"was ever in danger of being kidnapped by me or anyone else. After all, I am a retired Chicago police officer with no criminal record, and I was being favored by DCFS to care for the boy when his mother was still in rehab for *drug* addiction." He emphasized that too.

"Objection." The state's attorney stood up again behind her table. "Your Honor, we have two witnesses who will attest that Mr. Bentley not only assaulted Ms. Stevens but threatened to take her son. In fact—"

"Wait a minute." Harry was still standing. "Excuse me, Your Honor, but that is the main reason you will agree there is no probable cause to bring me to trial. One of those guys, Hector Jiménez, is Donita's pimp and drug supplier, and the other is a homeless vagrant who has been picked up in the neighborhood numerous times for shoplifting. He's mentally unstable. Neither one's testimony is worth a dime. My grandson's my witness. He'll tell you I didn't have anything to do with this and never threatened to kidnap him, though he would rather live with me than with his mother, given her sorry situation. You can even ask the social worker."

When Harry stopped speaking, the room remained silent as everyone watched the judge. Harry knew he had not been speaking like an attorney. He was just throwing out everything he could think of to make it clear he was innocent.

Judge Hollingsworth bent forward to study the papers on the bench before him, reading—Harry presumed—the details of the case against him. Finally the judge looked up and took off his glasses, putting one earpiece into his mouth as though he were puffing on a pipe. The he pointed them at Harry. "I appreciate your enthusiasm, Mr. Bentley, in spite of the fact that you thought you could wing this without counsel. However, I believe a crime has been committed, and it is quite possible that you were the perpetrator. Therefore I'm going to sustain the indictment, and we will sort out who's telling the truth at trial. You are to be arraigned ..." He looked at his clerk, who fiddled with her computer and then said something back to him so quietly Harry couldn't hear.

The judge continued. "Your arraignment is set for Wednesday, June 21, down at 26th and California." He shuffled the papers before him. "I'm willing to continue your I-bond if the State has no objections?"

He looked at the assistant state's attorney who shook her head.

"All right, then." He smacked his gavel and looked again to the clerk. "Who's next?"

Harry looked around, dazed. Was that it? He was indicted? The case hadn't been thrown out? Several people in the room were looking at him, but no one offered an answer. He turned and started for the back of the room then felt the hand of the deputy on his elbow. The man directed him to the clerk's desk. She was stamping several sheets of paper that she then handed to him.

How could this have happened? He should have taken Cindy's recommendation to get an attorney. But what could a lawyer have done? What could anyone have done? Like the judge said, this wasn't the trial. This wasn't the time to argue the pros and cons of the evidence. If it wasn't blatantly obvious that he was innocent and that the witnesses were bogus, then a trial was the only way to settle the matter.

But … going to trial for assault and attempted kidnapping?

He was hardly aware of pushing through the oak doors and walking through the marble-floored atrium, past the deputies who got grouchier by the hour as they stood there monitoring the metal detectors, and out to the parking lot.

Should he go talk to Captain Gilson, the head of the Review Board? Maybe he could pull some strings with the state's attorney to get this whole thing dropped. Certainly the state's attorney didn't have any ax to grind against him, did he? After all, for them this was just busywork, and they had far more crucial things to pursue. Why'd they even take on this case?

"Hey, Bentley. How's it goin'?"

Harry turned to see Matty Fagan standing in the doorway with his hand raised and a crooked grin on his face.

Harry waved him off and got into his RAV4.

Fagan! The irony of the real culprit being around while Harry got blamed was too much. If he didn't get out of there, he'd end up busting the guy's chops. Too much was at stake to take a chance of revealing what he knew. He revved the engine and spun out of the parking lot.

As he drove home, one question rose in his mind: What happened to the prayers? Did God listen at all? Did He even care? Maybe the guys didn't pray hard enough. But he shouldn't blame them. He hadn't even prayed once that morning himself. He didn't even know how to pray. Certainly those little *God-help-me* flares he'd been sending up from time to time weren't real prayers.

Oh God, what do I do now?

Chapter 21

HARRY COULD'VE GONE IN TO WORK and relieved Graven, but why? It wasn't like he needed the money that badly, and his top priority was clearing his stupid case.

He threw his court papers on the table and stomped into the kitchen to make some coffee. What was Fagan doing in court ... and talking to the state's attorney just before his trial? Did he have something to do with the state's attorney prosecuting him on such bogus charges? That didn't seem like his old boss's style. He thought back to Fagan's phone call: *"You got twenty-four hours to retract those lies or ..."* Or what? Catch him in some dark alley? Send a goon after him? Fagan would've confronted him head-on, threatening to tear him apart. But not this.

Still, maybe he shouldn't have deleted that phone call so quickly. On the other hand, what could he have done?

Harry stood there listening to the coffee gurgle through his coffeemaker. A sense of dread haunted him, the feeling that things were going down, coming from so many angles he couldn't keep up with them. Maybe he ought to bail on everything. Tell Gilson that he wouldn't be testifying against Fagan. Contact Donita and tell her she could have custody of DaShawn if she wanted. He'd back off if she'd withdraw charges. Send his mom to a nursing home, whether she needed it yet or not. Whatever she needed, he didn't feel up to being the provider. Quit his job at Richmond Towers and … and go fishin'! Maybe move down to Florida and really retire.

But that would mean leaving Estelle. Ah, who was he kidding? They didn't have that much goin' on yet. And her standards were so high, he'd probably never meet them anyway.

He took a deep breath and poured himself a cup of coffee. The truth was, he wouldn't have any chance with Estelle if he played the quitter on every front. And he wouldn't be able to live with himself either. No, he had to ride this thing through and pray that everything would ultimately work out.

Pray … Maybe that was what he needed to do.

"Yeah, God, so how am I supposed to learn how to do that?"

The question had no sooner left his mouth than the words, *the men's group,* came so distinctly to him that he jerked his head around to see who'd said them. Then he felt foolish. There was no one else in the room. It was strange though, as if the words had been spoken inside his head, somewhere between his ears and his brain.

Men's group, huh? Well, yeah, those brothers did pray, and he could probably learn a thing or two from them. Maybe he'd go again and let them pray for him. Couldn't hurt. But in the meantime, he had to fight his way out of his own problems.

Harry slumped into a chair, nursing his coffee. He still had an ace up his sleeve, one thing that would clear him and put Fagan away for good: that video DaShawn said he took on the cell phone. Why'd he let it go so long? That was a week and a half ago. He should've followed up immediately. Could he still track it down? It'd be like hunting for lost tax dollars in the city budget. But maybe he should try.

Okay, what were his options?

Fagan probably threw it away. Why would he keep a piece of property that could tie him to a crime? On the other hand, Fagan considered himself invincible, above the law. That might be his weak point. So what else might he have done with it? Tried to use it himself, passed it on to someone else, taken it home?... Of course, if he threw it away, there'd be no chance of retrieving it now. But if he'd thoughtlessly tossed it in the back of his cruiser ...

Harry got up and topped off his cooling coffee, got his phone, and punched in some numbers.

"Hey Cindy? Harry here. How ya doin'?"

"Tryin' to get some sleep, Harry."

"What? It's almost noon. Oh yeah, I forgot, sleepin' 'til noon is what cops do ... better than banker's hours. Maybe I ought to come out of retirement and go back on the force."

"Funny, Harry." He heard a loud yawn. "So what's up?"

"I need your help, Cindy—"

"What a news flash! That's what you're always sayin' these days." She paused. "Oh, I nearly forgot, today was your preliminary. How'd your case go?"

"That's what I'm callin' about. Remember I told you about that phone my son—I mean my grandson—used to video Fagan beatin' his mother and takin' her stash? I need to find it."

"Cell phone? You didn't tell me about a cell phone. What are you talkin' 'bout?"

"I didn't tell you about Fagan takin' the phone, the one with the video of him beatin' Donita?"

"Harry, you're losin' it. You didn't tell me, and since when can phones take videos?"

"But they can. High-end new ones, anyway." Harry sighed, and briefly filled Cindy on what happened.

"So if Fagan pocketed that phone, what do you want me to do about it?"

"That's where I need your help. Search his cruiser and see if—"

"Wait a minute. Wait a minute, Harry. First you want me to run a raid for you. Then you want me to get information from the state's attorney about a pending case, and now you want me to search my boss's car? I'm not gettin' involved in any more clandestine crap. I don't have a death wish like you seem to have. Trying to search his car is stupid. I could—"

"No, no. Hold on, now. All you'd have to do is go out to the motor pool and just casually look in his car. Check under the seat, look in the backseat, on the floor, maybe down behind the cushion. Wouldn't take but a couple of minutes. I'm not talkin' 'bout tearing the side panels off like you were searchin' a drug runner. Just give it a look. You can't miss it. The thing's hot pink."

"Pink?"

"Yeah, hot pink, my grandson says. And if he's still got it, he wouldn't have hidden it. He'd've just dropped it somewhere."

"Yeah, and when he comes by while I'm diggin' around in his vehicle, what do I say? 'Ah, gee, Matty, when we were makin' out in your backseat last night, I think I dropped my contact.'"

"Don't be so dense, Cindy. Hey, you're not … are you?"

"What do you think, Harry?"

"Sorry, that was outta line. But look, go in right now. You guys are takin' some comp time, aren't you? So he won't even be in the office. Anyone asks you what you're doin', just make up somethin', know what I'm sayin'?"

"Yeah, but … sounds kinda stupid to me. What chance is there that that phone would still be there?"

"Maybe not much, but it's the easiest and first place to search. I've gotta find it."

"And if it's not there, what are you gonna ask me to do next? Search his desk or his locker?"

"Yeah, maybe his desk. Hadn't thought of that."

"Not gonna do it, Harry."

"Come *on*, just the car, then. I can't go in there and snoop around. I need someone on the inside. Just this once, Cindy … for old times. Whaddaya say?"

There was a long pause. "I'll see what I can do. Hot pink, huh?"

HARRY HADN'T EXPECTED A RESPONSE from Cindy so quickly, but she called back within two hours. "Sorry, Harry. No cell phone … and before you say anything, I did take a peek in his desk. Only a quick one, but I don't think the phone's there either, so …"

"How 'bout his locker?

Silence stretched. "Come on, Harry. You know there's no way I can get into his locker without a bolt cutter. You want me to—"?

"No, no. I hear you, but …"

"Besides, I never see him using his locker. We all wear civvies, you know, so we're not changing all the time." She paused for a moment. "Hey, why don't you just go to the Review Board and tell them the whole story. Maybe they can get a warrant and do a real search."

"Yeah, maybe. I'll see. Hey, thanks, Cindy. I owe you one."

"You owe me a lot more than one, Harry. See ya."

Harry hung up the phone and stood there. If Fagan hadn't tossed it, the phone would have to be in Fagan's locker … or his house. Cindy was probably right: he ought to go to the Police Review Board. They could petition a judge for a search warrant. That'd be the only safe way to do it. He looked at his watch. Maybe he could still catch Captain Gilson this afternoon. He went into his bedroom and pawed through a box of papers until he found Gilson's phone number and made the call.

Gilson's secretary said he was out for the rest of the day but assured Harry that he ought to be able to reach him on Wednesday.

Now what? Harry paced around his apartment. All this crap had his whole life on hold. He oughta figure out what he was going to do about his mother, but he couldn't really do anything until he got these "issues" resolved. Yeah, he had issues.

Harry grabbed his car keys. He'd go visit her anyway, just to see how she was doin'. Maybe he could fix something for them both to eat—or carryout, that'd be easier—and then he'd drop on by the Bible study and collect a few more prayers for his "issues." Is that how it worked? The more prayers God logged into His "inbox," the more likely He'd be to answer them? Hah! He doubted anyone could force God to listen like that.

Duh! Harry knew true peace required far more than an imagination, in spite of John Lennon's song. Maybe the key was getting a really righteous person to pray for you, a genuine saint. Surely God would listen to a saint's prayer on your behalf.

Those guys in the Bible study were "righteous dudes," as they said on the streets, but Harry couldn't see any of them being notably holy. Ben Garfield, that old Jewish guy, was pretty crusty, and Carl Hickman … Harry was sure he had some dirt under his fingernails. Harry liked Carl. Of course, Denny Baxter and Peter Douglass knew a lot about the Bible, but Harry couldn't see them as saints either. Nothin' against 'em, really. But they just seemed too regular.

Maybe that kid, Josh, was the closest to a saint for takin' on the baby of a dead drug addict. That took some guts, but he was like any other new dad—overwhelmed by it all most of the time. And then there was that mariachi band guy. If he was a holy man, he was *definitely* in disguise.

No, those guys weren't saints, not in the sense of being so righteous that God would have to listen.

But they did pray like their prayers got through the ceiling. And Harry sensed God had actually answered a couple of them on his behalf. At least it'd felt that way for a hot minute. But now the walls were closing in, breaking down around him. He'd have to ask the guys tonight why God would pay any attention to their prayers.

Chapter 22

SERVING HIS MOTHER CHINESE FOOD from the little white carryout boxes didn't do much for Harry. Her attention remained glued to her TV.

"You want some more General Tao's chicken, Mama?"

"I like the lemon chicken. Why didn't you bring any lemon chicken? Move over, Harry. I can't see my show with you standin' in the way."

Harry sat back down. He didn't have the energy to try to break through to her with any meaningful conversation. The sense of dread that dogged him anytime he stopped long enough to take his emotional pulse left him drained.

He checked his watch. "Hey, Mama, I gotta go. You want any more of this? If not, I'm gonna put these out in the trash." Leftovers in her refrigerator usually stayed there till they grew fur. Heaven forbid that she would try to eat any.

She just stared at the TV.

Harry tossed the white boxes, came back from the kitchen, and kissed his mother on the forehead. "See you in a few, Mama."

"Bye, Harry." She looked up at him with a stern expression on her face. "Now don't you be out too late tonight. You know you got school tomorrow."

"Mama, I'm …" He shook his head. "Love ya, Mama."

He headed out to his car. Estelle was right. He needed a better plan for her. Sometimes she seemed with it, able to track what he was saying and able to take care of herself. Then a moment later, her mind could flip forty years into the past or into the TV show she was watching. And it seemed to be getting worse … another vapor in that cloud that hung over him.

Harry thought he might be late, but all the guys he'd met at the Bible study last week at Peter Douglass's apartment were still standing around talking when he arrived. A few minutes later, a tall, lanky white guy came in the door. Harry did a double take. With his grey hair and gentle smile, the man looked like Fred Rogers on that "neighborhood" TV show Rodney used to watch when he was a kid.

Carl Hickman slapped Harry on the back and pointed toward the new man. "Harry, meet Pastor Clark. He's one of the pastors at SouledOut Community Church. You'll have to come hear him sometime."

"I'll have to do that. Fact is, I was gonna come last week, but I had to work, last minute." Harry shook hands and nodded. "How you doin'?"

"You live around here, then?" asked the pastor.

"Not far. Met some of these guys at that women's shelter, and they roped me into comin' on over."

"Now you got that right." Carl laughed. "We use any means necessary: begging, bribery, hog-tie 'em, and if none of those work, we pray 'em in." He turned to the pastor. "We almost had to resort to drastic measures with this here brother, but now he's here."

Harry felt a little glitch somewhere inside. What was this about *praying him in* … into what?

Everyone soon found a seat, and they got right into the Bible study, picking up in Psalm 119 where they'd left off. When they got to the verse that said, "Trouble and distress have come upon me," Harry couldn't help feeling those words described his situation exactly. Then came verses that said, "I call with all my heart; answer me, O LORD" and "I call out to you; save me" and "I rise before dawn and cry for help…."

But did God answer the guy who wrote this? And why would He? Harry glanced around the room, his eyes stopping at the preacher. Would this white dude think his questions stupid? Oh well …

"Hey, I been wonderin', I know you guys pray an' all, like it says here in the Bible. But how do you know if God hears you? I mean, except for the pastor here, you guys don't strike me as such holy Joes or anything—not like whoever wrote this stuff in the Bible. So what makes you think God hears you when you pray?" There, he'd said it.

The pastor raised both hands in a *not-me* gesture. "Well, if these guys won't tell you, I will. I'm not any kind of a holy Joe myself. I'm no different than any of them. We're all just sinners saved by grace. Nothin' more."

The room fell quiet. Harry began to feel like maybe he'd insulted the pastor, though he couldn't see how. "Sorry, I wasn't meanin' anything. I was just askin', 'cause I was thinkin' about prayer the other day and wondering why God would listen in the first place."

Peter Douglass cleared his throat. "Truth is, none of us in this room—not even the guy who wrote those words in the Bible—has any reason to think God would listen. Look at the last verse in the whole psalm. The writer says, 'I have strayed like a lost sheep.' He wasn't perfect either, so there's gotta be some other way.

"Now, take that Bible you got there—and you can keep that one, by the way, okay?—and turn near the back to a book called

Hebrews. Go to Hebrews chapter four, verse fourteen." Peter waited until Harry and the others had found it and then read how Jesus Christ was the "great high priest" who had access to God because He'd never sinned, but He'd also lived on earth among humans so He understood our weaknesses.

"See that last verse?" Peter concluded. "It says, 'Let us then approach the throne of grace with confidence, so that we may receive mercy and find grace to help us in our time of need.'" He looked up. "That's the only way we can pray, Harry. Jesus gives us the pass that lets us come into God's very presence in prayer. No other way."

Harry stared at the Bible in his hand, nodding his head.

Pastor Clark cleared his throat and spoke in a mild voice. "There's another verse in Ephesians that makes much the same point. This is from the New Living Translation, chapter three, verse twelve." He hunched over his rather large Bible. "'Because of Christ and our faith in him, we can now come fearlessly into God's presence, assured of his glad welcome.'"

"All right!" Carl Hickman said. "Now that's off the hook, man. Know what I'm sayin'? If even I can talk to God and get a glad welcome … Whoo-ee!" He clapped his hands and shot his hand up, pointing one finger toward the ceiling.

It made sense. Nobody Harry knew was good enough to get God's ear on their own, but Jesus … now He was perfect, so of course, He could get in. If He invited us along, acted as a "priest" to make it right, then yeah, maybe God would listen. Even to Harry.

During the prayer time, several of the guys prayed for DaShawn, that he could come live with Harry soon. As Harry left, the cloud of dread that had been following him all day had somehow lifted. These guys were okay.

THE NEXT DAY, as soon the Richmond Towers lobby cleared of its own version of morning rush hour, Harry called Captain Gilson at police headquarters and told him about the cell phone. "My grandson says he took a video on it of Fagan beating Donita and holding bags of drugs—"

"*Supposed* drugs," Gilson shot back. "Just how are you gonna prove from a video that it was cocaine?"

"Okay, *supposed drugs*. But it's still totally incriminating. He beat up this woman but never arrested her for anything. That's his MO. Remember?"

"Maybe. But ... " *Bam!* It sounded like Gilson threw his phone across the room, followed by him calling Harry every name in the book, then some more clattering. "Bentley! You still there? You better be! You should've known better than to mix your personal business with this police case. What were you thinkin'? You're gonna blow the whole investigation."

Harry sighed and spun around in his chair to put his back to the front doors in case a resident came in. He'd half expected this kind of response from Gilson. "Look, I didn't blow the investigation. If Fagan has any idea I filed a report on him, it's because there's a leak in your office. And he doesn't even know I'm related to the woman he beat up! There's been no contamination."

"You hope. You're an idiot, Bentley! If you got by unnoticed, it was sheer luck. You know everything you did was out of line. This case is too important to get derailed by your foolishness. Now, stay away from Fagan! That's an order. Drop anything—and I mean *anything*—that might give him reason to link you to our investigation. We've put too many man hours in on this for you to trip us up now."

"Uh ..." *An order*? Gilson wasn't his boss. On the other hand ... Harry didn't want this whole thing to fall apart. He took a deep breath to calm himself and tried again. "But what about that cell phone? You could get a warrant and search his house or even his locker at work. That'd nail Fagan." *And clear me,* thought Harry.

"No way, José. You have no proof that cell phone's anywhere we could find it. If I pulled a warrant on him and didn't find it—which is probably what would happen—we'd blow everything. He'd start doing a mop-up and by the time we got an indictment from the grand jury, he'd have covered all his tracks. Heck, you don't even know for sure that phone has a video on it. I mean, I never even heard of such a thing."

"Wait a minute, Captain. I believe my grandson, and he says he took the movie! I mean, technology changes so fast ... Just call some cell phone store and ask 'em."

"Yeah, but if it exists and Fagan happened to see it, he'd've erased it, even if he kept the phone. It's no good, and I'm tellin' you: Stay out of it, you readin' me? I don't want to hear any more about you messin' with the evidence or hovering around Fagan. And that's an order, Bentley."

Harry flipped his phone shut without saying good-bye. "Yeah," he argued with thin air, "but I don't work for you, Mr. Police Review Board Captain. So you can't tell me what to do!" He banged a fist on the lobby desk, staring out at the traffic going by without seeing it. He was fuming, but he knew there was something he'd missed. He shouldn't have hung up on Gilson. Even if Gilson wouldn't go after the cell, he might be able to get the state's attorney off his case about DaShawn. He'd hesitated to tell Gilson about his personal motives for finding the video, afraid Gilson would dismiss the whole idea. But since he'd already done that, there was one thin shred of hope Gilson might help him with.

Merely punching in Gilson's phone number again was like eatin' crow before he even said a word.

"Ah, Captain Gilson. Sorry 'bout that. Didn't mean to cut you off. Let's see, you were sayin' back off and stay away from Fagan, right?"

"Yeah, and I'm serious. You understand?"

"I hear ya, but … there's one more thing." Harry paused and took a deep breath. "I need to ask a favor."

"What's that?" Gilson's voice dripped with skepticism.

"Well, it turns out that Donita—the woman who got beat up—is sayin' *I* did it and tried to kidnap her son, that'd be my grandson. 'Course that's crazy, but that's another reason I want to get a hold of that cell phone. It would clear me of those bogus felony charges—"

"*Felony charges*? You sayin' you actually have a case against you?"

"Yeah. She's just that crazy. But if we can't recover that cell phone, maybe you could put in a word with the state's attorney and get this case dropped. You could tell 'em it's tied up with a much bigger investigation and that you know I wouldn't have done any of that."

The silence on the other end of the line lasted too long, like a computer sorting a complicated problem.

"Don't think I can do that, Harry." He'd lost the edge to his voice. "I hear where you're coming from, and under most circumstances, I'd be glad to put in a good word for you. But in this situation, it actually adds to the depth of your cover, know what I mean?"

"What? What're you talkin' 'bout? That's crazy."

"Not really. You're the one who's been messin' around Fagan when you shouldn't have been, and by now he's probably got wind of it. If the state's attorney suddenly dropped the case, he'd have every reason to suspect someone had pulled some strings …

which is exactly what you're asking me to do. And we can't have him figuring that out. So—"

"Wait! Wait just a minute there. You got it wrong, Captain. Even if he did figure it out, there's no reason he'd think it had anything to do with an investigation against him. I mean, he'd just assume it got dropped because I had connections of my own. After all, he knows it's a bogus charge, 'cause he's the perp! Right?"

"Maybe. But I'm not willing to take that chance, Bentley. You're on your own with this one. But don't worry. If what you say is true, there's no chance you'll get convicted. It's just a matter of a little hassle, showin' up in court for a few months. Your lawyer can protect you well enough. I'm not gonna risk drawing any attention by getting it dismissed from the top down. You just stay outta trouble. You hear, Bentley?"

This time it was Gilson who broke off the phone connection.

Chapter 23

HARRY WATCHED THE CLOCK in the lobby of Richmond Towers, and as soon as he figured DaShawn would be out of school, he phoned Schaumburg just to keep in contact with the boy and—Harry had to admit to himself—to hear him say *Grandpa*.

And Harry was not disappointed.

"Hi, Grandpa. What's up?" came the bouncy greeting. "You comin' out to get me pretty soon?"

"Not yet, son. I'm still trying to straighten out that legal stuff so they'll give me custody. How's it goin' with you?"

"Okay, I guess, but …"

"But what?"

"I dunno. I don't really like it out here, know what I mean?"

"How come? Aren't they treatin' you right?"

"It ain't that. It's just … I dunno. I wanna stay wit' you, Grandpa, just like you promised."

Harry closed his eyes and sighed. He wanted to keep his promise—he *intended* to keep it—but was the kid playin' him? Puttin' the squeeze on for him to deliver on his promise? Harry rubbed his hand over his bald head. "Look, DaShawn, I'm doing everything I can right now. Some of these things take time. I'm real sorry."

"But how long? I thought it was just gonna be a couple days."

"I did too, but it's not something we can force to happen sooner. Know what I'm sayin'?"

"Guess so." There was a long pause. "Gotta go, Grandpa. See ya."

Harry hung up feeling sick to his stomach. His own grandson needed something from him, something understandable, something Harry wanted to provide but couldn't. He felt helpless. Back in the day, he'd never slowed down long enough for his family's needs to register ... but now he wanted to do the right thing but couldn't. It was like being disqualified from the game just when he was learning how to play.

Oh God! There had to be another card in this hand he'd been dealt.

Rodney. And why not? His son had been dealing with this mess long before he even knew about Donita and DaShawn. Harry slid off the stool behind the half-moon desk and went down the hall to the management office. Inside, he smiled warmly at the fifty-something, slightly overweight secretary. "Gretchen, just the person I wanted to see. Any chance I could give you a brief coffee break so I could use your computer for half a minute?"

"Well, I don't know, Harry. Is this business?"

"Hm. Frankly, no, it's personal." He stood there, smiling at her, gambling that she'd have a hard time denying him a few minutes of personal time on Richmond Towers' computer unless she'd never done the same herself.

"Well ..." She looked around. "I guess it would be okay ... for a few minutes. The boss is out now, but what about the front desk?"

"Don't you worry about that, and since Mr. Martin's out, he won't need you to type a letter in the next five minutes. So just go get yourself a cup of coffee or powder your nose or whatever. I'll only be a minute. Okay?"

As soon as Harry was seated before the screen, he called up the Web page of the Cook County Department of Corrections and entered Rodney's name. He scanned the details: Rodney was housed in the same place, Division 9, and he had visitation hours today, Wednesdays, between 9 a.m. and 9 p.m. All right! Harry slammed his right fist into his left hand and logged off.

"All done, Gretchen," he called. "Told you I wouldn't be long. Thanks!"

Back behind his desk in the lobby, he called Draven. If that guy would actually relieve him on time today, Harry ought to have time to go down to 26th and California and see Rodney. Maybe this was crazy. But if Rodney could provide even one more piece to the puzzle, it might help.

Draven didn't answer.

Harry hit Redial every fifteen minutes for the next hour and a quarter until … miracle of miracles, Draven walked in the door, five minutes before he was due to relieve Harry.

Harry wanted to throttle the young punk. "How come you never answer your phone?"

"Didn't figure you had anything to tell me I wanted to hear."

Harry clenched his teeth. He had to figure out some other way to relate to this jerk than slappin' him upside the head, which he felt like doing on a regular basis. Then an even better idea struck him. He stuck out his hand. "Draven, just wanna thank you for getting' here on time today. Appreciate it, man."

Draven's jaw hung open as a puzzled look washed over his face. He extended a limp hand in hesitant jerks as though he expected it to be rapped with a ruler. "You were calling me all afternoon just to tell me that … even before I got here?"

"Nope, but that's what I want to say to you right now. Have a good day." Harry grabbed up his newspaper and cap and got through the door into the parking garage before he burst out laughing. That one look on Draven's face had been worth a Benjamin, at least.

THE CLOCK IN THE WAITING ROOM said 8:20, and Harry's stomach grumbled before he heard his name called with the last group of visitors for Division 9. He took his seat in the small cubicle and waited for the prisoners to arrive on the other side of the thick glass.

Harry watched several prisoners file past before Rodney arrived and took the stool opposite him. He recognized the blank expression on Rodney's face, the look all institutionalized individuals learned in order to survive. They never revealed their hand until they knew the game. Display enthusiasm and someone would make a fool of them. Display disdain and they'd be targeted as a troublemaker. Better to remain noncommittal, blank as a mannequin until they knew what was going down. That way no one could single them out. Harry took a deep breath, sorry Rodney had been through all that. But at least he wasn't rolling his eyes.

"How's it goin'?"

Rodney pointed to his ear and shook his head. Harry moved his mouth right up to the clogged grill as Rodney leaned down slightly. "I said, how's it goin'? You stayin' healthy?"

"Yeah. Turned my ankle playin' ball the other day, but it's okay. How 'bout you?"

Wow. Now that was something new, Rodney asking if he was okay. Harry leaned close to the grill again. "I'm doin' good. But I got a problem." Harry could see Rodney draw back from the grill. "It's about DaShawn, your son DaShawn."

That got Rodney's attention. He leaned forward. "What about him? Is he okay?"

"Ah, yes and no. He's staying with this foster family out in Schaumburg, and I guess they're okay. But I want him to stay with me." Harry glanced to see if Rodney reacted. He didn't. "That's what DaShawn wants too. He stayed with me for a few days, and we got on real good. But …" Harry didn't really know what to say.

"So what happened? Why ain't he with you now?"

"It's Donita. She's filed some bogus charges against me, and until I get them cleared up, DCFS won't let me have him."

"What kind of charges?"

"Assault and kidnapping." Harry gave Rodney a sanitized summary of the situation, leaving out everything about Fagan other than some guy beat up Donita before Harry arrived on the scene.

Rodney rolled his eyes. "So why's she blaming you?"

"Not sure why, though it probably has something to do with protecting her pimp."

"Ah, that'd be Hector. So what you want from me?"

"Don't know. But I'm about out of ideas. I mean, eventually the case'll get dismissed—I'm not worried about that—but that could take a couple months, maybe longer, and I promised DaShawn I'd get him back with me as soon as possible."

Rodney sat back and looked at Harry for a long moment and then turned his head staring at nothing off to the side. There was a glint in the corner of Rodney's eye Harry hadn't seen before, and suddenly he realized Rodney *did* care about his boy, far more than Harry had given him credit for. Why had he decided his own son was such a no-good that he had no feelings for his boy? A lump caught in Harry's throat.

Rodney leaned close to the grill, his voice low. "Yeah, well, Donita has always batted that boy around like a Ping-Pong ball, grabbin' him when it served her purposes, then dumping him when she got too strung out to care. I always felt caught in her crosshairs, no matter what I did. If I knew how to keep that boy out of her clutches, I'd …" He shook his head. "Don't really know how to help you." He paused. "Sounds like you already know where Donita lives?"

"Yeah, but I can't approach her, or I'd mess up my case and be in real trouble."

"How 'bout Hector?"

Harry shrugged. "Same thing. Donita's named him as a witness against me, so I'd be tampering with a witness. But if you know where he lives, might be useful."

Rodney nodded. "Last I knew he had an apartment just west of the United Center." Rodney gave Harry an address on Warren Avenue. "He might flip Donita if you found a way to lean on him. Shouldn't be too hard, all the business he into. Know what I'm sayin'?" He shrugged.

"Hm. Have to think 'bout it."

Father and son sat there looking at each other for a few moments. Finally, Harry leaned forward again. "So how's your case goin'?"

"Nothin's happenin'. My next court date is in a couple more weeks. Then we'll see."

Harry took a chance. "You still haven't told me what it's about."

"Ah." Rodney shrugged. "It was bogus. You wouldn't wanna know."

"Maybe I would. I'm getting more acquainted with bogus myself, these days."

They both sat back. Rodney rolled his head like he was stretching the kinks out of his neck, and Harry knew he was going to say something.

Suddenly Harry remembered the video monitor and pointed his thumb toward it.

Rodney waved his hand. "Don't matter. They got me on a possession charge, supposedly my second one."

Harry couldn't help but grimace. His son, a druggie?

"Hey, I told you it was bogus." Rodney glared at Harry and pinched his lips into a hard line as though he was done talking, but after a moment he threw out his hands. "Look, at least I don't deal. That was Donita. Anyway, they set my bail at ten grand. I paid my bond and got out. Everything was cool, but the week before my court date I got a little antsy and headed on down to Atlanta to see a couple dawgs I's tight wit' when they lived up here. Then ... 'member that snowstorm last March?"

Harry frowned and shook his head.

"Yeah, you know. It was on Sunday, the fifth. Anyway, I had a round-trip ticket to come back that day. Had plenty of time, 'cept the storm shut down O'Hare, and my flight back got canceled. Missed my court date next mornin'. Didn't think it was no big deal. I was going to call my PD later that afternoon and have him work it out. But when I got home, I didn't have nothin' to eat back up in my crib, so I want out to the Jewel's, ya know, to do a little shoppin'. And wouldn't you know it, I got caught drivin' black three blocks from my apartment. They ran my ID, and it comes up with a warrant attached to my name. I tried to tell 'em no way. Couldn't be, not that fast. But they accused me of resistin' arrest and took me in." Rodney shrugged. "One of 'em was a real animal, man, nearly cracked open my head." Rodney pointed to a new scar above his right eye Harry had noticed on his previous visit. "Anyway, he brought me back up in here." Rodney shrugged.

For some reason Harry felt relieved. "So that's why you were denied bail?"

"Like I said, I was plannin' on surrendering, but then I just got picked up. Wasn't nothin' I could do 'bout it."

"Hm." Harry nodded. He'd wondered what Rodney had done that was so terrible that he'd been denied bail. Skipping a court date was more dumb than heinous, but it sure would get your bail denied.

The guard called, "Time's up." Rodney rose from his stool. He raised his hand in a half wave as he shuffled back toward his deck.

Harry didn't move. Things were bad, but not as bad as he'd sometimes imagined. At least Rodney was talking to him … and Rodney did care for DaShawn. Somehow that meant a lot. Maybe his family wasn't in total meltdown after all. In all this mess, he and his son had reconnected, especially over DaShawn. A connection they could build on once Rodney got out.

Maybe Rodney had learned his lesson and was ready to go straight. Harry wished he could bail him out. But he knew there was no chance. Even a good lawyer wouldn't be able to get him a second hearing after skipping bail. The most Harry could hope for was a speedy trial and a light sentence. But for second possession, skipping bail, and possibly resisting arrest … Leslie Stuart was probably right, it could be a couple of years.

Harry stood up and left the room. He was still the man on point for caring for DaShawn, but he was still no closer to gaining custody than he had been before.

Chapter 24

RAIN PELTED HARRY'S WINDSHIELD as he drove north on Western Avenue toward home. But when he got to Warren Boulevard, he turned east, looking for the address Rodney had given for Hector Jiménez. Lightning flashes lit up the neighborhood, but he got all the way to the large parking lots for the United Center, where the Chicago Bulls and Blackhawks played, before he realized that in the heavy rain, he had missed the address. He turned around and headed back, creeping along, trying to catch the building numbers. There. He hit the brakes. It ought to be the next building ... but all he saw in the flickering, soggy gloom was a newly leveled vacant lot.

So much for that. No telling where Hector was now. But what could he have done anyway without jeopardizing his case?

Somebody behind him laid on their horn, urging him to get out of the middle of the street. Yeah, yeah! He stepped on the gas and took off but felt like he didn't know where he was going. He'd run out of options. Wherever he turned there didn't seem to be any solution.

In frustration, he again headed for home.

"Oh God, I need a breakthrough here. I need something to bust this thing wide open. Otherwise, it's gonna drag on for weeks, perhaps even months before I can take DaShawn. And that's not fair to him, God. I made him a promise, and I need to keep it. He didn't ask for any of this mess." Harry stopped speaking. Was he praying? He even sounded a little like some of the guys on Tuesday night. But what was it they'd said about Jesus being the key or the pass that could let him into God's presence? Some of the guys always ended their prayers with: *In Jesus' name, amen.* Maybe he ought to try that.

"In Jesus' name, amen."

But Harry knew that wasn't quite it. Real prayer wasn't some kind of formula or magic incantation in which if you said the right words the door opened, otherwise you were shut out. Besides, Harry was sure some of the guys in the group just ended their prayer with *amen* or just stopped talking when they were done like most people did in conversation with one another. But that verse Pastor Clark had read said something like "*Because of Christ and our faith in Him*" we could come into God's presence. No, it was more than that … it said we could come *fearlessly* into His presence.

Faith in Christ—Harry remembered enough from when his mom took him to church as a child to know that *gettin' saved* and *comin' to Jesus* and *believin' in Jesus* was all about that faith in Christ and what it meant to become a Christian. He remembered revival services where at the height of the preacher's sermon, while everyone was hollerin' out "Amen!" and "Hallelujah!" and "Preach it, brother!", they'd say that the doors of the church were open and anyone who was "lost" should walk down that aisle and be saved.

But Harry wasn't in church right now. He was drivin' his RAV4 home in the rain. And if he were to get saved, what would he be saved from? This mess he was in? That'd be nice. Somehow Harry couldn't imagine it working like that. That was too much like those TV preachers his mama listened to.

Maybe he'd try the prayer thing again.

"God, I don't know much about prayin', but I wanna have faith in Jesus so I can … so I can come to You, and like the brothers said, so I can talk to You when I need to." He paused as he wheeled around a left-turner who had backed up traffic six cars deep. "Anyway, God, if You can hear me, I need some of that faith. And if You're listenin', please do something—anything, God—to break open this fix I'm in." He thought a moment as he pulled into a parking space behind his apartment, and then added, "In Jesus' name, amen." It couldn't hurt.

He sat in his dark car for a few minutes while the rain pounded on the roof. Surely it had to let up pretty soon, and as he waited, a calm came over him. Surely his troubles had to let up pretty soon too. Maybe God had heard him after all.

When the rain finally slowed and the flashes of lightning had moved east out over Lake Michigan, Harry popped the door and made a dash for his building.

Whew! Not bad. At least with a bald head, all you needed was a towel.

He bounded up the stairs, two at a time … until he got to the second floor. Then he grinned and began acting his age for the remaining steps to the landing for his floor, puffing only slightly. He needed to get back to working out regularly, lose a few pounds.

He stopped.

The door to his apartment was ajar, and there was a light on inside.

Harry never left his apartment unlocked when he went to work, and he wouldn't have left a light on in the morning.

He approached slowly, silently, and then realized he'd been making so much noise bounding up the stairs that everyone in the building probably knew he was home.

"Hello, who's there?" He pushed the door wide open and waited a moment before stepping in. "Hello?"

He took a step in, looked around, and froze. Fagan was sitting at the other end of his table like the chairman of the board, holding a can of Pepsi in his hand. His square face as flushed as ever, his flattop red hair sticking straight up, made him look like his blood pressure must be pushing 300.

"Hey there, Harry, my man. Hope you don't mind." He raised the Pepsi toward Harry, the can clasped in his sausage fingers. "I figured you'd be up to providing a little refreshment for your old boss while I waited."

Harry frowned at his former boss. "How'd you get in?"

"Through the door, of course." He grinned, turning his eyes into thin slits and revealing his yellowed teeth. "Ah, come on, Harry. You don't mind, do you? I just dropped by for a friendly chat. Sit down. Sit down. Hey, you want a Pepsi? I'd offer you a beer, but you don't seem to keep any in your fridge anymore."

"What're you doin' here, Fagan?"

"Hey, it's Matty, don'tcha know?" Fagan took a swig of Pepsi. The skin on his face looked a little crusty, like it would never recover from lifelong sunburn. "I'm just Matty. Like old times, hey, bro?"

"I ain't *bro* to you, not when you show up in my apartment uninvited. I'll ask you again, what're you doin' here?" Harry slid his hand into his pocket and grasped his cell phone.

"Go close the door, Harry, and come over here and sit down. We need to have a talk."

Harry noticed Fagan's right arm had remained under the table. He couldn't quite be sure, but it looked like Fagan's holster was empty. Was he holding his weapon in his lap? Harry's Glock was in his bedroom in the top drawer of his bedside table, but there'd be no way to get to it and defend himself. And Fagan knew that, so what was he thinking? Would he shoot him right there in his apartment where everyone in the building would hear? Did he now consider himself so far above the law that no investigation could nail him?

Harry deliberately did not go back and close the door. But he slowly pulled his cell from his pocket and sat down on the edge of the chair across from Fagan. With his elbows on the table, he held the cell in front of him so Fagan could see it. "So what's the agenda for this unscheduled meeting?" He was determined to not show any fear. "You here to invite me to one of our cookouts or something?"

"I'm here because I think there've been a couple of misunderstandings between us, Harry. And together I think we can clear them up to our mutual benefit."

"Oh, like what?" Harry leaned back in the chair, trying to calm himself as much as display an air of unconcern.

"For one, I understand you went to the Review Board about me, and that triggered some kind of an investigation. I called you, Harry, musta been ten days ago by now and asked you to clear up these rumors you were spreading. But you don't seem to have done that, and now they've led to some additional complications … for you, even. You get my drift, Harry?"

Harry stared at Fagan. The hair over the man's ears was turning white, and he wasn't aging all that well. Maybe his conscience was eating at him, but it hadn't dulled his cunning. How had he found out about Harry going to the Review Board? It was possible in the course of the investigation, that Fagan might have gotten wind of the fact that people were asking questions about him, but how'd he know that Harry was the source of the inquiry? Somebody on the inside must have talked.

"The thing is, Harry, it's my understanding that if you came to realize you were a little confused about those things you reported and let the Board know that you couldn't actually swear to them, the whole problem would evaporate, and that'd take a real load off my mind."

Harry could feel his jaw tightening and his teeth grinding. He rubbed the cell phone between his fingers like a lucky penny, feeling tempted to flip it open and dial 911 just to see what Fagan would do. But with a near-fatal curiosity, he wanted to know how Fagan thought he could get him to recant. Was Fagan making a raw threat, or did he have some other form of leverage in mind?

Harry took a deep breath. "So Fagan ..." He pointed. "Whaddaya got under the table, there? Let's get everything out in the open."

"What, this?" Fagan pulled his hand out and looked at the pistol in it as though he was surprised to see it. "Oh, yeah. Hey, you probably haven't seen my new weapon yet, have you? It's a new SIG, a P229 9mm. Real nice piece." Fagan bounced his hand up and down as though feeling the weight of it. "Great balance. You oughta try one sometime. But you know, it always pokes me in the side whenever I sit down. We need to get someone to design a new holster, don'tcha think?"

Harry recalled Cindy's warning about the rumors of Fagan "disposing" of various enemies. And sitting across from a desperate man who was playing with a loaded gun did raise his own blood pressure considerably. But if Fagan truly intended to off him, he'd probably do it in some remote place or fashion that'd look like an accident or random street robbery. Shooting him right there in his living room didn't make much sense. It had to be just a show to bully him, and Harry was determined not to be intimidated. He swallowed hard. "You could wear a shoulder holster or lose a few pounds."

"What?" Fagan's voice grated. "What'd you say about me losing weight?"

"You know, the spare tire. The butt of your pistol gets you right in the side when you sit down because of the overhang. Know what I mean?" Harry tried to laugh, but it sounded a little nervous. "Maybe you been throwin' too many of those backyard barbecues, Matty." Tense though he was on the inside, Harry felt emboldened by the puzzled look on Fagan's face. "Actually, that's what I thought you came over here for … to invite me to celebrate the Fourth with you guys, or something."

A snarl contorted Fagan's face. "Don't play the idiot with me, Bentley. You know why I'm here. I want you to withdraw that report."

"Yeah? Well you can kiss my—"

Fagan flipped the gun around, pointing it directly at Harry, and cocked it.

They stared at each other in silence. Harry slowly raised both hands to shoulder level, his cell still in his left hand.

The seconds dragged on. Finally, in a quick move, Fagan flipped his gun upward toward the ceiling and uncocked it, then laid it on the table in front of him. "Hey, you're right, Harry. Maybe I should lose a couple pounds, and I'm sure there's a better way to work out our little misunderstandings."

Harry lowered his hands to the table. His heart was pounding like a pile driver, shaking his whole chest so that he was sure Fagan could see it, but he'd not caved in.

Fagan sighed deeply. "You know, Harry, this can be a mutually beneficial conversation, and I was kind of letting it get one-sided. Guess that's why I'm not a union negotiator or a politician or whatever." He snorted a short laugh. "I'll tell you what; I do have somethin' that might interest you. You know, when I saw you at the courthouse yesterday, I knew I could be of help, but you just ran off. Probably had some important business appointment. I understand." He shrugged.

Harry was not impressed by Fagan's new casualness.

"Here's the deal, Harry." The man leaned forward and pointed at him. "It's come to my attention that you've got a little problem of your own, an additional complication, as I mentioned." He waved his hand. "I understand it involves some woman bringin' false charges against you, so you know how it feels. Well, I know the state's attorney who drew your case, and with just a word from me, I think she'd let it go. I'd be actin' like a character witness on your behalf, Harry. Shoot, she probably doesn't even realize the charges'll never stick, so I'd be givin' her a heads up, doin' her a favor, so to speak."

Harry went from trying to reign in his pounding heart to trying to focus his spinning head. Fagan was like a one-man intelligence agency, aware of everything going on in the department. And could he possibly have that state's attorney in his pocket? Harry was starting to think there was nothing Fagan wouldn't attempt.

Fagan raised both hands in a *come-to-Jesus* pose. "Do I gotta spell it out for you, Harry? Look, you scratch my back, I'll scratch yours. You tell Gilson you can't testify against me—give whatever reason you want—and I'll tell that assistant state's attorney to drop this stupid case against you, simple as that. We both win. Whaddaya say?"

Chapter 25

HARRY REALIZED HE'D LET HIS JAW DROP like Draven and closed his mouth. He turned his head to the side as he squinted at Fagan. "You're tellin' me you can just pick up the phone and tell a state's attorney to drop a case? Who do you think you are, God?"

"Hey, they don't call Chicago 'the city that works' for nothin', Harry. We get things done around here one way or the other. But nah, it's not as simple as me telling the state's attorney what to do. Let's just say I can make sure that her case would …" He shrugged and arched his fuzzy eyebrows in a *who-knows?* expression.

Harry slid his chair back from the table, leaned forward with his elbows on his knees, and cradled his head in his hands, ignoring that just minutes before Fagan had been threatening him with his gun.

No way did he want to give Fagan the satisfaction of his "deal." What, let him get away with the same kind of shakedown he'd pulled on so many others? Harry wanted to make a difference in the Chicago Police Department … but if he accepted the deal, he could keep his promise to DaShawn.

He stood up and forced a cool smile to try and show he was unruffled by the threats. "Get outta here, Matty," he said, deliberately using his old boss's more familiar name in a friendly tone. "Don't know what I'm gonna do, but I won't let you bully me into a hasty answer, not in my own house, for sure. I need some time to think. I'll call you in a couple days or so." He gestured toward his door like Fagan had overstayed his welcome at a party and needed to be sent home before he fell down drunk.

"Ah, Harry, I'd hoped for more. You know how these things are. Sometimes they take on a life of their own. I'm not sure I can promise how things will work out if you put this off." He stood up and—thankfully—holstered his weapon. "Like I said, I've got some connections, but those can erode." He shook his head. "You know the old saying: 'Don't put off till tomorrow what you can do today.' Know what I mean?"

Harry pointed to the door again, keeping his face placid.

Shaking his head again, Fagan walked to the door. "Call me, Harry."

Harry shut the door behind him, turned around, and leaned his back against the wall. He began shaking, his knees so weak he thought they might buckle. He started for the kitchen, thinking he just needed something to eat, then realized darkness was closing in from both sides. He stopped, leaned over, both hands on his knees, ready to allow himself to collapse gently to the floor if the blackness kept coming.

Slowly, he fought it back, stood up again, breathing deeply while his heart thudded in his chest. He was too old for this kind of drama. It was a good thing he'd retired from the force, but the way he'd gone about it hadn't freed him from the pressures of the job. They'd only ballooned.

He stared into his freezer trying to pick something to eat while a replay of Fagan's "deal" tumbled in his head. Finally he pulled out a frozen dinner and popped it in the microwave. While it was heating, he went into his bedroom and pulled open the drawer of his bedside table for a little Glock reassurance. His weapon was there all right, but when he picked it up, he realized the clip was missing. He checked the chamber. Empty!

Harry spun around, surveying is room. Fagan must have been in here, must have gone through his stuff, at least until he found his gun and unloaded it … a little extra insurance. But where was the clip?

He searched for half an hour, finally concluding that Fagan must have taken it with him. Finally, he gave up and went back into the kitchen, got his now-cool dinner out of the microwave and took it into the living room, sat in his chair, and switched on the TV to watch something mind-numbing while he ate. He needed something to drink. He'd take that Pepsi, now. He got up with a groan and went back into the kitchen, opened the fridge, and reached into the twelve-can convenience box. What his hand closed on was not a cold can, but the cold full clip from his Glock.

Harry held it up, staring at it. "That son of a—" He shook his head. Wrestling with fury at the invasion and pride that he hadn't caved in to Fagan's intimidation, Harry walked back into his bedroom and reloaded his weapon. He started to put it back in his bedside table, then thought of DaShawn. It was stupid to keep a loaded weapon in the house where a kid could access it. He knew of too many instances where a kid had stolen a handgun or shot a friend with one, simply because they had access. And he'd just had a lesson in how useless it could be unless you wore it wherever you went like a cowboy.

He was not a cowboy, and not even an off-duty police officer anymore.

He nodded and popped out the clip. He left it in the drawer of his bedside table and put the Glock on the top shelf of his closet. He'd have to get a lockable case before DaShawn returned.

When he was finally sitting in front of his TV, watching he-didn't-even-know-what, Harry was so tired he ate only a few bites of his cold dinner. The question was back: what was he going to do about Fagan's offer? He resisted. He'd make no decisions until the light of day.

THE LIGHT OF DAY ON THURSDAY morning only heralded the end of a sleepless night. His quandary still sat heavy on his mind. But a phone call from DaShawn before he left for work did make a difference.

"Grandpa? They're not gonna let me pass."

"What?" Harry could hear big sobs on the other end of the line. "Whaddaya mean?"

"They say I ain't gonna be a fifth grader 'cause I haven't been in class enough this year."

"Oh, wow. I bet that makes you feel terrible."

"Yeah. I don't want to repeat fourth grade again. I hate school. When can I come live with you, Grandpa?"

"I don't know, DaShawn. You know—"

"But Grandpa, you promised! You said you'd keep my room for me, so why can't I come home now?"

Oh boy, now he was calling it *home*. "You know what's going on, DaShawn. I gotta take care of these charges against me first. And I *am* keepin' your room for you. There's nothin' in it 'cept what you left here. Okay, buddy?"

A long pause was punctuated by with a muffled sob and a big sniff. "Yeah, guess so. But hurry, Grandpa. I don't like it out here."

"I'm doin' the best I can. Now you go on to school and do your best. Maybe we can work out this grade thing later. Okay?"

"O-o-kay Grandpa. But … aw, never mind. 'Bye."

Harry put down his phone, grabbed his cap, and headed for work. Family had to come first. That's all there was to it. If history or the press or even God judged him for giving a pass to corruption when he'd had a chance to address it, too bad. He couldn't let his own son down a second time … uh, he meant *grandson*.

On the way to work, Harry realized there were a couple of complications in Fagan's plan. First, was Fagan thinking clearly when he offered the deal? What if Harry declined to testify as Fagan wanted but Gilson subpoenaed Harry anyway? Of course, Gilson was trying to build a larger, stronger case against Fagan, but the report Harry had already signed might be enough to take it to the grand jury, then it would be out of Harry's hands. Had Fagan even considered that possibility?

The second complication was even more immediate: who was going to act first? He could call Gilson and tell him he didn't want to testify—that was Harry's end of the bargain. But what guaranteed Fagan would—or even could—pull the plug on Harry's case?

It all seemed too haywire, and Harry was afraid he'd end up on the short end. Still, DaShawn's call that morning haunted him. He had to do whatever it took to get DaShawn back.

The urgency of that goal simmered in the back of Harry's mind all morning while he wished the residents of Richmond Towers good day as they left for work or play or shopping—some never seemed to need to work. There had to be a more certain way for him to get out of his mess. If necessary, he was resigned to not trying to fight corruption, but he didn't want to get cheated out of fulfilling his promise to DaShawn.

Mrs. Worthington came out of the elevator and across the lobby to stand in front of Harry's desk, her white hair looking rather blue today. "Oh, Mr. Bentley," she said, digging in her purse, "has my cab arrived yet?"

Harry looked out the window. Why was it always a cab with this woman? Couldn't she simply turn her head and look for herself? "I don't think so, Mrs. Worthington. Did you call one already?"

"Of course, just before I came down. Why else would I ask?" With loose skin draping below her thin forearms, she started piling things from her purse on the end of the chest-high, half-moon counter above Harry's desk. "What did I do with those Tums? Would you have some Tums I could borrow, Mr. Bentley? My stomach's been acting up on me this morning, and I ... oh, here they are. Never mind."

She opened the plastic bottle and popped a green and pink wafer in her mouth.

Harry glanced out the window as a movement caught his eye. "Could this be your cab, Mrs. Worthington?" He needed to get her out of there, as quick as possible.

Hurrying her was the wrong idea. She swung around, causing her open purse to rake half of its contents onto the floor behind his desk. "Oh no. Oh no," she wailed.

Harry bent down to help her pick them up.

"No, no. I can do that. You go hold the cab for me."

"He's not gonna drive off this instant, Mrs. Worthington. He just got here."

"Nevertheless, I can manage. You just go on out there."

Harry complied, pulling the bill of his cap a little lower as he went through the revolving door. He held up his index finger indicating "just a minute" when he caught the driver's attention. The man nodded, and Harry turned to go back just as a harried Mrs. Worthington came bustling through the door, still trying to close the top of her purse.

He doffed his cap. "You have a good day now, Mrs. Worthington."

She didn't respond.

Harry shook his head and went back in as the cab pulled away. When he stepped around the end of his desk, his foot kicked something on the floor. He bent down. A cell phone, probably from Mrs. Worthington's purse. He ran out with it, but the cab had already disappeared into the traffic.

That woman was so scatterbrained, Harry almost had a drop of sympathy for her. Back inside, he left the cell on the end of counter to remind him to ask her about it when she returned, then sat back and began reading the *Tribune*. But for the remainder of the morning, that cell phone on the otherwise clear countertop seemed out of place and kept catching his attention.

Cell phone.

The *cell phone*. That was it! Donita's cell phone would solve his problems. Gilson had convinced him to put it out of his mind, but if he *could* retrieve it, he could clear himself no matter what Fagan did. And, if Fagan found some new way to threaten him, he could do whatever Fagan asked—withdraw his report or anything—and still nail Fagan simply by turning the phone over to the Review Board, anonymously, if necessary. Fagan would never need to know where it came from.

Harry went back over the facts: DaShawn was certain the phone contained a video of Fagan beating Donita and holding bags of drugs. He was also certain Fagan put the phone into his pocket and took it. Cindy had searched Fagan's car and desk and said he seldom used his locker. So, either Fagan took it home or he threw it away.

Harry tapped a pen on the desk, letting his mind review the backyard barbecue Fagan had thrown for the Special Ops team on Labor Day a couple of years ago. Harry had gone in the house to use the bathroom, but he'd been so drunk, he could hardly recall what the inside of the place looked like. He remembered a long hall and nice hardwood floors and a bright kitchen, but where were the bedrooms? Along the hall, probably.

What if he just went over to the house when no one was home and searched the place? Fagan had already broken into *his* place and pawed through enough of his stuff to disarm his weapon. Okay, tit for tat. And he wouldn't even need to toss Fagan's place, just creep it. Either the cell was in some obvious place, or Fagan had thrown it away. The jerk had no reason to think it contained incriminating evidence, so he wouldn't have hidden it.

The pen stopped tapping.

Yeah, that's what he had to do.

But how could he be sure no one would be home? Fagan had a wife and kids. They might be gone during the day, but that was a rather dangerous time to break and enter. *Breaking and entering*, oh yeah, now he was prepared to become a real criminal to get what he wanted. This was crazy!

Harry tossed the pen so hard it bounced across the lobby. No, it was simply the only option left open to him. Desperate men do desperate things! Isn't that what they always said? But he needed time, time to plan his little caper, case the place, try to figure out when the whole family might be out. He checked to be sure the lobby was empty, flipped open his cell phone, and dialed.

"Hey, Fagan. Harry."

"Harry, my man. How's it hangin'? Ready to do business?"

"I think so, but I'm gonna need a little more time. Know what I mean?"

A heavy silence weighed on the end of the line. Then … "Actually, I don't. Seems to me, all you gotta do is contact the Review Board, tell 'em you made a mistake and can't swear to all those lies you told. That shouldn't take any time at all."

Harry hesitated as he scrambled to think what to say. The most convincing excuse was the one closest to the truth. "Look. It's a sweet deal, Matty, and I'm workin' on my end of it. But I got a crisis goin' on with my grandson that I gotta deal with first. I need some time, but I promise I'll get back to you early next week."

"Harry, this don't make no sense to me. I thought the charges against you *were* about your grandson, and that's what this arrangement was designed to fix. Know what I mean?"

Harry's stomach tightened. Fagan knew far too many details of this whole situation.

"Seems to me, Harry, time is of the essence, at least for you. Now for me, I can wait. I can give you the time. Nothin's gonna happen to me all that fast. But you? Like I said, connections sometimes break down, accidents happen. You get my drift?"

Accidents? Yeah, Harry got his drift, but he wasn't gonna let Fagan bully him anymore. "Early next week, Fagan." He pulled the phone away from his ear and started to close it, then reconsidered. "Oh, by the way, there is something you need to work on in the meantime. You gotta figure out a way to verify to me that my case has been closed *before* I recant with the Review Board. I'm not gonna get suckered on this deal. You understand?"

Harry closed his phone. That'd give Fagan a little homework to do.

Chapter 26

THE NEXT DAY AT WORK, Harry got a call from Estelle. He had mixed feelings at the sound of her voice. On the one hand, he was eager for their relationship to progress. On the other, she was a bit too perceptive. Given the stuff going down right now, he felt a little like he was about to be caught looking at porn on his computer screen.

"Oh hi, Estelle. How you doin'?"

"Doin' good, Harry. Say, I was callin' to see if you were still planning on coming to church this Sunday."

Harry thought fast. "Uh, yeah. Don't see any problem with it. Why?"

"Well, I was just thinkin', since we've gone out a couple times with you pickin' up the tab, I wanted to invite you over to my place after church for dinner, if you'd like." She paused a moment. "I was thinkin' maybe some orange-smothered pork chops and holiday corn puddin' followed by peach cobbler."

Sounded great to Harry … except—

"'Course if you'd prefer something else, I do have another option or two—"

"No, no. That sounds like down home for sure ... it's just that ... who all were you thinkin' of?" He wasn't very eager to have dinner with Leslie Stuart.

"I was only thinkin' of you and me, Harry. But if you wanted to bring your mother—"

"Oh, no, no. You and me'd be just great, Estelle. I'm sure Mama can get along by herself."

"Good. And since Stu's visiting her folks in Indianapolis, I'll catch a ride home with the Baxters after church. That way you can take your mom home and get her settled before coming on over. And if it clears up—and warms up a little—we can eat out on the back porch, since you seem to like dining alfresco. Sound okay?"

"Sounds great to me."

He hung up and whooped, "TGIF, TGIF," doing a little happy shuffle with his feet. But the mantra didn't help his Friday pass more swiftly even though he now had something good to look forward to ... along with everything else, waiting for him once he went out through the revolving doors of Richmond Towers. Maybe he ought to say it like Estelle. He laughed at the memory of her, *"Thank ya, Jesus. Thank ya, Jesus,"* when he'd pulled his mother out from under the bed unhurt. He glanced around the lobby to be sure no one was there and said, "Thank ya, Jesus." He said it again, just a little louder, like he really meant it: "Thank ya, Jesus!"

So, was that a prayer?

He guessed so, but the last time he'd seriously tried to pray got him a confrontation with a crooked, gun-wielding cop. He'd asked God to do something—anything—to break open this mess over the charges he faced and get his grandson back. That was just before he found Fagan in his apartment. "Yeah, thank You, Jesus, for nearly gettin' my head shot off!" he muttered.

But he hadn't gotten shot.

And the confrontation had resulted in Fagan offering him a deal to solve his problem ... but at what price? The sacrifice of his integrity and letting a criminal go free? No way. If God wanted him to take such a deal, forget it. On the other hand, he could hardly believe God wanted him to commit a crime ... breaking and entering Fagan's house. It was just something he had to do—*a man's gotta do what a man's gotta do*. But he was pretty sure God wouldn't approve ... at least he didn't think so.

This religion stuff was ... he just didn't know. He wished he could really talk to someone about everything he was facing, get it all out there, including his little plan to retrieve that cell phone. But who would understand? Who could he talk to?

The day dragged slowly, causing Harry to watch the clock like he hadn't done since his part-time job as a grocery store clerk when he was a student down at the U of I.

When Draven didn't show at five, Harry began calling his cell phone. He redialed every five minutes until Draven finally answered around six-twenty. "Where are you? Why ain't you in here?"

"Uh, sorry. I'm on my way."

When "the door-dude," as Mrs. Fairbanks in the penthouse called him, hadn't arrived in fifteen minutes, which should have been enough time for him to get there, Harry began his phoning routine again, every call raising the tension higher.

Draven never answered, but at seven-fifteen he walked in the door.

"Ah, man, you're smashed. You're in no shape to work."

"Yeah, you're right." The young man held his arms out to his sides, tipped them to the left, and did a U-turn, making like an airplane heading back toward the door.

"Freeze." Harry said it like he was drawing a bead on the back of a fleeing criminal. "Where you think you're goin'?"

Draven turned around slowly, taking a little stutter step to the side to keep his balance. "You said I wasn't in any shape to work. Well, I agree. So I was heading home to sleep it off."

"You go out that door, and you're never coming back in again."

Draven raised his eyebrows. "Make up your mind. You want me to stay or you want me to go home? I really don't give a—"

"I'm not stayin' here the rest of the night, so you get back over here and pick up your shift. We'll deal with management tomorrow as to whether you keep your job."

Draven shrugged. "Whatever."

Harry didn't trust himself to come out from behind the desk to meet the guy, so when he saw that Draven was veering right, he went the other way and headed straight toward the parking garage and home. He'd done his part, waiting until his relief arrived, even though he was two hours and fifteen minutes late. He'd take that up with management. In the meantime, he figured the residents of Richmond Towers could get themselves tucked in bed by themselves. If they weren't warmly welcomed by "the door-dude," that'd be on Draven's head.

SATURDAY HE CAME IN to see what had happened.

Tony Gomez pushed his doorman's cap back a little on his head when Harry asked about Draven. "Oh, man, I think they fired him, Mr. Bentley. Now what we gonna do?"

"What makes you think they fired him?"

"Oh, when I came in to work, it was like an uprising down here. Mr. Martin was here, in the middle of the night, and some of the residents were yelling at him and sayin' Draven was sleeping on the chairs." He pointed to the lobby furniture. "Then that guy from the penthouse—what's his name, Fairbanks, he was on his way out—said Draven was stoned. He sure looked that way to me."

"So what happened?"

"Mr. Martin, he told Draven to come in today and pick up his check—minus last night's pay."

"Serves him right, but can he do that?"

"I guess so. He's *el jefe*, you know, the big boss." Tony shrugged, arching his brows over wide eyes.

"Yeah, but did he say what that means for us?"

"He not say nothin', man."

This was the last thing Harry needed to hear, but what could he do? "Look, Tony, this is your double shift right now, isn't it?" Tony nodded. "And Martin's not told me a thing yet, so we keep on the same schedule. But you probably better prepare to put in some overtime—talk to your wife or whatever—'cause the word might come down at the last minute."

Tony Gomez stood there shaking his head. Harry could see he wasn't very happy. "Look, Tony, this is what I'm gonna suggest. I'm gonna tell Mr. Martin that you and I will cover the day and evening slots, but until they hire another guy, we gotta let the graveyard shift go. It's only fair, unless he wants to pick it up himself, 'cause there's no way we can cover that many hours. Sound okay?"

"Sounds good to me, man. You know I can use a little overtime, but I got my day job."

It was the first time Harry realized that Gomez was working two jobs. Perhaps Tony was able to grab a few winks in the wee hours of the morning. Harry smiled to himself, recalling how he'd worked on perfecting the ability to snooze a little yet come quickly awake to greet residents when they came in. Maybe they ought to install some kind of an electric eye that would be a reliable alarm for the night guys, at least. 'Course, nothing could have brought Draven to full attention quick enough.

Harry got the call later Saturday afternoon.

"But Mr. Martin, there's no way two men can pull twenty-four/seven."

"It'll only be until we find a replacement."

"Then this is my suggestion," said Harry. "Tony and I will do the day and evening shift. Almost everyone is in by midnight, and anyone leaving early in the morning is in too much of a hurry to care whether someone's at the desk or not."

"This building is committed to twenty-four-hour doorman service," Mr. Martin insisted. "It's in the contracts."

"Look, Mr. Martin, I'm not working a sixty-hour week, not even temporarily. If you feel the residents won't cut you a little grace in this emergency, then hire a temp."

The line was silent. That was a good idea, probably one Martin hadn't even thought of. Harry didn't think he was much of a manager—salesman, maybe, but not a manager. Finally, Martin responded. "I'll look into that. But can you come in Sunday evening?"

Sunday evening ... Harry sighed. That might cut short his time with Estelle. But at least the guy was asking rather than demanding. "Yeah, I'll be there ... Want me to tell Gomez 'bout the new schedule?"

"If you would, please. I'd appreciate it."

ON SUNDAY MORNING, Harry parked in the large lot for the Gateway shopping center and, with his mother, followed Estelle's lead toward one of the peripheral buildings. Painted in a bold red script across the windows of the storefront were the words *SouledOut*

Community Church. Harry hung back. He hadn't been to church for a lifetime, but had it changed this much—church in a mall? Then, remembering to be the gentleman, he stepped forward and held the glass door for his mother and Estelle. Over their heads—his mother seemed to keep shrinking these days, even with her wig—Harry surveyed the large, low-ceilinged room. The walls were painted coral and salmon with blue trim. Only the many bright banners—*Hallelujah; Sing to Jesus; Praise Him, Praise Him; Jesus Is Lord; Ride On, King Jesus*—distinguished the décor from a cheery Mexican restaurant. In front of him stretched several semicircular rows of sturdy chairs upholstered in a rich tweedy material that picked up the colors in the walls. People stood around in little groups, chatting. Carl Hickman broke away from one group and made a beeline toward Harry.

"Hey my man, Harry. Good to see you, bro."

"Yeah, I promised my mom and Estelle I'd bring 'em, so ..." He shrugged and continued glancing around, noting other brothers from the Tuesday evening Bible study: Peter Douglass, Denny Baxter, and the preacher, Pastor Clark, up near the front going over a sheet of paper with a tall, attractive black woman. He remembered seeing her at the shelter at Fun Night. Wait, could she be Peter Douglass's wife? Whew!

Behind them several musicians were setting up, tuning guitars and bass, doing sound checks, testing the keyboard, and *tada-da, tada-da, tada-da, crash* on some nice traps. Harry brought his attention back to Carl, who was saying, "... things going with your grandson?"

"Oh, DaShawn? Talked to him a couple days ago. He's okay." Wait a minute, these guys didn't go for shinin' one another on. They put it right out there on the table, whatever it was. He gave a nervous laugh and glanced to the side. "Actually, Carl, he's not doin' so well. Seems they won't let him pass to the next grade. Bummed him out. Guess he missed too many days of school this year."

"Ah, that's cold, man. Especially for a kid like that."

"Yeah, I just hope we can get it worked out later."

The tall black woman was at the mic. "Good morning, brothers and sisters! Could we find our seats and get ready to praise the Lord?"

Harry leaned close to Carl. "Is that Peter's wife?" He nodded toward the front.

"Who, Avis? Oh yeah, that's her."

"Hm."

Harry nodded to Carl, then followed Estelle and his mother. He would have preferred sitting in the back, but they filed into the third row, all the way to the center. No easy exit from there. What if he had to go to the restroom? In fact, where were the restrooms? Probably through those far doors.

The band exploded with a rousing beat, and Peter Douglass's wife began to swing her hands in an arc to meet over her head, signaling everyone to join in clapping. "Come on, saints! Let's practice singing with those elders in heaven." A PowerPoint suddenly lit up the wall behind the band with the words.

You are worthy. You are worthy,
To receive glory and honor and power, amen.
For You have created all things,
All things for Your pleasure, they were created, amen.

Holy, holy, Lord God Almighty,
Who was and is and who is to come!

Harry's mother sat down, and he started to follow her lead when he noticed that no one else sat except for a few of the elderly people. Well, he wasn't elderly. He looked around. There had to be a couple hundred people there, rather equally mixed black and white, with a few Latinos. Harry didn't know if he'd ever been in church with white people ... except for a couple funerals for cops, killed in the line of duty, but that didn't count. You had to be there. This was kind of like the men's group ... and down at the end of the row he saw Ben Garfield, looking like an overworked Jewish grandfather with a wiggling tyke in each arm. Harry thought he might know a little bit about how Ben felt, trying to keep up.

Harry picked up the beat and joined in the clapping. No reason to draw attention to himself. The song repeated itself, and Harry squinted at the words on the wall.

Several other songs followed, and Harry admitted the music was pretty good. He'd always liked music, even gospel music on the radio and the songs he remembered as a boy. When the singing ended and everyone sat down, a black man stood up to preach. Estelle leaned over. "That's Pastor Cobbs, one of our pastors for SouledOut." But even though Pastor Cobb put a lot of energy into his preaching—so much so that he had to wipe his face with a little red towel every once in a while—Harry was thinking about finding that cell phone.

Before he knew it, the pastor was asking people to come forward for prayer, and Harry hadn't really heard a thing he'd said. So what was he doin' in church, planning a B&E?

Chapter 27

THE STAIRS UP TO ESTELLE'S APARTMENT were narrow, each worn wooden step creaking under Harry's heavy tread. She might live on the top floor—the second floor of the Baxter's two-flat—but this sure wasn't a penthouse. The door at the top of the stairs stood ajar, the intoxicating aroma of genuine home cooking drifting out to greet him.

"Hello," Harry called, knowing Estelle was expecting him since she'd buzzed him in down below.

"Come on in! I'm back here in the kitchen."

Harry stepped into an airy living room with melon-colored walls and filmy lime-green curtains. After one look at the gleaming hardwood floor, he leaned against the wall and lifted one foot to balance like a stork as he began to remove a shoe.

"Harry, you still here?"

"Yeah, just takin' off my shoes."

"Oh, you don't have to do that."

Harry peeked down the hallway. On the right were three doors. On the left was a large archway leading into the dining room. Through it he could see the kitchen doorway. Estelle stood there with some kind of a casserole in her mitted hands. She gestured with her head. "Just come on back."

He retied his shoe and stepped gingerly into the hallway, noticing that the first door on the right was open and led into an off-white bedroom trimmed in burgundy with matching bedspread and curtains. Could that be Estelle's bedroom? No, no, he wasn't going there … yet, or maybe ever. Harry had gotten the message: Estelle was firm about marriage coming first. And he had to admit, old school wasn't so bad. At least, it reduced the precedent for a lot of suspicion.

He walked through the sparsely furnished dining room and took up a stance like the cool guy he was—he hoped—leaning against the kitchen doorjamb. The workspace was small, and Estelle looked to be managing just fine. He'd only get in her way if he got in there and displayed his culinary ignorance. Still, he thought he ought to offer, and close quarters with the charming Estelle might not be so bad.

"Need any help?"

"Sure. Whaddaya think, Harry, should we try eatin' out on the deck?" She nodded over her shoulder toward the back door.

"Okay by me."

"Good. Maybe you could go out and set the table. There's the plates and stuff." She pointed to the settings stacked on the end of the counter just inside the door. "You can take them on out there. I already cleaned off the table and chairs. And when you come back, I'll have a pitcher of water for you. You want ice?"

"Yeah, sure." He hesitated a moment.

"Oh, if you want to wash your hands, the restroom's across the hall, the next door past Stu's bedroom."

Okay, so that enticing lair wasn't Estelle's bedroom, after all. As he headed for the restroom, he resisted the temptation to go the few extra steps to peek through the door that had to lead into Estelle's room.

A few moments later when he got out to the deck, he put down the table settings and surveyed the small yard below backed up by a two-car garage against the alley. That alley … He let his gaze drift along it, noting the various backyards.

Something was too familiar.

Oh heck! He ducked his head, not really able to hide. There was nothing to hide behind. But across the alley and one house over stood Fagan's building—he'd almost forgotten that it faced the street just south of the Baxters' place—and he'd been in that yard before.

His memories were still veiled by the alcohol haze of that Labor Day barbecue, but the more Harry studied the layout, the more he recalled the party Fagan had hosted for the whole SOS team. Fagan had been king of the grill that day, turning out brats and chicken and hamburgers as fast as the crew could eat them. On the covered back porch had been two large ice chests full of beer. A table beside them held the hard stuff—Jim Beam, Seagram's, Smirnoff, Bacardi—and someone had even brought a bottle of Chivas, all to Harry's delight.

He remembered planting himself in a sky chair hanging from the limb of a large elm tree. But there was no elm tree now. Perhaps it fell victim to Dutch elm disease. Harry had sat in that chair, letting its swinging motion fan the buzz of booze into a perfect storm until he staggered up the porch steps and into the house looking for a restroom. Now, in his mind, he traced the layout of the first floor: The kitchen, then—

"Harry, you didn't set the table yet, and here I'm bringing out the food." Estelle stood behind him with a platter of sizzling pork chops.

"Oh, sorry." Maybe eating out here wasn't such a good idea. What if Fagan came out, looked up, and recognized him? "Uh, you sure it's not too cold out here for you?"

"I'm good. It's up to you."

Harry hesitated. Sitting up there in Estelle's "bird's nest" would be a good way to case Fagan's place. Might learn something.

"Nah. Let's eat here." Harry waved his hand, and Estelle went back in while he distributed the plates, silverware, and napkins, keeping watch on Fagan's place out of the corner of his eye.

Estelle returned with a corn pudding casserole, a dish of buttered green beans with slivered almonds and shaved parmesan cheese, and a bowl of rice and peas, carrying all three like an experienced waitress. Amazing.

Rice and peas … He loved rice and peas. "Hey, I thought you said you didn't do Jamaican."

Estelle pouted. "When did I say that?"

"When I was askin' you to go sailing."

"Sailing? Oh, yeah. No, no. I just wasn't gonna take no mojo from you. But these here ain't real pigeon peas, just red beans. Tastes nearly the same, though."

"Looks good to me."

"Go ahead now, you sit down, and I'll be right back."

She gestured to the chair on the far side of the table before going back inside. But that would put Harry's back to the alley. He glanced after Estelle, then sat on the side where he could see the alley … and perhaps hide behind her, if need be. When Estelle returned, she hesitated for a moment, eyeing him a little skeptically, then shrugged and placed a small vase with a single purple iris in it in the center of the table.

"There. I think that's everything? Oops. Forgot something."

She returned a moment later and placed a small gravy boat near Harry. "This is some extra orange glaze for the pork chops if you want. Okay?"

Harry inhaled its tangy aroma and rubbed his hands together. "Mm. This is great!"

Estelle sat down with a *whumph* and unfolded her napkin into her lap. "You want to do us the honors, Harry?"

Harry had no clue. Did she want him to serve the meat or … or what? Then it hit him: She was expecting him to say grace, to actually pray out loud. What was he supposed to say? All he could remember was, *"God is great. God is good. Let us thank Him for our food. Amen."* A little lame for an adult prayer.

"Uh, you know, this being your house and all, maybe you should be the one to do the prayin'."

"Okay, whatever. Just didn't want to presume, in case you thought it was the man's role or somethin'." She bowed her head and began praying before Harry realized it. "Father God, we thank You for this blessed day and for the chance to worship You this morning. Now please bless this food …"

Harry tuned out. She was speaking just like the men in the Bible study, talking to God like He was sitting right there at the table with them. This was something he still didn't understand. It was so obvious they believed what they were doing was reality. To Harry, any kind of prayer had been like grasping at straws of hope that God might—just might—hear his desperate requests … occasionally if … if Jesus paved the way, like Pastor Clark had said. But Estelle and all the brothers prayed like they were God's kids, welcome to walk right into the—how had that verse put it?—right into "the throne of grace." Yeah, he remembered those words.

" … Amen." Estelle smiled at him, picked up the platter of pork chops and handed them to Harry. "Help yourself, now. As you can see, there's plenty, so don't be bashful."

Harry piled food on his plate and took a few bites. Estelle took a drink of water and cleared her throat. "So, what did ya think of church this morning?"

He swallowed. "Oh, pretty good." Harry couldn't help glancing beyond Estelle's shoulder to Fagan's house. "I liked the music."

"Well, if you like music, you ought to hear our gospel choir. You got a voice, Harry? Maybe you oughta try singin' with 'em. And Oscar Frost—he wasn't there today, either—but you oughta hear that man on that sax of his. Like honey from heaven."

She took a couple more bites, then wiped her mouth. "Harry, what's the matter with you? You've hardly eaten a thing. Don't you like it?"

"Oh, sorry. Yeah, it's great." He shoveled several bites into his mouth, determined to pay attention to Estelle's meal. But the sound of childish chatter made him glance at Fagan's house again. Two kids were coming out of the back door—a boy maybe as old as DaShawn, dressed in a Cubs uniform, and a blonde girl of about six, outfitted in pink—pink top, pink pants, and pink gym shoes. Even a pink floppy hat with elastic under her chin. Both children dragged roller luggage—the girl's was pink—bouncing them down the steps and coming toward the garage.

And there was Fagan and his wife coming out, too. Also bringing luggage. Harry dodged his head to the side so he was mostly hidden by Estelle, should Fagan look up.

"Harry Bentley, you haven't heard a thing I've said! Whatchu lookin' at anyway?" Estelle looked over her shoulder like there might be a giant caterpillar crawling up her chair.

"Sorry, Estelle. It's nothin'." Fagan and his family had disappeared into their garage now, so Harry straightened up and smiled at Estelle. "What were you sayin'?"

The garage door across the alley came up, and Harry could see Fagan loading the luggage into the trunk of his silver Chrysler Concorde. Then a door slammed, but the noise came from below the deck where Harry and Estelle were eating. Harry could hear a man's voice saying, "I'll get it a little later."

Estelle was still glancing behind her, trying to see what had captured Harry's attention. She turned back, squirming in her seat and adjusting her shoulders back and forth like a hen settling into her nest. "Well, it ain't nothin' when you don't even hear what a body's sayin', Harry Bentley."

She busied herself eating, looking down at her plate and chewing hard. Harry knew was she upset.

"Hey, I'm sorry, Estelle. Really." Still, he glanced down at the alley again. The voice belonged to Denny Baxter, who was now walking toward the alley, carrying a large black trash bag. Baxter opened the bin and tossed it in, wiped his forehead with the back of his hand, and turned toward Fagan's open garage. "You guys headin' out somewhere?" Harry heard him call. In spite of Estelle's irritation, Harry couldn't retrieve his attention as Fagan responded.

"Yeah, sendin' the family down to Florida. Promised the kids a trip to Disney World if their grades were good enough. So ..." He shrugged and slammed the trunk.

"You not goin' with 'em?"

"Nah. Can't get away right now. Too much poppin' around here."

Harry took a bite of the corn pudding, flecked like lights on a Christmas tree with small chunks of red and green sweet peppers. He forced a look at Estelle. She still looked mad, busying herself with cutting a bite of her pork chop. Harry shook his head and looked back down to the alley. Right now Fagan was more important.

"Well, you guys have a good trip." Denny Baxter waved and turned back up the walk to his house as Fagan's car backed out of the garage and headed down the alley.

"This corn puddin' is fabulous!" Harry smiled when Estelle looked up. But his mind was working on the plan: Fagan's family would be out of the house for a few days. Now was the time to get in there and find that cell phone! All he had to worry about was finding out when Fagan was on duty. Cindy could probably help him with that.

"You thinkin' 'bout some other woman, Harry Bentley? 'Cause I can't figure nothin' else that would so captivate a man's mind when we're tryin' to have dinner together."

Harry leaned back in his chair and sighed deeply. "I'm sorry, Estelle. No, it's not some other woman—" At least not the way she meant it. "It's ..." What could he say? "It's just this situation with my grandson. It's like I'm lettin' him down. Leastwise, that's the way he sees it. You know, he called last Thursday all upset 'cause they won't pass him on to the next grade. They say he's missed too many days of school this year."

Estelle riveted him with a long stare. She was probably trying to decide whether to believe his distraction wasn't some other woman. Finally her expression softened, but her eyes squinted a little. "I thought you said all this was gonna get cleared up when you went to court last week."

He shoveled in a huge bite of green beans. "Love these." He swallowed and took a drink of water. "But didn't quite work out with DaShawn like I hoped." The squint relaxed, but Harry still wasn't sure Estelle believed it had only been DaShawn that had distracted him. "It's gonna work out, sooner or later. In the meantime, my grandson's the one who pays, and that really has me in knots."

"Sounds like somethin' that can only be handled with prayer."

Harry shook his head. "I don't know. I tried prayin', but it don't seem to work. I've pretty much given up on God." He wanted to tell Estelle the whole story, how the last time he prayed, he'd ended up facing a man with a gun—within minutes. He knew it wasn't quite that simple, but … He wanted to tell her about the deal Fagan offered, the deal that forced him to choose between his grandson and his own integrity. He wanted to tell her how he'd concluded the only way out was to burgle Fagan's house, the house right across the alley from where they now sat, and *that* was the reason he'd been so distracted, not some woman.

But he couldn't. He couldn't talk to her about any of those things.

Estelle sighed. "Well, Harry, all I can say is that sometimes God's shortest path between two points doesn't look very straight to us, but He has His ways, and they always work out for our good in the end. You just need to keep on prayin', tell Him everything, how you feel, how you're disappointed in Him. Tell Him everything."

"You don't think He'd get mad if I told Him how I feel?"

"You don't think He already knows?"

Chapter 28

HARRY WANTED TO SEARCH FAGAN'S HOUSE for Donita's cell phone that very afternoon, but by the time he helped Estelle clear her deck table—she wouldn't hear of him actually washing the dishes—and thanked her for the wonderful meal, it was time for him to head down to Richmond Towers to relieve Gomez. It also had been over an hour and a half since Fagan had taken his family to the airport, definitely enough time that he might be returning any moment, even if they'd flown out of Midway Airport on Chicago's southwest side. Harry needed a more secure window of time if he was going to break into someone's house. And besides, it was still daylight.

"Estelle, I can't tell you how much I enjoyed the dinner. I hope you'll forgive me for being a little preoccupied, but I'm sure things'll settle down pretty soon."

"Hm. They usually do."

"Do what?"

"Settle down. Things usually settle down if we just trust the Lord. Know what I'm sayin'?"

"Oh yeah." He grinned, feeling a little like she was the Sunday school teacher and he was a fourth grade student. Then again, when it came to this God thing, he was barely even a student. "Maybe if you think about it, you could send up a little prayer."

"Oh I do. I pray for you every day, Harry Bentley."

"You do?"

"Of course. Got you on my list."

He didn't know what to say to that. At first, the idea of her praying for him every day sounded special, like maybe he meant more to her than he realized. But when she said he was on her *list*, that meant there were other people on it too. He didn't know what to think. But some extra prayer was good … wasn't it?

Even though he was a little late leaving Estelle's, Harry drove around the block and past the front of Fagan's place. Still didn't look like anyone was home. All the front blinds were pulled. He made one more lap, looping around the block to the south this time rather than drive by the Baxters' where someone might recognize him. Harry crept by Fagan's house as slow as he could without attracting too much attention. Maybe he would come back tonight after he got off work and stake out the place for a while, get the pulse of the neighborhood.

He was ten minutes late relieving Gomez by the time he got to Richmond Towers.

"Sorry 'bout that, *amigo*. Hope I didn't mess you up too much."

Tony Gomez shrugged but didn't look Harry in the eye. "When we gonna get a replacement for that night guy? This weekend schedule's killin' me."

"Don't know. But when I come in tomorrow morning, I'll check with Mr. Martin. Maybe I can light some kind of a fire under him."

Heading toward the revolving door, Gomez glanced back. "Yeah, you do that, man, 'cause now I'm gonna be late to my other job."

Harry waved and then sat down on the swivel stool. There were crumbs on the desk counter, like Gomez had been eating cookies. Harry went to the cabinet for a rag and cleaning spray. He set to work cleaning the counter, the desk, the chairs, the lobby tables, handprints off the glass doors. The doormen weren't expected to be custodians, but somehow it calmed Harry's nerves, maybe like doing penance for being late … or perhaps some kind of indulgence for the break-in he was planning.

That was stupid. There was no connection. He threw the rag and spray back in the cabinet and went back to his seat, opening the Sunday *Tribune* to the sports page.

The White Sox were playing the third game of a series with Cleveland. He got out the little TV to see if the game was still on, but by the time he got it turned on, he'd just missed the end of the ninth. Sox 8, Indians 10. Bummer.

A commotion outside in the access drive caught his attention. He flicked off the TV, adjusted his cap, and came out from behind his desk, ready to do his doorman thing.

Mrs. Fairbanks and her boys were getting out of their rented minivan … along with an old lady and—Harry walked toward the doors, a scowl deepening the grooves between his eyebrows—what was that? A yellow hairball of a dog bounced out of the van, its rear end wagging right and left while its front paws bounced alternately up and down like the sidewalk was as hot as a skillet. The younger boy snapped a leash onto its collar and headed toward the park while the older boy—the smart-mouth—came toward the lobby.

"Mom says she needs a luggage cart," he said as he came through the door.

"No doubt." Harry grabbed the cart with its brass arch for hanging clothes and headed out. "Could you hold open that non-revolving door for me, son?"

The boy gave him a look, probably didn't like being called *son*—Harry made a note not to do it again—but obliged as Harry wheeled the cart to the curb side.

"Mr. Bentley!" The Firecracker from the penthouse threw her arms wide and gave Harry such a hug that he almost stumbled backward. It lasted only a second before she stepped back and looked at him with surprise on her face. "What are you doing working on Sunday? I thought the door-dude—"

Harry burst out laughing. "The 'door-dude,' as you so aptly call him, got himself fired. I have to fill in until they hire his replacement. And who is this lovely lady?" Harry tipped his head in a little bow toward the older woman, who stood beside the car looking flustered at keeping track of all the items in her arms.

"Oh … This is my mother, Martha Shepherd, from North Dakota. Mom, this is Mr. Bentley. He's the doorman here at Richmond Towers, and also a good friend."

Harry doffed his cap. "I'm very pleased to meet you, ma'am—"

The barking hairball came bouncing up, followed by a breathless boy. Mrs. Fairbanks grinned. "And, uh, this"—she did a Vanna White toward the dog—"is Dandy, my mom's doggy companion." The little yellow mutt danced and turned circles in front of the old lady until he got his rump scratched and a pat on the head, then he bounced over to Harry and sniffed his shoes. Harry stood stock still, hoping the dog didn't mistake him for a fire hydrant.

When all seemed safe, he replaced his cap and looked at Mrs. Fairbanks, giving her what he hoped was a welcoming smile. "I see. You've multiplied." She seemed to have a habit of bringing home strays. What would her husband do this time? He decided to venture an inquiry. "Are you expected?"

She flushed and looked down at the dog.

Uh-oh! She hadn't told him, but she recovered quickly and grinned. "Uh, I hope so. It was kind of a last-minute thing. I left a message …"

"Mm. A message." Harry lifted bags out of the rear of the minivan and piled them on the cart, the older boy helping with a couple of them. When Harry had balanced the heavier ones, he looked at her. "Would you like me to call upstairs and tell Mr. Fairbanks you've arrived?" It might temper his response if he had to face her down here in public.

Mrs. Fairbanks gave him a wan smile. "Uh, that would be great. Thanks, Mr. Bentley. We can load the rest of the bags."

Harry went inside and called the penthouse while the family cleaned the trash out of the van and Mrs. Fairbanks parked it in a visitor space. The phone rang and rang until the answering machine picked up. No sense leaving a message, so Harry hung up as everyone came into the lobby, pushing the overloaded luggage car.

"No answer upstairs," he said to Mrs. Fairbanks.

A puzzled look crossed her face as she stopped.

"You need some help getting that upstairs?" Harry wasn't supposed to leave the door, but …

"No, that's okay. We can make it. Got two good helpers."

Uh … yeah. And would that be the dog and the old lady? "Well, you have a good evening now, Mrs. Fairbanks."

It was an hour later when Mr. Fairbanks came in like he was on a fashion runway, flashing the golden tan on his face, silver shades, open-necked silver-and-black silk shirt, and gray slacks.

"Evening, Mr. Fairbanks."

The man glanced Harry's way but said nothing as he slid his card through the slot in the security door.

Harry was glad he was not stationed at the top of the elevator to usher Mr. Fairbanks into the penthouse. He had an idea there'd be some sparks flying up there tonight. What was that girl thinking anyway, bringing home a dog and another old lady—mother or not? On the other hand, she was just being a normal human being with normal family issues. It was the stuffed suit that made it a problem. But Harry couldn't worry about that. He had his own issues … big ones, bigger issues than anyone around here could ever guess.

He was planning a felony!

AT MIDNIGHT, Harry put the little sign on the desk that read, "Doorman temporarily off duty. Sorry for the inconvenience," locked the desk, and left for the parking garage.

Even though he was tired and would have to be back on duty by eight in the morning, he took the extra time to drive over to Fagan's. He cruised slowly down the one-way street, looking for a parking space within sight of the brownstone. He wanted to just sit there for a while, observing what he might not have noticed in a drive-by. No legal parking spaces left, but there was a fire hydrant directly across the street from Fagan's. Adjoining cars impinged on the no-parking strip, but there was enough room for Harry to back his RAV4 in. If a cop came along—highly unlikely in the middle of the night—he could pull away.

He switched off the engine and sat there staring at Fagan's house, the blinds still pulled. A dim light glowed behind the living room window, probably on a timer as a "security" light since it didn't seem bright enough for reading and there were no bluish background flickers from a TV. With the family gone, Harry guessed Fagan might leave the blinds pulled day and night. That would be good for him. Neighbors wouldn't notice a stranger moving around inside the place. Funny how some people felt more secure with all their blinds pulled, when what the blinds actually did was prevent the residents from seeing what was going on *outside*, like a stranger sitting in a RAV4 across the street casing your place.

The windows along the side of the house ... did any of them match up with windows in the adjoining houses so that people might look in? And were those blinds pulled too? Harry quietly got out of his car and crossed over for a closer inspection. There were a few windows neighbors might look in, but then they or the neighbors' windows might be blinded as well for privacy.

A walk ran up the east side of Fagan's place with a gate about midway. Was it locked? Harry couldn't tell, but he looked for other avenues of escape, places around the house where he might hide if necessary. And where should he park? He needed a place close, but not on this one-way street and not any place where he might get blocked in.

He went back to his car and sat there for a few minutes with the windows down, absorbing the feel of this quiet neighborhood. He could hear sirens in the distance, but he'd been here at least ten minutes and hadn't seen anyone other than a few passing cars. Of course, it was nearly one o'clock. And it wouldn't be this quiet if he did the job in the day, with people coming and going.

He started his engine and drove around the block and down the alley that divided the Baxter side of the block to the north from the Fagan side of the block to the south, the same alley he'd overlooked when sitting on Estelle's porch. He rolled slowly along, bouncing over the speed bumps, until he found a wide spot near the end, just before coming to the next cross street. Signs announced, No Parking, Violators Will Be Towed at Owner's Expense. Below was a phone number for Lincoln Towing, one of Chicago's most notorious companies for grabbing people's cars. But the signs were old, and Harry doubted anyone would call on a car that sat there for no more than twenty minutes. It was not as if this was someone's designated parking space. Most important, the spot was close to Fagan's house and Harry could go either north or south when he came to the cross street.

He headed home, his mouth feeling dry, even though he'd cased the place and had a plan. Now all he had to do was confirm when Fagan was out of the house, and he wouldn't have long to find that window of opportunity before the family came back from Florida. He'd prefer the cover of dark for the job, but it might be easier to find a time during the day when Fagan was gone.

But how could he know for certain?

Chapter 29

MONDAY MORNING, JUNE 12, and Harry knew his time was running out. He'd put off responding to Fagan's deal about as long as he could. All he needed was a clear window of time when he could be certain Fagan wasn't home. He chuckled to himself as he drove to work. If he was a *real* cat burglar, he'd go right in when Fagan was home asleep. But even though he'd studied crime for twenty years, it had been as a law enforcement officer, not as a practitioner. He knew how guys got caught—what tripped them up and what he must avoid—and how many crimes went unsolved, but he was not about to creep Fagan's house when the man was home.

Besides, Fagan had a gun. And nothing would please him more than to catch Harry in his house. *Blam!* Even if Harry was unarmed, Fagan'd work it so it was a justifiable homicide and end up free of his troublesome snitch.

Harry stopped at the Dunkin' Donuts on Bryn Mawr Avenue and picked up breakfast: a couple of maple frosteds and a large coffee. He should be eating better and exercising more, but there'd be time for that when he got his life in order.

Maybe for a job like Fagan's he should go in packin' heat, a little protection from his Glock, just in case. No, no, no! That was an amateur's mistake, something a gangbanger or a strung-out addict might do. He wasn't going to shoot anyone. If he got caught, he'd just take his lumps like a man. And he'd be careful so even if he did get caught, they wouldn't be able to prove he intended to steal anything. Then he might get off with nothing more than criminal trespass, a Class A misdemeanor. The only thing he planned to take was that cell phone, and how could Fagan prove Harry'd stolen it if Fagan didn't have it in his house legally? If caught, that argument should be enough to keep him from being convicted for residential burglary, which was a Class 1 felony, and would get him four to fifteen years.

On the other hand, if he was armed, there would be no way to plead down to a misdemeanor.

He jumped back in his car and drove on to work, sipping coffee on the way.

No, he wouldn't take his Glock. Keep it simple, in and out, nothing but the cell phone. Still, he could feel the adrenaline pumping as he turned onto Sheridan Road and approached Richmond Towers. He understood now how career criminals could get off on their crimes—the challenge of it, the planning and calculating, outsmarting the mark, the lure of a big score. Yeah, what if Fagan had a shoebox full of that cash he'd been collecting on his raids? It's not as though he could deposit it in his regular bank account where the IRS might ask how he got it. Like the cell phone, how could Fagan file a complaint if Harry stole all his stolen loot?

Harry flushed that idea as he turned into the parking garage. He couldn't go there, not even in his mind. Focus! Focus! Focus! He was after one thing, the one thing that would clear his name so he could keep his promise to his grandson while not sacrificing his integrity as a cop. That was it; nothing more than the hot pink cell phone.

By the time Harry walked into the lobby with his coffee in one hand and his bag of doughnuts in the other, it was less than eight hours since he'd been there on duty the night before. He set his breakfast on his desk—the lower level, below the crescent counter—so it wouldn't be obvious to the residents that he was eating on the job.

Ding! The elevator doors opened and Mr. Fairbanks and his boys emerged. The boys, each carrying a sport bag and dressed in shorts, knit tops, and sneakers, came into the lobby. Mr. Fairbanks remained in the secured area, talking on his cell phone. He looked the suave businessman, as usual.

"So where you boys off to today? Looks like some fun."

The older boy gave Harry a dead-eye look, but the younger one—Paul, as Harry recalled—piped up. "We start sailing camp today down at ..." He turned to his brother. "Where was that place?"

"Burnham Harbor. Come on, let's go." The older boy headed toward the frontage road exit.

"Yeah," said Paul as he started to follow, "we're going to sailing camp at Burnham Harbor."

Mr. Fairbanks flung open the security door, phone pulled away from his ear. "Hey, where you think you're goin'? Car's this way, in the garage."

The older boy turned and gave his younger brother a shove. "Told ya."

Harry shook his head. Some pecking order! He stroked his beard and looked up toward the ceiling as though he had x-ray vision. Had Daddy made peace with the two new waifs the Firecracker brought home, or had the dog and the old lady been ejected sometime during the night as fast as the homeless bag woman had been sent packing a couple months before?

He had his answer within a half hour when Mrs. Fairbanks came down accompanied by her elderly mother and the bouncy yellow dog.

"Mornin', ladies. Off to see the Windy City?"

"No, no. Just going to work. Thought I'd take Mom along to see Manna House."

"And ..." Harry scowled and stared down at the wiggly canine, who obviously wanted nothing more than to be with his people.

"Oh, you mean Dandy?" Mrs. Fairbanks smiled like sunshine. "Surely you've heard about pet therapy, Mr. Bentley, how soothing animals can be for people in institutional settings. We're just doing a little field test." They jostled their way through the revolving door to the frontage road where they'd left the van in a guest parking space.

Hm. A field test, huh? Harry shook his head. This spunky woman seemed more likely to be headed for a crash test. And who would be there to pick up the pieces?

THE DAY DRAGGED BY. Shortly before five in the afternoon, when Gomez was due to come in, Harry called Cindy, his old partner. It seemed the only way he could discover when Fagan would be on duty and his home would be vacant.

The phone rang again and again. Harry thought it'd gone to voice mail when he heard a weak, "Yeah."

"Cindy? That you?"

"Yeah." She sounded like she was talking in a bucket.

"What's a matter? You got a minute?"

"Not really." There was a smothered moan.

"Cindy? What's goin' on? You okay?"

"No. I'm in the hospital, Harry, waitin' for this Vicodin to kick in so they can stitch up my arm."

"Stitch?… What happened?"

"Got myself shot, Harry. But I'm okay. Just a flesh wound. Hey, I can't really talk right now."

"Oh, man. You gonna be okay? You want me to come to the hospital? Where you at?"

"Stroger. And, no, I don't want you to come down here. I'll call you later."

The line went dead, and Harry was tempted to redial. But as he imagined the hospital emergency room, he knew he should leave her alone. Was anybody there with her? Had this happened on the job? Why was she just sitting there *waiting* to get her arm sewed up, and answering her own cell phone, no less? Well, he knew the answer to that one: It was Cook County Hospital's emergency room, and she might wait all evening before they finished treating her.

He frowned. How had she answered her cell phone while in the ER? He thought you couldn't make calls from within a hospital.

Maybe he ought to go down there anyway as soon as Gomez arrived. So what if Cindy said not to come? His partner needed help.

When Gomez arrived to relieve him, Harry hurried out to the parking garage and almost dialed Cindy before starting his RAV4. But what if they were working on her arm right then? He resisted and drove out of Richmond Towers. Should he go home or head down to Cook County Hospital? He turned into a McDonald's and ordered something to eat while he considered his options. But once he'd finished, he couldn't wait any longer. Surely she'd be out of the ER by now.

He dialed. It rang and rang until this time it did go to voice mail. "Uh … Cindy, this is Harry. Call me on my cell as soon as you can, okay?" He thought for a moment. "If you need anything, just let me know. I'll be there for you."

So, what did no answer mean? Was she okay? Was she in surgery or had she been admitted? How bad was it? But when he got home and still couldn't raise Cindy on her cell, he called the hospital to see if she'd been admitted. But the answer was, "Sorry. No Cindy Kaplan in our system." Good news? Or was she registered under some other name, like Cynthia Kaplan or who knows what?

He was about to leave the apartment and drive down there on his own when his phone rang. He sighed with relief as he saw the caller ID. "Hey Cindy. So where are you? You okay?"

"I'm okay, Harry. I'm home, and Mom's doin' her Jewish mother thing, lookin' after me. My dad's fussin' and fumin', so I don't need anything … except maybe rescuin' if this keeps up for more than twenty-four hours."

"You gonna be okay?"

"That's what they say, but I don't know. This thing hurts like my arm's been through a meat grinder. And I may end up as a desk jockey for a while. I don't know about goin' back on the streets."

"Sorry to hear that." He was quiet a few moments. "So what happened? How'd you get shot?"

There was a deep sigh on the other end of the line. "Well, this one was a legitimate raid. We had a warrant and everything."

"With Fagan? What the … ? Cindy, you should've gotten out of that unit when I did, Cindy."

"Maybe." She was silent.

"Uh … you still haven't said how you caught one."

He heard a big sigh. "I'm probably gonna have to tell this story twenty times before the investigation's over, so might as well tell it once to you. But no questions, okay?"

"Yeah, yeah."

"All right, so we came in on this guy. His apartment was dark, all the shades down, TV blaring. He was sitting across the room on the couch with a coffee table in front of him so we couldn't see his feet. Anyway, I went through the house securing the other rooms to make sure no one else was in there while Fagan and this rookie we had with us began askin' him questions. He wasn't really a rookie, but new to the unit. And my partner, Art, some help he was. He just stood back by the door covering the whole thing. Anyway, when I got back into the room, the rookie had worked his way around the other end of the coffee table and was gettin' in position on the guy's left side. I approached his right side, knowin' we were gonna have to take him into custody and cuff him. Just then the rookie yells, 'Gun!' and draws his weapon on the guy.

"I saw the gun, too, then. The guy had hidden it on the floor, under his foot, and was reaching for it. Instead of pulling my weapon, I lunged for his arm to keep him from getting to his pistol. Fagan came across the coffee table and so all three of us were grappling with the guy when the rookie's weapon went off. I don't know if it was intentional or just the result of the scuffle, but the bullet went into the perp's shoulder, through his lung, and out his side where it clipped my arm. It didn't hit the bone, but it sure hurts like fire."

Harry pulled the phone away from his ear and stared at it a moment as though he couldn't believe the words coming out.

"Whoa!" He put the phone back to his ear. "So, the perp, did he buy the farm?"

"Nah. He's gonna be okay. They got him all sewed up before they finished fixin' me, from what I heard. Actually, that's good. We aren't facing a kill and trying to prove whether it was good or not."

"But ..." Harry left the word hanging.

She sighed. "I'll probably spend all day tomorrow answering questions for Internal Affairs. 'Course Fagan and that rookie are gonna be there all night. And Art, too, since he played the 'objective observer' through the whole thing, the lout. At least they let me come home for a while."

"They questioning Fagan right now?" Harry couldn't help his mind going to the possibility that this might be his perfect opportunity to search Fagan's house.

"Well, you know, Harry. They want to get the story as soon as possible before it starts evolving in our memories. Internal Affairs took a statement from me when I was in the hospital, but I was hurtin' so much I could hardly think straight. I'll have to go over it again and again tomorrow. No doubt about that."

"But you're sure they're questioning Fagan tonight?"

"Yeah, I'm sure. He wasn't injured. They'll keep him and that rookie isolated from each other for as long as they need. You know the drill. They'll have to tell their stories a dozen times and fill out a ream of paperwork, especially Fagan, him being the senior." Cindy was quiet a moment. "Maybe I'll luck out and by tomorrow Internal Affairs'll be satisfied that we're all telling the same story and not put me through the mill. Who knows?"

"Well, for your sake, I hope so."

But for his own sake, Harry was satisfied that Fagan would be busy until well into the night going over the details of the shooting and filling out reports. And he would not be home.

Neither would Harry.

Chapter 30

THE STREETLIGHTS HAD COME ON, but it was still twilight when Harry drove slowly over to Fagan's place. He cruised by twice, and was going to park and wait until it got darker. *Keep it cool. Don't be impatient.* Then he remembered that given Chicago's nearly universal street and alley lighting, it never would get much darker.

He circled the block and drove down Fagan's street one more time. Except for the perpetual dim light behind the pulled blinds in the living room, all looked dark. He drove around to the alley and backed his RAV4 into the space at the end. It was well positioned for a quick getaway. He shut off the engine, got out, and stood motionless for a minute, then two, and stretched it to three. All was quiet ... for the city. Just some late-night cicadas whining like leaf blowers in the trees, a pimped-up ride throbbing down the next street with its booty-buzzer amped up so high it shook the whole neighborhood. Once it faded a couple of blocks away, the laugh track of a TV sitcom cackled from an apartment window. Sirens in the distance. And somewhere a car alarm went off. Harry waited until it stopped.

All seemed normal.

He walked down the alley, fast enough so anyone who saw him would think he was there on business, but not so fast as to attract any attention. Past the Baxters' on the left. He glanced up at Estelle's apartment. Dark. Maybe she was at the shelter or work. After one more quick look around, Harry ducked into the narrow walkway along the side of Fagan's garage.

He waited before entering the yard just to take another pulse of his environment. Was there a neighbor somewhere, standing at a window, looking down on Fagan's yard? Would they be able to see Harry, dressed all in black, with a black golfer's cap on his head? Harry sniffed: barbecue smoke. Someone was grilling, and they'd be in and out of their house, maybe standing on their back porch or in a backyard while they attended to dinner. Would they notice him? He hadn't seen anyone, but he had to be alert. He didn't need anyone seeing him if he could help it.

From a nearby apartment the angry voices of a domestic squabble rose and fell. He listened for a moment, unable to discern the words but finally satisfied that it wasn't about to erupt into violence. He didn't need some neighbor calling the police.

After two deep breaths, Harry strode calmly across the yard and up onto the back porch. He stopped to look back and survey any avenue from which he might be observed ... including Estelle's back porch. At least Fagan's porch roof gave him some cover. He turned to the back door and tried the handle. It turned easily, but the door didn't budge. Probably a deadbolt ... no surprise. Fagan was a cop and would obviously take reasonable precautions. Beside the door a table sat in front of a frosted window, perhaps the same table on which Fagan had spread the booze for his party. The window was small and high, probably into a bathroom. It would be a tight squeeze, but possible.

He moved the table and tried the window. Stuck. Harry looked around for anything to pry it up. He'd rejected bringing burglary tools. Their possession would increase the severity of a charge if he were caught. But maybe he should have brought something. Harry spied a small garden trowel in the corner of the porch. He tried it on the window without success.

Keeping the trowel with him, he came off the porch and looked down the sidewalk along the side of the house toward the small gate. Not a good idea. Too open. Anybody glancing that way might see him, bending down, working a window. He went around to the other side of the house. No sidewalk here. Just hostas, weeds, bushes, and other plants Harry couldn't recognize in the dark. A six-foot-high wood fence separated Fagan's property from the neighbors. He could take his time here. The first and second windows were solid, but the third one, the one closest to the front yard yielded … a little, at least on the bottom right corner. It was a casement window, hinged at the top to swing up and into the basement. Apparently, it was latched on the two bottom corners.

Kneeling in the dark, Harry puffed as he forced that corner open an inch or so. It was a start. He wedged the trowel into the other corner and pried. Something seemed to give a little, and Harry pulled harder. Then with a crash, it broke free, and Harry went rolling backward in the dirt and weeds.

He froze. Had he attracted anyone's attention? His heart was pounding hard enough that he couldn't be sure, but he heard no doors open, no one yelling, "Who's out there?" Slowly he came up to a sitting position and then to his knees. The window swung freely in, with enough space for him to crawl through. He held it open and shined his mini LED Maglite into the dark basement. It was a storage room, piled high with boxes and suitcases, and a couple old window air conditioners. He'd have to be careful climbing over all that junk.

Harry rolled over on his belly and went in feet first. He brushed away the dirt he brought with him, then closed and locked the window on the side that had been open. On the other side, he'd pulled out the screws from what looked like rotten wood. No way to secure that, but he tried to brush away the telltale signs and make it look like it had been that way for a long time.

He made his way out of the storage room and found the stairs up to the first floor.

He used his Maglite as sparingly as possible. You never could tell when someone outside might notice a flash through a hole in the blinds and call the cops, though there weren't that many curious neighbors—the best kind for the homeowner, Harry admitted to himself. But right now he was hoping for neighbors who minded their own business and expected everyone else to look out for themselves.

The first thing Harry did was secure his avenues of egress. If Fagan came home unexpectedly, he'd most likely park his car in the garage and come in the back door. So the solid front door with no window was Harry's most likely escape route. Though secure from outside, all that was required from inside was to turn the knob and the standard deadbolt lock. Harry tested it quietly. No problem.

Next … the kitchen. That door was also secured with a deadbolt as Harry'd suspected. But because the door had a window, a double cylinder deadbolt had been installed, requiring a key from either side to open it. Harry knew most people kept the key for such locks in a nearby place in case of fire … he found it hanging on a nail only a few feet away. He put it in the lock and tried it. Smooth. He relocked the door, left the key in the lock. He didn't want to waste even a moment finding it in the dark and inserting it if he needed a quick escape.

Scanning the rooms of the first floor as he moved through the house, he crept up the squeaky stairs as quietly as possible. What was he doing? There wasn't anyone here—and if there were, he was already sunk. He coughed out a laugh to relieve the tension.

A glistening wood-floor hallway on the second floor led to the back of the house with a large window at the end. It was propped open a few inches, held up by something at the side—perhaps a book on edge. Harry did a quick survey. Two kid bedrooms opened off the right. A bathroom and a couple of closets on the left. He came back up the hall. Across the front of the house, Harry found what he was looking for: the master bedroom with its own large closet and the master bath.

This was the most likely place for Fagan to dump unwanted stuff from his pockets when he came home too tired to figure out where to put it away. It's what every guy did at the end of a long day.

A quick scan of the bedroom showed a king-size bed … unmade. Harry sighed with relief. Wife and kids still away, and not expected back tonight. Underwear and socks cluttered the carpeted floor. The door to a large closet stood open, displaying off-the-rack suits, shirts, and sports jackets. Harry thought he recognized a couple of Fagan's dumpy regulars. On the other side of the room a door opened into the bathroom.

A small TV hung from a ceiling mount, the unset timer on the built-in VCR winking zero-zero-zero. How could the guy stand that thing blinking at him all night?

Two matching chests of drawers and one dresser lined the walls of the room. But the dresser and one chest were obviously feminine—a bra hanging out of a half open drawer. Bottles of skin creams, perfumes, and an open jewelry box on top. Harry didn't even look. He wasn't a thief. Only interested in the other side of the bed, Fagan's side, and Fagan's dresser.

The top was piled high with junk just like he had imagined—keys, pens, a tipped over bottle of Aleve with a couple pills spilled out, a half-full can of Budweiser, another can on its side surrounded by a stain of skunky, dried beer. Folded papers, crumpled credit card receipts. A Chicago Cubs bobble-head doll of Derrek Lee. Pennies, nickels, quarters. A blackjack—what was he doing with a blackjack? Hair wax, probably to make his flattop stand up straight, and ... Harry started for a second at the sight of a handheld technical gadget. Just the TV remote.

But no pink cell phone.

Harry opened the top drawer and pawed through Fagan's underwear and socks, crumpled ties—why didn't he hang 'em up? What a mess, but good for Harry. Fagan couldn't possibly notice that someone had been in his stuff. But no phone. He tried each drawer, still with no luck.

Harry checked his watch. He'd been in the house ten minutes. This was taking longer than it should. He didn't want to be here. He wasn't a burglar. Slinking around wasn't his style. The urge to run rose to a near panic, and Harry took a grip on himself. He turned to the top of Fagan's bedside table. A thick paperback—Ken Follett's *Pillars of the Earth*. Harry's eyebrows went up. Not bad reading. He'd thought of Fagan as more of a low-life, like the crumpled magazines below the book: *Hustler* and *Guns and Ammo*. He pulled open the little drawer. There lay Fagan's new SIG, the same piece he'd waved around trying to intimidate Harry in his own apartment—must have his other gun with him. A second full clip of bullets lay next to it. Harry started to pick up the gun, to feel its balance like Fagan had done when pointing it at him. No, no. He was here for only one purpose. No time to review old scores.

He turned away, scanning the cubbyholes in the headboard of the bed: a digital clock radio—he checked his watch; the time was three minutes slow—a tissue box, a saucer with the remains of a half-eaten … what was that? A pastrami sandwich? Harry could smell its sour tang, like the inside of an old dumpster. Ha, ha! All Harry had to do was keep Fagan's wife away a little longer, and the man would kill himself with food poisoning.

He checked his watch again—fifteen minutes. It was time to get out.

But the closet floor looked like a gold mine, the perfect place where Fagan might have tossed a useless thing like a stolen cell phone, letting it be buried among old sneakers and scuffed shoes, unmatched dirty socks, the wrinkled pants from Fagan's dress blue uniform. A set of exercise dumbbells—two pounds, three pounds, five pounds—obviously unused, given the amount piled on top of 'em. Harry was too old to be stooping down here for so long going through someone else's junk. He felt stiff as he rose in defeat.

On the shelf above the hanging clothes, the beam from the Maglite spotted a shoebox, wrapped with heavy rubber bands. Harry touched it. Heavy, definitely not shoes. Its sides were solid, supported by whatever was inside … like stacks of money, thousands, perhaps tens of thousands. Harry put the butt of his Maglite in his mouth and manipulated it to illuminate the box as he reached for it with both hands. A quick look wouldn't hurt. Hey, it could be evidence that might help put Fagan away.

No. He stopped. Chasing rabbit trails was the kind of delay that got amateurs caught. He came for one thing, and that was all he could focus on. Besides, the need to get out was becoming more intense. He was crazy to be doing this. There was nothing in this room. Maybe he'd been mistaken. Maybe …

He made a quick search of the bathroom. But why would Fagan hide a cell phone in the linen closet or the medicine chest? Doing his cop thing, Harry lifted the top of the toilet tank and looked inside—the classic place where no criminal ever stashes stuff anymore because all TV cops check there first. Oh well. Harry shook his head at wasting even a moment to look. He was losing it.

He came out of the bathroom and swept the room one more time with his light, then dropped to his knees and looked under the bed. Slippers, dust balls—large ones—socks, more magazines, nothing that looked like a—

What was that? A noise downstairs. Someone was opening the front door, the key working noisily in the lock, then a kick to the door as it swung open, followed by loud talking: "No, no, I tried to tell you, I don't have time for that." It was Fagan's voice. "Look, they kept me six, no, almost eight hours down there grilling me over that shooting, and I ain't gonna …"

Fagan! Talking on his cell phone! Could it be the pink …? No, he'd never be using that one. But the man was home, and Harry was trapped upstairs, away from either exit.

Chapter 31

HARRY SWITCHED OFF HIS FLASHLIGHT and stood up slowly, listening to Fagan talking on his phone and walking toward the back of the house. He held his breath. Would Fagan notice the key in the back door? Why had he come in the front door? Had he just stopped by the house for a minute?

Keep it calm, Harry. What were the options?

If Fagan had dropped by just to pick up something, he might leave soon, giving Harry a chance to escape. But if Fagan came upstairs … Harry glanced at the bedside table with Fagan's gun in the drawer. He took a step toward it, his heart thudding in his chest.

Fagan was certainly armed and might shoot Harry on sight. If it was between him or Fagan, he had a right to defend himself … though the courts wouldn't see it that way, since he was the intruder. Think, think! Could he live with himself if he killed the man? Why not? The man was a scumbag! Still …

Something teased the edge of Harry's consciousness, some kind of a solution. *Focus, man. Don't panic. Think it through.* Harry took a single, deep breath. He imagined Fagan grabbing a beer, maybe a sandwich. Then climbing the stairs, flopping down on the bed, and flipping on the television. So far, nothing had tipped Fagan off that an intruder was in his house.

That was it! Just keep it that way. Harry'd find a place to hide until Fagan was asleep … or until he left the house the next morning, if necessary. He glanced around the bedroom. Not here. Maybe one of the kids' rooms.

Harry stepped silently across to the door, glad for the carpeted floor in the master bedroom. He could hear Fagan still talking on the phone: "So what time will your flight be in?… I can't pick you up then … So, get a cab." It sounded like Fagan was in the kitchen now. Refrigerator door slammed, several beeps, and then the hum of the microwave. Harry smiled. Good, very good. He was getting himself something to eat. No suspicions so far.

Harry moved quietly into the dark hallway. Light from the alley streamed through the window at the end of the hall and reflected off the wood floor. Still, to steady himself, Harry dragged his fingers along the wall at shoulder height. This was no time for a misstep.

The microwave below screeched the end of its cycle just as Harry's heel touched the floor for his next step. But as his weight rolled onto that foot, the hardwood floor protested with a loud creak. Harry froze too late to pull his weight back before another pop sounded.

"Hold on," Harry heard Fagan say.

Harry's whole caper was coming unraveled, and he was about to be caught. He swore silently and held his breath, teetering off balance, not daring to shift his weight.

"I said, hold on a second. I'm tryin' to get this wrapper off my dinner, and it's burnin' my fingers."

Harry breathed. Fagan hadn't noticed the creaking floor, but Harry hesitated to take another step. Maybe Fagan would hang up and turn on the big flat-screen TV Harry had seen in the family room. He strained to hear.

"What? You want me to find the prescription number for her inhaler? Give me a break.... Why doesn't the doctor there write a new one?... All right, all right. Hang on."

If that prescription was upstairs, Harry was toast. He had to move, and move fast. The door to the first bedroom was just a few feet down the hall, the hall with the squeaky floor. He slid his right foot forward and put weight on it. Hardly a sound. Left foot ... *creak!* Harry grabbed the wall for balance, but his hand hit something, perhaps a picture, knocking it to the floor with a crash. Glass shattered.

Two quick steps. He ducked into the bedroom, and stood stock-still in complete darkness.

"What?... Shut up a minute. No, no. Something just fell and broke upstairs ... I don't *know* why ... Okay, okay. I'm goin' up to check."

Harry heard Fagan's heavy tread on the stairs. He wished he had Fagan's gun. Surprising him in such close quarters could be deadly even if the guy had no intention of shooting him. Fagan was puffing at the top of the stairs as he flipped on the hall light and swore. "It was this picture ... No, the one of all of us at your mom's last year. I told you it wasn't hung well enough. Now there's glass everywhere. Where's the broom, anyway? Forget it. I'll find it." Fagan turned the other way, toward the master bedroom.

Of course ... the medicine cabinet in the master bath. That's where they'd keep any prescriptions. This might be his only chance. He peeked out the door. The stairs were too close to Fagan's bedroom, he didn't want to go that way. The other way ... yes, the window at the end of the hall. Could he crawl out onto the porch roof before Fagan heard him? Even if he couldn't, maybe he could duck into the end bedroom. At least he'd be farther away from Fagan.

Harry didn't worry about the creaky floor. Fagan was too busy in the bathroom. He got to the window to find the wood weathered and rough, the old frame stuck in its tracks. Harry swore silently and heaved, putting his entire weight into the effort. It broke free, and the book that had held it open fell out onto the porch roof. Too late to worry now whether Fagan had heard the noise. He raised the window all the way up. There were no counter weights to hold it up—probably broken cords. He scrambled through the opening onto the roof but lost his grip on the window as he turned around. With a crash that sounded like someone hitting the house with a sledgehammer, the window fell. He swung around, away from the window and plastered himself against the outside wall.

A second later he heard Fagan charging down the hall, slamming each door open, yelling. "Who's there? I know you're here! I got a gun, and I'll blow your head off."

Harry stood frozen. The light from the hall window onto the porch roof was suddenly matched by a second light coming out of the window to his right … the end bedroom. He was stranded between the two. All Fagan had to do was open the window and catch him standing there on the porch roof.

He could still hear Fagan crashing around … again opening doors to the hall closets, the bathroom, then the bedrooms, doing a more thorough search this time. He heard a thump, perhaps Fagan dropping to the floor to look under the bed. More swearing. Then yelling into the phone. "I'm tellin' you, someone's here. I heard him, twice … Maybe he ran downstairs while I was in the bathroom. I'm gonna look down there … No, I haven't called 911. How could I? I'm still on the line with you … All right, all right! Yeah, I'll call you back."

Harry heard Fagan stomping back down the hall and down the stairs.

He gasped. It was the first breath he'd taken since climbing out onto the porch roof. But should he stay there? What if Fagan did call the cops? They could see him on the roof by standing out in the yard, even if he laid flat. He had to get down, get away.

He moved past the bedroom window, still brightly lit, and glanced in. Everything was pink—bed, furniture, wallpaper—the little girl's room, obviously. And then he saw it—a hot pink item the size of a deck of cards on the dresser directly across from the window. But it wasn't a packet of cards.

It was a cell phone, *the* cell phone … Donita's cell phone with the incriminating video. Harry knew it.

Now every nerve was on edge. He had to get that phone! It was almost within reach. Who knew when he'd get a better chance? How long did he have before the cops came? Not long. Still, he had to risk it. He could see that the latch on the bedroom window was locked. No luck there. Turning back to the hall window, he tried to raise it. It wouldn't budge. What? How'd it get stuck? Must have been when it crashed down.

He wedged his fingertips into the crack under the weathered window and pulled with all his might. A lip of wood splintered free, but as his hands flew up, two of his fingernails on his right hand caught on something sharp and tore loose. *Ahhh!* He had to bite his tongue to keep from crying out. He bent double clutching his hand to his stomach, bobbing up and down to overcome the pain. When he finally gained some control, he examined his hand in the light from the alley, tears blurring his vision. It looked like the nails on his two middle fingers had been torn completely out by the roots … and it felt like that too. No wonder this torture could produce a confession to anything.

Stupid, stupid! And he was bleeding, too, threatening to drip DNA everywhere. Might as well leave his calling card. He had to get out of there.

Below he heard a *bam* as the back door was flung open … and then a yard light went on. Fagan was stomping around the porch. "Yep! Somebody's been here too. This table's been moved." Was Fagan muttering to himself, or was he on the phone to the police. This was getting worse.

The back door slammed again, and Harry crept over to the edge of the porch roof. It wasn't that far down, maybe ten feet. If he could slide over the edge and hang from the rain gutter, he could easily drop to the ground. It seemed like his only option. He lay down on his stomach, swung his legs out into space, and let his body slide slowly over the edge. But his weight got harder and harder to hold the farther he went. What if Fagan came back out and saw his legs and torso hanging down from the edge of the porch roof? Now he was at the tilt point … another inch and he'd drop, suspended only by holding onto the gutter. Would it hold?

In the next second, none of that mattered. He slid over the edge but couldn't hold his own weight with his injured fingers. The pain was so great he cried out and let himself drop to the ground. He landed at an angle, his right foot hitting a bucket and twisting as he collapsed to the ground. A stab like fire shot up his leg and took away his breath, but Harry didn't even take time to look. His cry of pain and the crash was enough to rouse the whole neighborhood. As fast as he could, he limped across the yard, along the side of the garage and into the alley just as Fagan's back door slammed again.

"Who's out here? I know you're here!"

Harry stood stock still, breathing heavily, easy for anyone to see by the alley light if they were out there, but he couldn't run, not on his injured ankle. It felt like it might be broken. He tried putting a little weight on it, wincing with the pain. But it didn't buckle. He took another step. He had to get away. His car was half a block away. Could he make it?

He listened. Fagan must have gone back inside. It was now or never. He shuffled along a few feet, steadying himself along the backs of the garages. The pain was so intense, he feared he might pass out. Hanging on to some garbage bins, he huddled down between two of them to give himself a break, get on top of the pain.

Breathe, steady in and out, in and out, no hyperventilating. Isn't that the way women managed childbirth? Slowly, his control returned. He lifted his golf cap and wiped the sweat off his head. "Oh God. What am I doin'?" he groaned. "I could've gotten myself killed. And now I'm all messed up. How am I ever gonna get that phone? You gotta help me, God. If You're there, if You care at all about what's just and right, please help me get outta this. I promise I won't commit no more crimes. Promise!"

As his breathing returned to normal, Harry saw blue flashing lights reflecting off buildings and down gangways. Police radios cackled on Fagan's street. Soon they'd be combing the entire area, and if they found a beat-up old man sitting in the alley between two trash bins, they'd certainly take him in for questioning. Harry glanced down at his fingers in the glow of the copper-colored alley light. The blood looked black. If the cops saw that, they would for sure do a little checking around Fagan's house and find the evidence to place him at the scene.

He had to get out of there!

Pulling himself up, he tested his ankle. He could feel it swelling in his shoe, but he managed to put some weight on it. He took a step in the direction of his car, but the lights of a squad car swung into the alley—headlights, blue lights, and spotlights. Harry snatched his cap off his head, he hoped before they noticed it, and raised the lid of the trash bin beside him. He let the cap fall inside and made a show of slamming the lid, turned, and headed up the sidewalk alongside the garage toward a house like any resident who'd just come out to empty the trash.

It was the Baxter house.

Harry glanced up at Estelle's windows. All dark. Just as well. He couldn't climb the steps to the second floor right now even if he wanted to. It was hard enough trying to walk normally, aware that the cruiser was getting closer and closer. In spite of the pain, Harry forced himself up the few steps to the Baxters' porch and tried the back door just as a spotlight outlined him. It was unlocked, and without missing a beat, he stepped into the kitchen and closed the door.

If they didn't come after him, he might make it.

Harry waited a moment, then realized he'd better announce himself or he'd have a lot more explaining to do.

"Hello? Anybody home? Denny? Anybody?"

Chapter 32

HARRY COULD HEAR MUSIC and the roar of something that sounded like a passing jet coming from the front part of the house. The sounds stopped. "Yeah, who's there?"

"Me. Harry Bentley."

Denny appeared in the doorway to the dining room. "Hey, Harry. How you doin', man? Come on in."

"Sorry 'bout that. I knocked, but no one answered, and the door was open so ..."

"No problem. We're just having a guys' night in, me and Carl. Wives went over to the church to make a new banner, so we decided to watch an old *Star Wars* movie. Hey, you want a soda?"

"Sure." Harry glanced through the window at the blue-and-white lightshow ricocheting in the alley while Denny opened the refrigerator. He moved away from the window so when Denny faced him again there would be less chance of him noticing what was happening outside. But just then Carl came strolling into the kitchen and looked right at the window.

He frowned as he craned his neck to see out back. "Oh, man. What's goin' on out there?"

Harry shrugged. "Who knows? It's like a circus out there, man." How could he distract them? "Hey, I'd go for that Pepsi there, if it's okay."

Denny handed Harry a can just as loud banging rattled the back door. "You need a glass?" he said, moving toward the door.

"Nah." Harry quickly opened the can and took a sip. He leaned against the counter as though he'd been standing there for half an hour. He knew who was at the door.

Denny opened it. Harry could see him recoil involuntarily. "Oh … hey. What can I do for you guys?" He tried to look up and down the alley. "What's goin' on out here, anyway?"

"Ah, got a report of an alleged burglary in the neighborhood, so we're checkin' around. Any of you guys been outside recently?"

Denny turned slightly toward Harry.

Harry shrugged. "Just came in, but I didn't notice anything." He glanced at Carl whose face was unreadable. "I, uh … I went up to visit Estelle … upstairs," he explained for the sake of the cops. "But she don't seem to be home, so I dropped in on my buddies here."

The cops—both white—looked at Denny. Now why did they do that? Carl could've been the homeowner. But they were expecting the white man in the room to validate Harry's story. On the other hand, what'd he have to complain about? He'd been "misrepresentin'"—as the kids on the street say—since he came in the door.

Denny picked up. "Oh, yeah. He's a good friend of ours. We're just watchin' a movie."

"Okay. If you see anything out of line … you know." The cops nodded and backed out of the doorway.

Denny raised his hand in a half-wave. "Hope you catch the guy. Our neighbor had bikes stolen right off their porch … in the middle of the day, no less."

The door closed and Harry sighed. His arm was trembling, the pain from his fingers pounding. He glanced at the stone-faced Carl. Had he noticed?

Doing his best to hide his limp, Harry followed the two men into the Baxter's living room, eased into the recliner, and scooped some onion dip with a couple of chips. Denny picked up the DVD controller to restart the paused movie with its pod racer shivering on the screen when Carl held up his hand.

"Harry ... what happened to your fingers, man? You got blood all over them. Fact, Jodi's gonna kill you if you get it on her recliner."

Harry jerked his hand closed, rotating his wrist up so he could see clearly for the first time the ugly destruction of two fingernails torn completely off. Now that the other aspects of his "crisis" had settled down a little, the throbbing from his fingers seemed to be increasing. "Uh, this? Oh, man. You got some napkins, Denny? Sorry."

Carl passed over a pile of napkins. "You need more than a couple napkins, Harry. Better get a bowl with some water and ice in it, Denny."

"Sure thing." Denny headed for the kitchen.

"And your pant leg, Harry. It's all torn below your knee and covered with mud."

"Oh, yeah. Well, I tripped when I got of my car and went down. Musta jammed my hand right into the curb. Didn't realize I was such a mess."

"Hm." Carl's face hardened, eyelids dropping a little lower.

Denny came back with a clean washcloth and a plastic mixing bowl of water with ice cubes floating in it. "You need some Band-Aids? Oh, man, you might need more than these little plastic things we got."

"Nah, nah. Couple of 'em oughta do. But hey," he called as Denny left the room again. "You got any Tylenol or somethin'? This is almost a number ten, if you know what I mean."

"Sure. Be right back."

"Really appreciate this, you guys."

Carl snorted. "Yeah, you oughta." It wasn't loud enough for Denny to hear, but Harry heard it. Then Carl spoke up. "You know, Estelle *is* home, so is Stu, so I don't think you could've been up there."

"Ah ..." He thought quickly. "Really? Their place looked so dark when I came down the alley, I just figured ..."

"Hm. But you tol' those cops you went up there."

Harry shrugged. "Guess I misspoke. What's the difference?"

Denny handed Harry a bottle of pills and a box of Band-Aids and sat down, while Carl leaned forward on the edge of his seat, his gaze as steady and cold as a rattlesnake.

"You know what, Harry? I don't think you're bein' straight with us. I think you're connin' us."

Harry popped a couple of Tylenol. "Whaddaya mean?" He didn't really want to know.

"I'm just sayin', Harry, takes one to know one, know what I'm sayin'? I've done my time out on the street. An' you're sittin' there, shakin' like a leaf in the wind. Somethin' ain't right. So, what's goin' on?"

Harry waved his good hand while he let the other one soak in the ice water. At first the cold had made the pain worse, but now his fingers were beginning to numb up. And his ankle had simmered down to a dull throb, now that the weight was off it. "Ah, it's nothin', just that fall I took. Musta hit the ground a lot harder than I realized."

"Come on, man. Quit your jivin'. Who you think we are? Denny, shut that TV all the way off, would ya?"

The screen went blank.

"All right. Now, Harry, this is what I think. I think you the dawg those cops are chasin'. Only question is, why? What you up to, man?"

Harry looked at both men. Denny had made a tent with his fingers, his eyes closed, but he wasn't sleeping. Carl's stare wouldn't let go of him. He felt as if the trembling was spreading throughout his whole body, though when he looked at his hands and legs, they appeared steady. He closed his eyes and breathed deeply, trying to calm the internal static.

He now knew for sure that the pink phone was in Fagan's house. He had failed to get it, but he wasn't about to go back in there to get it. That little prayer he'd said in the alley had been for real. He'd asked God to help him out of his mess and had promised God—God Almighty, the Man upstairs, the One you're not supposed to mess with—he'd promised Him he wouldn't commit any more crimes. He didn't know if God had heard him or not, but … he wasn't sittin' in jail, which is where he deserved to be. Maybe God had given him one more chance.

But he'd better quit playin' with Him!

Harry blew out a long breath. "All right. You're right. I'm the one they're lookin' for. Ah, man, you guys ain't gonna believe this." He'd wanted to tell Estelle all about what was going on, but he'd been afraid it would put too much stress on their relationship. But here with these guys, perhaps …

Carl grinned, breaking the dead-eye look he'd had ever since Harry had come in. "You might be surprised, brother … Go on."

Harry sighed, closed his eyes, and whispered one more prayer, then told his story, his whole story, everything from his decision to blow the whistle on Fagan to Fagan beating up Donita and taking the cell phone with its incriminating video to the deal Fagan had offered him to get his case tossed so he could get his grandson back.

Denny shook his head. "So you were *in* Fagan's house trying to find that phone?"

"Yeah, and I saw it, too. It's right there in his daughter's bedroom, on her dresser."

"You're sure that's the one?"

"I'm positive. Couldn't be anything else. It's the right color: hot pink. And if it was her own phone, why didn't she take it on vacation? What better way to keep connected with kids if they get lost or something? No, Fagan just gave it to her to play with because the kid likes pink. That's the phone I need."

They were silent for a long minute, causing Harry to wonder if he'd overloaded their circuits. Then Carl pointed at him. "Harry, seems to me God has answered your prayers every time you prayed. Each step has brought you closer to gettin' your grandson. But you can't see it, man. You keep tryin' to solve the whole thing by yourself instead of trusting God. What I think you oughta do is trust Him to take it all the way."

Harry looked back and forth at the two of them, expecting an explanation. Finally, he said, "So, how am I s'posed to do that?"

Carl just shrugged and leaned back in his chair like that wasn't his problem.

Harry rubbed his hand over his bald head. "Oh, so you guys don't have any better answers than I did. What? You think I should sit back and wait until this case I've got goes away then … then after I've ignored my grandson's needs for who-knows-how-long, *maybe* the case will get dismissed. By then, Donita could have custody of him again. DaShawn don't want that! I don't want that, and I hope God doesn't want it either, or He ain't any kind of a God I want to follow."

The silence remained. Denny had closed his eyes again, like he was in some other world, maybe reliving the pod race from the *Star Wars* movie. Harry guessed his question had finally stumped them. But he didn't want them to not have an answer. He was tired of pulling this whole load by himself. He wanted to believe in God—a God who was good, who heard his prayers, who actually cared about an ordinary guy like himself. If God was like that, he'd give Him a chance. But his two friends just sat there, one with his eyes closed and the other staring down at the floor.

Finally, Denny opened his eyes and took a deep breath. "You know, you can't put conditions on God, Harry. You can't tell Him you'll only follow Him if He behaves like you want Him to behave. He's not a vending machine. He knows more than you. He knows everything, so you have to let Him be God. I think God probably does care about your desire to help your grandson. You want a good thing. And it's for sure God loves your grandson … more than you do, if you can imagine that. But what if your grandson never comes to live with you? Can you trust God with that? At some point you have to come to the point of deciding whether you're gonna trust God with everything, with your whole life, no matter what the outcome."

Harry threw up both hands, scattering droplets of ice water into the air. "But why would I do that? What's the point?"

"What you're really saying is, 'What's in it for me?' Right?"

"I guess. But …"

Denny shrugged. "It's not a bad question, but your perspective's too small. You want to tell God, 'I'll follow You, God, if You let my grandson live with me and smooth out some of these other issues in my life.' God's offering a much bigger deal. He's saying, 'I love you so much, that I gave My Son, Jesus, in place of the death you deserve. And if you put your trust in Him, you'll be able to live forever in relationship with Me.' Now that's a much better offer, wouldn't you say?"

Harry shifted uncomfortably. "Yeah, I guess." He'd been getting along pretty much without God for fifty-eight years. Things hadn't been all that good, but he wouldn't call it hell, if that's what they were getting at. He'd heard preachers talk about hell. Scared the crap outta him as a kid, but now ... True, his marriage had failed. He'd been an alcoholic, technically still was one. For the last ten years he'd lost contact with his son, who was now in jail. And he couldn't get custody of his grandson ... and had almost gotten himself shot or thrown in jail trying. But hey, that was life. Even these guys had their problems, and this last mess of his was all tied up with trying to do the right thing—trying to take care of his grandson and blow the whistle on police corruption. If he wasn't trying so hard to do the right thing, he could forget about the whole mess and go back to copacetic.

But he couldn't ... and somewhere down deep, he wanted to know God the way these guys did.

Carl leaned forward in his chair. "So what you thinkin', man? I can see those gears a grindin."

Chapter 33

HARRY PULLED HIS HAND OUT of the cold water and examined his two injured fingertips. The blood was washed away, and the pain had diminished—maybe the Tylenol had kicked in. He dried his hand with napkins, then looked up at Carl. "What I'm thinkin' is, I wouldn't be in this mess if I wasn't tryin' to do the right thing. Know what I'm sayin'? That oughta count for somethin'. I figure I'm as good as the next guy, maybe better than most."

Carl's eyebrows went up like their corners were hinged. "Oh, you think so, huh? Well, maybe you are ... better than most people, that is. But that don't count." He got up and came toward Harry. "Here, let me help you with those Band-Aids."

"Whaddaya mean it don't count? I thought that's what this was all about ... bein' a good Christian and all."

Carl shook his head as he finished wrapping the bandages around Harry's fingers. "If my relationship with God depended on me bein' good enough, you can be sure *I* wouldn't make it, man. Not this sorry brother." He returned to his seat. "You see, the thing is, we all mess up." He looked at Denny. "What's that verse?"

"You mean, 'All have sinned; all fall short of God's glorious standard'?"

"Yeah, that's the one. Nobody's perfect."

Harry snorted. "'Course not."

"Yeah, but God is. He's so perfect He can't have sin around. So how you gonna have a relationship with Him if you ain't perfect? How you gonna be in heaven with Him when you messed up?" When Harry didn't answer, Carl continued. "And you know what hell is? It's being separated from God forever and livin' with your sin in your face twenty-four/seven. The Bible says it's like fire."

"Yeah, but ..." Harry looked back and forth between Carl and Denny. "I thought God was all about love and forgiveness."

"You right. And that's the point—"

Denny broke in. "Remember when we said the only way we could enter God's presence was if Jesus gave us a pass? That's because Jesus suffered the punishment we deserved. Because He is perfect, His sacrifice covers us. Well, that's not just for prayer. That's forever and in every way."

"That's what I was sayin'," Carl added. "God's perfect, but He's also all love. He even sacrificed His own Son so we could be with Him forever. But He won't force you."

Harry frowned. "Whaddaya mean?"

"He wants a relationship with you, but you have a choice to accept it or not."

"And that's what I was saying." Denny jumped in. They reminded Harry of two rookies, eager to tell about the last twenty seconds of their first game. "God's offering you a much bigger deal than being a magic genie for you in this life." He paused a moment. "That doesn't mean He doesn't care about your daily problems. He does. But that's not the most important. Once we get our relationship with Him straight, it's a lot easier to accept His plan for getting us through the day-to-day stuff. Know what I mean?"

Harry frowned. He could see what these guys were saying, and as they talked, he felt a strong tug somewhere deep inside him. What would it be like to have that kind of relationship with God? But did he want it enough to trust God with getting DaShawn back or putting Fagan away or even his relationship with Estelle? It felt like giving over control of his whole life!

"But what if ..." He stopped for a moment, not knowing how to ask the question. "What if I go for the 'big deal,' like you said, but don't like some part of the 'plan'?" The way things were going, what if God didn't want him to have his grandson?

Denny and Carl looked at each other. "First of all," said Denny, "God won't make you do something just because you've signed on with God's team. Sometimes it takes time to learn to trust that His plan is best." Denny rubbed his chin. "Did you know that all the apostles except John died as martyrs?"

Harry shook his head. What did that have to do with his grandson?

"Well, tradition says they did. I doubt any of them *liked* that plan. And in several cases they could have rejected the plan by denying Christ. But because they believed God's plan was best—in the big picture—they accepted their destiny."

"What do you mean, 'big picture'?"

"It's been said, the blood of the martyrs is the seed of the church. Their willingness to die for their belief in Jesus caused the church to grow. That's the big picture. God's love has been spread over the whole world. In our men's group, we studied the book of Romans, where it says God works all things together for our good, but that doesn't always mean it's easy or comfortable. We have to learn to trust."

Harry leaned forward in the recliner, resting his elbows on his knees. It felt like a huge decision, bigger than getting married—

which he'd done without much thought—and bigger than blowing the whistle on Fagan, which he had thought about, struggled with for weeks. But there was still something deep inside him—like his desire to take care of his grandson—that told him it was right. It was a desire that had intensified bit by bit ever since he'd come to know these guys, like a hunger that could only be satisfied by saying yes to a life with God.

Harry was about to ask how he'd go about starting that kind of relationship with God, when a door slammed in the back of the house.

"Sounds like the girls are back," Denny said.

The guys stood up, Harry wincing when he put weight on his ankle. "Hey, it's been good," said Carl. "Let's keep talkin'."

Harry nodded. "Yeah. Heavy stuff." He gave each of the men a back-slap hug as the two women came into the living room, one white, one black, laughing and talking.

"So whatchu mens been doin' up in here while we was over at the church? You eat up all Jodi's good stuff?" The thirty-something black woman with sculpted braids scooped up a bite of dip with a chip. With her mouth full, she gave Harry a quizzical look and stuck out her hand. "Hey, how ya doin'? Didn't I see you at church Sunday? I'm Florida, Carl's *better* half."

Harry glanced at Carl, then grinned. "Name's Harry … Harry Bentley."

"Oh yeah! You and Estelle—"

"Flo! Come help me carry in the sewing machine and stuff, would you? How are you, Mr. Bentley? I'm Jodi Baxter."

"Oh I'm fi—" The pain in his ankle cut him off as he stepped forward to shake her hand. "Fine, doin' just fine."

Carl followed the women out. "Let me get that thing. Is it still in the van?"

Once the others were out of the room, Denny turned. "Look, Harry, I know this thing about your grandson has been heavy on your mind, and I don't know what God's plan is for you. But all the guys have been praying, and we're not gonna quit. You keep praying, too, Harry. I know you were feeling like every time you prayed, things got worse."

Well, he sure has that right, Harry thought.

Denny extended his hand in an appeal. "But like Carl said, that might not be the case. Each step may have brought you closer to your grandson than you realize."

"Yeah, but then"—Harry laughed nervously—"Carl as much as said that I keep messing it up by trying to do things in my own power. I don't even know what that means." He shrugged. "Am I supposed to just wait around? Not do anything?"

Denny scratched the back of his head, as though Harry had totally stumped him. Finally he spoke. "Tell you the truth, I don't know what you're supposed to do or what the final outcome will be. But I do think you knew that breaking into that man's house was committing a crime and wasn't the right thing to do, not the God thing. *That,* at least, was trying to force the situation in your own power. All I can say is, you keep on praying, and when the time comes for you to do something, ask God if it's the right thing."

"And He's gonna tell me?"

"Well … yeah. I actually believe He will if you're sincere about doing it His way, if you really want that relationship with Him. You know, there's a verse in Proverbs that says, 'Seek his will in all you do, and he will direct your paths.' I believe that's a promise you can count on, Harry."

"Yeah, maybe." Harry looked down at the floor and stroked his beard with the back of his good hand, then looked up again. "Where would I find that verse if I, you know, can't remember it?"

"Oh, uh, Proverbs three, verses five and six." Denny studied Harry, his eyes squinting slightly. "You can find Proverbs near the middle of your Bible, right after the Psalms, which is pretty big. Can't miss it."

"Yeah, okay. Thanks. Guess I better get going before this leg stiffens up on me so I can't walk."

AFTER THE NIGHT HE'D HAD, Harry nearly expected to find his car had been towed. But it was still where he'd left it. Even driving with his bum right ankle wasn't too bad, but climbing the stairs to his apartment was another matter. Dragging one leg up a step at a time didn't seem so hard in itself, but by the time he got to his third floor, he was puffing like he'd run a mile. The pain had worn him out. He worried that he might have broken something.

What a stupid thing to have attempted!

He plopped down in his recliner and raised the foot rest. Get the weight off, get that thing elevated. He flipped on his TV. Letterman ... Leno ... *Antiques Roadshow*. He clicked it off and sat there in the silence, only the faint music of the never-sleeping city drifting in through his open window.

He'd been lucky, really lucky. Or maybe ... maybe someone, maybe God had been looking out for him, giving him another chance. How many would he get? He turned and dug through the stuff on the end table beside his chair. Somewhere there, he'd left the Bible the guys had given him. There it was. He leaned back and flipped through it until he found the place Denny had told him to look. Following his finger until he found verse five, he read, "Trust in the Lord with all your heart; do not depend on your own understanding. Seek his will in all you do, and he will direct your paths."

That included a little more than Denny had said. He reread the first part again. "Trust in the Lord with all your heart; do not depend on your own understanding." Well, he'd surely been depending on his own understanding. He had to admit that.

Suddenly, he had an urge to try and pray again. But this was different. He wasn't crying out in a moment of crisis. He just wanted to talk to God. "God, if You're there, I'm sorry for what I did tonight, and I … thank You that I'm not in jail … or dead. Would You, uh, please forgive me, 'cause I want to trust You." He waited for a few moments, not knowing what else to say. "Guess that's about it. Good night."

Harry closed his eyes, relief washing over him. Within minutes, he fell asleep and spent the whole night in his recliner.

Chapter 34

IT WAS NOON THE NEXT DAY at work when Harry pulled out his cell phone to call DaShawn. He flipped it open and discovered five missed calls, all from the same number. He listened to the first one.

"Hey Bentley, this is your old team leader. We got a deal or what? Get back to me." Each subsequent call ramped up the frustration until Fagan was swearing every other word. Harry got the message and deleted them one by one. He'd turned the ringer off before creeping Fagan's house the night before and had forgotten to turn it back on. Now Fagan was going berserk.

He turned the ringer back on. Should he call Fagan? Or let the guy stew a little longer? Harry had no idea. Was this one of those situations where God was supposed to *direct* his path? He was tempted to call Denny Baxter and ask. But that seemed useless. It wasn't Baxter who had promised to help him out. It was God. What had that verse said? "Seek his will … and he will direct your paths." Did that mean pray?

Guess it couldn't hurt.

"Okay, God," Harry muttered while watching the doors in the lobby of Richmond Towers to be sure no one walked in on him. Did he have to pray out loud for God to hear? "Anyway, what am

I supposed to do here? Looks like it's time to fish or cut bait. This guy wants an answer. What do I tell him? Should I even call him? I'm sure he's getting madder by the hour. 'Course You probably already know that, don't You. So … what's the plan?" Harry sat there a moment, looking around the lobby. "Oh, yeah. Amen. No … in *Jesus'* name, amen." He still wasn't entirely sure what was meant by Jesus being the one who got you into God's presence.

He waited. Would God answer?

SHORTLY BEFORE FIVE THAT AFTERNOON, Mrs. Fairbanks came in through the frontage road door followed by her elderly mother, the two boys, and the dog. What a parade.

"Well, well, where has everyone been today, down to see the city?"

"Not really." The Firecracker was untangling herself from the dog leash. "Dandy, just sit down, would you? Sit!" She sighed, and gave Harry a stare as though all her snap and crackle had fizzled. "Mom spent the day with me at Manna House, and we just picked up the boys from sailing camp." She dredged up a tired grin. "At least we made it back in one piece."

Harry nodded. "Well, welcome home."

"Yeah … home …" She looked at her mom and then held out the dog leash to her oldest. "P.J., would you take Dandy? You all go on up. Here's the keys for the door. I'll be there in a minute." She swiped her card, and held the security door open while the menagerie traipsed through and headed toward the elevator. Then she came back to stand before Harry's half-moon desk, eyes downcast as though she were reading something on the empty counter.

Harry eyed her, aware that something was wrong. "So, what's up? Somethin' I can do for you?"

"No ... it's just that ... I'd *like* this to feel like home, but Philip's put his foot down and said I've gotta find some other place for Mom." She looked back up at him. "You know of any good retirement homes in the area that might have an opening?"

He stroked his beard and looked out at Sheridan Road. "Not really. I'm kind of in the same place. Estelle Williams has been tellin' me my mom shouldn't be living alone any longer, but I don't know what to do."

Mrs. Fairbanks nodded her head and started to turn away. "Oh, hey ... speakin' of Estelle Williams"—she rallied her sparkle—"you know her birthday's comin' up, don't you, a week from Friday?"

Harry assumed a frown, trying to display intense bewilderment as to why the Firecracker would be telling him about Estelle's birthday.

"Don't give me that look, Mr. Bentley. You and Estelle are a confirmed item. I have it on good authority. So, just thought I'd save your bacon—you don't want to forget the lady's birthday, you know."

Harry gave in and grinned. "No, of course not. Thanks."

"Good." She headed toward the security door.

"Hey," he called after her, "you planning any kind of a party or anything ... you being the program director and all?"

"Not really. Can't throw a party for everyone's birthday. We'll probably sing to her at lunch or something. But you can't forget her!" She grinned and went through the door.

Harry chuckled to himself as he spun around on his stool. He'd have to think of something.

The door to Sheridan Road *swished*, and he looked up to see ... Fagan! What was he doing here? Huh! Harry knew the answer, but how had the guy discovered where he worked?

Fagan came steaming across the lobby, his face flushed as if he were coming in out of a Chicago blizzard. Uh-oh, had this guy discovered he'd been the one to creep his house?

His old boss pointed a rough sausage finger at Harry's face. "What's the matter with you? You don't even answer my calls! We got business … or had you forgotten?"

Whew! It wasn't about his little crime spree. Harry turned his head with measured slowness to look out at the street where Fagan's unmarked cruiser was parked. "That's a no parking zone out there, you know." He turned back to Fagan, stalling, trying to calm himself. Should he be praying right now? "I know that being a top cop on official business, you wouldn't get a ticket. But this time of day, the traffic's rather heavy. You're liable to get your fender clipped."

"Bentley, what the hell is the matter with you? I thought you wanted your little problem cleared up so you could … get on with your life … get your grandson or whatever. You're not takin' this seriously."

"Oh yeah, I am. I'm just tryin' to look out for you, Matty."

"You what?" His slits for eyes opened wide enough for Harry to actually see the whites. "Geez, Bentley!" He threw both hands up. "I oughta just walk out of here and leave you to your own fate. I'm tryin' to help you here, don'tcha know?"

Harry leaned forward and lowered his voice to a growl. "This isn't the place or the time, Fagan. Now you listen to me. My relief's due any minute. So you go on over to that bar on Touhy—what's it called?—The Office. I'll meet you there soon as I can."

It was a stare-down until Mrs. Worthington came sweeping in through the frontage road door. "Oh, Mr. Bentley, I want to thank you so much." The silver-haired woman marched right up to the desk and planted her arms on the counter, nearly pushing Fagan to the side. "That night doorman always used to give me the willies. You know what I mean? And then"—she said it like she was God announcing the sixth day of creation—"you got rid of him for us. I can't thank you enough."

Harry glanced at Fagan, who was slowly backing away from Mrs. Worthington's chatter, a snarl on his face. He pointed at Harry and mouthed, *"You better show!"* before turning and walking out to the street. Other residents were pushing through the revolving doors and passing through the lobby, but Mrs. Worthington remained planted in front of Harry.

"You know what I think, Mr. Bentley? I think we ought to get all the residents in Richmond Towers to sign a petition to Mr. Martin recommending he give you a raise. What would you think of that?"

Harry tried to smile. "You do that, Mrs. Worthington. You go right ahead and do that."

"That I will. That I will. Now, let me see." She put her finger alongside her cheek. "It's almost five, and if I remember correctly, that's when you get off. Right? So I was wondering if you could come up and—"

He was already waving his hands in front of her. "Sorry, Mrs. Worthington. It's out of the question. If it's not against union rules or building rules, then it's against my rules. Besides I have another appointment, and ..." He looked through the glass security door to the garage door. "And here comes Mr. Gomez right now, so gotta go. You have a good evening, Mrs. Worthington."

Harry tossed his empty Dunkin' Donuts coffee cup in the trash, grabbed his cap, and left.

Fagan was sitting at the bar, but Harry headed straight for a booth near the back and sat down so he could face the front door. Let Fagan come to him. He had been praying all the way from Richmond Towers to The Office—out loud, at that. At least with the advent of hands-free cell phones, he didn't look strange talking to thin air in his car. He'd asked God to show him the path, but so far he hadn't gotten any text-messages or heard any voices from heaven. Still, he had come to the point of realizing he couldn't do this on his own, and who else was there to turn to but the Lord? Did that count as "Trust in the Lord with all your heart"? He didn't know. How did you trust *anything* with all your heart? He was just trusting as much as he knew how.

Fagan picked up his frosty mug of draft, slid off the bar stool, and sauntered back to Harry's booth, calmer now, at least, than when he'd charged into the lobby of Richmond Towers. "You want a brew?"

Harry shook his head. "Sit down, Matty."

Fagan sat on the bench seat with a *whoosh,* squeezing his ample stomach behind the table as he slid in. He stared at Harry for a few moments. "So, what's the word? We got a deal?"

Oh God, how should he answer? And then an idea came to Harry, at least that's the only way he could describe it. Without calculating how Fagan might respond, he began to speak. "Look, Matty, let's get some things out on the table. First of all, I know you were the guy who beat up Donita Stevens. I saw you come out of that building … one of your regular, unreported raids—"

"Ah, Harry, there you go again, tellin' lies about me. When you gonna learn that's a big mistake? After all, it'd be your word against mine … and the victim's word, the word of two witnesses … not to mention the other guys on my team, who'll all swear we were on the south side on a stakeout." He grinned like a Cheshire cat. "Maybe, you just fell asleep that morning, sittin' there in your little black-and-silver SUV. Maybe you just *dreamed* you saw me comin' out of the building. Who knows, it was kind of early. And what were you doin' parked outside her place, anyway? Puttin' yourself at the scene, Harry? That wasn't very smart. Now you're tryin' to get your case dropped. You oughta leave that to me, Harry. So ... as you were sayin' ..."

Harry's stomach lurched. He'd hoped for a little shock value in telling Fagan he knew he was the one who beat up Donita. But Fagan already knew it. He'd seen Harry's SUV parked on the street. In every hand, Fagan seemed to hold all the cards.

"All right, all right, Matty." Harry paused. Where was God now? "All right, I will tell the board that I'm not prepared to testify against you, if ... if you'll return that cell phone you took from my grandson."

"What? What are you talkin' about?"

"The cell phone. My grandson says you took it away from him so he wouldn't call 911. He wants it back."

Fagan grimaced. "You're not gonna put that kid on the stand trying to claim I was in there are you?"

"Not if you return the phone."

"Huh?" Fagan let his lip rise up over his teeth as he squinted. "You're crazy, Bentley. You've gone over the edge. I offer you a deal that can put your whole life back on track, and all you want is some techno trinket. You know, Bentley, I oughta walk out of here, leave you sittin' there with nothin'. 'Cause if anyone ever put you on the stand, it wouldn't take but a minute to demonstrate that you'd lost touch with reality, know what I mean?"

"The phone, Fagan. That's all I'm askin'."

He looked Harry right in the eye. "I don't know anything about no phone."

"Yes you do. Think! Look, Fagan, I'm not wired or anything. You can check me out if you want. So forget all the denyin'." Harry sighed, shaking his head. "Hypothetically, let's suppose my grandson *thought* you took away the cell phone when he *imagined* you were hittin' his mom. Remember?"

Fagan stared at him, not admitting to any details.

"My grandson—the kid with the big hair—was sitting on the floor in the corner. He pulls out a phone and starts punchin' the buttons. You don't want him callin' for help, so you snatched it away and dropped it in your pocket. He's very clear about that. You walked out with a pink phone in your pocket."

"Pink?" Finally Fagan was playing along enough to continue the conversation.

"Yeah. Not Barbie pink. Hot pink, almost like raspberry." Harry leaned forward as he saw recognition dawn in Fagan's eyes. "You remember now?"

"A pink phone? Yeah, maybe. What about it? 'Course, I'm not sayin' I was even there at this alleged place or did any of those alleged things." He looked around the bar as though someone was eavesdropping. "But hypothetically, let's just suppose there was a pink phone. Why do you want it?"

Harry leaned back. He had him on the hook. Now he needed to be careful how he played the line so as not to lose him. He placed his hands flat on the table. "Look Matty. Sooner or later that case against me is gonna fall apart and get dropped. No one's gonna believe those two stooges Donita's lined up as witnesses. I don't need you to clear my name for me. But in the meantime, my grandson's upset … very upset. He keeps tellin' me about this cell phone." He smiled as warmly as he could and leaned forward, extending his hand halfway across the table. "Come on, Matty. You got kids. Aren't there times when you'd do just about anything for 'em? If I can't provide a home for him right now, I'd at least like to do something. Get that phone back. You can understand that, can't you?"

Fagan stared, his eyes narrowing down to their normal slits in his puffy face. "I don't know. Somethin' ain't right here, Bentley. You went to all the trouble of filing a complaint against me—became my sworn enemy, determined to ruin my whole career, my life. It was like you thought you were some kind of crusader or somethin' ... but now all you want is a pimped-out cell phone? That don't make no sense to me." He turned his head to the side, studying Harry out of the corner of his eye.

Harry remained silent, looking steadily back, trying not to give Fagan a cold stare or a haughty look or a cynical *gotcha* smile. Just plain Harry makin' a simple request. But inside he was praying, hoping God could hear silent requests as well as spoken ones.

Fagan took a long pull on his beer and wiped his mouth with the back of his hand. "All right. Let's suppose I give you this alleged phone ..." Fagan paused.

Harry resisted rolling his eyes. Why did some cops talk that way? It wasn't an *alleged* phone. The only thing being alleged was Fagan's possession of it.

"Let's suppose I give you this alleged phone, how do I know you'll withdraw your report against me?"

Harry had known this was an issue from the moment Fagan first proposed a deal between them. How could either party be assured the other would deliver?

Oh God, what's the next step on this path?

Chapter 35

HARRY LOOKED FAGAN IN THE EYE. "You have a cell phone with you?"

"Whaddaya think I am? Some kind a girly man, carrying around a pink thing like that? You gotta be kidding? I gave … If I ever had that alleged phone, I'd …" He waved his hand to the side, like tossing away trash.

Harry nodded. "No, I meant your own phone, your personal cell phone. You got it with you?"

"Oh, sure, of course."

"All right. Here's the plan." Harry pulled out his phone and laid it on the table. "You call the Review Board office. Use my cell so the number will register as coming from me. It's after hours, so no one's gonna pick up. You punch your way through the phone tree until you get to Gilson's voice mail. Then you continue holding the phone so you know that I haven't cut it off or anything while I make my statement retracting my report." Harry paused. "That good enough for you?"

Fagan sat there, finally nodding his head just a little as he squinted his eyes. "Pretty good, Bentley, pretty good. But how do I know you haven't set this up with Gilson ahead of time so all he has to do is hit the Delete button and it all disappears? Then we're back to square one with no proof that you withdrew your charges."

"Why would I set up such a ruse with him just to get a cell phone?"

"Why don't you just go buy your grandson a new cell phone?"

"'Cause that's the one ..." Oh God, gotta get Fagan's mind off why this phone is important. "I don't know. Maybe it's got all his numbers in it. Anyway, how about this? After I leave my message on Gilson's answering machine, I'll call you—your cell, office, whatever—and leave the same message there. Then you have an audible copy of me retracting my charges. That good enough?"

"That's not very much, given how your report could ruin my life."

"Well, it would be enough for any lawyer worth his salt to shoot holes in my report. And Gilson would know that too. He wouldn't even try to rely on my report in court." Harry watched Fagan. He could see the man was almost convinced. "Besides, you were the one who asked me to withdraw my report in the first place. Apparently at the time, you thought withdrawing it was worth something, and now I'm willing to do it. You don't have to call in any favors with the state's attorney or anything. Just gimme that cell phone."

Fagan lifted his mug and downed the rest of his beer in one draft. "All right. Let's do it. But not here."

"Of course not. But there's one more thing: I want to see that pink cell phone sittin' right between us when we make the calls. I need to know you got it."

Fagan grinned. "I was wonderin' 'bout that, Bentley. Would you go through all this without even knowin' for sure that I had it? Maybe you're not so dumb after all. Heck, I don't even know if

I can find it. Gave it to my daughter to play with." He slid to the end of the bench and hoisted his bulk to a standing position. "But let me tell you one thing: if I find it, your statement better be unequivocal. No jackin' me around. You're withdrawing the report and refusing to testify to any of the charges in it."

Harry followed Fagan's cruiser in his own RAV4, pulling up behind him when he parked in front of his house. He lowered his window as Fagan got out and walked back toward him.

"Wait here, Bentley. I'll see what I can do. Like I said, I don't even know if she still has it." He went up the walk and into his house.

Harry waited. He was so close. *Oh, God, take him right into that room, let that phone still be on the dresser where it was.* He waited some more. How long was this gonna take?

The door opened. Fagan stepped out and came straight to the passenger side of Harry's car and got in. He reached into his shirt pocket and pulled out the hot pink cell phone. "This it?"

Harry reached for it.

"Nah, nah, nah … not until you make those calls."

Okay, there it was … he hoped … and he hoped it still had the video on it as DaShawn had described. He didn't dare insist on viewing it, because that'd reveal its value, and Fagan would never agree. So, was he buying a pig in a poke or—*"Trust in the Lord with all your heart"*—could he believe that God had directed this path?

Harry pulled his own cell phone out of his pocket and handed it to Fagan.

Fagan took it hesitantly, eyeing Harry. "So, what's the number? You don't think I have it memorized, do you?"

"Go to Contacts and go down to OPS."

"OPS?"

"Yeah, Office of Professional Standards. Make the call, and follow the prompts until you get to Gilson's voice mail. Captain Roger Gilson. He's the head of the Review Board."

"I know. I know." Fagan put the phone to his ear, taking it away to press various numbers as he navigated the phone tree. Finally, he thrust it back at Harry. "You better make it good."

Harry took a deep breath as he eyed Fagan and put the phone to his ear. "Yeah, this is Harry Bentley, CPD, retired. I'm calling in regard to a report I made several months ago before the Independent Police Review Authority concerning Matty Fagan ..." He glanced at Fagan. "That is, Lieutenant Matthew Fagan. I made a number of accusations in that report concerning his conduct. And I am herewith withdrawing all those complaints and giving notice that I will not personally attest to any of them in any investigation relative to my earlier report. I will not testify against him. Again, this is Harry ... Harold Josiah Bentley, and I'm calling at"—he checked his watch—"at 6:51, Tuesday evening, June 13, 2006."

He nodded at Fagan, and Fagan shrugged. Harry closed the phone. "Good enough?"

"How should I know?"

"What do you mean? You were the one who wanted me to withdraw the report. What'd you expect that would accomplish?"

"But I don't know if it'll work, if that'll stop the damage you already did."

Harry swung around and grabbed a fist full of Fagan's collar and yanked him toward him. "You rotten ... If you weren't sure this was what you wanted, why'd you ask for it?"

"Easy, easy, man." Fagan tried to brush away Harry's hold on him. "I'm not backin' out on the deal. Here's your pink phone." He handed it to Harry. "But how about that call to me? My little insurance policy?"

Harry released Fagan's collar and took Donita's pink cell and slipped it into his own pants pocket. "Yeah." Then he handed his own phone back to Fagan. "Go ahead, dial wherever you want me to put it."

Fagan dialed the number for his own cell phone. It rang and buzzed in Fagan's pocket, but he didn't answer, letting it go to voice mail. Then he handed Harry's phone back to Harry.

Harry put it to his ear. "This is Harry Bentley, CPD, retired...." He continued reproducing his earlier message as accurately as possible. When he finished, he stared at Fagan. "You ain't worth what I have to scrape off my shoe when I walk in the park. Get outta my car."

Fagan sneered at him and opened the door. "You never were a very good cop, Bentley. Didn't have the right connections." Fagan got out and headed up his walk, his head slightly hanging to the side, shoulders rolling with his bulk.

Harry started his RAV4 and roared out of there before he did something stupid. Tires squealed around the corner and the next one, and then he was driving down the street in front of Estelle's apartment … and the Baxters' place. He felt the urge to stop and run in and tell Denny the good news. He'd done it! He'd gotten the phone.

He pulled to the curb. But this was Tuesday evening, and Denny and his son would be at the men's Bible study. So much the better. Harry punched the gas and headed for Peter Douglas's house. He'd be late for the Bible study, but who cared. It was a good thing he had a new circle of friends, or he might have ended up partying with the old gang—Jack Daniel's, Jim Beam, Johnnie Walker, or whoever happened to be around.

Several minutes later, Harry found a parking spot half a block from Peter's house. He got out and hiked up the block, taking long strides that made his ankle ache. No matter. As he walked, he pulled out the pink cell and flipped it open. The screen was black. Of course. It was off. He pressed the button, and it filled with animation as it powered up. Harry clicked on Menu, then scrolled down to Videos, and clicked on the first one, which he assumed would be the most recent. The screen flickered. He saw a brief image of a man with his fist pummeling someone who had to be Donita. Then it went blank, beeped, and the screen swirled with the words, *Powering Off.*

He slammed his fist on the steering wheel. Okay, okay, the battery was dead ... not surprising after two and a half weeks. But "Yeah!" Harry punched the air. The video was there, and that had to have been Fagan. The question was, was he clearly identifiable when the whole video was viewed? He'd just have to find a charger that matched and see. But chances were good.

He took the front steps to Peter's building two at a time, then settled for a calmer pace as his ankle protested when he started up the stairs. By the time he got to the third floor, he was taking one step at a time, dragging his lame foot up to meet it. But he made it and could hear someone speaking inside followed by warm laughter. He knocked on the door and turned the handle.

"All right, Harry," called out Carl. "Come on in, my man."

Harry went all around the circle, receiving hugs and apologizing for being late.

"No problem," said Peter. "Have a seat right there."

"I've actually got an excuse for why I'm late." Harry pulled out the pink cell phone and held it up. "I did it! I actually did it," he said as he sat down. "I'll tell you all about this later."

Harry sat there trying to look like he was paying attention, but his mind was racing a thousand miles a minute about what he needed to do next: get a charger and charge the cell, show the video to Ms. Stuart so she'd return DaShawn, apologize to Gilson for withdrawing his complaint but give him the phone so he could prosecute Fagan without Harry's testimony. It'd be more conclusive anyway. Then—

Denny Baxter was saying something that caught his attention. "I think that's what it means in Psalm 35:18, where it says, 'I will give you thanks in the great assembly; among throngs of people I will praise you.' If we don't give God the credit when He does something for us, it's like we're taking the credit for ourselves."

He'd been going to tell the guys—without going into too much background—how he'd outsmarted a real crook to get the cell phone that would clear away the last obstacle to getting his grandson back. And that was all true ... except it made him look like a smooth operator—when the truth was, he'd had no plan going into the meeting with Fagan. And even as the confrontation had proceeded, he'd been outmaneuvered at almost every step. His only plan had been to commit a crime to get the phone, but God not only protected him from the consequences of that foolishness but ... well, maybe it was God who had dropped the idea into his head to ask Fagan for it. *"Seek his will in all you do, and he will direct your paths,"* the verse had promised, and God had come through.

Maybe he'd better give God the credit and not try to make himself look good.

Chapter 36

HARRY DIDN'T TELL THE WHOLE GROUP how he'd gotten the cell phone or how he hoped to use it to clear his name so he could get his grandson back. There were still too many details, and he hadn't yet seen all that was on the video. Also, though his trust of the group was growing, he wasn't sure how many people he wanted to know that he'd actually committed a crime the night before in his abortive attempt to retrieve the phone. But he was careful to say that God had given him the idea to *ask* for the phone at the right moment ... and God had made sure his request worked. Of course, Denny and Carl knew the details, and Harry received their knowing smiles and back slaps after the meeting broke up.

Carl grinned so wide his face lit up. "Didn't we tell ya you could trust the Lord? Now how 'bout that, man? But even if things don't work out sometimes like you think they should, you still gotta trust the Lord. It's the only way."

Harry hung around talking until it was too late when he left to find an open store to buy a charger that would fit the pink cell phone. And the next morning, the sign on the RadioShack only four blocks from Richmond Towers said it wouldn't open until 9 a.m.

He could hardly wait as he smiled and wished the residents a good morning as they headed out for the day. Mrs. Fairbanks again took her mother with her to work. "You have a good day, now, Mrs. Shepherd, and don't you let those young people get too rowdy over there at Manna House. That daughter of yours can throw a wild party, you know."

"Mr. Bentley, you know that wasn't a wild party. And besides, my mom just might be able to cut a rug as well as the next person."

"I wouldn't doubt that." He gave the old woman a little salute.

Mrs. Shepherd just smiled and nodded at Harry. But as they headed out to the van, Harry heard her say, "That Mr. Bentley's quite unusual for a black man, isn't he? I kinda like him."

Harry sighed. Some things never seemed to change.

At nine o'clock, Harry put the little "Sorry, be back soon" sign on the counter—an early coffee break he hoped Mr. Martin wouldn't mind or even notice—and left for the RadioShack store even though some stragglers were still drifting through the lobby of Richmond Towers. He couldn't wait any longer.

He had to get a special adapter along with the charger—all of which cost more than thirty bucks—but he didn't mind. He had to see that video. When he got back, he plugged it in behind the desk. How long did you have to charge a dead battery before it'd work? He'd give it at least ten minutes.

Eight minutes later, he unplugged the phone and turned it on, flipped through the menus until he got to the video, and pressed the Play button.

There it was, just like DaShawn had described it, even with sound, though all he could hear was a bunch of yelling. He watched as Fagan hit Donita again and again, shaking the bags of drugs in her face—oh yeah, *alleged* drugs. But there was no doubt. It was clearly Fagan, and he was definitely beating up Donita. Furthermore, there was a date and time stamp on the lower righthand corner of the screen.

Bingo! He had him!

And he had his own get-out-of-jail-free card, as well.

The video didn't last for more than fifteen seconds, but that was enough to incriminate Fagan. Harry watched it again and again until the phone closed down as the battery drained.

He plugged it back into the charger and opened his own phone, punching in a few numbers, and then stared out on Sheridan Road until he got an answer.

"Ms. Stuart? This is Harry Bentley. I think I've got some good news for you … or rather for me and my grandson, I guess I should say."

"Oh great. Has your case been dropped?"

"Not yet, but it will be. I've got something I'd like to show you right away. I think you'll agree that it will clear up any doubt."

"What's that, Harry?"

Harry looked around even though the lobby was empty. "I'd rather show you in person. It's not the kind of thing I can discuss over the phone, if you know what I'm sayin'."

There was a pause. "Actually, I'm not sure what you are saying, but I'm glad to take a look at whatever you've got. When can you come in?"

"I … uh, I was hopin' you might be able to come up this way, since I'm workin' today."

"Well, I've got a pretty full day myself—in the field, mostly on the south side…." She left her words hanging, signaling that it was up to Harry to find a solution.

He would have begged Mr. Martin to give him a couple of hours off in the middle of the day to go down to DCFS if Ms. Stuart had been available, but what good would that do if she weren't there? He grimaced. Guess he had to tell her now … at least part of it. He cleared his throat and spoke in a lower tone. "Actually, what I've got here is a video that proves I didn't have anything to do with beating up DaShawn's mother. That should clear the way for me to get DaShawn back, right?"

"A video? You're kidding. Where'd you … I gotta see that. Look, maybe I could drop by this evening on my way home. That be okay?"

Harry wasn't usually a clock watcher, but that Wednesday the hands moved as slowly as they had the summer he was seventeen and worked in the cafeteria of Cook County Hospital washing food trays eight hours a day.

At one point he called DaShawn. He wasn't going to tell him that the problem was solved until he knew when the boy could actually move in, but he just wanted to hear his voice, see how he was doing. Unfortunately, he was told DaShawn was at some day camp program. Day camp during the summer, oh yeah, Harry would have to learn all about that … like the Fairbanks boys, who were in sailing camp. Who had done all that for Rodney? His wife? Or no one?

In the middle of the afternoon, Harry's phone rang. He didn't recognize the number, and there was no caller ID. "Hello."

"Bentley? What's with this message you left for me?"

The voice was familiar … "Gilson? Captain Gilson?"

"You bet your sweet bippy it's me." *Sweet bippy*, what a flashback to the seventies. "What's goin' on? I want to know why you're jerkin' me around. You can't just cancel your report like reservations at the Marriott. You're on the line here, man. You'll testify to what you reported, and you'll testify when I tell you to. Understand?"

"Now hold on, Captain. I don't think you're gonna be disappointed, but there's been a change I need to talk to you about."

"Change? There's not gonna be any change. We've been investing a lot of man hours in this ... all initiated by your report. I'm not letting you back out."

Harry took a long breath. He didn't know how much to tell Gilson over the phone.

"Bentley, you still there?"

"Yeah, I'm here, but that's what I've got to talk to you about ... You available tomorrow morning if I come in to see you?"

"It'll be a waste of your time and mine if you think I'm letting you back out of this."

"I still need to talk to you ... in person."

There was a pause and the sound of some papers being shuffled. "Be here at nine, and not a minute later." The line went dead.

Harry sat there thinking. He'd made a deal with Fagan, but the guy was corrupt, so why worry about fulfilling his end of the deal? Maybe he should go ahead and testify as planned. And what was the difference between testifying and supplying separate evidence that would put Fagan away? He took out a handkerchief and wiped the sweat off his head. The difference was, he'd be going back on his word if he broke the deal. Fagan might not see the difference if Harry turned over the phone. To him it might seem like a technicality, but Harry knew the difference. He hadn't promised to protect Fagan from prosecution. He had just agreed to withdraw his report. The phone was separate evidence.

No. He had to keep his word ... even if it was only for his self-respect.

But if he was going to go to police headquarters in the morning, he'd better make arrangements with Mr. Martin to come in late ... maybe not until noon.

Walter Martin didn't appreciate Harry's request, but Harry pushed him. Richmond Towers hadn't yet hired a replacement for Draven, so they had to get by with two doormen even if they were allowing the midnight-to-morning shift to go unstaffed.

"Mr. Martin, I think you've got to realize that things come up—emergencies, illness, days off, for heaven's sake. You can't get by with just two of us. I mean Gomez is already working the weekends. He's about ready to drop. And this thing I've gotta do tomorrow is … Well, there's no way I can get out of it. It's a legal thing, hanging over from my old job as a cop. Know what I'm sayin'?"

Mr. Martin didn't like it, but he finally agreed and promised to hire a third person.

"Thanks. I'll be in as soon as I can. But you know, you ought to hire one and a half more people. Let the halftime person be a floater to fill in for stuff like this."

"Yeah, and where am I going to find someone like that, who'll come in at a moment's notice? Draven's been calling every day, begging me to take him back, and I'm about ready to do it just to fill the slot."

Harry didn't stick around to argue with him.

It was nearly seven when Leslie Stuart buzzed Harry's door that evening. It looked like she'd had a long day when she came in, pale hair hanging straighter than usual, eyes a little hollow.

"Thanks for comin' over," said Harry. "Here take this seat at the table, and have a look at this." He flipped open the pink phone, pressed a couple of keys, and held it out to her.

The social worker watched with a blank expression on her face as the fifteen seconds of action played out. Then she looked up at

Harry. "What am I seein' here, a clip from some TV show? I don't see how this has anything to do with you getting DaShawn back."

Harry's eyes got big. "You don't know what this is? This is what really happened to Donita! That's her … getting beat up, and the guy that's doin' it is a rogue cop Internal Affairs is trying to put away. It's my evidence! It proves I didn't touch her. Her story about me beating her up and tryin' to kidnap DaShawn is totally bogus. Don'tcha see?"

"Let me see that again."

This time she hunched forward, staring intently at the screen while a frown puckered her forehead. "That's not you!"

Harry laughed. "'Course not … not unless it was before I got my color and lost my hair. No, that's Lieutenant Matty Fagan, head of Chicago's elite anti-gang and drug unit. He goes around beating up people and stealin' their drugs so he can sell 'em on the street himself."

She looked at Harry with shock. "He can't do that. It's illegal! He'd go to jail."

Harry pulled out the chair on the other side of the table. "We're workin' on that. But don't you see? The reason I showed you this before turning it in as evidence is because it completely clears me of the charges. So now you can go out tomorrow and bring my grandson back to me."

She grimaced. "Not sure I can do that until your case is cleared."

"Why not? You can see it wasn't me who beat up that woman."

"Well, I saw it, but I can hardly write that up in my report. What am I supposed to put down? 'He's still under indictment, but I know he's innocent?' That won't fly. What I need is the official dismissal of charges against you, something I can point to, case number and everything."

"Oh come on." Harry rolled his head back and around. "That's gonna happen. It just hasn't happened yet. But you've seen the evidence, so just … act on that."

"Look Harry, I'm on your side. I want to get your grandson back to you as soon as I can, but there are legal things involved here. I can't just transfer him to you until this is officially cleared up. You're just gonna have to be patient. When does your case come up again?"

"A week … a week from today is the arraignment. They'll drop it then."

"Well …" She slid her chair back. "I'll be ready to act as soon as that happens, and that's a promise."

She got up, and Harry reluctantly followed her to the door.

"Don't be discouraged, Mr. Bentley. I agree, that video proves you are innocent, so we'll get it worked out as soon as possible."

THE NEXT MORNING Harry didn't let Gilson start in on him. As soon as he entered the captain's office, he held the open phone out in front of him. "Here, I want you to see this." He pushed the key.

Gilson craned his neck forward and squinted at the small screen. "Here, let me see that." He grabbed it out of Harry's hand. "Who is this?"

He pressed the key to replay it while Harry stood silently, waiting for him to comprehend what he was watching.

He glanced at Harry for an instant. "That Fagan?" He pressed the key again. "It is Fagan! That's him. Wow!" He left his mouth hanging open.

"That's the cell phone I told you about, but you were afraid that it might not exist, so you wouldn't get a search warrant to go pick it up."

"How'd I know it existed for sure?"

"'Cause I told you."

"Yeah, but you were just speculating. You *hoped* it existed. How'd you get it? Can we use it as evidence?"

Harry grinned. "Fagan gave it to me when I asked him for it. Now I'm turnin' it over to you. No reason that shouldn't be admitted in court."

"He just gave this to you?"

"He had no idea what was on it, but I did." Harry shrugged. "So …"

Gilson leaned back in his chair. "Sit down, Harry. Sit down. This is great. This should put the icing on the cake. I think we got him."

Harry did not take the seat as offered. "Uh … icing, yes. Cake, no. At least not from me. I was serious when I said I was dropping my complaint. I won't be testifyin' 'bout the report. You gotta do the rest on your own."

"Whaddaya talkin' about?"

Harry filled him in on Donita's charges against him, the deal Fagan offered to fix his case, and how he ultimately got the phone from Fagan by promising to drop his report.

Gilson threw up his hands. "But you don't have to do that. You don't have to keep your word to a crook."

Harry shrugged. "Maybe, maybe not. But I do keep my word to myself, and I said I wouldn't testify. So there you have it. But there is one thing I'll do … in exchange for a small favor from you."

The captain frowned. "What's that?"

"I'll sign a statement concerning where I got the phone to begin your chain of custody record, provided you speak to the state's attorney and get that case against me dropped. Otherwise … "

"Otherwise what?"

"Otherwise I'll have to use that phone in my own defense. And my guess is, you don't want it to surface prematurely, not before you're prepared to indict Fagan. Am I right?"

Gilson sat with his elbows on his desk, tapping his fingers together in a tent before his face. "All right, I'll speak to the state's attorney."

"Good. Before Wednesday, 'cause that's my arraignment, and I don't want to have to go back into that courtroom for *any* reason. It's gotta be over. Understand?"

Gilson straightened. "You watch how you speak, Bentley. Who do you think is the boss around here?"

Harry smiled, letting his eyebrows arch. "In this case, I am, Captain. So don't be late." He turned and walked out, his grin lasting all the way to the car.

Chapter 37

On Sunday, Harry picked up his mom and Estelle and went to SouledOut Community Church for the second time. He still felt awkward, but walking in beside the regal-looking Estelle in her flowing green and purple—whatever she called her African-looking outfit, complete with a matching head wrap—made him feel more ... more at ease. He stood a little taller, breathed a little deeper. This wasn't so bad. And there were more people he recognized this time: Denny Baxter and his wife, the young Baxters holding their little one in their arms, Carl Hickman and his wife, Flo, and the Jewish guy with the twins from the men's group.

As Harry made his way into a row beside Estelle, he noticed the back of Peter Douglas sitting in the front row, and there was his wife, Avis, standing in front. She raised a hand as the band began to play and called out, "Good morning, church! Let's find our seats and begin our worship this morning with 'Shout to the Lord'!"

The two preachers—one black and one white—rose from their seats behind Avis and raised their hands as everyone began to sing: "*Shout to the Lord, all the earth, let us sing ...*"

Harry tried to find where they were singing in the words projected on the wall. "*Nothing compares to the promise I have in You ...*"

He tried to follow along. It was like learning dance steps when everyone else knew the music. Did they? He looked around. Most people were singing with obvious delight. That's when he saw someone else he knew: the Firecracker, Mrs. Fairbanks. He nodded and winked. Her mouth dropped open, and she covered it with her hand as though she were stifling a laugh.

The worship went on and on, too long, Harry thought, until he made more effort to listen to the words. They were thanking God and telling Him how good He was. Yeah, okay, maybe it was something he needed to learn more about.

When the singing and praying—talking right out loud to God—was over, Avis invited everyone to be seated. One of the pastors stood up—the white guy, Harry couldn't remember his name—and asked all the fathers to stand. Harry looked around, not knowing what was happening, but he went along.

"This is Father's Day, a special day in which we want to honor and pray for every father in the room ..."

Harry stood with the other men, surprised that he hadn't even realized it was Father's Day. He'd always thought of himself as a man of honor, but he'd never considered it much of an honor to be a father. Now Mother's Day, that was different. He always remembered his mom on Mother's Day, but Father's Day? He could hardly remember his own father, so the day had never meant anything to him. And maybe that was one of the reasons it had gone so wrong between him and Rodney. He'd never considered being a father all that important. It was just something that happened, the result of biology. Oh yeah, back when Rodney had been a baby, he'd been all excited and proud of what he'd done—what any healthy male could do, he later admitted—but ... when he got too busy and he didn't know how to relate to the kid, he'd just kind of backed off. And being a father became, at the most, a duty, and not one he enjoyed.

Harry tuned back in. The preacher was praying. " … and Father God, help us, each one of us, to be a father like You, one who listens like You, one who cares like You, one who is there like You. In Jesus' name, Amen."

"One who listens … one who cares … one who is there … " Yeah, that's exactly the kind of God he wanted. And now he was starting to get to know Him, just beginning to trust that God did listen, did care, and was there for him.

The thoughts swirled in Harry's head throughout the rest of the service and preoccupied him so much afterward that he knew he wasn't responding to people very warmly, but he couldn't help it. To be a father like God, to have God as your father, it was awesome. And perhaps he was being given a second chance at both.

To escape the hubbub, he guided his mother over to the table with the large coffee urn and made himself useful filling her cup and the cup of Firecracker's mother. "Mom, this is Mrs. Shepherd. She's stayin' in the building where I work." They smiled and exchanged greetings while Harry looked around for Mrs. Fairbanks, but she was busy talking with Denny Baxter's wife. At least, hanging out with the mothers didn't require much more than, "Cream?" "Sugar?" and a smile.

Later, as they headed out to the parking lot, Estelle turned to him. "You okay, Harry?"

"Sure. Why?" But he knew why.

"Oh, I don't know. You just acting like you walkin' in a fog. Thought I'd ask, that's all."

"Nah. I'm fine." He helped Estelle and his mom into the car. Estelle sure didn't miss much.

As he went around to the driver's side, a red car zipped to a stop so close to him that he instinctively jumped back.

The driver's door opened … and Leslie Stuart got out. "Hey." She grinned. "Thought I might miss you. Traffic was terrible this morning. I have no idea why."

Harry frowned at her and then turned as the passenger door opened and DaShawn stepped out, a huge grin on his face. "Happy Father's Day, Grandpa." He came running around the front of the car and with arms wide crashed into Harry so hard it knocked him back into the fender of his RAV4.

"DaShawn!" It was all he could say as he gave the boy a hug, then untangled himself and held the boy at arm's length as he looked him up and down. The short hair looked good on him, made him look older, more muscular. He was wearing an oversized white T-shirt over some undershirt, a pair of baggy red gym shorts, the bottoms of which hung down to his knees. Boat-sized basketball shoes cradled his feet. But Harry had no doubt they filled the shoes. What a style! Harry grinned and pulled him in for another hug. "Someday somebody gonna grab those shorts of yours, and pants you, son. You know that, don'tcha?"

"Better not try."

Harry looked over his grandson's head at Ms. Stuart, his eyes misting.

She held up her hand. "Now technically, this is just a visit. But I've checked it out. There's no reason he can't visit you for a few days until we get this all worked out. So …" She grinned. "Happy Father's Day, Mr. Bentley.

"Oh, and just in case," she added, her long hair falling over her shoulder as she unlocked her trunk. "I brought all his stuff."

"Includin' my new basketball, Grandpa."

When DaShawn and Harry got in and slammed the doors, his mother said, "Harry, you didn't tell me Rodney was here today. This is so nice."

"No, Mama." Harry turned around in his seat. In all the confusion, he'd forgotten. "This isn't Rodney, Mama. This is DaShawn, Rodney's son.... My grandson, and your great-grandson. Isn't that nice?"

DaShawn grinned and said brightly, "Hi, Grandma."

A puzzled expression clouded her face and she pulled her arms in a little tighter to her chest. "He sho' do look like Rodney … and talk like him too."

"And you remember my friend"—Harry gestured toward Estelle—"Estelle Williams?"

"Sure do. Hi, Miss Estelle."

"How you doin', DaShawn. Your grandpa been sayin' such good things 'bout you."

HARRY FELT LIKE CELEBRATING. But all he could think of on short notice was to take everyone out to dinner. DaShawn chose Old Country Buffet over on Lincoln Avenue, "'Cause they got lots of everything." Though it wasn't the best place for conversation. Harry sat down beside his grandson and didn't know what to say, anyway. He just sat there watching the boy out of the corner of his eye as he took a huge bite of fried chicken. It felt like a miracle, them being together again.

Estelle finally guided his mom to their table, their plates piled high, and helped her get seated. "Hey … aren't we goin' to thank the Lord for this food before divin' in?"

DaShawn looked up at Estelle who was staring down at him like a stern teacher. "You mean pray? Right here?" He looked around like he thought someone was going to throw food.

"I sure do. We didn't snap our fingers and make all this food outta nothing', ya know. It came from the Good Lord, and we owe

Him some thanks." She pulled out a chair and sat down across from Harry. "Harry."

Oh no. There she went again, expectin' him to pray … and out loud at that when he didn't even know what to say. Now *he* felt like the one people might throw food at. But this time he couldn't think of a convenient excuse to pass on the responsibility the way he had on her back porch when he suggested she pray because it was her house. He had to do something. She was reaching her hand across the table to take his while she grabbed his mother's hand and nodded directions to DaShawn, her lips pursed, eyes wide, expecting the boy to follow her example.

Harry closed his own eyes. "God … our Father … I … I can't believe what You've done for me. I … I want to thank You for bringin' my grandson back, for keepin' him while he was away. And I want to thank You for protectin' me from my foolish ways by makin' a way outta no way …" The words were an echo of someone praying when he was only a boy. Suddenly, their meaning crashed over him like a giant storm wave rolling across Lake Michigan, and he couldn't get his breath.

"That's right, that's right, now. You know it's right," his mom said in her high-pitched voice like she was in church.

Harry had to bring this thing to a close before it got out of control … before he lost control. He caught a breath. "And … and bless this food we're about to eat. Amen."

He looked up. The people around him, the room, the lights were all glistening and a little distorted. He blinked and blinked again. Then cleared his throat. "Well, now can we eat?"

"Amen to that," said Estelle. She turned her head, courteous enough to not stare at him while he caught the corner of his eyes with his napkin.

AFTER HARRY TOOK HIS MOTHER and Estelle home, DaShawn jumped into the front seat of the RAV4, and they started driving south. At Foster Avenue he turned east, going under Lake Shore Drive and creeping along through the lakefront park down toward Montrose Harbor. So many people were out enjoying the warm weather. Latinos, Cambodians, African-Americans, Caucasians, Chinese, Indians, Pakistanis, Middle Easterners—families grilling, flying kites, playing games and music … all the richness that made it Chicago in the summer.

Harry felt blessed.

"Hey, Grandpa, there's an empty court. Want to stop and shoot some hoops?"

Harry chuckled. "Why not?" He pulled into a parking spot. DaShawn got his new basketball from the back, and together they walked in silence over to the court, just taking in the day. Harry was still wearing his church clothes, but he didn't really care. He was with his grandson.

They shot hoops together and played a little one-on-one, laughing and teasing. Harry played through the hurt from his injured fingers until his ankle began to shoot pain up his leg. Then he begged off and found a bench. After all, it had been only a week since his foolish escapade. DaShawn flopped down on the other end. Together they stared across the little bay the lakefront made toward Chicago's Loop, taking in the Hancock Building, Sears Tower, Aon building, and other magnificent spires raking the sky like the limbless trees of some ancient, crystal forest. No words were needed.

There are only a few times in this life when everything feels just right, when all the troubles of the world—even personal troubles now behind or still to come—melt into insignificance compared to the perfection of the moment. And Harry knew this was one of those moments. He savored it. And wondered how he could make it last. It crossed his mind that this must be what heaven is like, what being with God is like, a place and time so perfect that no evil could penetrate. No wonder God could not allow evil in His presence. No wonder the only way to God was through Jesus.

Had God given him this moment so he could know that giving up his petty plans and his way of wrestling with life was a trivial sacrifice if in exchange he could have this kind of peace forever? It would be worth it, worth anything. How had Denny Baxter described it? Something about, *if you put your trust in Jesus, you'll be able to live forever in relationship with God.*

Harry looked over at DaShawn sitting on the other end of the bench, relaxed, one foot on top of his basketball. A relationship with God—that's what he wanted for himself ... and for his grandson.

Chapter 38

IT WAS SUNDAY EVENING before it dawned on Harry that he had agreed to work late the next day so he could take Wednesday morning off for his court case. But now that he had DaShawn, the only solution was to arrange for the boy to stay with his great-grandmother.

"But why can't I stay at your place, Grandpa? I'll be okay."

"I'm sure you would, but I can't take any chances. What if DCFS checked up on us and found that I'd left you home alone all day? Look, we'll pick up some videos, and I promise, I'll work on finding a better alternative as soon as I can."

No one seemed to notice that Harry arrived a little late for work at Richmond Towers Monday morning. He quickly busied himself passing out newspapers and whistling up taxis for the departing residents.

"Mr. Bentley, Mr. Bentley!" The Firecracker came running up like her hair was ablaze. "Did you see Dandy outside this morning?" She pointed toward the frontage road exit. "We … lost him last night."

"Sure haven't, Mrs. Fairbanks." He watched her wheel around and head toward the revolving door, followed by her youngest son. Harry called after her, "I'll keep an eye out and let you know soon as I do." He'd thought about telling her his good news about his grandson, but this didn't seem like a good time. He shook his head. It was gonna be one of those days.

Thirty minutes later mother and son returned without the dog, tears running down the boy's face, and headed straight for the elevator. The next Harry saw of Mrs. Fairbanks, she was crossing the lobby again, this time with her mother. The little wave she gave him as they went out to Sheridan Road looked more like the Firecracker had fizzled.

But when she got home that afternoon—alone—she had recovered her spark. "Hello, Mr. Bentley! Guess what? *Estelle*"—she winked at him—"is looking after my mother at Manna House for a while. Ought to ease things upstairs—oh, did Dandy show up?"

"Haven't seen him, Mrs. Fairbanks. Your boys went out again after you and Mrs. Shepherd left this morning, but they came back empty-handed … and then they took off on their trip, so I kept a lookout for the dog whenever I could." He'd actually only thought to glance outside a couple of times. "Never did see him, though. Sorry."

She shrugged. "Well, thanks anyway. I'll go change my clothes and do another run through the park. Oh—the other big news. I quit my job at Manna House. Didn't want to, but I need to spend more time with the boys … long story."

Harry let the frown lines deepen in his forehead. Something didn't seem right. The boys were gone. It had looked like a serious trip with lots of luggage, so why the rush to spend time with them now?

"Tell you more later, okay?" She gave him a quick wave and headed for the elevator. "Right now I've got to run."

The house phone rang, and Harry picked up.

"Hey, Bentley, how's it goin' out there?" It was Walter Martin, the manager.

Harry looked around the lobby. "Everything's fine, Mr. Martin. What can I do for you?"

"Actually, it's what I can do for you, Bentley. I heard what you said the other day about needing another doorman, so I rehired Balor Draven, and—"

"You what?"

"Now hold on. I think he's ready to turn over a new leaf. He's agreed to be on time and show up in the proper uniform. And he said he was glad to take whatever shift you give him and fill in any time you need a sub. So I'm going to give him another chance."

Harry didn't respond. He'd thought he was finished with that jerk.

"Bentley? You still there?"

"Yes sir."

"Okay, then. He's supposed to come in on Wednesday afternoon to get his new schedule, so you have it ready for him." He hung up before Harry could respond.

Draven … Well, he'd test that lout. Harry glanced at his watch. Five o'clock. Too bad he wasn't here right now. He'd have him pick up this extra four hours he'd traded with Gomez so he could make his court date Wednesday morning. But there'd be other occasions. He slid up onto his stool to take the weight off his sore ankle.

Norman Gardner, the bulldog who'd gone ballistic when the Fairbanks boys set off the car alarms in the parking garage, came strolling into the lobby, dressed like he was going to the opera. Harry put on a broad smile. Couldn't hurt to try making friends with the crusty old coot. "Lookin' mighty sharp, Mr. Gardner. Something special tonight?"

"Oh, hello, Harry. Yes, it's our sixteenth anniversary, so me and the missus are doin' the town tonight. I was just waiting for our ride. You haven't seen a Northshore cab out there have you?"

Before Harry could answer, Mrs. Fairbanks came running out of the elevator, through the security door, and up to the desk. She reached across and with a wild look in her eyes grabbed Harry's arm. "Mr. Bentley!" She turned to Gardner. "I'm sorry! It's urgent!"

Gardner shrugged and went back through the security door before it swung closed.

Gasping like she'd run a marathon, the Firecracker continued. "What did you mean, the boys took off on their 'trip'? *What* trip?"

Harry shrugged. "What did *I* mean? Don't you know? It just looked like they were going on a trip is all. Your man and the boys came out that security door each pulling a big suitcase, you know, the kind with wheels—"

"*When*? When did they leave? Did they take a cab?"

Harry shook his head. "Didn't ask me to call a cab. But they came through the lobby, *mm*, maybe 'round two o'clock, and went out that door." Harry jerked his thumb toward the frontage road exit. "Car must've been parked outside."

She grabbed her purse off her shoulder, dumped the contents on Harry's half-moon counter, and snatched up her cell phone.

Harry frowned. "Mrs. Fairbanks. What's the matter? Are you—?"

She held up her hand, listening to the phone. "No signal." She ran outside to the frontage road, and Harry could see her punching the keys again. She put the phone to her ear, a look of horror growing in her face until she yanked it away, looked at it and then threw it at the building, where it bounced off the glass doors and spun to a stop on the sidewalk. She bent over, hands on knees, and Harry could see her sobbing so hard he thought she might collapse.

He hurried out and gently supported her, helping her stand. But she turned around in his arms and began beating on his chest. "*No, no, no, nooo* ... ! Oh God, oh God, he took my boys away!" Then she went limp as though all the air was whooshing out, crying as if her world had come to an end.

Finally spent, she pushed Harry away and stumbled across the road to the nearest park bench. Harry shook his head, retrieved her cell phone, then went inside to get her purse and a bottle of water. "Here," he said when he got back to her, "drink something. It'll help."

"Mr. Bentley, you don't understand." She looked up, her face blotchy red, nose and eyes still wet. "He's gone. The boys too. I'm locked out. Can't get in. And ... and he even cut off my cell phone." She broke into sobs again.

Harry sat down beside her, his arm loosely around her shoulders until the crying subsided. She finally turned to face him. "You don't happen to have a master key or something? All my personal belongings have been thrown out into the hall upstairs, and my key won't work in the lock!"

Harry spit out an expletive. That was cold, and the jerk had even involved him in his low-down scheme. He nodded slowly. "I've got keys, but don't get your hopes raised. A service guy came in this morning, said he had an appointment with Mr. Fairbanks. I didn't think anything of it, just called the penthouse and your husband buzzed him in. Honey, if your key doesn't work, I don't think mine will either. But come on ... come on now. Let's check it out."

None of Harry's keys worked. He stood there outside her penthouse, scratching his beard and surveying the piles of the poor woman's belongings. "He's not supposed to change the locks, ma'am. We'll get it switched back ... for sure by tomorrow."

"I don't care about the lock. He took my boys. He took my boys!"

"But where? Where would he take them?"

She stared blankly at the floor and spoke as though in a dream. "Probably sent them back to Virginia, to their grandparents. I don't know. How could he do that?"

Harry shook his head. People were capable of some crazy things. For some reason the memory of his recent burglary popped into his mind. Yeah, real crazy. "What are you going to do?"

"I—I don't know. I need to think."

"Well, come on now. Come down to the lobby and sit. You can have my chair at the desk."

"No, no … you go on." She held her head in both hands, fingers entwined in her curls like hair combs. "I need to think!"

"You sure?"

She nodded. "Please. Just … leave me alone." She backed up against the wall and slid down to the floor, sitting there cross-legged like Little Orphan Annie.

Harry hesitated. "Well, you let me know if there's anything I can do, okay?"

He didn't see her for the next hour and was about to go up and check on her again when she came in through the revolving door from the frontage road and park. How had she slipped out without him noticing? But this time it was the old bag lady who was leading her back into Richmond Towers … and they had the yellow dog in tow.

"Well, how 'bout that?" Harry muttered, giving them a smile.

The bag lady approached Harry, chin high, just daring him to kick her out again. "Mr. Doorman, would you please call us a cab. We're goin' to Manna House where we're welcome!"

The shelter? That was a big comedown from the penthouse. But the woman worked there—guess they'd help her figure something out.

As Harry helped them into the cab—he had to bribe the driver to take the dog—he reassured the Firecracker, "Don't worry about those suitcases and stuff upstairs, Mrs. Fairbanks. I've got a car. I'll bring it all later tonight when I get off work."

It meant picking up DaShawn from his mother's even later. But he knew what it felt like to lose a kid. He couldn't turn his back on her now.

DaShawn had survived the long day with his great-grandmother, but he wasn't happy about it. Tuesday wasn't quite as long, but Harry took DaShawn to a movie that night—even though he would've liked to go to the men's group at Peter Douglass's house to share his good news.

But when DaShawn found out Harry was going to the courthouse Wednesday morning, he begged to go along. "I wanna stay with you, Grandpa."

Explaining his court case to DaShawn took some doing. Harry knew the boy didn't have much respect for his mother—didn't even want to live with her—but he didn't want to make it worse. At some point his grandson would have to come to terms with what she was, but Harry hoped that could happen without causing him to resent all women.

His case was first on the docket, and he didn't really know what to expect. It was the same courtroom, same judge—the Honorable Samuel Hollingsworth—and same middle-aged woman prosecuting him. But had Gilson reached out to the state's attorney's office like he'd promised? Harry knew if he'd had a lawyer representing him, the attorney could have communicated with the prosecutor, and they'd know what was going to happen this morning, but he didn't know if he could do that himself as a defendant.

He glanced over at the state's attorney, dressed in what looked like the same gray suit as last time, only slightly more rumpled. She seemed all business, shuffling through her folders, and didn't give Harry a clue what was to come.

Harry sat behind his defendant's table, his tension rising, wondering how DaShawn was dealing with all this. He looked back. The boy had his head down, hopefully reading the book Estelle had given him. Or maybe he was just too depressed to look up. After all, his grandfather was on trial for beating up his mother. What a scandal! DaShawn knew it wasn't true, but just to hear such accusations flying around between family members could make a kid feel like his whole world had gone crazy. If things got dicey, Harry could call his grandson as a witness, but he'd rather not. He remembered how Donita had treated her son when the police came, ridiculing him for sticking up for Harry. *"He don't know nothin'…. Don't pay him no mind."* What if DaShawn got hammered like that on the stand? No, he didn't want the boy involved any more than necessary.

Harry surveyed the people in the courtroom, family and friends of other defendants, a couple of cops probably waiting to testify in some case. But where were Donita, her pimp boyfriend, and that Gummy guy? He thought they'd be there as witnesses against him … After all, Donita was the one bringing charges against him. Was their absence a good sign or a bad sign? Well, one good thing. DaShawn wouldn't be caught in the middle.

Finally, the door to the judge's chambers opened and the bailiff ordered everyone to rise, calling the court into session, "… the Honorable Samuel Hollingsworth, presiding." The tall, gray-haired man in the black robe swooped in and took his seat behind the bench. He adjusted his wire-rimmed glasses and leaned over to speak to his clerk. She read Harry's case number, and immediately, the state's attorney stood up and went around her table and up to the judge. She said something Harry couldn't hear while pointing back over her shoulder in his direction.

The judge looked up at him. "Mr. Bentley, are you still without representation?"

"Yes, Your Honor. I mean, I'm representing myself." For the second time in dealing with his case, he wondered if he'd made a grave mistake.

"Then you better get yourself on up here, don't you think?"

Harry grabbed a notepad and a pencil and hurried to stand beside the state's attorney as they both faced the judge. He arrived just in time to hear her saying, "... No, Your Honor, the State of Illinois has no further interest in that."

The judge removed his glasses and massaged both sides of his nose with his fingers. Maybe that was how it got so long and thin in the first place. Harry nearly laughed at his private thoughts.

The judge replaced his glasses and with elbows supporting himself leaned forward over the bench. "Well, Mr. Bentley, looks like you lucked out this time. Case dismissed." *Bam!* He banged his gavel. "But as a former police officer, you ought to know better. Do not make light of this court again by coming in here without representation. You understand?"

"Case dismissed"? Had he heard right? Gilson *had* gotten to the state's attorney. Harry's knees wobbled. Puff of smoke, and it was over. He felt like yelling, "Thank ya, Jesus!" just like Estelle did sometimes.

"Mr. Bentley, did you hear me?"

"Uh, yes, Your Honor. That's good advice. But there won't be a next time."

"I should hope not." The judge looked at his clerk. "What's next?"

Harry stood a moment longer before the bench until he realized the state's attorney had returned to her table and was opening her next thick folder. He hustled back to the defendant's table and picked up his own folder—thin, with nothing in it but the copy of his arrest record and a few other papers he'd accumulated. Two dark-suited lawyers hovered nervously at the side of the table for him to clear out so they could set up for their next case.

Harry was happy to accommodate. He hurried down the aisle. "DaShawn, come on. Let's go."

"Is it all over, Grandpa?"

"Yep, all over."

He turned his cell phone back on as he and DaShawn got to their car, parked on the second level of the parking garage. It beeped that he had one missed call. "Get your seat belt on DaShawn. Gotta check this message."

It was from Cindy. "Hey partner, hope you get this before your case this morning, 'cause there's something I think you need to know. Fagan just got a call, some woman really yelling at him. I couldn't hear it all, but I'm pretty sure it was the mother of your grandson, the one he beat up. She was screaming like a banshee so that he had to hold the phone away from his ear. That's how I heard. He kept mentioning a Jiménez too. Didn't you say that was the name of her pimp? As far as I know, we don't have anything official going on with any Jiménez right now, so … Anyway, Fagan kept saying, 'Don't worry, you'll get your five hundred.' That's what really caused me to take note. But once he said, 'Nothin' for that bum. He's a no-count.' Course he could've been talkin' about a couple of informants. I don't know. But I thought I oughta tell you. Hope everything works out."

Harry just sat behind the wheel without starting the car. Five hundred to Donita? Wait … could Fagan have engineered this whole thing to get him to drop his report? He thought through the sequence of events. When Harry showed up after Fagan's raid and found Donita beat up, she'd started ranting and raving at Harry when the other cops came in, but he thought that was nothing more than her hotheaded jealousy over losing DaShawn. But later when he and Fagan were "negotiating," Fagan had said he'd seen Harry sitting in his car on the street outside Donita's apartment spying on him. He'd tried to intimidate Harry for being "at the scene" … but maybe that was the key. Maybe in seeing him there, Fagan had gotten worried that Harry would use that incident in his report, so he went back later to buy Donita's silence.

If Fagan returned to Donita's place a second time—after she came home from the hospital—she would've been frightened, but once she learned he was there to get Harry, she would've been all too willing to add her own rants about him taking her son. Yeah … Fagan picked up on that, built it into a felony case against Harry, offering her money if she'd name him as her attacker and press charges for attempted kidnapping.

Harry shook his head, dumbfounded. Fagan probably helped her recruit Jiménez and Gummy as witnesses. The plan had almost worked too. In fact, Harry had agreed to bury his complaint, and Fagan might've walked … if it hadn't been for that pink phone.

"Yeah, the pink phone." Harry put his key in the ignition. "I wouldn't put the whole scheme past that …" Harry glanced at DaShawn and kept to himself the foul name he had for Fagan. He could kill that guy, but why? The Review Board would soon put him away, and nursing the anger would only destroy his own copacetic. Besides, he had what he wanted. He grinned at his grandson.

"Hey, buddy, let's go celebrate."

Epilogue

"HEY," HARRY SAID as he and his grandson headed back along Belmont Avenue to Giordano's Pizza to celebrate their court victory, "I got an idea. Friday is Estelle's birthday, and I think we should prepare a very special cake for her. Whaddaya say?"

DaShawn turned to Harry and squinted his eyes a little. "Grandpa, you two an item?"

"What? What you talkin' 'bout, boy?"

"I'm just askin', that's all."

Harry braked the RAV4 for a signal and sat there waiting for the green. He could tell the kid it was none of his business. On the other hand … "I guess you could say, I'd like to be, but I'm not sure we're there yet. We've only been out a couple times … well, three, technically, but …"

The light changed, and he stepped on the gas. "So, you got a problem with that?" He looked over to see the boy's response.

DaShawn shrugged. "She's okay."

"Ah, she's more than okay. She's a queen. And you should take note so you'll know what to look for someday."

"Who, me? Not me."

"Yes, you. Watch and learn. Watch and learn."

They rode in silence. As DaShawn watched out the side window as the storefronts passed, Harry realized his instructions were all too real. The boy would learn by watching. The question was: what would he learn? How he'd treated Rodney's mother probably had far more to do with how his son had turned out than Harry cared to admit.

He'd make sure DaShawn had a different model as long as his grandson was with him. "I can tell you, she's a queen, Estelle's a real queen. She's just not my queen … at least not yet." He grinned and scratched his gray beard. "But I'm workin' on it. I'm workin' on it."

AT ELEVEN-THIRTY FRIDAY MORNING Harry got his first chance to test Balor Draven. In addition to giving the guy what was typically called the graveyard shift—midnight until eight in the morning—Harry had asked him to come in and spell him for a couple of hours in the middle of the day so he and DaShawn could deliver their birthday cake to the lovely Estelle Williams.

To Harry's amazement, Draven arrived five minutes early, dressed properly and only a little blurry-eyed. Couldn't blame him for that. The guy barely had time to catch a nap and a bite of breakfast after pulling an all-nighter.

Harry nodded his thanks and hurried out of Richmond Towers to go pick up DaShawn from his mother's. He still hadn't worked out a better arrangement for his grandson's days, but … one thing at a time.

Plans for the cake had begun at Vogue Fabrics in Evanston and proceeded to Emely's Cake Decoration shop on Western Avenue in Chicago. It was nearly noon when Harry picked up DaShawn, and they hurried over to the decorator's, hoping the masterpiece would be ready as scheduled. They had to get to Manna House in time to present it before lunch was over.

"That's a big cake." DaShawn's eyes widened at the work of frosting art with its creamy swirls of high-peaked pink and yellow sugar roses and beautiful blue script declaring, HAPPY BIRTHDAY ESTELLE.

"Almost good enough to eat, too, wouldn't you say?"

"Yeah, and I love sponge cake!" DaShawn giggled.

They carried the cake, safe in its box, out to the car and raced over to the shelter.

Parking the car on a side street, Harry checked to be sure the cake hadn't slid around in the back of the car getting smashed, then he let DaShawn carry it up the steps to the door of Manna House while he rang the bell. They waited … and waited. Harry shook his head. "Probably already downstairs eating." Finally the door swung open and there stood the Firecracker.

"Mr. Bentley! Don't tell me—you're here because … ?"

"Uh … you said this was Estelle Williams's birthday, didn't you?"

She sighed, "Yeah, I did. But with everything that's happened this week, guess who forgot?" She rolled her eyes. "Come on in." She led them into the foyer, the sun streaming through the stained glass windows on either side of the door casting colored patterns on the floor, then seemed to notice DaShawn for the first time. "Who's your young helper there?"

Harry grinned. "That's right, you two haven't met. This is my grandson, DaShawn. He's living with me now." He put his hand on DaShawn's shoulder. "This is Mrs. Fairbanks. She's, uh … from Richmond Towers where I work. Here let me take that." Harry took the cake so DaShawn could shake hands.

The Firecracker turned to Harry. "I didn't know you had a grandson. I—I'm happy for you." She got a funny look on her face.

Harry could've kicked himself. He hadn't even asked if she'd found her sons. "You doin' okay? Your boys … ?"

"They're okay. Just … trying to get them back is all." She shook herself and managed a smile. "Look, you two can go on down. They've already started eating."

"Uh … is there a way I can sneak this in without Estelle seeing? We'd like it to be a surprise."

Mrs. Fairbanks peeked through the clear top of the cake box. "Wow. I guess we're gonna pig out on cake today. Here, let me carry it. She won't even notice what I'm carryin' when she sees you." She winked at Harry.

DaShawn noticed and grinned. "So you only still workin' on it, huh, Grandpa?"

"Always workin' on it." He threw his arm over his grandson's shoulder as they went down the stairs. "Never stop workin' on it. That's somethin' I learned the hard way." He was thinking about how he had lost his wife through his own neglect.

Estelle Williams was at the far end of the counter when they entered the dining area. In spite of the big white apron and food-worker's hairnet, she looked great to Harry in her bright blue tunic with silver decorations around neck and sleeves. She cocked her head to the side and raised an eyebrow. "Harry Bentley, what are you doing here? And with that fine grandson of yours. Hey, everybody, this is Mr. Bentley's grandson, DaShawn."

Several people looked up from the tables where they were eating and called out, "Hi, DaShawn," like a Greek chorus.

"You boys want somethin' to eat? Still got plenty. Chicken pasta salad with walnuts and grapes and some almost-hot garlic bread. Pretty good, if I do say so myself." She didn't wait for their answer, but began serving up two plates.

Harry noticed that the Firecracker had managed to deposit the cake box on a long empty table at the back of the room. Great! He waved and nodded at Josh Baxter—the young guy from the men's group—sitting at a table on the other side of the room with his wife Edesa and their beautiful foster baby. Josh gave him a thumbs-up. He was ready.

Estelle joined Harry and DaShawn with a plate of her own at a table with several other women, including Mrs. Fairbanks and the bag lady—Lucy, they called her. Harry proudly announced that DaShawn had just come to live with him. Everyone was friendly enough, but Harry noticed that most of the women were rather reserved about telling anything more than their names. After all, what could they tell? Where they were from? What they did for work? The usual introductory chit-chat by which people positioned themselves before others? These were homeless folks, after all.

When most people had finished eating, Harry leaned over to DaShawn and whispered in his ear to go in the kitchen and get a large knife. Then he stood up and began tapping on the side of his glass with his spoon. Estelle grabbed his arm and whispered, "Harry, what are you doing?"

He smiled down at her but raised his voice so everyone could hear. "Could I have your attention, please? She probably wouldn't tell you herself, but today's a special day for Miss Estelle Williams. I wonder if we could all join in singing 'Happy Birthday' to her?"

A loud, gravelly voice started it right off—turned out to be the bag lady, Lucy—and everyone followed along in about three different keys. Before they finished, Harry had retrieved the cake from the box and set the magnificent creation before Estelle just as DaShawn arrived on the other side of the table with a huge butcher knife. "This do, Grandpa?"

Harry grinned as Estelle's mouth dropped open. She seemed totally flustered. "Okay, Estelle. If you'd do us the honors, I'm sure everyone is eager to try a piece."

He sat down as Estelle stood up protesting that he shouldn't have, but obviously pleased. She turned the base on which the cake sat a few degrees so she could see it more squarely. In doing so, her thumb brushed the frosting, and she put it in her mouth. "Mm, that frosting's good."

Yells of "Make a wish!" ... "But there ain't no candles." ... "Make a wish anyway." ... "Ohh, now that's real purty!" rang out as the women gathered around.

"You know, this cake is too beautiful to cut," she protested sweetly, quickly taking off her apron and hairnet when Josh Baxter waved a camera.

"Cut that cake, Estelle," Lucy commanded. "Don't drag this out forever."

Estelle lined up the blade to cut the cake exactly in half and brought it carefully down ... but it didn't go in beyond the depth of the frosting. She sawed it back and forth a little. Nothing resulted but a groove across the frosting. She frowned and pointed the tip straight down, pressing it into the center of the cake with no effect other than to create a big dimple in the surrounding frosting that rebounded when she withdrew the tip. "That's funny!" A puzzled frown pinched her forehead. She tried a different place. The knife only went one inch deep. "What ...?" she mumbled.

Josh took another photo while the women crowded in closer.

Harry raised his eyebrows and shrugged like an innocent boy. "Go ahead, Estelle. Cut your cake. We're all waiting."

She tried once more, again without success. Then with a more determined frown, she glanced at Harry and raked her finger across the edge of the cake, scraping off the beautiful frosting along a two-inch swath. Josh took another picture as she put her finger in her mouth. "This ain't no cake like I ever made!" She lifted the knife over her head with both hands and plunged it into the middle of the cake. This time the knife went in, though it took an extra push on Estelle's part. She lifted the knife and the whole cake came with it.

Gasps from the women and another flash from Josh's camera.

"Harry Bentley, what is this?" She put it back down and scraped off more frosting. "This ain't no cake. There's a foam pillow in here!"

The entire dining room was gasping with laughter. "What is it?" ... "What? No cake?"

"Ah, he gotcha good!" yelled Lucy.

Harry was laughing now, so hard he could hardly stay seated.

"Harry Bentley! I oughta throw this whole frosted pillow in your face, but I'm too ... I'm too ..." And then she picked it up and did just that.

More screeches. More photos. More cheers. DaShawn was hopping up and down, pointing at his grandpa, laughing loudly.

Someone brought Harry a damp towel from the kitchen. When he'd finally wiped the frosting off his bald head and caught his breath, he stood up, still chuckling. "Happy birthday, Estelle. We really do have some cake for you." He grinned as Josh and Edesa Baxter brought out a real sheet cake from a side room, decorated with the same yellow and pink sugar roses and HAPPY BIRTHDAY ESTELLE written on it in pink frosting.

Estelle shook her head. "I ain't cuttin' no more cake ... not today, that's for sure. You gotta cut this one yourself, Harry Bentley, or no one's getting' any."

"It's a deal ... if you let me give you a hug first."

"With that frosting still in your beard?" Estelle rolled her eyes. "Oh, okay. If you insist."

The residents and staff of Manna House laughed and cheered as Harry embraced her, but he looked over her shoulder and winked at DaShawn. "Insist? Well, I'm workin' on it. I'm still workin' on it."

Acknowledgments

My sincere thanks goes to ...

Allen Arnold, Senior VP and Publisher of fiction at Thomas Nelson Publishers, for suggesting the idea of writing a "parallel novel" featuring one of the male characters from Neta's Yada Yada House of Hope series.

My wife, **Neta,** for "loaning" me Harry Bentley and wrestling with me for months as we coordinated the details of our intertwined stories.

Colleen Currat, Karen Evans, Carl Fowler, Julian Jackson, Neta Jackson, Sue Mitrovitch, and **Julia Pferdehirt**—readers who improved the story and helped me avoid many blunders.

Jennifer Stair and **Neta Jackson**, most excellent editors.

Kristen Gilliam, Leslie Martinez, and **Aerin Mitchell**, neighborhood girls, for the "Strawberry shortcake" jump rope rhyme.

Jeffrey Malik Pittman, Jr., our young neighbor, who posed for the cover photo.

Julian Jackson for assistance with the cover design.

LaVergne, TN USA
03 August 2010
191884LV00003B/29/P